Louis Loewe

Diaries of Sir Moses and Lady Montefiore

Vol. II.

Louis Loewe

Diaries of Sir Moses and Lady Montefiore
Vol. II.

ISBN/EAN: 9783337112233

Printed in Europe, USA, Canada, Australia, Japan

Cover: Foto ©Raphael Reischuk / pixelio.de

More available books at **www.hansebooks.com**

DIARIES OF
SIR MOSES AND LADY MONTEFIORE.

REPRODUCED FROM A PHOTOGRAPH ON PORCELAIN

DIARIES OF
SIR MOSES
AND LADY MONTEFIORE

COMPRISING THEIR LIFE AND WORK AS RECORDED
IN THEIR DIARIES FROM 1812 TO 1883.

WITH THE ADDRESSES AND SPEECHES OF SIR MOSES; HIS CORRESPONDENCE WITH
MINISTERS, AMBASSADORS, AND REPRESENTATIVES OF PUBLIC BODIES;
PERSONAL NARRATIVES OF HIS MISSIONS IN THE CAUSE OF HUMANITY
FIRMANS AND EDICTS OF EASTERN MONARCHS; HIS OPINIONS ON
FINANCIAL, POLITICAL, AND RELIGIOUS SUBJECTS, AND
ANECDOTES AND INCIDENTS REFERRING TO MEN
OF HIS TIME, AS RELATED BY HIMSELF.

EDITED BY

DR L. LOEWE,

MEMBER OF THE ROYAL ASIATIC SOCIETY OF GREAT BRITAIN AND IRELAND; OF THE SOCIÉTÉ
ASIATIQUE OF PARIS; OF THE NUMISMATIC SOCIETY OF LONDON, ETC. (ONE OF THE
MEMBERS OF THE MISSION TO DAMASCUS AND CONSTANTINOPLE UNDER
THE LATE SIR MOSES MONTEFIORE, BART., IN THE YEAR 1840).

In Two Volumes

WITH ILLUSTRATIONS

VOL. II.

LONDON
GRIFFITH FARRAN OKEDEN & WELSH
NEWBERY HOUSE CHARING CROSS ROAD
AND AT SYDNEY
1890

CONTENTS.

————o————

CHAPTER I.

CHAPTER VII.

CHAPTER VIII.

CHAPTER IX.

CHAPTER X.

CHAPTER XI.

CHAPTER XII.

CHAPTER XIII.

CHAPTER XIV.

CHAPTER XV.

CHAPTER XVI.

CHAPTER XVII.

CHAPTER XVIII.

CHAPTER XIX.

CHAPTER XX.

CHAPTER XXI.

CHAPTER XXII.

Contents.

CHAPTER XL.

CHAPTER XLI.

CHAPTER XLII.

CHAPTER XLIII.

CHAPTER XLIV.

CHAPTER XLV.

DIARIES OF

SIR MOSES AND LADY MONTEFIORE.

CHAPTER I.

1847.

SIR MOSES PRESENTED TO THE QUEEN ON BEING MADE A BARONET—UKASE OF THE CZAR—THE AFFAIR OF DEIR-EL-KAMAR—SIR MOSES' INTERVIEWS WITH LOUIS-PHILIPPE, M. GUIZOT, AND LORD NORMANBY—SATISFACTORY MEASURES OF THE FRENCH GOVERNMENT.

THE Diary of the year 1847 continues to refer to gratifying events. Sir Moses orders medical supplies at the Apothecaries' Hall for his dispensary at Jerusalem, is presented to her Majesty on his being created a baronet, and on March 29th he receives a letter from the representatives of the Hebrew community in Kowno, conveying to him the gratifying intelligence that the Emperor of Russia had issued a Ukase, dated 10th December 1846, permitting the Jews to remain in that town free from molestation. But on May the 2nd I find an entry which must have occasioned him much pain, as it refers to an accusation brought against his brethren at Deir-el-Kámár. Fortunately he was in possession of all the papers relative to the subject, and could at once refute the charge in a letter to the *Times*, of which the following is a copy—

"SIR,—My attention has been directed to a paragraph which appeared in yesterday's *Times*, being an extract from the *Union Monarchique*, Paris paper, which extract purports to contain a narrative of the abduction and murder by the Jews of Deir-el-Kámár, near Beyrout, of a Christian child; that, after the lapse of three days, the corpse had been discovered in a field, that the hands, feet, and side of the child had been pierced, and that it had also been bled in the neck. Happily, I am in possession of intelligence of the 5th and 6th of April from a correspondent at Beyrout, in whose veracity I have every reason to confide, and am thus enabled to furnish a correct statement of the circumstances.

"It appears that on the day preceding Palm Sunday several Christian boys joined some religious procession, agreeably to the custom of the place. In the dusk of the evening one of the children, about the age of four years, having strayed from the others, lost its way among the gardens and vineyards. On the following day, when it became known that the child was missing, the fanatic populace attributed its disappearance to the Jews; their Synagogue and houses were tumultuously searched, but, of course, without success; and subsequently the child was found in a vineyard, exhausted by cold, hunger, and fatigue, from the effects of which it soon afterwards expired. This, however, did not silence the clamour of the ignorant multitude, and eventually the affair was referred to the Governor-General. The accused persons had been placed in confinement, but on their brethren undertaking for their appearance in due course, the Governor gave instructions for their immediate liberation, and he has directed an investigation before the judicial tribunal.

"I am happy to say that Colonel Rose, Her Majesty's Consul-General at Beyrout, kindly interfered on the occasion, and that, thanks to his humane intervention and the good sense of the Governor of the district, my poor brethren were protected against the frantic violence of their accusers.

"I had hoped, Sir, that even in the East the absurd, yet cruel, calumnies urged against our faith had ceased to obtain credence; but where ignorance and superstition prevail to so great an extent, it is more a subject for sorrow than surprise to find the occasional resuscitation of the bigotry of a bygone age; but, Sir, I cannot refrain from expressing my deep regret that this melancholy event should have been recorded so inaccurately and in so adverse a spirit by the journal in question.

"I am anxious to obviate its mischievous tendency by an authentic version of the circumstances, and I entertain no doubt, though fully conscious of the value of the space I seek to occupy, that you will kindly admit this letter into your columns, as you will thereby give at least an equal circulation to the true, as you have unfortunately given to the erroneous, statement; though I believe that even without contradiction few would attach any credence to the imputation thus unhappily revived.—I have the honour to be, Sir, your obedient humble servant,   "MOSES MONTEFIORE."

"GROSVENOR GATE, PARK LANE, *May 2.*"

Returning to the Diary, we read that on 27th May he and Lady Montefiore had a gracious reception at the Queen's Drawing Room; and on the 28th, they received an invitation from the Lord Chamberlain by command of the Queen to Her Majesty's Ball on Friday, 11th of June, an honour, however, of which they were unable to avail themselves owing to its being Sabbath.

June 20th.—An accusation having been brought anew against the Jews in Damascus, Sir Moses and Lady Montefiore received numerous petitions from representatives of the Hebrew communities in Jerusalem, Beyrout, and Damascus, to intercede on their behalf with the French Government, the Christians in Syria being generally considered under the protection of France.

They at once resolved to go to Paris, and obtain, if possible, from King Louis-Philippe, a declaration of his disbelief in the charges brought against the Jews.

In the present instance it was Monsieur Baudin, "Le Gérant du Consulat de France" (as the French Minister in Paris described him), who, on the occasion of a child disappearing from Damascus (the child, however, was afterwards found at Baalbeck), called upon the Moslem Governor to have a search made in the houses of the Jews, reminding him, at the same time, of the accusations brought against the latter in the year 1840.

July 3rd.—Sir Moses walked to the Foreign Office, having an appointment for that day with Lord Palmerston. He acquainted the Minister with the contents of the letters he had received from the East respecting the late charges brought against the Jews, also with the translation of M. Baudin's letter to the Governor of Damascus. Sir Moses praised the conduct of the British Consuls on the unfortunate occasion, and spoke highly of Mr (now Sir Richard) Wood. His request to Lord Palmerston was that he would repeat to the Consuls the instructions he had formerly given them, to protect the Jews from lawless persecution, and also to give him a letter of introduction to Lord Normanby in Paris to assist him in procuring a private audience of King Louis-Philippe. His object was to obtain from His Majesty a declaration, similar to one made by Augustus III., King of Poland, in 1763, of his entire disbelief in the ignorant delusion about the Jews and the use of blood in the Passover cakes, and to induce him to give directions to his Consuls, not to countenance any charge of the kind. Sir Moses found Lord Palmerston fully aware of all that had passed, as the latter repeated to him the contents of Sir Moses' last letter from Damascus. The Governor had behaved extremely well to the Jews, and Lord Palmerston had sent him the thanks of the British Government.

Lord Palmerston kindly complied with both his requests, and said he would give him a letter from the Government to Lord Normanby, in order that it might remain on record in his office.

July 7*th*.—Before leaving for Paris, Sir Moses and Lady Montefiore accepted an invitation from Monsieur Zohrab, the Turkish Consul, to attend an entertainment on board a large and powerful new steamship built by White of Cowes for the Turkish Government. They met the Turkish Ambassador, Sir Stratford and Lady Canning, and many other distinguished persons there, who were all most kind and attentive to Sir Moses and Lady Montefiore.

On receipt of Lord Palmerston's letters of introduction, Sir Moses started for Paris, where he at once called on the Marquess of Normanby. His Lordship was extremely kind, and paid great attention to what Sir Moses had to say, but could only regret Sir Moses' inopportune arrival. The King was somewhat annoyed at the differences with England, and although Sir Moses might go direct and obtain an interview, still it might be difficult for Sir Moses to move the King—who was then an old man—sufficiently to induce him to get Monsieur Guizot to take the matter up. Lord Normanby was unwilling to incur the jealousy of Monsieur Guizot, but although the British Ambassador entertained little hope of Sir Moses' success, he said that he would reconsider the matter.

July 17*th*.—Sir Moses received a note from his Lordship, saying that he would be glad to see him to-day (Saturday), between one and two o'clock. "In spite of the burning sun," Sir Moses writes, "Dr Loewe and I walked there (the sanctity of the Sabbath preventing the use of a carriage). His Lordship said he had read over all my papers in respect to the declaration I wished the King to make; he believed it would be impossible to obtain it, and thought I must give up the idea.

"The memorial would therefore require curtailing and altering, and he would look at it if I brought it on Monday at about the same time. On that morning he should see the King of the Belgians at the Palace, and would consider how I might be introduced to the King of France; as I had been presented before, it was not requisite for his Lordship to present me himself."

Paris, *July* 20*th*.—The following entry is contained in the Diary :—

"Monsieur Guizot received me kindly, and by no means as a stranger. He attended to the recital of what had occurred at Damascus, and said in reply that Monsieur Baudin was not a Consul ; but I said he represented the French Government, and the people believed he spoke their sentiments. Monsieur Guizot then said he would write a very strong letter himself to Monsieur Baudin,* and would speak with the King on the subject, and I should hear from him. I immediately went to Lord Normanby, and informed him of all that had passed ; he thanked me for calling, as he was just going into the country for a couple of days, and was happy he had been able to facilitate the accomplishment of my object."

August 5th.—Sir Moses went to the Foreign Office to see Monsieur Le Sage, the head of the department. The latter, having mislaid the papers, had to go over the whole business again, but eventually promised to write to Monsieur Baudin, who had exceeded his duty in expressing his own opinion as that of the French Government.

August 9th.—Monsieur Hude came to Sir Moses from Baron James de Rothschild, and brought him the following note, written by the King's own hand, to Monsieur Guizot :—

"DIMANCHE, 8 *Août* 1847.

"MON CHER MINISTRE,—Je recevrai Sir Moses Montefiore demain aux Tuileries pendant que vous serez occupé à faire la Clôture, c'est-a-dire à une heure précise. Veuillez donc l'en faire prévenir. Je n'ai pas d'autre moment a' lui donner comme vous le savez.—Bon Soir. "L."

Sir Moses at once put on his uniform, and went to the Palace of the Tuileries a little before one o'clock. The King was in Council, and it was ten minutes before two when the Ministers left to go to the closing of the Chambers of Peers and Deputies. Two minutes after he was conducted through a splendid picture gallery and several large apartments into a room, in which the officer who was his conductor left him.

The King immediately entered, and said, " I am very happy to see you, Sir Moses ; you are come from England." Sir Moses then informed His Majesty of the object for which he had solicited the honour of an audience, in compliance with the wishes of his co-religionists in the East. He informed His Majesty of the unfortunate occurrence at Damascus, and

* Refer to Appendix for Monsieur Guizot's letter.

asked permission to read him a paper containing the particulars of his petition, to which the King graciously assented, asking if there was sufficient light, as the blinds were closed. The King paid great attention while Sir Moses read, and when he came to the part which mentions the Jews of France, His Majesty observed, *that he was happy to have been the first to have given them every civil right, and hoped soon to see the example followed in every country;* he fully concurred in the sentiments expressed in Sir Moses' statements. His Majesty very graciously took the paper, when Sir Moses had finished reading it, and said he would give it to Monsieur Guizot, who took as keen an interest in the matter as he did himself, and would attend to it. When Sir Moses mentioned the loss of the child at Deir-el-Kámár, he immediately said, "But it has been found, and there is an end of the matter." His Majesty could not have been more gracious, and Sir Moses was satisfied that the Government would give such directions to their officers in the East, as would prevent their again acting in so cruel a manner with regard to the Jews. On his taking leave, the King inquired if he intended leaving Paris, and said that he was going to-morrow to the Chateau d'Eu, where he would be happy to see Sir Moses at all times.

Sir Moses left the Audience Chamber by the wrong door, and after wandering through two or three rooms, endeavouring to find his way out, he met the King. He very good humouredly said, "You have lost your way; I will show you," and most kindly walked with him through two large rooms which brought them to the end of a long picture gallery, where there were many officers and servants. Here the King bade him farewell. Sir Moses felt the greatest confidence that the great object he had at heart had been blest with success.

Paris, August 10*th.*—He called at the Foreign Office to return Monsieur Guizot his thanks, and the latter repeated his assurance respecting the protection of the Jews in the East.

August 28*th.*—This morning Sir Moses received a letter from Monsieur Guizot as follows:

"PARIS, *August* 23, 1847.

"SIR,—The King has forwarded me a letter which you addressed to him on the 9th instant, on the subject of the prejudice unfortunately existing in the East against the Israelites, which has given rise to the accusation of their shedding human blood for sacrifices. You express the desire that the agents of His Majesty in the East should be instructed not only to abstain from doing anything which might tend to strengthen this prejudice, but to use all means in their power to combat and destroy it.

"The Government of the King regards the imputation in question as false and calumnious, and its agents are, in general, too enlightened to think of abetting it in any way. The Government would deeply regret their doing such a thing, and would not hesitate to censure them severely for it. This is what the Government has done in the particular case to which you refer, regarding the disappearance, in April last, of a Christian child of Damascus, and also regarding the accusation which the agent of the French Consulate appears to have been emboldened to bring before the Pasha in this matter. No direct information having reached me on these subjects, I asked the King's Consul at Damascus for an explanation, and commanded him in the event of the facts which had been stated to you proving true, to express my severe disapprobation to the agent, who upon a simple rumour would have ventured such an accusation against a whole people.—Accept, Sir, the assurance of my highest esteem.   (Signed)   "GUIZOT."

"Sir Moses Montefiore, &c."

August 30*th.*—Sir Moses called on Viscount Palmerston, and communicated to him what had passed between His Majesty the King of the French, Monsieur Guizot, and himself. He gave his Lordship a copy of his Memorial to the King, and of Monsieur Guizot's letter to himself. Lord Palmerston expressed his happiness at receiving so favourable an account, and said he trusted his endeavours would have the desired result, and that the French authorities at Damascus had certainly encouraged the charge against the Jews.

In the same year we find Sir Moses Montefiore's name gazetted (September 24) as Deputy-Lieutenant of the County of Kent, an honour which he highly prized. Later on he laid the foundation stone of the Canterbury Synagogue, and addressed the assembly. On his return to London he presided at a meeting of the London Committee of Deputies of the British Jews, which had been convened by him for the purpose of considering the propriety of an address from that Board to Pope Pius the Ninth, to express their thanks to the Sovereign Pontiff for the benevolent solicitude he had manifested for the welfare of the Israelites under his dominion, and for the judicious measures he had adopted to improve their condition. It was resolved to prepare an address to be first forwarded to Lord Palmerston, and then with his consent to be presented by Baron Charles de Rothschild of Naples to the Pope, who, in due course acknowledged the receipt of the same, in a courteous letter addressed to the President by Cardinal Teretti.

December 18*th.*—He had the satisfaction of learning from the evening papers that Lord John Russell's motion for the removal of the civil and political disabilities affecting Her Majesty's Jewish subjects had been carried on the previous night, the numbers being 250 "Ayes," and 186 "Noes,"—majority, 64.

This pleasing event was followed by another: the reception of a letter from the elders of the Hebrew community of Damascus, in which they expressed their gratitude to him for his exertions on their behalf with the French Government.

CHAPTER II.

1848.

IN the early part of the year 1848 Sir Moses was occupied with the question of agriculture in Poland and Russia, and had several interviews with Baron Brunnow on the subject. A plan, drawn up by Mr Posener of Warsaw, in connection with the tenancy, treatment, and improvement of farms, fields, and estates generally in the dominions of the Czar, was submitted by Sir Moses to the Ambassador, who fully approved of it.

At home his interest was centered in the Bill for the removal of Jewish disabilities, which was read a second time on the night of the 11th February, and passed by a majority of 73, there having been 277 for and 204 against it. Sir Robert Peel, in his memorable speech on this occasion, spoke in most flattering terms of Sir Moses.

Lady Montefiore's interest in politics was also much sustained by her regular interchange of visits with Mrs Disraeli, who was a near neighbour.

April 9th.—In consequence of the threatening Chartist riots, much alarm was felt at the meeting of the rioters which was convened for the morrow, and it was found necessary to take measures for the protection of the Bank of England, the parapet of which was lined and covered with sand-bags, to form a breast-work.

April 10th.—Sir Moses was at Mount Street at half-past eight this morning. Mr Graham, a magistrate, was in attendance, and remained with him till three, swearing in about 450 special constables. "It has been," he says, "a day of much anxiety for the public peace, but, thank God! the Chartists' meeting has proved a complete failure." At three o'clock he went to the Alliance and the Irish Bank, where all the clerks had been sworn in; some were to remain till late in the evening. Sir Moses returned afterwards to Mount Street, where he remained till five.

May 11*th*.—Sir Moses and Lady Montefiore attended the first Drawing-Room of the season.

May 25*th*.—Sir Moses proceeded to the House of Lords. "Sir Augustus Clifford," he writes, "was so good as to procure for me a place at the Bar, and at six o'clock a place near the Throne. The debate for the removal of Jewish disabilities lasted till half-past one. It was a painful excitement. The majority against us was thirty-five, much greater than was expected."

The Duke of Cambridge, on that occasion, although one of the opponents of the Bill from conscientious motives, made a speech in which he expressed himself favourably towards the character of the Jews in general, and more especially towards that of Sir Moses.

His Royal Highness the Duke of Sussex, however, also from conscientious motives, supported the Bill. The course taken by the latter prince, it may be observed, has been amply justified by the experience of the last forty years. In this country, as well as in all others where Jews have been admitted into the legislature, their presence has unquestionably had no unfavourable effect on the administration of the law.

On the 7th of July Sir Moses and Lady Montefiore made a little excursion to Scotland, and on their return to town attended a soirée at the Marquis of Salisbury's. Whilst they were passing the evening here, visitors of a different description had availed themselves of the temporary absence of Sir Moses and Lady Montefiore to effect an entrance into the drawing-room at Park Lane, whence the thieves succeeded in abstracting every article of gold and silver, as well as the Hamburg medal and many other valuable testimonials and mementoes.

In November they took an active part on a Committee which had been formed in Ramsgate, for providing relief for one hundred and sixty emigrants who had been saved from the ship *Burgundy*, and in December they provided one hundred of the London poor with blankets, again sent medical supplies from Apothecaries' Hall to their dispensary in Jerusalem, and visited the London Hospital and several other charitable institutions.

The reader will probably remember that in the year 1840, when Sir Moses appealed to Cardinal Riverola, head of the Capuchins in Rome, for the removal of the libellous and malicious epitaph in the Church of the Capuchins at Damascus, respecting the supposed murder of Padre Tomaso, His Eminence promised him his aid; but the events of Deir-el-Kámár and Damascus having given undoubted evidence of the spirit of hatred and persecution which still filled the hearts of the people, Sir Moses entertained serious doubts as to the fulfilment of that promise, and resolved to go there himself to ascertain the actual state of affairs.

The French Government having so forcibly expressed their disbelief in the accusations brought against the Jews, and having so severely censured the Agent of the French Consulate in Damascus, he thought, in the event of the epitaph in question being still in existence, he might now be able, with the assistance of the French Government and the Cardinal, to get it removed.

Independently of his own feelings on the matter, he was desirous of complying with the urgent prayer of the representatives of the Hebrew community at Damascus, who addressed several letters to him on that subject. "We have reason," they wrote, "to be greatly distressed on account of this epitaph, as by it the feelings of hatred and revenge entertained by Christians towards Jews may be perpetuated through coming generations. Whosoever sees the inscription is filled with hatred and indignation against Israel."

Many important meetings which he, as President of the Board of Deputies of the Congregation of British Jews, had to attend, and various engagements of communal interest, prevented Sir Moses and Lady Montefiore leaving England before May the 16th.

This delay, however, was productive of considerable pleasure to them, inasmuch as they were thereby enabled to receive the congratulations of their friends on the result of the debate in the House of Commons respecting the second reading of the

Oaths Bill (May 7). The numbers were—For, 278; against, 185; majority, 93.

Accompanied by Colonel Gawler, a gentleman who took a great interest in the colonisation of the Holy Land, and had published several valuable papers on the subject, and by the Rev. Emanuel Myers, they left Dover for Calais, reaching Marseilles on the 24th of May and Alexandria on the 5th of June.

There Sir Moses sent the Admiral's letter to Captain John Foote of the *Rosamond,* who invited him on board his ship the next day to meet Said Pasha. His Highness received Sir Moses very kindly, and expressed pleasure on meeting him again.

They left Alexandria on June 14th on board the steamer *Le Caire,* arriving at Beyrout on the 16th, where they entered the Lazaretto for twelve days.

Sir Moses presented Lord Palmerston's letter to Mr Niven Moore, Her Britannic Majesty's Consul General, who assured him of his readiness to assist him in the object of his journey to Damascus. Deputations arrived from all parts of the Holy Land, and especially from Damascus, offering their greetings of welcome and their services, but it was found desirable, in order to avoid any unnecessary excitement, to request the representatives of the deputations to return to their respective towns and await the arrival of Sir Moses there.

Dr Frankel, the doctor in charge of Sir Moses' dispensary at Jerusalem, was sent for to accompany the party to Damascus, and letters were written to the four Holy Cities, viz., Jerusalem, Hebron, Tiberias, and Safed, apprising the communities of the arrival of the travellers.

They passed twelve days in quarantine, not altogether without anxiety on account of Lady Montefiore, who was confined to her apartments for several days by illness. The heat of the weather was very oppressive, and the presence of the graves of some unfortunate travellers who died whilst in quarantine, affected their spirits very much, and conjured up gloomy reflections.

One morning a very large black snake was killed close to the door of their house. It measured six feet ten inches in length, and its bite would have been fatal. They were told that great numbers of them might sometimes be seen in the grounds of the Lazaretto.

Happily the number of letters which required their attention, and the frequent calls from their friends, did not allow them to remain long in this desponding state.

June 19th.—Colonel Moore communicated to them some news which afforded them much pleasure. The Emperor of Russia had conceded to all his subjects in the Holy Land, whose passports had expired, the right of placing themselves under British protection, which, in fact, was allowing them to become British subjects. The British Government had approved of the measure, and at this moment, the Consul said, the Russians and Poles in Syria might, if they chose, be British subjects.

June 27th.—They left the Lazaretto, proceeding to Damascus, where they arrived on July 3rd, taking up their quarters in the house of Isaac Haim Farhhi.

Her Majesty's Consul, Mr (now Sir) Richard Wood, was foremost in his attention to them. The members of the Hebrew community were rejoiced beyond description on seeing those who had made so many sacrifices for them ; but, while these manifested their great happiness, there were others, still under the influence of the ancient prejudice against the Hebrews, who could not suppress their chagrin at the presence of Sir Moses and Lady Montefiore in Damascus.

Sir Moses being desirous of ascertaining for himself whether the objectional inscription was still in existence, repaired to the Church of the Capuchins, where, to his great sorrow, he saw the stone, bearing the inscription in Italian and Arabic. He immediately had it copied in the presence of Fratre Giovannida Termini Pref° dei Mis F. Cappucciai, and Fr. Domenico de Sewazzo Mis F. Apos° Cappño, and determined to return, with as little delay as possible, to England, in order to appeal to the English Government, and, through them, to the French and Turkish Governments, for the removal of the tablet.

History affords many examples of fanaticism, but never has there been one more scurrilous and malicious than this. It has been repeated from father to son, and has insensibly become an accepted tradition. Every possible endeavour, Sir Moses thought, should be used to prevent history being tarnished by this new proof of falsehood and defamation.

Great was the anger of the people when they heard of his having been in the church and procured a copy of the epitaph. It was reported that the French authorities intended to celebrate a grand mass in commemoration of the death of Padre Tomaso, which they would attend in uniform and in their official character.

Sir Moses had frequent interviews with the principal Jewish inhabitants, and arranged with them to have some new Jewish girls' schools.

Sunday, July 7th.—They left Damascus and directed their course to Safed, where they arrived on the 15th inst. Here they encamped in tents till the 18th, then proceeded to Tiberias, where they accepted the hospitality of Mr Abulafia. On Friday they set out for Nazareth, remaining there over Sabbath and Sunday. Here a most serious incident happened, for, in the middle of the night of Saturday, they heard a terrible yelling and shouting near their tent; a woman was howling dreadfully at the loss of her child, which she said the Jews had murdered for religious purposes. Fortunately the child was soon found, and the Governor took immediate steps to punish severely the persons who had attempted to bring against Sir Moses and Lady Montefiore an accusation like that brought against the innocent Jews of Damascus. They left Nablous and went to Jerusalem, where they arrived on the 26th, remaining there for a week.

They paid a visit to Hebron for three days, returning again to Jerusalem, and from there directed their course to Jaffa, and embarked on board the *Grand Turk* for Beyrout, where they arrived on Friday, August 10th, taking apartments at the Hotel de Bellevue, to wait for the arrival of the steamer *Le Caire*.

During their sojourn in Beyrout, among the numerous visitors who called on them was Colonel Churchill, who was dressed as an Arab chief; he purposed making a tour in the mountains, and then publishing an account of his travels. Mr Moore, the English Consul, paid them long visits, and assured them that the Jews should receive every protection. Sir Moses spoke to him of the dread which the Jews of Tiberias had of increased taxation, and also of the missionaries at Jerusalem.

August 14*th.*—Signor Finzi, the British Consular Agent at Acre, who had made the journey expressly to see him and Lady Montefiore, paid them a visit. He was a very good and charitable, but not a wealthy man, whom they had seen ten years previously, when they visited the Holy Land the second time. He received no salary from the English Government for the reason, one may suppose, that there are too many in Syria who would be glad to serve in that capacity, even if they had to pay the Government for it, on account of the honour which the office confers upon them. Sir Moses, in appreciation of his services, requested his acceptance of a valuable uniform with gold embroidery and large gold buttons. The reader will perhaps smile at the choice of this present, but those who know the East, and the importance a military dress there imparts to the wearer, will understand the motive Sir Moses had in enabling a good man without means, who was a co-religionist and an English official, to appear on grand occasions as well dressed as other Consuls.

The weather being very hot and oppressive, Sir Moses thought it would strengthen him to take a little trip on the water, and invited Signor Finzi to accompany him in a small boat with four men and Ibrahim the cook, to the mouth of the Nahr-el-Kelb, a distance of seven miles by sea, and nine or ten miles by land. Colonel M. Gawler had gone there in the morning to copy the Assyrian inscription.

Though the boat was small and there was a heavy swell, the voyage was pleasant enough until they endeavoured to enter the river, when by some mistake they took the wrong channel, and the boat grounded in the surf, and the waves threatened to overwhelm it. All the men jumped into the water, and two of them seized Sir Moses and carried him on to dry ground. He was greatly alarmed, but with the assistance of Signor Finzi happily escaped with the fright and the wetting.

The Colonel soon joined them, and then proceeded to view the inscriptions, of which however he could only make out that the figure was dedicated to the Emperor Antonius. I myself had visited this spot ten years previously, and made a rough sketch of the tablet and figure at the time. The "Nahr-el-Kelb" is known to the student of ancient history by the name of Lycus, the "river of the wolf or dog," whose bark could be heard as far as Cyprus. It is of great interest to the archæologist. The view of the river when coming from Beyrout is very beautiful. A bridge of three arches is built across it, and there are three high and imposing rocks in the immediate vicinity; to the left of the bridge several waterfalls are visible between the foliage of the trees, and the scenery is altogether very grand. After crossing at the ford called Nahr Antelias, the traveller comes to Ras Nahr-el-Kelb; here the guides generally direct the attention of the traveller to the top of the promontory, where they allege a colossal figure of a dog used in former ages to stand on a kind of pedestal hewn out of the rock. During a tempest the figure was hurled into the sea, and a piece of rock is shown under the water, bearing a resemblance to a dog, and which, they say, is part of the very figure once standing on the top of the rock.

Sir Moses enjoyed the little excursion, and returned to Beyrout in good spirits.

August 16*th*.—After entrusting Signor Finzi with his offering for the poor at Haifa and Acre, and forwarding £537 to Jerusalem on behalf of the Hebrew community of Warsaw, Sir Moses bade farewell to his friends and left for Alexandria, Malta, and Marseilles, where they kept quarantine. Sir Moses was suffering from indisposition, caused by the great heat of the weather, and was made very uncomfortable by hearing that every one who could was preparing to leave Marseilles on account of the cholera, which was raging fearfully in the town. His anxiety was relieved by Clot Bey, first physician to Mohammad Ali Pasha, who assured Sir Moses that he was quite free from fever, and would soon be better. Clot Bey was most kind, coming to see Sir Moses as often as possible until his recovery, and when they left the Lazaretto, he presented Lady Montefiore with some Egyptian antiquities, with which she was greatly pleased. Clot Bey promised to pay them a visit in Ramsgate, where the Egyptian souvenir he gave to Lady Moses is still preserved in her cabinet at the Judith College, among other antique treasures. During the short stay of Sir Moses at Marseilles he made it a point of visiting the gasworks of the company of which he was a director, and so acquainting himself fully with the working of the establishment. At the hour for divine service he went to the house of prayer to return thanks to

God for his safe return from the East ; and last, though not least, he felt it his duty to pay a visit to an old invalid aunt, Miss Lydia Montefiore, whom he did not know, and who did not remember him. Although very aged and in bad health, she was in good spirits. She chatted with Sir Moses for a long time, and showed him a portrait of his grandmother, Esther Hannah Montefiore, taken when she was a young woman. Miss Montefiore assured Sir Moses that she had always endeavoured to follow the example of her parents, and would live and die a Jewess. She sent her blessing and good wishes to Lady Montefiore, who sent her a handsome souvenir in return.

The travellers soon left Marseilles, and arrived in Paris on the 11th September. Sir Moses called on the Ambassador, Lord Normanby, on the President of the Consistoire, the Chief Rabbi, the different members of the Rothschild family, and some of his own near relatives who happened to be in Paris. They all took a great interest in the exertions of Sir Moses and Lady Montefiore for the benefit of their co-religionists, and Sir Moses was glad of an opportunity to tell them of the result, and to enlist their sympathy still more for the good cause.

After a short stay in Paris, they continued their journey to England, and soon arrived in Folkestone, where they found Mrs Gawler, who had come to meet her husband. Sir Moses and Lady Montefiore here bade adieu to the Colonel and Mrs Gawler, as they were anxious to go to Ramsgate as quickly as possible. Immediately after their arrival there they attended divine service in their own Synagogue, to thank God for their safe return home.

CHAPTER III.

1849-1852.

FROM the 16th of September to the 16th of October Sir Moses spent his time partly in Ramsgate and partly in London, pursuing his usual occupations. He continued to attend the meetings of various financial companies and associations of communal and educational interest. He also devoted much time to political matters, expressing his opinions lucidly to his friends, although to strangers he would usually protest that he was no politician. As a rule he would either read or have read to him most of the political leaders in the daily papers. At this period he received a copy of the pamphlet written by his nephew, Mr Arthur Cohen, Q.C., and entitled "A few Arguments in favour of the Jews Bill." Sir Moses spoke very highly of the ability displayed by Mr Cohen in this pamphlet, as well as in a letter he had received from him at the same time on the subject of religion.

During this month they undertook two journeys to Frankfort-on-the-Maine, one for the purpose of consulting with his friends there on the subject of the Damascus inscription, and the other in compliance with an invitation from Baroness Charlotte and Baron Anselm de Rothschild to the wedding of their daughter with Baron Willie de Rothschild.

On his return to London, one of his first acts in the cause of education was the gift of a hundred guineas to the " Merchant Taylors" for a medal to the best Hebrew scholar, and in grateful remembrance of past services he was able to offer Mr Richard

Wood, Her Britannic Majesty's Consul at Damascus, a cadetship at Addiscombe for his nephew, whilst his remittances to charitable institutions, and the forwarding of medical supplies to Dr Frankel, in Jerusalem, for the dispensary, showed that he was ever mindful of the requirements of the needy.

We now come to the year 1850, the first two months of which Sir Moses devoted to making selections from papers he had received during his stay in Damascus, relative to the removal of the infamous inscription in the Capuchin Church, and when he had completed the work, he called on Lord Palmerston to request his assistance in the matter.

On that occasion he also conveyed to his Lordship the sincere gratitude of the Russian and Polish Jews in the Holy Land for having been received under the protection of the English Government, the Czar having granted the necessary permission. Lord Palmerston promised to write to Lord Normanby on the subject as soon as Sir Moses had furnished him with further particulars, and, as a matter of fact, had already informed one of the consuls, who had interfered with the religious observances of the Jews, that such conduct was against the wishes of the English Government.

In March he was present at a grand dinner given by the Lord Mayor to the Mayors of the several towns and other cities in connection with the Grand Exhibition of the Industries of all Nations. Prince Albert was in the chair; there were three hundred persons present, and the Prince made a good speech. Sir Moses contributed £100 towards the object in view.

In the same month he attended a meeting of the Elders, to inform them of an invitation he had received from the Great Synagogue in reference to the establishment of a West-End branch, towards which, under certain conditions, he and Lady Montefiore offered to contribute £500.

A few days later he was present at the Mogador Committee, when it was agreed to send 500 dollars for the relief of the poor.

At the end of the month of May he was much disturbed by the issue of a Ukase against the Jews of Moldavia and Wallachia, ordering all those who had hitherto dwelt in the villages to quit the same without delay and remove to the towns.

An appeal, signed by a great number of Moldavian and Wallachian Jews, had been forwarded to him, in which they said that, apart from the considerations that they had committed no wrong justifying so severe a decree as that of their expulsion from the villages, many thousands of their brethren would be cut off from the possibility of earning a livelihood, and would thus become reduced to penury. Their religion, they said, would be looked upon with derision and scorn; and all the accusations and calumnies which their enemies had ever raised against them in justification of this harsh measure were fictions and fabrications of their own. "We implore you," they wrote, "give ear to the supplication of your brethren, and intercede in our behalf, that the decree in question may not be put in execution."

About the same time distressing accounts reached him from the Jews at Rome. The supplicants said: "We are now more oppressed than ever; no Christian is allowed to be in a Jew's house, either as servant or companion. The Pope will receive neither an address nor a deputation from the Jews."

This was the same Sovereign Pontiff to whom an address of deep gratitude had been presented for his kind and humane treatment of the Jews.

"Wait on the Lord, and keep His way," said Sir Moses, in the words of the Royal Psalmist; "better days will yet come."

In June Sir Moses dined at the Merchant Taylors' Hall, where he met Sir Robert Peel, Lord Hardinge, Lord Salisbury, the Bishop of Oxford, and Mr Gladstone. In reply to inquiries made by some of these gentlemen, he took the opportunity of communicating the information he had received from Moldavia and Rome.

Lady Montefiore states in her Diary that she fulfilled this month the promise she made to the Duchess of Leinster, in presenting Her Grace with two plants of the cedars of Lebanon, which she had brought from the spot.

In July the labours of Sir Moses in connection with the Exhibition commenced, and he presided over a large meeting of the City Committee at the Mansion House for carrying into effect the scheme of the "Great Exhibition of the Industries of all Nations in the year 1851."

News arrived from Damascus, this time of a very gratifying character, and Sir Moses lost no time in communicating the same to the morning papers. It appeared that Osman Bey had, by order of the Sultan, remodelled the Council at Damascus, which, up to that moment, had consisted exclusively of Moslems to the number of twelve, and had formed a new Divan of Moslem, Catholic, Greek, and Jewish members.

He invited the Chief Rabbi to summon a meeting of the leading members of his community, and to elect a person of integrity and talent as a representative to attend the Council, and the choice fell on Solomon Farhhi, one of the sufferers in the lamentable affair of 1840.

During the same month he had the opportunity of witnessing in England another step towards the emancipation of the Jews. "Baron Lionel and Baron Anthony de Rothschild," says an entry in the diary of July 26th, "and others, came into the Lobby of the House of Commons. Baron Lionel went with J. Abel Smith to the Voting Office. At two the Speaker went into the House to prayers; in a few minutes afterwards we were admitted under the Gallery, Mr Smith having put our names down. Baron Lionel de Rothschild, introduced by Mr John Abel Smith and Mr Page Wood, appeared at the Table of the House, and requested to take the oath on the Old Testament; he was very much cheered, but was desired to withdraw, when Sir Harry Inglis moved a resolution to refuse his request. A long and most interesting debate then followed, and at nearly four the question was adjourned till Monday, at twelve o'clock. Mr Bernal Osborne, Mr Page Wood, Mr Joseph Hume, and several others spoke in our favour, and many against, but none with any bitterness."

July 29*th*.—"Baron Lionel was permitted to take the oaths on the Old Testament by a majority of 54, the numbers being 113 for, and 59 against."

This gratifying event was now the general topic of conversation among members of the House, and the Jews were delighted at the result.

November 7*th*.—Sir Moses again attended a meeting of the Committee of the Great Exhibition at the Mansion House, was called to the chair, and received a vote of thanks.

Subsequently he went to the Guildhall to take the oath of qualification for the City Lieutenancy, the Lord Mayor having remained for the purpose, and he then proceeded to Ramsgate.

On December 16th he had an interview with Lord Palmerston, who gave him the promised letter to Lord Normanby, the English Ambassador at Paris ; and on the 24th of December Sir Moses and Lady Montefiore proceeded to the French capital, with the object of obtaining an audience of the President of the Republic to solicit the removal of the inscription in the Church of the Capuchins at Damascus.

On his arrival at Paris he was well received by Lord Normanby, who thought that the inscription might be replaced by another, Sir Moses observing that this would quite satisfy the Jews there. General Lafitte, who was then Minister of Foreign Affairs, also granted Sir Moses an interview, and advised him to wait a few weeks, as he was expecting a report from the French Consul-General at Damascus on that very subject. Meanwhile, through the good offices of Lord Normanby, Sir Moses obtained the coveted private audience with Louis Napoleon at the Elysée, and gives the following description of it in his diary :—

" He received me most graciously, said that Lord Normanby had apprised him of my wishes, and that he was glad to see me ; asked me to be seated, and sat down himself. I requested his permission to read him my address. He listened to it with the utmost attention, and several times intimated his approval of the sentiments. When I had concluded he said, 'I am sensibly affected by your address ; I will give immediate instructions, and write very strongly. I am very happy in having it in my power to serve the cause of truth.' "

The words of the then powerful President of the French Republic could certainly not have been more satisfactory, and Sir Moses had every reason to be pleased with the result of his audience.

Before leaving Paris he had an opportunity of seeing Monsieur E. de Valbesen, the French Consul, who had just arrived from Damascus. That gentleman, however, did not give Sir Moses the information which he had so much at heart, and which would have interested him most.

Sir Moses and Lady Montefiore now returned to Ramsgate for a few days' rest, and then proceeded to London, where Sir Moses, who had been appointed Chairman of the Fine Arts Section of the Great Exhibition, had many committee meetings to attend.

On January 20th they paid their first visit to the Exhibition, which was not nearly completed. In his zeal for the promotion of the welfare of the Holy City, and with the object of drawing the attention of the public to the superior talents of his co-religionists in Palestine, Sir Moses exhibited two beautiful vases executed by Mordechai Schnitzer of Jerusalem, and consented to the request of Messrs Mortimer & Hunt of New Bond Street to allow the silver testimonial (produced by them from a design of Sir George Hayter) presented to him and Lady Montefiore on their return from Damascus to be also shown.

At this time a Committee was appointed by Parliament to investigate the subject of divorce. Sir Moses, ever watchful, called on the Chairman, Dr Lushington, and requested him to afford the Chief Rabbi an opportunity of expressing an opinion on the subject, in the event of the interests of the Jews being in any way affected by the measure to be brought before Parliament. This Dr Lushington promised to do, adding that if any Bill were introduced he should recommend that the Jews be exempted therefrom. Sir Moses referred to Lord Lyndhurst's Act, but Dr Lushington gave it as his opinion that the Jews were not affected by it; upon which Sir Moses observed that the Registrar-General thought differently, and would not grant a certificate.

March 4th.—A cry for help reached his ears from Suram in Georgia, a province of the Caucasus, the Hebrew community in that place having unfortunately been exposed to great suffering in consequence of an unfounded accusation brought against them. They now appealed to him to intercede in their behalf with the Russian Government. He lost no time in going to Baron Brunnow, who suggested that Sir Moses should write a letter to Prince Woronzow, the Governor-General of Georgia, and undertook to forward the same through Lady Pembroke. Sir Moses accordingly prepared an address to the Prince, which he submitted to the Count for his approval. The latter read it, and promised that he would himself write in support of the good cause. A few months later Sir Moses received a reply from Prince Woronzow (dated Tiflis, May 14), conveying to him the assurance that his request had been complied with, that the persecutions had ceased, and that the Jews had nothing more to complain of.

May 1st.—Sir Moses and Lady Montefiore went to the opening of the Exhibition. The building was already very full on their arrival, but Lady Montefiore secured a good seat. The

Queen and the **Prince entered at twelve.** The procession was a splendid **one, and the Palace presented a** magnificent scene. The ceremony passed **off extremely well,** without the slightest hitch, to the great delight **of** the **spectators.** Sir Moses' attention was drawn to the Russian Division of the Exhibition, where an apparatus was exhibited for ascertaining **the** value of gold and silver coins and other metals without **the** use of **fire or** chemical analysis, also to a calculating machine **for simple and** compound addition, subtraction, multiplication, **division, and extraction** of square and cubic roots, both invented **by Israel Abraham** Staffel of Warsaw. Being most anxious **to befriend** so clever a young man, **he at** once invited him **to his house, and** after impressing upon him the necessity of raising **and maintain-**ing the standard of **education in** Russia and Poland among **his** co-religionists, made **him a handsome** present.

During his visit to the **Exhibition,** representations were **made** to him regarding **the** desirability of exempting his co-religionists from signing their names on Saturday when entering the build-ing, writing being prohibited **on the Sabbath,** and he at once applied **to** Captain Elderton, **who promised to** entertain the request.

The same day **he went to the House of Commons,** where he had the satisfaction of hearing the Emancipation Bill read a second time and passed by a majority, though only **a** very small one, there being 202 for the Bill and 176 against it.

In June he gives evidence of his generosity by presenting two of his young friends, on being taken **into partnership by the** head of a business firm, with a sum **of £500, accompanied by** his best wishes for their prosperity.

In appreciation of the services which Sir **Robert Peel had rendered** to the country, Sir **Moses took a** great **interest in a** proposal for the erection of a statue **to** him, and gave **his vote in** favour of the model by Mr Henry Weekes.

Fully justified in his hopes **of** continued progress in political matters affecting the Jews in England, he now again turned his attention to the Holy Land, and **to a scheme** which had been occupying his mind **some** considerable time.

It had long been his ardent desire **to** establish a hospital in Jerusalem, and as the maintenance of such an institution neces-sitated considerable capital, he entered into correspondence with his friends **on the** subject, spent several hundred pounds **in** having proper plans drawn up by English and foreign architects, and consulted medical authorities in the large hospitals respecting various modern improvements which had been introduced. Count Pizzamano, the Austrian Consul at Jerusalem, also took a lively interest in the scheme, and promised to assist Sir Moses to his utmost.

During July and September he and Lady Montefiore visited Plymouth, Exeter, and Yarmouth, and on October the 15th we find them again in London at the closing of the Exhibition. "We were there," says Sir Moses, "at half-past nine; secured capital seats. The ceremony commenced at twelve, and was concluded before one. Prince Albert, the Bishop of London, and Lord Canning were the only persons who spoke; there was a large orchestra, and many singers; the building was very full."

On November the 11th he records in his Diary the loss he sustained by the death of an old and esteemed friend, Matthias Attwood, who was one of the original founders of the Imperial Continental Gas Association. He was often the subject of Sir Moses' conversation in connection with financial operations; and his portrait, to which he used to call the attention of his visitors, was conspicuously placed near the entrance to the Gothic library at East Cliff. In the course of the same day Mr Gladstone introduced to him Lieutenant Pym, who was going in search of Sir John Franklin, and Sir Moses made him a present of some beautiful furs.

During the year 1852 he devoted much time to important meetings in his own community, and on the 3rd of May accompanied the Chief Rabbi to Manchester for similar communal purposes.

A few days later, Dr Thompson of Beyrout came to inform him that he was on his way to Constantinople to obtain a firman for a railway route by the Euphrates Valley to India, and that he then proposed forming a company for the purpose under Colonel Chesney. Sir Moses understanding that an easy road would then be made from Aleppo to Damascus, thence to Safed and other places in the Holy Land, felt much interested in the scheme, and promised to communicate with his friends on the subject.

May 17th.—He gave a large dinner party in honour of the Lord Mayor, and in the course of the evening took the opportunity of conversing with several gentlemen present on the subject of Colonel Chesney's proposed railway scheme.

CHAPTER IV.

1852.

"ON June 21," Sir Moses writes, "at six o'clock in the
morning I received a telegraphic note, informing me
of the arrival of his Highness Mohammed Said Pasha, Prince
héréditaire d'Egypte," who very shortly afterwards became
Khedive.

"I went," Sir Moses writes in his Diary, "to the railway
station, and at ten minutes to eight his Highness arrived. He
immediately got into our carriage, and, as we were driving off,
the Turkish Ambassador came to receive him and followed us
to Park Lane. The Pasha was attended by Mr Zohrab, Mr
Galloway, two physicians—Dr Gaëtani Bey and Dr G. A. Haage,
Zoulfikar Effendi, Ali Capitan, his Secretary, and four Mamelukes, his servants. They all came to Park Lane. The Pasha
took a pipe and coffee, and then all, together with the Ambassador, went down to breakfast. At twelve His Highness, myself,
Mr Zohrab, and Mr Galloway went to Greenwich. The physicians
and secretaries followed in our carriage. We went on board
His Majesty's yacht, the *Hásseid Háïr* or *Good Omen*, Captain
Longridge, a screw steamer magnificently fitted up In about
two hours we got under way, and ran down to near Gravesend
at the rate of twelve miles an hour. On our way back there
was an elegant dinner served on board, and on coming to anchor
at Greenwich I went on shore with Mr Galloway, the Pasha and
his suite remaining on board.

"*June* 22*nd*.—We went in our carriage to Greenwich, met
there Mr Galloway and Gaëtani Bey, and went on board His
Highness's yacht. After paying our respects to him, he and all

the party went on shore. He chose the large carriage. I and
Mr Galloway and Gaëtani Bey accompanied him to the Royal
Observatory. Professor Airy very kindly showed His Highness
and all the party his astronomical instruments and explained
their use. We then rode to Park Lane, where my dear wife had
prepared a splendid entertainment for His Highness and party ;
there were ten at table. In the evening the Pasha had many
visitors, including the Turkish Ambassador.

"*June 23rd.*—The Turkish Ambassador called on the Pasha
at about twelve ; they went to Lord Malmesbury, who introduced him to the Queen and Prince Albert at Buckingham
Palace. The Government sent Captain E. Stopford Claremont,
of the Royal Canadian Rifles, to attend on His Highness during
his stay in England. The Turkish Ambassador called at eleven
for the Pasha. They went with Captain Claremont to Mrs
Disraeli's grand reception, with which the Pasha was much
pleased.

"*June 24th.*—The Pasha received an invitation from our
beloved Sovereign to dinner at the Palace to-morrow, also from
the Duke of Northumberland to dinner on Saturday, and for
Friday, 2nd of July, from Lord Hardinge. The Prince went to
Vauxhall soon after ten o'clock.

"*June 25th.*—At half-past eight I was in the park with the
Pasha to see the Guards drill ; they were reviewed by Prince
Albert and the Duke of Cambridge, who both rode up and spoke
to him. At eleven Captain Claremont and myself, with the
Pasha, went to Wormwood Scrubbs to see a review of three
cavalry regiments by the Duke of Cambridge, and returned at
one o'clock to Park Lane. The Pasha went in the evening to
dine with Her Majesty.

"*June 26th.*—The Pasha went this morning to Woolwich
with Captain Claremont. All the foreign Ministers left cards
for His Highness to-day, also the Duke of Cambridge, Lord
Derby, Lord Palmerston, &c. I called on Baron Brunnow ; he
spoke much about the Pasha. The Pasha dined with the Duke
of Northumberland, and gave his arm to the Princess Mary of
Cambridge. He returned soon after, much pleased with his
day's amusement. He smoked a pipe, gave me one, and remained chatting with us for some time. He was received at
Woolwich with all the honours usually paid to a prince of the

blood. The Pasha assured us that our dinners were better than any he had eaten elsewhere. He has ordered the yacht to sail to-morrow, but we do not go with him to Ramsgate, as he must pass the morning with the Duc de Montpensier.

"*June 27th.*—The Pasha went to Richmond to breakfast with the Duc de Montpensier. They afterwards rode to Claremont to see the Queen of the French and other members of the French Royal family. We did not expect him back to dinner, but he returned to Park Lane at six o'clock, and we fortunately had a very good dinner to offer him. In the evening the Turkish Ambassador came and stayed till ten o'clock.

"*June 28th.*—The Pasha went with Mr Zohrab to see Maudsley's manufactory of steam-engines. The Ambassador came in the evening to smoke a pipe with the Pasha.

"*June 29th.*—The Pasha breakfasted in the parlour, and had afterwards a numerously attended levée. He then went to the Duchess of Cambridge with the Turkish Minister.

"*Park Lane, July 2nd.*—This morning my dear wife and I went to Woolwich to be present at the review given to His Highness Said Pasha. Our carriage was placed in a capital situation, close to the colours, near which the Duke of Cambridge, Lord Hardinge, and General Fox were to review the troops. The Pasha dined with Lord Hardinge.

"*Saturday, July 3rd.*—The Turkish Ambassador came at 7.30, and the Pasha accompanied him to dine at Lord Palmerston's.

"*Park Lane, Sunday, July 4th.*—Just returned from seeing His Highness Said Pasha set off for Portsmouth. His Highness expressed his high gratification for our attention to him during his stay in London, and insisted upon Judith's acceptance of a very beautiful and richly embroidered dress as a small souvenir. I hope and believe that not only His Highness but all his officers have been pleased with our desire to make them comfortable, and I trust that, by God's blessing, His Highness will be a friend to our co-religionists in Egypt and the Holy Land when he becomes Viceroy of Egypt.

"His Highness partook of a splendid breakfast with all his party before they left. The Turkish Ambassador and his brother came at nine, and half-an-hour later I went with His Highness and the Turkish Ambassador and Captain Claremont in His

Highness's open carriage to the Waterloo Station, my carriage and that of the Ambassador following. There were several persons connected with His Highness at the station to see him off.

"His Highness has been very kind, good tempered, and affable during his sojourn with us, and repeatedly told us that he was more comfortable with us than he had been anywhere else since his arrival in England.

"At one to-day I delivered into the care of Said Agha a parcel which was left by His Highness, to be given to him when he called for it."

July 5th.—Sir Moses received a note from Mr Zohrab, informing him of the Pasha's safe arrival on board his yacht at Portsmouth, and Sir Moses now considered himself free to pursue his usual occupations.

The next day he was present at the Guildhall, when the candidates for the city of London addressed the Livery. The show of hands was declared by the Sheriffs to be in favour of J. Masterman, Lord John Russell, Baron Lionel de Rothschild, and Mr Crawford. On the following morning Sir Moses rode to the city at an early hour, and voted at the Guildhall for Baron Lionel de Rothschild. By five in the evening his return was perfectly secure, but Alderman Solomons was not equally successful, to the great regret of Sir Moses.

July 9th.—Captain Hopford Claremont having written to say that His Highness the Pasha requested Sir Moses to lend him his travelling carriage, and to send it to Dover, Sir Moses and Lady Montefiore determined to pass the Sabbath at Dover, and to see His Highness again before he left England. They directed their coachman to take the carriage by train to Dover, and taking with them six pounds of the finest hothouse grapes as a present for the Pasha, they proceeded to Dover. On their arrival they went to the Ship Hotel, where rooms had been taken for the Pasha, and dinner ordered.

His Highness soon sent for Sir Moses to come and dine with him. He was very chatty, and said he should leave to-morrow for Ostend, but Captain Claremont told Sir Moses that the Pasha had changed his plans twenty times, and might do so again. Sir Moses told the Pasha that his travelling carriage was already at Dover at His Highness's service, and that he had taken care that it was in good order. His Highness was in good spirits, "and would, I have no doubt," Sir Moses says, " have gone back with me to Park Lane or to East Cliff, if I had invited him."

July 10*th*.—" The Pasha has," Sir Moses observes, " at length left the English shore, and probably for ever. I hope he will remember the kindness and attention shown to him by the British Government as well as by individuals, and that he may, whenever in his power, serve the British interest, and befriend my brethren in the East."

" The Pasha is," Sir Moses writes, " a young man with a good heart, but somewhat of a spoiled child : he is extremely sharp, quick, and discerning, positive in his manner, but at the same time, most courteous. For his great size he is very active, and enjoys excellent health. May good fortune and happiness attend him, and may the Almighty shield him from the temptations of ambition.

During the latter part of this year, Sir Moses attended various meetings of the Board of Deputies of British Jews, convened for the purpose of preparing a draft deed for making parliamentary grants to educational institutions. Whilst engaged in making preparations for another journey he received the news of the death of one of his aunts, which caused him much grief, but in consequence of his public character, he was not allowed long to brood over private misfortunes. On this occasion it was the oppressions suffered by his brethren at Tunis which roused him to intercede with the authorities on their behalf; and he addressed a petition to the Bey accordingly. Before the close of the year he and Lady Montefiore had the gratification of receiving a very kind letter from Said Pasha, thanking them for their hospitality, and offering Sir Moses his services in the East.

His attention in the years 1853 and 1854 was principally directed to communal matters in his own congregation, and to an extensive correspondence with Hebrew communities in foreign countries.

He received a communication from the Rev. S. M. Isaacs, a minister of one of the Hebrew communities in New York, referring to the " North American Relief Society," an institution founded by Mr Sampson Simon and himself (the Rev. S. M. Isaacs) for the purpose of creating a capital, the interest of which was to be annually appropriated to the support of the poor Israelites in the Holy Land.

He made the first remittance of the amount to Sir Moses, and requested that he would forward the same to Jerusalem. Sir Moses acceded to his wishes with pleasure, and continued to forward the remittances of that society, amounting to £145 every year, until his death.

The Rev. S. M. Isaacs also informed him of the death of a great philanthropist, Juda Touro of New Orleans, who had left the North American Relief Society $10,000, and a further sum of $50,000 for the benefit of the poor Israelites in Palestine; the latter sum subject to Sir Moses' control, conjointly with the executors.

Knowing the interest Sir Moses took in Jewish communal affairs, Mr Isaacs gave him all the particulars respecting his wealthy friend, who desired to benefit the poor, without distinction of creed or nationality. "Mr Touro," he wrote, "has left princely legacies of $20,000 for the hospital recently established at New York, $40,000 for educational purposes, and $80,000 to various synagogues. He has also left munificent gifts (more than $200,000) to Christian charities.

His remains are to be interred at Newport, Rhode Island, where his family are buried. He has left $10,000 for the endowment of the office of minister there, has given a synagogue worth $50,000 to the Hebrew community at New Orleans, and endowed it richly; he has also given a hospital, munificently endowed, to his co-religionists in New Orleans.

Sir Moses immediately expressed his willingness to forward the remittance of the North American Relief Society to the Holy Land, and to accept the trust of the Touro legacy, respecting the application of which I shall give the reader full particulars as I proceed further.

At the same time he received a communication from the Holy Land which gave him great pain. It conveyed the intelligence that there was great suffering in Palestine, and Sir Moses at once addressed the Chief Rabbi on the subject.

"For the sake of Zion," he writes to him, "I cannot remain silent, and for the sake of Jerusalem I cannot rest, until the whole house of Israel have been made acquainted with the lamentable condition of those of our brethren who devotedly cling to the soil sacred to the memory of our patriarchs, prophets, and kings.

"Thrice having visited the Holy Land, it was my earnest desire fully to inform myself as to the condition of our brethren there, for whom my deepest feelings of commiseration were excited, in regard to the amount of misery endured by them.

"Poverty in the East differs vastly from the like calamity experienced in Western Europe, inasmuch as the capability to relieve is in the East confined within the narrowest bounds, and restricted to a very limited number. Such being the general outline of the condition of our brethren in Judea, my feelings were most naturally aroused in their behalf.

"But, reverend sir, judge to what extent my sympathies are now awakened, when—as I informed you, from the harrowing intelligence it has been my painful lot to receive, both from direct and indirect sources—I learn that 'fathers in Israel'—men profoundly learned in the law, who, so that they may die near the graves of their forefathers, submit to live in the most abject poverty—are now impelled by the very love they bear towards their children to sell them to the stranger, 'so,' to use their own words, 'that their offspring may be spared death from starvaton.'

"Reverend and respected sir, I am loudly called upon by our brethren in the Holy Land, as the annexed letters will show, and farther prompted by the voice within me, to urge their claims on the notice of the congregations of Israel, and to request their immediate and liberal assistance.

"Aware, however, reverend sir, of your great anxiety for the physical amelioration of our suffering brethren, and how watchfully you note their spiritual welfare, I am induced to put you in possession of the documents and appeals which I have received from the Holy Land, with the assurance that your powerful co-operation, in the shape of a pastoral letter addressed to the Jews of Great Britain and America, or the exercise of the same in any other mode your wisdom may dictate, will, with God's blessing, not only tend to remove the present appalling misery of our starving brethren in Zion, but spare us the humiliation of its recurrence."

The Chief Rabbi, the Rev. Dr N. M. Adler, expressed great sympathy in his reply to Sir Moses, and addressed a pastoral letter to the wardens and members of the United Congregations of Great Britain, the result of which was that an appeal was made on behalf of the starving Jews in the Holy Land, which realised £19,887.

The Chief Rabbi and Sir Moses were appointed trustees of the Appeal Fund, and a committee was nominated, consisting of the following gentlemen: Mr Henry Louis Cohen, Mr S. L. de Symons, jun., Mr Philip Lucas, jun., Mr A. J. Montefiore, and myself, the Rev. A. L. Green acting as honorary secretary.

In the month of February, at Scarborough, Sir Moses was attacked by a most dangerous illness, which confined him to his bed for forty-three days. He was attended by a physician and a surgeon, both very eminent men, who visited him regularly three or four times a day.

On the 5th of March Lady Montefiore wrote in reply to my inquiry: "In compliance with your request I snatch a moment from the sick couch of Sir Moses to give you the pleasing information that our medical attendants pronounce our dear invalid to be improving since yesterday. He has suffered severely, and been in danger; but now I trust, with the Almighty's blessing, that he will progress towards recovery."

In his Diary he makes an entry on the 27th in the following words :—

"Though I am still extremely weak and nervous, yet Scarborough, being bleak and cold at this season, and exposed to the prevalent north-east winds, I was advised to return home as soon as possible, and to-day is the first time I am able to write."

At the end of March Sir Moses and Lady Montefiore returned to London, and found the town in great excitement on account of war having been declared with Russia. Sir Moses, although still weak, had to receive a great number of friends, who called to congratulate him on his recovery, and took the opportunity to ask his opinion as to the effect the war would have on the financial world, as serious consequences were feared. He gave them his opinion, which afterwards proved entirely correct. He also attended an important meeting of the Alliance Assurance Company, but was advised by his physicians that so much exertion was not good for him in his weak state, and induced to go to East Cliff for rest. Some months later he had occasion to call at Belvedere House, Erith, the seat of Sir Culling-Eardley, the great-grandson of Gideon Sampson, a Jewish capitalist of the eighteenth century. Sir Culling showed to Sir Moses the tombstone of Gideon Sampson, which he had caused to be removed from the cemetery of the Portuguese Jewish congregation in London, and to be placed close to a new church which he had built in that locality. Many members of the Hebrew community disapproved greatly of the removal of the stone, as it had a Hebrew inscription expressing the grief felt by the deceased at having left the community.

Sir Moses brought the subject of the distress in the Holy Land and the appeal that was being made to the notice of Sir Culling, who gave a very handsome contribution towards the fund, and promised to interest himself as much as possible in securing donations from friends and acquaintances. Among the numerous contributors there was one known to Sir Moses and myself by the signature of "Anonymous," who always greatly encouraged the study of Hebrew literature and the sacred writings in Tiberias. For many years he used to remit his donation to Sir Moses, with a request to forward it to the Holy City, though his position in society and the tenor of his conversation would generally have led his friends to think that he was unfavourably disposed towards the tenets of the Mosaic code. Among Sir Moses' correspondents there were many who, on subjects of religion, expressed sentiments differing considerably from those which they expressed in their usual intercourse, showing that there are, unfortunately, a good many persons in society who have not the moral courage to express openly what they feel in their hearts, from fear of incurring the displeasure of those whose opinions, from motives of interest, they are impelled to court.

CHAPTER V.

1854-1855.

JULY 25th.—The *Times* published the news of Abbas Pasha's death and Said Pasha's succession. Sir Moses immediately addressed letters of congratulation to the new ruler, expressing at the same time the hope that under his benign sway a new era of prosperity would begin in the Holy Land.

August 5th.—Mr Gershon Kursheedt, one of the executors of the late Juda Touro, of New Orleans, arrived to arrange with Sir Moses about the legacy of fifty thousand dollars left at his disposal for the purpose of relieving the poor Israelites in the Holy Land in such manner as Sir Moses should advise.

Sir Moses, at the first interview he had with this gentleman, suggested that the money should be employed in building a hospital in Jerusalem. Mr Kursheedt immediately assented, and Sir Moses gave him the plan and drawing made about a year before, and he said the thing was done. He was most happy, as it settled the principal business he had in England; the co-executors had given him full power to agree to any plan Sir Moses should propose. A letter was prepared by a solicitor to that effect, which Mr Kursheedt signed.

A remittance of £1200 from the Appeal Fund was now forwarded to the Holy Land, and instructions were given to the representatives of the various communities to have Loan Societies in each of the four Holy Cities. Letters were addressed to the Baroness James de Rothschild in Paris and Baron Amschel de Rothschild at Frankfort, to apprise them of the legacy of the late Juda Touro, and of the manner in which it had been decided to employ it.

Sir Moses, however, had soon to learn that Mr Kursheedt had been induced to alter his mind, and had withdrawn the consent he had given to the building of a hospital. The 15th of August, it appears, had been fixed by Sir Moses for communicating the consent of Mr Kursheedt to the American Consul in London, but at the appointed hour, when Sir Moses met Mr Kursheedt at the Alliance, the latter, to Sir Moses' great surprise, said that he must decline going with him to the American Consul, and could not sign the proposed memorandum.

August 22nd.—Sir Moses went to Lord Clarendon to acquaint him with his desire to obtain a firman from the Sultan, giving power to purchase land for agricultural purposes, buildings, &c.; as also to build a hospital in Jerusalem with a Synagogue attached to it. His Lordship said he had written to Lord Stratford de Redcliffe, but there were great difficulties regarding the land ; as to the hospital, he had heard that one for the Jews had been opened only a month since. This was the hospital known by the name of the " Rothschilds Hospital." Sir Moses informed his Lordship of the Juda Touro bequest, and received a promise that he should be assisted in his good work whenever necessary.

September 19th.—He called on Mr B. Osborn at the Admiralty, to request that he would give him a letter enabling him to see the Russian Jewish prisoners of war at Sheerness.

That gentleman acceded to his request, and gave him a letter to the superintendent of the dockyard, Captain Tucker. An opportunity of seeing them was thus afforded him, and by the permission of the Captain he left many tokens of his benevolence to be distributed, according to the judgment of the superintendents, among the men, women, and children.

September 20th was the day on which the great battle on the left bank of the Alma was fought. In commemoration of the victory of the English, Her Majesty graciously appointed a " Royal Commission of the Patriotic Fund" for the collection and distribution of the money pouring in for the widows and orphans of our soldiers, sailors, and marines who had died in the war, to which Sir Moses at once contributed £200.

At the Board meetings of the Alliance Marine and Alliance

Fire Assurance Companies, and at the Imperial Continental Gas Association, Sir Moses, being in the chair, successfully pleaded in favour of the fund, and obtained donations to the amount of £600 from the three offices.

The Central Jewish Consistory of France having petitioned the Emperor to extend the privileges about to be obtained for the Christians in Turkey to Jews who might be subjects of the Sultan, he was most anxious that an application of a like import should be made to our Government without delay. He communicated with the London Committee of Deputies of the British Jews, and an address to that effect was sent to Lord Clarendon.

As President of the Board of the same committee, accompanied by the solicitor and secretary of the same, he called on the Lord Advocate of Scotland on the subject of the Scotch Birth Register Bill, and it was intimated to him that the wishes of his ro-religionists would be complied with.

As one of the trustees of the appeal fund, he forwarded remittances for the relief of the poor in the Holy Land, a duty which frequently necessitated his attendance at the committee for whole days together.

He consulted an eminent physician regarding his health. The latter examined his heart and lungs, and informed him that his heart was feeble, there was poison in his blood, and his digestive organs were not perfect. The disheartening statement of the doctor, however, did not prevent him from continuing his labours, nor stop his preparations for another journey to the East.

The trustees of the appeal fund on behalf of the suffering Jews in the Holy Land published their first report, in which they enumerated the several appropriations of money they had made up to date, giving at the same time the detailed particulars of the grants awarded for immediate relief, those made in augmentation of the funds of existing charities, and the sums set apart for the establishment of institutions designed to relieve distress, and to encourage and promote industry.

"With reference to the future," the report stated, " it was the intention of Sir Moses to proceed shortly, accompanied by Lady Montefiore, to the Holy Land, to ascertain, by personal inspection and examination of the several charities the extent to which the temporary and provisional relief, already mentioned, had proved effective, and to organise the best means which might be devised for the appropriation of the remainder of the funds, with the view to the utmost benefit of the supplicants, and, at the same time, to the effectual accomplishment of the intentions of the benevolent contributors."

Before they set out on that mission, there was still a great deal of communal work in connection with the London Committee of Deputies of British Jews to be done. There was the new Marriage Act, in which a clause had to be inserted to exempt the Jews from Lord Lyndhurst's Act regarding affinity and consanguinity, and it was the duty of Sir Moses, as president, to take the necessary steps in the matter. He also attended various meetings of the "Assyrian Excavation Fund," and was present at the meeting of the City Lieutenancy at the Guildhall, where he took the oath of qualification.

March 25*th.*—Sir Moses called on Lord Palmerston, and informed him of his intention of going to the East with the object of erecting a hospital at Jerusalem and encouraging the cultivation of land in Palestine, which would be greatly promoted by the security afforded by the presence of Turkish troops, officered by Englishmen, and by the Sultan allowing Jews to purchase land. He also wished to secure the removal of the inscription from the tombstone in the Church of the Capuchins at Damascus. His Lordship said that the hospital was a desirable institution. The superstition of the Turks, he believed, created obstacles which prevented Englishmen from buying land in Syria, but it might be obtained on long leases. As for the troops, they wanted all the men they could get now for the war. He however wrote a letter to Lord Stratford de Redcliffe, and another to Lord Cowley, which he handed to Sir Moses, wishing him every success. Lord Clarendon, he said, would give him letters to the Consuls.

On the 17th April Sir Moses proceeded to Windsor for the purpose of assisting at the presentation of an address to the Emperor of the French on behalf of the Commission of Lieutenancy. The Lord Mayor had already preceded him, and they at once went to the Castle. "There," the entry in the Diary records, "we were soon admitted to the presence of the Emperor. The Lord Mayor read the address, to which His Majesty made a very kind reply. The Lord Mayor then presented Colonel Wilson, as the mover of the address, and Mr Moon, as the seconder, with myself. The Emperor most graciously said to me, ' I remember having already had the pleasure of seeing you in Paris.' "

April 19*th.*—Sir Moses and Lady Montefiore went to the Guildhall to witness the presentation of the city address to the Emperor and Empress of the French. " It was impossible," Sir Moses said, " to have been present at a more gratifying sight." " The Emperor's reply was most distinctly heard in every part of the hall."

April 25*th.*—With the concurrence of Lady Montefiore, Sir Moses, accompanied by the author, started for Paris, where he at once called on Lord Cowley, the British Ambassador, and informed him of his earnest desire to place a petition into the hands of the Emperor, in which he begged for a letter to the French Consul at Damascus, to enable him to secure the removal of the infamous inscription from the Church of the Capuchins. A few days later Sir Moses received a letter from Lord Cowley to the effect that he had placed the petition into the hands of the Emperor Napoleon.

April 30*th.*—Sir Moses called on his Lordship to thank him for his courtesy, and then rode to the Tuileries to put his name in the Emperor's book. We then left Paris.

Preparations for the fourth journey to Jerusalem were now made with great expedition, and Tuesday, the 15th of May, was fixed for our departure.

Before leaving England Sir Moses had the satisfaction of receiving a further sum of about £3000 in addition to the £5028 of the Juda Touro legacy already remitted to him on the 24th of February, and Mr Kursheedt was now, it appeared, in possession of full powers regarding the building of the hospital in Jerusalem.

Sunday, May 13*th.*—Sir Moses and Lady Montefiore started for Dover, where they were soon joined by their relatives, Mr and Mrs H. Guedalla, by Mr Kursheedt, and myself.

After calling on the Wardens of the Synagogue to give them instructions regarding the distribution of some of his offerings, he took leave of the numerous friends who had come expressly to Dover to see us off. We reached Calais at one. In spite of the recent gales the sea was tolerably smooth.

Sir Moses' carriage having been very much injured by the rolling of the ship, it was found dangerous to use it, and to his great vexation no coach-maker in Calais could repair it ; he was therefore obliged to send it back to London.

All our luggage—an immense number of packages—had to be taken out, and marked with our names. "The railway charges," Sir Moses says, "will be immense, but I must submit to the disappointments and vexations I am doomed to meet."

His servants made everything comfortable, but in order to be ready to start at two in the morning, Sir Moses did not go to bed at all. This was a peculiar habit of his which I noticed on all his journeys. However tired others around him may have been, he would sit up and write or arrange his numerous memoranda.

We left Calais on May the 17th, and proceeded *viâ* Cologne and Dresden to Prague, where we remained during the Pentecost festival, visiting the celebrated ancient Synagogue, known by the name of "Alt-Neu-Schul," the restoration of which, after a great fire, dates from soon after the year 1142, and the ancient burial ground, in which there is a tombstone bearing the Hebrew date of 4366 A.M., corresponding to 1280 of the Christian era.

The short stay of Sir Moses and Lady Montefiore in that city was made particularly gratifying to them by the great number of deputations they received from communal, educational, and literary institutions.

The Rev. S. L. Rapoport, the spiritual head of the community, spoke to them on several occasions on the subject of the Holy Land, and the necessity of securing protection to its Hebrew inhabitants.

May 25th.—We left Prague for Kolin, where we attended the examination of the pupils of the Hebrew Communal School, under the direction of the eminent Chief Rabbi Frank ; and Sir Moses and Lady Montefiore, as a token of their satisfaction with the teachers and pupils, left a sum of money with the school committee for the purpose of having a medal struck, with their Chief Rabbi's name on it, to be given as a prize to the best scholar.

We left Kolin early in the morning, and reached Vienna the next day.

Monday, 28th.—Baron Anselm de Rothschild called. He conversed with Sir Moses on the subject of the journey, and offered his services. Lord Westmoreland invited Sir Moses to dinner. The representatives of the Hebrew community and most of their members came to pay their respects, and expressed their wishes for a happy and successful journey.

We remained in the Austrian Metropolis three days, and then proceeded *via* Laibach to Adelsberg, making a halt in the latter town for two days, for the purpose of visiting the famous grotto, which, in honour of Sir Moses and Lady Montefiore, was illuminated by one thousand candles.

The formations produced here by the union of the stalactites and stalagmites are of the most pituresque beauty and effect, and the guides have a variety of names for them. One they call "the throne," another "the altar," and a third they call "the Synagogue."

One might almost be justified in assuming that they introduced the latter appellation on the very day of our arrival for the special purpose of paying Sir Moses a compliment. Sir Moses at all events appeared to regard it as such. He accepted from the guide a beautiful piece of stalactite as a souvenir of his visit to the grotto, for which he gave him in return a very handsome present. It was preserved in his library to the day of his death.

June 3rd.—We continued our journey to Trieste, where we remained five days. As in Prague and Vienna, solemn services were held in the Synagogues, both German and Portuguese, which were brilliantly lighted for the occasion, and addresses were delivered by the ministers and spiritual heads of the Hebrew community.

On Sunday, June 17th, we arrived at Constantinople, and took up our quarters with Mr Abraham Camundo at Galata. During the first days of his arrival, Sir Moses delivered his letters, and called on Lord Stratford de Redcliffe, Ali Pasha, the Grand Vizier, Rechid Pasha, and Rifaat Pasha, being most anxious to hear from Mr Pisani what arrangements had been made by the Turkish Minister regarding his audience with the Sultan.

"*June 25th.*—Received a note from Mr Pisani, stating that the Secretary of the Turkish Government had informed him that the Sultan would receive me at a private audience on Thursday next.

"*June 27th.*—Dr Loewe brought me a note from Mr Pisani, informing me that the Turkish Ministers, being desirous of showing me some mark of the high esteem they entertain for me, expressed the desire of conferring upon me the honour of the Medjidjeh.

"*June 28th.*—Soon after two o'clock Mr Et. Pisani came, and he accompanied me and Dr Loewe to the Palace. We were shown into a large handsome room, and served with pipes and coffee; the mouthpiece of the one I had was worth at least £200, and the cup-stand was ornamented with diamonds. Having sat some time, an aide-de-camp of the Sultan informed us that the Sultan had gone to the New Palace, and wished to see me there. About ten minutes afterwards we were met by an officer at the first gate, and I had to walk round the Palace; at least it took us twenty minutes before we reached the door. Here we entered by a private gate, and walked up to the Sultan in a splendid room, though but partially furnished. His Majesty was standing, and, on Mr Pisani presenting me to him, he graciously said he remembered me very well, and was happy to see me again. I then informed His Majesty of the purport of my visit in nearly the same words that I had addressed to his Ministers, and prayed His Majesty to grant me his countenance and support and his compliance with my petition to the Porte. His Majesty replied that it was his happiness and duty to do all in his power to promote the welfare of his subjects; that he would grant my request, and was happy to do so for my philanthropy and humanity.

"I expressed my gratitude, and then introduced Dr Loewe as having accompanied me on my former visit to His Majesty, and as having made a translation of a hieroglyphical inscription on the obelisk in the Atmedan (Hyppodrome). Mr Pisani was here my interpreter. We then bowed, and backed out of His Majesty's presence. We were conducted out of the Palace through a magnificent marble arch to the carriage.

"I feel deeply indebted to Lord de Redcliffe, who has by his great kindness aided my endeavours to assist my co-religionists in Palestine. May God reward him. Amen.

"I entreated Mr Pisani to obtain the firman for me by Monday next, and he promised to do his best. He rode with Dr Loewe and me as far as the Arsenal, where he took leave of us.

We returned to Mr Camundo's, much delighted with the success of our mission, but excessively fatigued.

"*Friday, 29th.*—My dear Judith and I walked to the British Embassy, and were most kindly received by Lord and Lady Stratford de Redcliffe ; we were there nearly two hours. His Lordship had been informed of all that had passed at my audience with the Sultan, and was pleased with the result. He will give me a letter to Mr Wood (now Sir Richard Wood) at Damascus, respecting the inscription in the Capuchin Church, and will endeavour to obtain my firman on Monday next. He spoke for some time to me respecting the Holy Land, and the purchase of land there. A few years since three Englishmen bought an estate of 40,000 acres, with much good timber, within two miles of the Sea of Mormora, within a mile of a town, and with good roads, for £15,000 sterling.

"Lady Stratford was most courteous, and walked with Judith and me through her garden ; it is quite a paradise. They wanted us to stop and dine with them, but on account of the Sabbath in the evening, we could not accept.

"*July 1st.*—Mr William Doria of the British Embassy came with his Káwáss, and accompanied me to the Porte, and to Ali Pasha, the Grand Vizier. Dr Loewe went with me. His Excellency claimed acquaintance with me, and confirmed in the most flattering manner all that His Majesty the Sultan had promised me. He said the firman should be ready in two or three days. Ali Pasha is a mild and agreeable man, and expressed much pleasure in assisting my philanthropic efforts.

"*July 2nd.*—Dr Loewe accompanied me to Rechid Pasha. We smoked a pipe, and had coffee with him. He will send me to-morrow letters of introduction to the Governors of Beyrout and Jerusalem. On my taking leave, he said I should write to him from England, if I should at any time desire anything for my co-religionists. I gave him a copy of Dr Loewe's Circassian and Turkish Dictionary ; he conversed with the Doctor about it."

CHAPTER VI.

1855.

ARRIVAL AT JERUSALEM—MISS ROGER'S DESCRIPTION OF THE JEWISH GIRLS' SCHOOL THERE—SIR MOSES PURCHASES A PIECE OF LAND—ORIENTAL METHODS OF BARGAINING.

ON July 3rd Sir Moses writes: "Mr Pisani informed me he had received the firman for the building of an hospital, and also that for myself, which, according to the usual practice, he had forwarded to the Ambassador for transmission to me; adding in his note, 'I also have the satisfaction to announce to you that the Sultan has been pleased to confer upon you the Medjidjeh of the second class.'

"This distinction will, I hope, convince the people in the East that His Imperial Majesty the Sultan and his Government approve of my efforts for my co-religionists.

"*July 4th.*—I went with Dr Loewe over the two hospitals at Therapia. They were in perfect order, and most of the inmates were convalescent. We saw some cholera and fever patients, and a number of soldiers, some of them most severely wounded. Later on we walked to Lord Stratford de Redcliffe's. He said my firmans were all ready, and they should be sent to the British Consul at Pera for me, as was usual; I should get them to-morrow morning. At the same time he presented me with the order the Sultan had conferred upon me. He would, he said, inform the British Government of it in his despatches, and would add his wish that Her Majesty the Queen would allow me to wear it, as he knew it would afford the Sultan much pleasure. I presented Dr Loewe to Lord Stratford. On taking leave he wished me again every success."

July 5th.—Sir Moses had now received all the letters and important papers promised to him; and not wishing to lose a day unnecessarily, gave orders for our departure, having previously expressed his warmest thanks to Mr Abraham Camundo for the hospitality he had received at his hands.

We left Constantinople on board the *Impératrice*, much pleased with the result of our mission, and directed our course towards the Holy Island.

Wherever practicable Sir Moses went on shore to acquaint himself with the state of the Jews in the locality, but where this was impossible, deputations came on board and presented addresses. He thus had ample opportunities to ascertain the exact condition of his brethren in Smyrna, Rhodes, Messina, Scandroon (Alexandretta), Latakia, Cyprus, and Beyrout, and at the proper time Sir Moses availed himself of his information to the advantage of those who stood in need of his intercession with their respective governments.

On July 18th we arrived at Jerusalem. On nearing the spot from which the Holy City is first seen by the traveller, we dismounted as usual for a short prayer, and were met by thousands of people who came to greet Sir Moses and Lady Montefiore. His Excellency Kiamil Pasha, the Governor of Jerusalem, sent an escort of horsemen. The Haham Bashi, at the head of the members of his ecclesiastical court, the representatives of the congregations, deputations from schools, and the most influential citizens, came to meet the travellers and welcome them to the Holy City. A guard of honour was drawn up by order of the Pasha, and the people generally evinced their pleasure by continually firing off guns and pistols as a sort of *feu de joie*.

Tents were then pitched outside the city, at the corner of the Máïdân, nearest the walls.

Information having already been given to the authorities in Jerusalem that Sir Moses would be the bearer of important official documents, many persons called to ascertain their nature. To the British Consul, to whom Sir Moses had special letters of introduction from the British Government, he showed the firman he had obtained, by the intercession of Lord Napier, for the rebuilding of an ancient synagogue belonging to the German Hebrew congregation, and also a Vizierial letter, enjoining the Governor of the Holy City to give him every assistance to enable him to carry out his benevolent intentions.

Mr James Finn, Her Britannic Majesty's Consul, presented Sir Moses officially to the Pasha, who received him with great kindness.

In the presence of the Council of the City Effendis the firman was read out. The Pasha and the members of the Council remained standing whilst it was being read.

Many complimentary speeches then followed.

Sir Moses afterwards went to the barracks to see the Mosque of Omar and the adjacent courts and buildings from the roof; and paid a visit to the commandant to thank him for the attentions he had shown to him. On leaving the house a guard of honour was turned out, presenting arms as he passed, the commandant himself walking with him along the street as far as the spot where the sedan chair was waiting for him.

The day following being the anniversary of the destruction of the two temples, was kept by all of us in solemn devotion, attending Divine service, and abstaining from food and drink during four-and-twenty hours, which in the hot weather in Jerusalem requires some resolution.

Neither Sir Moses nor Lady Montefiore showed any sign of faintness or exhaustion, and whilst others hastened to take a glass of water as soon as stars appeared in the sky, they proceeded, but slowly, to prepare for the breaking of the long fast.

July 26th.—They received an invitation from the Pasha to see all the places held in veneration by Moslem, Christian, and Jew.

The Patriarchs of the Greek, Armenian, and Latin convents also invited them to visit their convents. Sir Moses, however, was not able to accept them all; he had but one object in view in coming to Jerusalem, which was to help the poor and destitute, and his attention was entirely directed to that, no time being at his disposal even for subjects which, on other occasions, would have greatly interested him.

"Sir Moses, on his arrival at Jerusalem," as stated by him, subsequently, in the trustees' report to the committee, "had the pain of witnessing the deep distress prevailing in the several communities; and it was an aggravation of his sorrow to find that his presence had long been looked forward to as a panacea for all future suffering, many having supposed that Sir Moses would have had the power to relieve from every ill and to provide for every want.

"The mode of proceeding, however, having been previously

determined upon, the greatest energy was devoted to carrying out the settled plans.

"Representatives from the Holy Cities were invited to meet in Jerusalem, each of them to be provided with statistics relating to the general affairs and necessities of their respective congregations, and to be furnished with the number, nature, working, and condition of their various institutions, especially of those recently established by trustees of the Appeal Fund in London.

"The attendance of skilled practical agriculturists was also requested, that they might be consulted as to the practicability of setting on foot an agricultural scheme.

"On the 27th July the first meeting was held with the representatives of Safed.

"The accounts connected with the Free Loan Society, the Lying-in Charity, and the Institution for the Encouragement of Needlewomen and Laundresses,* produced by their respective representatives, were minutely examined and found correct; and it was shown that the several committees had faithfully discharged their duties. As there was every reason to be satisfied with the results presented in the working of these institutions, Sir Moses deemed it desirable that the funds should be augmented, to enable the committees to continue their benevolent work.

"The desirability of cultivating land was patiently discussed at this sitting, and the mention of numerous well-authenticated facts raised great hopes of success.

"The views entertained by Sir Moses having been confirmed by the best evidence, a committee of practical agriculturists —men distinguished by their probity, and of acknowledged skill—was, without further delay, appointed, to aid in the selection of land, and to advise as to the fitness of the persons to be employed in its cultivation.

"Assisted by this committee he selected thirty-five families from the Holy City of Safed, provided them with means to commence agricultural pursuits, and also secured for them the protection of the local governors.

"Some orphan lads were also provided for, by being placed under the care of the committee to be trained as agriculturists.

"A district in the vicinity of Safed, called Bokea, having

---

* All of which had been established by the trustees in the year 1857.

been pointed out as a most desirable spot for agricultural purposes, sufficient means were granted to give employment to fifteen families to be engaged in the cultivation of that fruitful region, the whole of them being placed under the supervision of the agricultural committee at Safed.

"The claims of Tiberias were next considered, and the reports of the working of the several institutions in this Holy City being most satisfactory, the funds of these institutions were also augmented. The claims of all those who petitioned for assistance to enable them to engage in agricultural pursuits were then considered, and means were afforded to thirty families to enable them to realise their wishes.

"It was found necessary here to make some changes in the establishment for weaving, owing to the difficulties experienced by the English instructor, in consequence of his inability to communicate with the young artisans in their own tongue, and, to remedy this defect, Sir Moses made arrangements to engage an intelligent person, qualified in all respects to superintend the establishment.

"He continued, however, to place his entire confidence in the committee for supervising the weaving establishment at Jerusalem, as they had hitherto, in all their proceedings, strictly conformed to the written instructions of the trustees."

With the concurrence of the Jewish authorities in Jerusalem, Sir Moses and Lady Montefiore succeeded in founding a girls' school in that city, in which, in addition to other subjects necessary to be taught to the daughters of Israel, instruction in dressmaking, embroidery, and domestic occupations forms a prominent feature of the plan of education. Sir Moses was fortunately enabled to secure for this establishment one of the best houses in the Jewish quarter. The fitting up of the school was entrusted to thirty-five Jewish mechanics, who completed their several contracts in the most satisfactory manner.

They also succeeded in finding adequate instructors for the school among the ladies of the community, and they had the gratification to find that, on the very next day after the establishment of the school had become known in the city, 144 girls attended, and the names of 400 girls, many of them belonging to the best and most pious families, were registered in the school books.

Miss Mary Eliza Roger, in her "Domestic Life in Palestine," gives a full description of that school, from which I here subjoin some portions, to give the reader an idea of its efficient working at the time.

"On Thursday, May 28, 1856," that lady writes, "I was invited to visit the new schools for young Jewesses, established by Sir Moses Montefiore. . . .

"While we waited for admittance, I looked up at the windows. Two were square, unsheltered openings. A third jutted far out from the wall, and through its quaint and fanciful wooden lattice we could see bright and rare flowers. The fourth was a large square oriel window, supported by a stone bracket, and protected by an iron balcony. A crowd of happy-looking children were peeping from it. One dark-eyed little creature had a red-cloth tarbush on the back of her head, and a rose in her black hair. The others wore soft muslin kerchiefs of various colours tied tastefully on their heads.

"We entered the door, crossed a small court, and were led up an open staircase on to a terrace, the low, broad walls of which were converted into a garden. . . .

"We were politely received in this court by a Spanish Jewess, who conducted us into a light, cheerful room, containing animated groups of girls, varying in age from seven to fourteen, perhaps. I counted thirty-one children, but the full number usually assembled there was thirty-five.

"Eight forms and a double row of desks gave quite a European character to the room, and the raised pulpit-like seat of the teacher indicated order and authority.

"The girls were nearly all engaged at needlework, and our guide exhibited to us, with evident pride and pleasure, a considerable stock of wearing apparel, the result of one week's work in that room. The simple garments were very nicely made, considering that most of the little workers did not know how to sew six or seven months before. The mistress could not tell us what was done with the work when finished, as it passed from her hands at the end of each week. The children looked busy and bright. Some of them were singularly beautiful. One tall and stately girl, of about fourteen, was acting the part of monitor, and she answered our questions in Arabic with the utmost modesty and self-possession, and glided among her little pupils with native grace and dignity. All these children were natives of Palestine; they spoke Arabic, and wore the Arab costume. . . .

"After lingering for a short time to enjoy the prospect, we were led to another room equally large, light, and airy. Here we found about thirty children, under the care of two female teachers. One tiny little creature was learning a Hebrew lesson, and carefully spelling words of two letters. Another child of seven or eight was reading, with very little hesitation, some Scripture history. The other children were seated comfortably, and with perfect ease and freedom, yet without disorder, upon mats, or on the deep-carpeted window seat. There I recognised the happy faces which I had seen from the street below. They looked up at me smiling, as much as to say: 'We know you again ; we saw you waiting at the door.'

" They were all at needlework, and I could not help observing the extreme delicacy and beauty of their hands. If, as it is said, this is the distinguishing feature of noble birth, then these young daughters of Israel are of princely race. Some of the little hands were stained with henna, and almost all the nails were tinted, and looked like the delicate rose-coloured shells we find on the sands on English shores.

" The children were uniformly neat and clean, and there was a picturesque variety of costume there that struck us pleasantly, contrasting with our recollections of the ugly uniforms in some of our public schools at home and abroad. . . .

" These two rooms were set apart expressly for the children of parents belonging to the Sephardim congregation, consisting of the Spanish and Portuguese Jews settled in Jerusalem.

" We were now led downstairs again to the open court, which we crossed, and, after ascending another stairway, we found ourselves in the school of the Ashkenazi congregation, formed of German, Russian, and Polish Jews. Here there were fifteen children, and they all seemed to be under seven years of age. They were much more fair, though less beautiful, than those in the other rooms. They were sitting very much at their ease, perched upon the sloping desks, with their little feet resting on the forms. How thoughtful and kind it was to allow them this freedom during the hot weather! There was not a sign of fatigue, or any expression of rebellion against restraint, on any of the young faces around us.

"A little girl of five years of age, with pink cheeks, blue eyes, and hair almost white, was reading aloud from some Hebrew volume, and was evidently interested by it. I cautiously inquired whether she knew by heart all that fell so fluently from her lips. I was assured that I was listening to genuine reading.

"We went downstairs to the second German rooms, where most of the girls were between thirteen and fifteen years of age, and the rest younger. We heard two of the eldest read with emphasis several pages from the life of Moses—a book written expressly for the use of women and children. It is a paraphrase of the Bible history of Moses, in a curious harsh dialect, being a compound of Hebrew and German. It is printed in Hebrew characters, and embellished with quaint and curious woodcuts in the style of the followers of Albert Dürer.

"In these rooms fifty-five pupils generally muster."

Turning again to the administration of the Appeal Fund, the reader will learn that, independently of the several grants made to the respective institutions, a considerable sum was entrusted to the elders of the communities, to be distributed among the necessitous poor of Jerusalem, Hebrew, Jaffa, and other congregations.

Having surmounted the difficulties and impediments which he had to encounter, Sir Moses eventually succeeded in purchasing a track of land to the west of the Holy City, adjoining the high road from Jerusalem to Hebron, in a most beautiful and salubrious locality, and within a few minutes' walk from the Jaffa and Zion Gates. Here a considerable number of our co-religionists and others at once found employment on the land, and in the building of the boundary wall.

Sir Moses being the first Englishman to whom the Ottoman Government granted the permission to purchase land, I give some particulars connected with the transaction.

Ahhmed Agha Dizdar, who had been Governor of Jerusalem during the reign of Mohhammad Ali, and who since the year 1839 had stood in friendly relations with Sir Moses, was the owner of the land in question. When Sir Moses broached the subject of the purchase to him, his answer was : "You are my friend, my brother, the apple of my eye, take possession of it at once. This land I hold as an heirloom from my ancestors. I would not sell it to any person for thousands of pounds, but to you I give it without any money: it is yours, take possession of it." " I myself, my wife, and children, we all are yours." And this was his reply to Sir Moses day after day, whenever he was asked the price for which he would sell the said property.

Ultimately, after a whole day's most friendly argument, which almost exhausted all my stock of Arabic phraseology (having acted as interpreter between him and Sir Moses), he said to me : " You are my friend, my brother ; by my beard, my head, I declare this is the case. Tell Sir Moses to give me a souvenir of one thousand pounds sterling, and we will go at once to the Ckádee."

The moment I informed him of the Agha's price, Sir Moses lost no time, and counted out one thousand English sovereigns, did them up in a roll, and proceeded to the English Consulate, together with the Agha and his friends, where the sale was effected.

On our arrival at the Máhhkámeh (hall of justice) to have the purchase confirmed, we found all the members of the Meglis assembled, and the Judge, or Ckádee, with his secretaries, present.

Questions were put by the Judge, both to the seller and the purchaser. The purchase money was counted, and the contract of sale was read aloud, and witnessed by all present.

The wording of the document is to the effect that, " By permission of the Sublime Porte and the Imperial Throne, may the Lord of Creation preserve them, and in conformity with the letters on that subject from the Grand Vizier to Sir Moses Montefiore (Baronet), the pride of the people of Moses, the man of prudence, &c., the son of Joseph Eliyahu (here also follow a number of complimentary titles), Sir Moses purchases a piece of land for the purpose of establishing thereon a hospital for the poor of the Israelites who reside in Jerusalem, and does with it as he pleases."

" Sir Moses Montefiore, Baronet," the contract continues, " presented himself as the purchaser before the Legislative Council in presence of the members of the Council of Jerusalem, to purchase the land hereinafter described with his own money, not with that which belongeth to another, from the vendor, Sir Ahmed Agha Eldizdar (the support of the great men), son of Sid Fadh-ed-din Agha."

The contract then defines the exact limits of the property,

and the Chádee attests the correctness of the deed of purchase. Sir Moses returned to his camp, and gave orders to remove his tents to the land which had become his own property, whilst I proceeded to measure it, inscribing the initials of Sir Moses' name in large Hebrew characters on a piece of rock forming the angle of its boundary line upon the road, the right side of which, when coming from the Jaffa Gate, leads to Bet-essefáfa.

August 15*th.*—In the presence of a numerous concourse of spectators of various religious denominations, Sir Moses and Lady Montefiore had the satisfaction and happiness to lay the foundation-stone of the proposed hospital, in the presence of Mr and Mrs Guedalla, Mr Gershon Kursheedt, one of the executors of Juda Touro, the American philanthropist, and myself.

CHAPTER VII.

1855-1856.

BESIDES the various acts of benevolence already accomplished by Sir Moses in Jerusalem, there is one for which the community cannot be sufficiently grateful.

He entreated His Excellency Kiamil Pasha, the Governor of Jerusalem, to remove from the Jewish quarters the public slaughter-house, which had become extremely offensive in consequence of the vast quantity of refuse which had accumulated ever since the time Jerusalem had been conquered by the Khaleefa Omar.

The Pasha immediately acceded to his request, and the slaughter-house was removed to a place outside the city walls. Before leaving the Holy City Sir Moses promised the representatives of the community that he would recommend the committee in London to erect a windmill in Jerusalem, with a view of superseding the expensive method used there for grinding corn. The poor, he said, should then have their flour at a reduced price.

Having concluded his arrangements with the several congregations of Jerusalem, and given his instructions to the representatives of Safed and Tiberias, he prepared to depart from the Holy City.

The next day we left for Hebron, where the result of his enquiries as to the conduct and management of the several institutions in that Holy City was likewise most satisfactory. The disturbed state of the country unfortunately occasioned much suffering to the inhabitants of this district, which induced Sir Moses to devote a considerable sum to the relief of the immediate necessities of the poor.

The country round Hebron being at that time much disturbed by the revolutionary acts of Abd-er-rahhman, the notorious oppressor of the Jews, Kiamil Pasha had encamped there, with a battalion of soldiers and two brass field-pieces, to be in readiness to proceed against any disloyal subjects of the Sultan.

He summoned the Sheikhs of the surrounding villages, and there were several among them who declared that they would only pay their taxes through Abd-er-rahhman, whom they considered as their local chief.

In consequence of this the Pasha proclaimed him a rebel, and nominated his brother Salâmeh in his place as Nâzeer (chief inspector) of the district.

The wife of Abd-er-rahhman and his sister, hearing of the presence of Sir Moses, called on Lady Montefiore, entreating her to speak to Sir Moses and obtain the removal of Salâmeh from his new office, which, she said, belonged to her true and faithful husband. She also brought a letter from Abd-er-rahhman himself, who called even on all the Jews whom he so often ill-treated, to intercede on his behalf with Sir Moses; but of course Sir Moses would not even see her. I had nearly half-an-hour's conversation with her, when she and his sister made many promises of the kindness with which Abd-er-rahh-man would in future treat the Hebron Hebrew community. I requested them to leave our camp as soon as possible, as some of the Pasha's soldiers, who were near our tents, might notice their presence, and consider themselves justified in bringing them before the Pasha to make their representations to him. Sir Moses being desirous of establishing a dispensary for the benefit of all the poor inhabitants at Hebron, he wanted to purchase the field where we were encamped, and therefore sent for the owner, who, on being informed of the object for which the purchase of his field was required, after long consideration gave the laconic reply, " Ten purses " (equivalent to £50). Sir Moses agreed to the price, and gave orders to have the deed of sale prepared. On the following day the owner of the field made his appearance early in the morning. We thought he came to tell us the hour when to appear before the Ckádee. To our great surprise he said, on reconsideration, he thought he could not sell the land under £500. Sir Moses would not hear of paying such an amount, and the consequence was, that the poor of Hebron lost the dispensary, which it was his intention to supply with medicines in the same way as he did to the one at Jerusalem.

We left Hebron and proceeded to Jaffa, where some property was purchased, with a house and well, affording an abundant supply of excellent water. A number of poor Israelites were at once engaged upon the land, which is known by the name of the " Biera," and is situated near the estate of the Wurthemburg Templars. The amount distributed was £10,932, 10s.

After a number of personal interviews, and after carefully considering documentary evidence, Sir Moses and the other trustees arrived at the conclusion that the future well-being of the Israelites in the Holy Land must, under Providence, depend upon active support being accorded to the institutions established there for the promotion of agriculture and industrial pursuits.

We left Jaffa for Alexandria, where we arrived on the 1st of September. Three of the Pasha's boats, specially sent to take Sir Moses and Lady Montefiore, brought us on shore, where carriages were in readiness to take us to the Palace, which His Highness, Said Pasha, now the ruling Prince, had ordered to be prepared for their reception. On our entering the Palace we met a great many attendants ; the table was decked with costly ornaments, and with numerous dishes filled with French and Egyptian viands, the best wine and liqueurs, and ices of every description. There was a French *chéf* superintending the culinary department, and his constant anxiety was to please Sir Moses and Lady Montefiore.

The latter, however, had their own cook with them, who arranged their daily meals, consisting of a few plain dishes. This man soon pacified the *chéf,* and aided him during our stay in the Palace in the selection of the dishes which were most palatable to His Highness' guests.

Each of Sir Moses' party had his special attendants ; from morning till evening they would be in readiness to serve pipes, coffee, ices, &c. Every now and then an officer from the Palace came to ask if we wished for anything. Not knowing what to ask for, because every one really had all he could possibly require, we said, rather by way of a joke than anything else, " A tooth brush ; " within half-an-hour's time there appeared a whole box of tooth brushes, sufficient to open a store with. Another of us thought he would ask for " a clothes brush," and a quantity of these articles was within a short time at his disposal. One of the officers gave us to understand that it would please His Highness if we were to ask for some really valuable object to take with us as a souvenir, but this we, of course, courteously declined to do.

The next day we were invited by His Highness to be present at the investigation of the Leopold order, which the Emperor of Austria had sent to His Highness in recognition of the attention he had shown to the Archduke of Austria during his recent visit to Egypt. We met all the dignitaries of state there, the consuls, and high officers of the army. After the ceremony we were all presented to His Highness.

The reception given by His Highness to Sir Moses was most cordial ; he frequently expressed the pleasure it afforded him to see Sir Moses in Egypt. He paid Sir Moses a long visit, and constantly showed him every possible attention.

Sir Moses received numerous visits from representatives of educational, charitable, and financial associations of every nationality in Egypt. Among the latter there was Monsieur de Lesseps, who had a long interview with him, explaining the importance of the Suez Canal. Sir Moses, however, did not appear to regard the undertaking as likely to prove successful from a financial point of view.

Friday, September 7th.—We went on board the *Valetta*, and ultimately arrived safely at Dover on Wednesday, September 19th.

The greater portion of September and October was spent partly at East Cliff Lodge and partly at Park Lane, Sir Moses being busily employed in reporting to the English and Turkish governments on the result of his journey. He was again elected President of the Board of the London Committee of Deputies of British Jews.

On the 4th of December he accompanied the Lord Mayor and the Court of Lieutenancy to Buckingham Palace, to present an address to the King of Sardinia, where, as seconder of the address, he was introduced to His Majesty by the Lord Mayor ; and at the end of the month Baroness Meyer de Rothschild invited him to be present at the opening or consecration of the Baronial Hall at Mentmore, where, he notes in his Diary, " Dr Kalisch read prayers, also several psalms, and affixed mezuzas or phylacteries to the doors. A splendid breakfast and dinner followed the ceremony."

At the beginning of 1856 he paid much attention to the communications received from the various committees appointed in the Holy Land to superintend the institutions established there by the trustees of the Appeal Fund ; and conjointly with the Chief Rabbi he published the second report, embodying the statements I have already given in one of the preceding chapters.

The trustees, upon the suggestion of Sir Moses, made an agreement with Messrs J. J. and T. R. Holman of Canterbury to erect a windmill at Jerusalem.

He also attended meetings convened for the purpose of discussing a scheme for a railway from Jaffa to Jerusalem.

Accompanied by the Secretary of the Board of Deputies of British Jews and myself, he went to Count Strzelsky, at whose house he met the Hon. Mr Ashley, Sir Culling Eardly, Mr Uzielli, Mr Baxter, Mr Barkley, and Mr Redhouse, and remained in consultation with them for several hours.

April 7th.—He had an interview with Lord Palmerston, of which he gives full particulars in his Diary. To Sir Culling Eardly, who came to him previously to their going to see his Lordship, he said, that " to prevent the possibility of his (Sir Culling) being under any mistake with regard to the object he (Sir Moses) had in view respecting the railway to Jerusalem, it was his opinion that, when finished, it would not induce fifty Jews to return to the Holy Land, but he had no doubt it would greatly conduce to the improvement of their situation ; that he would have nothing whatever to do with it if the undertaking was to be regarded as a sectarian measure. " The men we should have for directors," he said to Sir Culling, " must be those whose names are well known for wealth and connected with other railways, but on no account with religious societies."

Sir Culling Eardly, understanding Sir Moses' object, agreed to his views, and they both proceeded to Lord Palmerston. Sir Moses told his Lordship what had been stated before, adding that he had desired Sir Culling Eardly in the first instance to ascertain whether the project had his approval, and if so, whether Lord Palmerston would grant a royal charter limiting the liability of the shareholders to the amount of their subscriptions; also whether he would make an application to the Turkish government for its consent, and a grant of land on each side of the road, or a guarantee of a minimum rate of interest, as might be agreed upon.

Lord Palmerston heard Sir Moses most patiently, and said he considered such a work would be extremely useful to the Turkish Government. It would enable them to move their troops with greater facility, and the country would become more settled; at present, not a month passed but he received accounts from the consuls of outbreaks. It would also increase the commerce of the country, which would improve the revenue of the Porte and the commerce of England. He would have recommended Sir Moses going to Paris to see Ali Pasha, but this morning he had heard from Lord Clarendon that Ali Pasha was coming to England, and Sir Moses would better see him here.

With regard to the Báláklava railway, he hoped Sir Moses would give him a good price for it, though it would be some time before it could be given up; upon which the latter said he hoped his Lordship would make them a present of it.

"It was clear," Sir Moses writes in his Diary, "that Lord Palmerston is very much in favour of the project."

May 20*th.*—Sir Moses received a note from Sir Culling Eardly, saying that the Grand Vizier, Ali Pasha, would receive the deputation on the following day.

May 21*st.*—At twelve o'clock he was at Claridge's Hotel to meet the other members of the deputation, Sir Culling Eardly, the Hon. Mr Ashley, Mr Oliphant, and some others. They were with the Grand Vizier for nearly two hours, and he agreed to receive and to forward to Constantinople their proposal for the railway, with either a grant of land, or a guarantee for interest of capital, but not both.

It was arranged they should all meet on Friday to prepare a paper for the Turkish Government.

May 20*th.*—Sir Moses and Lady Montefiore went to Belvedere House, the beautiful seat of Sir Culling and Lady Eardly, where they found a very large party to meet the Grand Vizier,

Ali Pasha, the Turkish Ambassador, Musurus Pasha, the Danish Ambassador and his wife, and many more distinguished persons. After luncheon there were several good speeches respecting the proposed railway.

May 31st.—Sir Culling Eardly had another interview with the Grand Vizier; it being Sabbath, Sir Moses was prevented from going. In the evening he received a note from Sir Culling, expressing his regret that the Grand Vizier had appointed that day for the interview, and begging that he would go on Monday to the Grand Vizier, as the latter would leave soon. Count Strzelsky sent him the paper which he had agreed to deliver to the Grand Vizier, and Sir Moses signed it.

June 2nd.—He met Count Strzelsky at Clarendon Hotel, where he had an audience of the Grand Vizier, to present to him the paper regarding the Jerusalem Railway. He read it very carefully, and promised to recommend it to the attention of the Sultan.

Sir John Macneil, whom Sir Moses saw a few months later, advised them to have a railroad from Jaffa to Lidda, and thence a macadamized road for carriages across the mountains. A railroad, he said, would cost from £4000 to £4500 per mile, the other £150. He thought the Government would not give land, and would guarantee only 6 per cent., as the road would not pay.

Count Strzelsky then went to Constantinople, and on his return, about the 8th December, he told Sir Moses, in the presence of Sir Culling Eardly, Sir John Macneil, Mr Ashley, and others, all that had passed there regarding the Jaffa railway; and that the Government would only guarantee 6 per cent., and give no land.

Sir Francis Palgrave evinced much sympathy for the Jews in the Holy Land, and had frequent interviews with Sir Moses to consider the best mode of serving their cause. He thought they should be placed under the immediate protection of the Sultan, like the Armenian Protestants. Sir Francis continued for many years to take an interest in their welfare, and Sir Moses always appreciated his suggestions, referring to the improvement of their occupations.

Early in this year the Jewish Disabilities Bill again excited attention both in and out of Parliament.

On April 9th Sir Moses writes :—" Whilst sitting under the gallery of the House of Commons, together with Baron Lionel de Rothschild, Sir J. L. Goldsmid, and the Lord Mayor, during the debate for altering the oath so as to admit Jews as members of Parliament, I had the happiness of witnessing another step towards the attainment of religious liberty. The Bill was passed by a majority of 35."

On May 7th he was present at the banquet given at the Mansion House by the Lord Mayor to Her Majesty's Ministers, and the day following he joined the procession of the Court of Lieutenancy to Buckingham Palace, to present addresses of congratulation to the Queen on the happy restoration of peace. The bells rang merry peals at midnight, every one was rejoiced, and there was no doubt of the truth of the good tidings.

As President of the London Committee of Deputies of the British Jews, he was much occupied this year with the Dissenters' Marriage Bill, containing a clause (constituting the twenty-second section), which was objected to by the Board in a former Bill. He signed the address to the King of Sardinia on his arrival in England ; also a letter of thanks to the British Government for the kindness extended by them to some of the Hebrew Russian soldiers taken prisoners at Kertsch; and finally brought under the notice of the Foreign Office a petition to the Prince of Servia from two thousand Israelites dwelling under his sway, to ameliorate their condition, and obtain all the rights of citizenship. He also paid much attention to the Carmara case, referring to the family of that name in Constantinople, who fell victims to Sultan Máhmoud's Government. The chief of that family having had claims of a considerable amount on the Sultan's Treasury, the debt appeared to have been cancelled by the sudden execution of the creditor, at night, in his own house, without trial. One night after he had retired to rest there was a violent knocking at his door, and an officer, with whom he was on friendly terms, entered. This officer had been charged, by the Sultan's commands, to murder him with the aid of a band of authorised assassins. The Sultan 'Abd-ool-Megid, on consideration of the injustice done, allowed the family a pension.

On the occasion of the Sultan's issuing the firman, Hháti-hoomáyoon, in which His Majesty granted equal rights and privileges to all his subjects, irrespective of their religious creeds, Sir Moses received the following letter from Lord Stratford de Redcliffe, dated February 23, 1856 :—

"MY DEAR SIR MOSES,—Before this letter can reach your hands you will have learnt from the public prints what amount of success has finally crowned our long-continued efforts in the cause of humanity and freedom of conscience. I take the liberty of sending you a copy of the Sultan's firman, together with a French translation.

"I shall be disappointed if it does not afford you as much satisfaction as I have derived from it myself.

"Excuse the haste in which I write, and pray, believe me, with every good wish.—Your faithful, &c.,

"STRATFORD DE REDCLIFFE."

Sir Moses, fully appreciating the attention paid to him by his Lordship's most valued communication, addresses him as follows :—

"DEAR LORD STRATFORD DE REDCLIFFE,—The exceeding kindness and consideration of your Excellency in gratifying me with your communication of the 23rd ultimo, which I have to acknowledge with the deepest and most cordial gratitude, are indeed such as I could not have ventured to anticipate, considering the numerous, the serious, and the complex matters which are constantly claiming your Excellency's attention.

"I feel that it might be obtrusive to tender on the part of my co-religionists any expression of thanks for your Excellency's noble and triumphant efforts, by which they, in common with all the other subjects of Turkey not professing the Mahomedan religion, have obtained the inestimable boon conferred by the Sultan's firman, copies of which you so kindly and promptly transmitted to me ; for I am sure nothing could enhance the gratification which your Excellency must experience in having so successfully laboured to accomplish an achievement of beneficence so grand in its scheme and so extended and comprehensive in its operation.

"Permit me, then, simply to offer you my most sincere and heartfelt congratulations.—I have the honour to be, &c.,

"MOSES MONTEFIORE."

CHAPTER VIII.

1857.

FIFTH VISIT TO THE HOLY LAND—MALTESE JEWS AND THEIR
GRIEVANCES—CAIRO, JAFFA, LYDDA, AND GEEB—ARRIVAL
IN JERUSALEM—THE APPEAL FUND INSTITUTIONS.

IN order to ascertain the reasons for Sir Moses' return to Jerusalem after so short an interval since his previous visit to the Holy City, I must ask the reader to revert to the narrative I have given of his previous pilgrimage in 1855. It was undertaken for the purpose of alleviating the sufferings of the poor, and of establishing various benevolent institutions there in the hope of preventing the recurrence of distress. The object of his present journey was to give personal supervision for a short time to the workings of those institutions.

Sir Moses began making preparations for this, his fifth journey, in February. He resigned the presidency of the London Committee of Deputies of British Jews, and made an agreement with Messrs J. J. and T. R. Holman, millwrights of Canterbury, conjointly with the other trustees, for the erection of a windmill in Jerusalem at the cost of £1450. He attended a meeting at Count Strzelsky's, and agreed with the other gentlemen present that nothing could now be done in the matter of the Jerusalem railway; he, however, advanced his share of the expenses, and withdrew altogether from the scheme.

On February 25th Sir Moses and Lady Montefiore, accompanied by Dr Hodgkin and Mr Gershon Kursheedt, left England for the Holy Land. Proceeding *via* Rome and Naples, they soon arrived at Malta, where Sir William Reid, the Governor, gave them a very friendly reception, drawing their special attention to the school for young gardeners at St Antonio, the ladies' school, and to his (Sir William's) experiment in rearing silkworms on castor-oil plants, an experiment which Sir Moses proposed trying in the Holy Land.   The Governor likewise showed him his collection of implements for the improvement of Maltese agriculture.   The ploughs were from New York, and were very light.   His Excellency presented Sir Moses with one of them for the Holy Land.

The next day Sir Moses received a deputation from the Maltese Jewish community, who complained of the great intolerance in the island, but gratefully acknowledged their indebtedness to the English Government for the protection it extended to them.

Friday, May 1st.—Mr Laurence Oliphant, a gentleman whom Sir Moses had last met at Sir Culling Eardly's, and who was now on his way to China, as secretary to Lord Elgin, breakfasted with him.   Mr Oliphant took a great interest in all matters relating to the Holy Land, and conversed freely with him on certain schemes which might serve to improve the condition of its inhabitants.

On May 5th they arrived at Alexandria, where, all the hotels being full, they accepted the hospitality of Mr Galloway.

Believing the Viceroy to be at a palace he had built in the desert, three hours' distance from Alexandria, near the Lake Merotir, where several regiments of his soldiers were encamped, Sir Moses went there the next morning with his friends, but to his great disappointment he found the Viceroy had gone four hours farther into the desert with most of his troops, and was not expected back for a day or two.

There were only a few servants left in the palace.   Sir Moses and the other gentlemen walked to His Highness's large European tent, where they remained three hours to repose and refresh the horses.   About an hour after their arrival a capital dinner was sent in to them.   Sir Moses himself only partook of bread and coffee.

Thursday, May 7th.—A special train having been engaged to take the Earl of Elgin and his suite to Cairo, Sir Moses was permitted to avail himself of the same.   When on board the steamboat crossing the Nile he was introduced to his Lordship, whom Sir Moses describes as a very handsome, chatty, and agreeable person.

At Cairo he received a deputation from the Hebrew congregation ; visited the Synagogue, a large handsome but plain building, and called on the Governor, who had been to his house in London when His Highness Said Pasha was staying with him. Thence Sir Moses proceeded to the Citadel. He was invited to breakfast with Dr Etia, the physician of His Highness Hálim Pasha, on the occasion of a religious festivity, but was prevented from accepting the invitation by the overpowering heat of the day and the consequent fatigue he experienced.

After remaining a few days at Cairo, they left the hospitable roof of Mr Galloway, and proceeded to Jaffa, where they were received by Mr Kháyát, the British Vice-Consul, Ahmed Agha Dizdar, the former Governor of Jerusalem, and by the representatives of the community. "Jaffa," Sir Moses writes, "appears much larger, and a great number of houses have been built since we were last there, only twenty-two months ago." The English Vice-Consul had built a house with warehouses attached to it, which, he told Sir Moses, cost him £10,000. Everything had doubled in value in a few years, and houses and land could now only be bought at extravagant prices. He thought, with or without the English, there would soon be a railway to Jerusalem. Ahmed Agha Dizdar, who had brought five soldiers under his command to accompany Sir Moses and Lady Montefiore while in the Holy Land, joined their dinner party, and made them offers of valuable land.

May 17*th*.—They visited the garden, or Biara, as it is generally called, which had been bought by Sir Moses for the Trustees of the Appeal Fund, and remained there for an hour, examining the reports handed to him by Mr Minor, and inspecting the plantation of new trees. Subsequently he visited the house and garden of the English Vice-Consul. "He has," Sir Moses says, "30 acres outside the town, and wishes to sell it for £1000; he also possesses large plantations of orange, mulberry, lemon, and palm trees. Our own garden could be better managed, but it is 40 acres in extent, and a splendid piece of land."

May 18*th*.—Sir Moses and Lady Montefiore left Jaffa. The Governor of the town passed half an hour with them before they set off, and wished to ride out of the city with them, but it being Rámádan, Sir Moses prevailed on him to desist from his intentions, as he was fasting. Ahmed Agha, with many of his horsemen, as well as the British Consul of Jerusalem and the Vice-Consul of Jaffa, were with them. Ahmed Agha and the

Consul of Ramlah, with an officer from Jaffa, rode with them all the way to Jerusalem.

On the road they had some Turkish music, and as they passed the several villages they were met by the Governors and their officers. After a pleasant ride of four hours they arrived at Lydda, and encamped there, in a beautiful vineyard a short distance from the town. They had two sheep cooked for Ahmed Agha's men, who, after sunset, made a great feast, and were very merry. For Sir Moses Lydda was a place of special interest, on account of its having been famous during the second century for its Colleges and Synagogues. Mr Galloway, the other gentleman who was with Sir Moses, only came to Lydda to ascertain what facilities the place offered for the projected railroad to Jerusalem. It will perhaps be remembered that, at one of the meetings held in London in connection with this project, one of the gentlemen present proposed having a railway from Jaffa to Lydda, and from there a macadamised road over the hills to Jerusalem.

On May the 19th they started for Geeb. Sir Moses remarks that the road was exceedingly bad, through dry beds of former torrents, over desperately stony hills. They rode for an hour and a half in darkness, and, Sir Moses confesses, in great terror. He could not see his horse's head, but they followed Ahmed Agha as well as they could. Lady Montefiore was greatly alarmed, more so, Sir Moses says, than she had been in all her life; but after retiring to rest she soon recovered her courage.

May 20*th.*—They arrived at Jerusalem, and were most cordially received by all the inhabitants, who appreciated the object for which they came. After having attended several meetings of the representatives of the Holy City to hear the reports they had to give them of their communal affairs, they visited the dispensary under the direction of Dr Fränkel, the weaving establishment, and the girls' school.

Eight persons belonging to the weaving establishment stated that they were able to get a living. One said he could now keep his wife and family; another observed, "The bread gained by the labour of the hands was most sweet;" a third said that "formerly when he rose in the morning he knew not where to get a morsel of bread, now he enjoyed his regular meals, and blessed the name of God"; and a fourth remarked that "formerly he carried stones in some gentleman's garden for a scanty pittance, now he earned, comparatively speaking, sufficient to live comfortably." All agreed that the weaving master was a good man, and they preferred the present house in which the work is done to the old one which they used to occupy.

Sir Moses and Lady Montefiore describe their visit to the girls' school in terms conveying to the reader the idea of their satisfaction.

"We were delighted with it," they say. "There are three class-rooms. No. 1 has eight forms, with forty-five pupils, belonging to the Portuguese community, with four teachers. No. 2 has seven forms, with forty pupils, with two teachers; and No. 3 has also seven forms, and forty pupils, with only one teacher, but an excellent instructor."

"Nos. 2 and 3," they continue, "were German children, and very clever indeed. The schools and scholars will bear comparison with any in England."

On their return home from the day's excursions, they invited the ladies' committee of needle-women to attend a meeting which had been convened there, and Sir Moses then entrusted them with the entire management of the Society. The ladies all expressed themselves as greatly pleased with the charge, and promised to attend the school, and themselves give out the needlework to all the pupils.

With regard to those whom the Committee had enabled to engage in agriculture in Safed and the Bokea, Sir Moses was told that eight had the misfortune to lose their cattle by death or by theft, and only one succeeded in making a profit. At Tiberias the work of agriculture had met with even less success. The prevalence of drought caused the death of the cattle, and the ravages of cholera prevented the men from attempting to ameliorate their condition.

The principal cause of the unhappy issue of this first agricultural attempt, however, must be ascribed to the insufficiency of the amount which the Appeal Fund Committee considered themselves justified in advancing to the Safed and Tiberias poor. The latter had neither houses, barns, stables, nor agricultural implements, nor had they any means of their own to live upon till the gathering in of the first produce of their fields.

We can now record most gratifying instances of the results

of agriculture pursued by the poor in the Holy Land who had the good fortune to meet with friends in Paris and in other places, in Germany, Poland, and Russia ; and the general opinion of those who know the Holy Land is that agriculture, when properly attended to, may be considered the best means of securing a useful and comfortable life to the poor who, from religious motives, may prefer that country to any other.

With reference to the Jaffa garden, which was then cultivated by two Jewish families, Classen and Litman, under the superintendence of the former tenant of the estate, Dr Hodgkin and Mr Galloway made a report, at the request of Sir Moses, in which they state as follows :—

" In the year 1856 they expended 28,700 Egyptian piastres, whilst their income only amounted to 27,544 piastres."

When Sir Moses bought this property for the Appeal Fund Committee, with a view of encouraging agriculture among the Jews, it contained no less than 1407 trees of every description. Knowing that similar gardens and fields in possession of the natives were very profitable, he was rather surprised at this result. Still he contented himself with the hope that the property would increase in value, if it were once decided to have a railroad to Jerusalem, in which case that place would be a great acquisition for the directors for the purposes of the Jaffa railway station , and, in the meanwhile, three poor families were deriving some advantage from its cultivation.

From that time up to the present the expenses have, on an average, not been less than £40 a year.

Offers were made by some persons to pay a high rent for the property, but they could only do that, they said, after having had possession of the land for at least ten years ; and to this Sir Moses did not feel inclined to agree.

A few days later he inspected the preparations which were then being made for the erection of the windmill, and held special conferences in the garden with the elders of the several communities regarding the hospital he intended to build on a spot not far from the mill.

The spiritual heads of the German congregations, however, considered it advisable to have alms-houses instead of a hospital, " as such an institution had been built within the last year by the Baroness Bettie de Rothschild in memory of the late Mayer de

Rothschild, and although not large enough for the numerous poor in Jerusalem, still," they thought, " it might probably soon be enlarged by the same lady for the accommodation of a greater number." " Moreover, for the sake of preserving peaceful relations between all parties in Jerusalem," they added, " it would be desirable to be satisfied for the present with one hospital."

Sir Moses consented to their suggestion, notwithstanding the great trouble he had taken in the matter, and the heavy expenses he had incurred by having elaborate plans of the building made, and having gone to Constantinople to obtain the special permission of the Sultan for it.

Thursday, May 21st.—Count Pisamani, the Austrian Consul, informed him that he would proceed in a fortnight to Constantinople to get a firman for a highway or carriage road from Jaffa to Jerusalem.

The Emperor of Russia, he was told by the same gentleman, had sent £50 to the poor Jews of the Warsaw congregation at Jerusalem. His Imperial Majesty had also given permission to his Jewish subjects in Poland to send money to the Holy Land. Sir Moses and Lady Montefiore were much pleased with this gratifying news.

The Loan Society, established by the Appeal Fund Committee, was next examined, and found to have done much good. The necessity of having such an institution was proved, and it was decided by Sir Moses to continue it, although in some cases the loans could not be recovered on account of the abject poverty of the borrowers.

Sir Moses received and paid visits to the Governor, the Consul, the patriarchs of various religious communities, visited, as on former occasions, most of the places held in veneration, and having obtained all the information in connection with the institutions established by the Appeal Fund, left Jerusalem on the 7th June, arriving at Alexandria on the 11th of that month.

The attention shown to Sir Moses and Lady Montefiore by the Pasha of Egypt has already been described by me when referring to their visit to Alexandria in the year 1849. On the present occasion the friendly feeling of His Highness was, if possible, even more strongly displayed.

Sir Moses was impressed with the idea that any act of kindness shown to him by the Pasha might leave a favourable impression on the Egyptian population, inasmuch as the latter would notice His Highness' friendly sentiments towards a member of the Hebrew community, and it might possibly induce them to cultivate more friendly relations with his co-religionists. He had entered in his Diary full particulars of the reception given to him also on the present occasion by order of His Highness. One of the Pasha's palaces was prepared for him, the viceregal boats, manned by sailors and soldiers in full uniform, were sent to meet Sir Moses, and royal carriages were in waiting to drive his party to the Palace. Magnificent entertainments were arranged for him. There were elegant repasts served by thirty attendants. The Governor of Alexandria came to offer his services, and carriages and horses with runners at the side were continually at his disposal.

"The morning after our arrival," Sir Moses writes, "the Governor sent to inquire after our health. In the course of the day Lady Montefiore, accompanied by Mrs Tibaldi, paid a visit to the Princess, who received her with the utmost kindness, and made her promise to spend a day with her.

"I returned the Governor's visit, accompanied by my friends and the officer appointed to attend me during my stay in Egypt. His Excellency received me at the Grand Palace, came to the top of the staircase to meet me, and showed every possible mark of respect.

"He invited me to pay him a visit at Cairo, which I promised to do."

June 15*th.*—In accordance with a previous arrangement with the Governor, Sir Moses and Lady Montefiore proceeded to Cairo ; there they again had a princely reception in the palace. "The breakfast," Sir Moses says, "was magnificently served in truly regal state ; not less than thirty-two servants were in attendance."

At six o'clock in the morning, attended by the civil engineer, a colonel in the Egyptian Army, and their own party, they set out in three carriages for the railway, and proceeded on the line to Tuck, through the desert for forty miles. The railway was well finished thus far, and works in construction for carrying the line three hours further. It is expected to be finished by the end of June. "The scene in the desert," Sir Moses says, "was most interesting ; hundreds of camels, thousands of men as busy as ants; at present there are ten thousand men at work!"

Magnificent as the palace was which they occupied, the millions of mosquitoes and their innumerable associates, stinging their faces and hands, did not permit them to remain an hour at rest in their apartments, and they had to leave them for the adjoining gallery; there they passed the night on chairs. They were glad, when the morning came, to ride to the Synagogue, where they felt the soothing effect of a cool and refreshing breeze (the building excluding the rays of the sun, and conveniently permitting the currents of air to pass), which the palace in the previous night could not offer them.

They left Cairo in the Pasha's carriages, accompanied by several officers, for the railway, where every arrangement had been made for their journey to Alexandria, which place they reached at 5 A.M. Ahmed Bey, one of the officers of the Pasha, was waiting there to receive them. They proceeded immediately to the palace, with three carriages, two outriders, and runners.

June 18*th.*—Sir Moses attended divine service at five in the morning, and met in the house of prayer the newly appointed spiritual head of the community, who happened to have entered into office on that day for the first time. The Rev. M. Hazan, a native of Jerusalem, who had recently filled a similar office at Corfu, had been appointed Rabbino Maggiore in Alexandria. His name is well known in England, as he took an active part in the deliberations on subjects connected with reform movements in the Synagogue.

June 19*th.*—We find Sir Moses and Lady Montefiore on board the *America*, Captain Florio, in the harbour of Alexandria; and on Sunday, June 21st, they were on their voyage to Trieste, where they arrived on the 27th, and proceeded, *viâ* Adelsberg, Laibach, Vienna, and Hanover, to England.

On Sunday, July 19th, they arrived at Ramsgate, after an absence of five months.

CHAPTER IX.

1857.

SIR MOSES reported to the Rev. Dr N. M. Adler and the
other gentlemen of the Holy Land Committee the result
of his observations in Jerusalem on the various institutions
established there by the trustees. He also had many interviews
with Holman of Canterbury on matters connected with the
erection of a windmill in the Holy City, and the preparation
of a balance sheet of the Appeal Fund occupied a good deal of
his time. But he was not permitted to devote his attentions
exclusively to the Holy Land. His Highness the Pasha of
Egypt, as a proof of his confidence in the kindness of Sir Moses
and Lady Montefiore, entrusted them with the care of his son,
Toussoun Pasha.

This young Prince, although of a most amiable disposition,
was rather self-willed, like many other young people in an
exalted position, and thereby caused some anxiety to Sir Moses
and Lady Montefiore, who deeply felt their responsibility for the
Prince's well-being during the time he was under their care.
Among the suite of the Prince was a physician, against whose
advice the Prince often rebelled, and it required all the tact of
Lady Montefiore, and sometimes all the firmness of Sir Moses,
to make the young Pasha submit.

Sir Moses had for some time to relinquish his favourite
pursuits in connection with the Holy Land in order to study the
comforts of the Prince.

Thursday, August 20th.—Mr S. A. Hart, the Royal Academician, was commissioned by Sir Moses to paint a full-length portrait of the Prince.

The young Prince was entertained in a variety of ways, in Eastern and European style.

Almost day after day there are entries such as " The young Pasha continues well, which is a great happiness to me," or " The Prince is in high spirits and excellent health ; he grows tall and strong," showing his great anxiety of mind during the period of the young Prince's residence with him.

Toussoun Pasha's visit to England was now drawing to a close, and as Monsieur Jules Pastré had arrived to accompany the young Prince on a visit to Monsieur de Lesseps, Sir Moses made arrangements for his departure. Sir Moses and Lady Montefiore accompanied the Pasha to Dover, where they parted from him.

Monday, September 25th, being the Hebrew Day of Atonement, Sir Moses and Lady Montefiore this day attended the services in the Spanish and Portuguese Synagogue from before seven o'clock in the morning until nearly the same hour in the evening without intermission. Sir Moses records in his Diary the pleasure he felt in having been called upon during the service to read publicly the chapter referring to the day from an ancient scroll of the law presented by his grandfather to this Synagogue.

Soon afterwards, on the 7th October, Sir Moses and Lady Montefiore again attended a solemn service at the same place. This day had been appointed by special command of Her Majesty to implore the blessings of Heaven upon her arms for the complete and speedy restoration of tranquillity in India. The Jews having proved themselves at all times and in all countries loyal to the Government under whose sway they live, it may readily be imagined that the Jews in England joined heartily in the prayers offered up on that day, and no one could pray more fervently than did Sir Moses and Lady Montefiore for the continuance of God's blessing on Her Majesty, for the success of her armies in the field, and for the speedy restoration of peace. Before long the happy tidings were received that the Mutiny was at an end, the East India Company became extinct as a ruling body, and on the 1st November a public proclamation was read in front of the Government House in Calcutta, declaring that the Queen of England had assumed the direct control and sovereignty of India.

I now invite the reader to follow me to the Bank of England. There, on our arrival, we are shown a pile of papers, and from them we gather that Sir Moses had absolutely forgotten the existence of £50 Three Per Cent. Annuities standing in his and Lady Montefiore's joint-names and had not claimed the dividends thereon since the year 1847. There is happily no record of such an oversight on the part of Sir Moses in connection with his administration of the property of others.

It was now high time for him to think of the trust he held of the benevolent Juda Touro legacy, and to commence the building of almshouses in Jerusalem. He gave orders to a Ramsgate architect, Mr W. E. Smith, to prepare a plan for a number of such houses at a cost not exceeding £6000.

Mr Smith's son at once proceeded to Jerusalem, to obtain information respecting the cost of labour and materials.

Within a month after the departure of the Egyptian Prince, Sir Moses and Lady Montefiore received letters of thanks from the Princess, the wife of the Viceroy; from the mother of the young Prince, and from the Viceroy himself, who officially acknowledged the kindness shown towards his son, the letters having been forwarded through the Foreign Office in London. They were at the same time informed that the marble bust of the young Prince, executed by Miss Susan Durant, had been submitted to Her Majesty. The year, however, did not end without causing Sir Moses some uneasiness, occasioned by the unsatisfactory state of Lady Montefiore's health and by financial matters. There was a great monetary crisis which threatened to affect many banks. A deputation from the bankers and discount houses of Lombard Street had been to the Chancellor of the Exchequer to endeavour to induce him to authorise the Bank of England to make an issue of notes regardless of the Act of Parliament. As one of the directors of the Provincial Bank of Ireland, Sir Moses had some anxious days, the run for gold having alarmingly increased at Dublin, Limerick, and Cork, until the Bank of England announced the receipt of a letter from the Government, authorising them to extend the issue of bank notes on undoubted securities, not under the rate of 10 per cent. This notice stopped the panic in England, and it was hoped would have the same effect in Scotland and Ireland.

Sir Moses says: "We have made every arrangement to send 50 mille gold to-night; if needful, 100 mille to-morrow, and 50 mille on Thursday. This is, I think, all that caution and prudence can require for the week, and hope all demand for gold will cease before that time ; if not, we have plenty of Consols, new Three Per Cent. Bank Stock, and India Bonds, besides an immense amount of bills we have discounted. I wish every bank was as well prepared for a severe run as, thank God, we are." Still the anxiety must have been very great.

The panic in England was followed by a monetary crisis at Hamburg, and there was great apprehension of many failures in London and other commercial places. During this time Lady Montefiore had been suffering from illness, and was still very poorly. She was frequently attended by eminent physicians, who recommended her a change of climate.

At the beginning of 1858, just as they had arranged to return to East Cliff to allow Lady Montefiore the benefit of rest, Mr Arthur Cohen (the present Queen's Counsel and Member of Parliament) and his brother called on them with a message from his parents, to the effect that they were desirous of passing a couple of months with them in a warmer climate. Both Sir Moses and Lady Montefiore, ever delighted to have an opportunity of evincing their affection towards their brother and sister, at once changed their plans, and made arrangements to take a trip to Italy, and thus avoid the inclemency of an English winter.

Lady Montefiore, recording the day of their departure in her Diary, invokes the blessing from Heaven. "May every evil," she prays, "be averted from us, and may joy and thankfulness fill our mind throughout our projected journey."

Sir Moses, wishing good acts to accompany them, as it were, like guardian angels, handed on that day a cheque for £100 to the treasurer, as his donation to the Lord Mayor's Commemoration Scholarship for the Jews' College, and bestowed various gifts on charitable institutions and deserving individuals.

They then left London for Dover.

On March 20th the travellers reached Florence, where, unfortunately, Lady Montefiore was taken seriously ill. Two eminent physicians, Dr G. Levy and Professor Pietro Ciprani, held frequent consultations. Dr Canham, the physician who attended her at Ramsgate, was also sent for, and it was not until the 13th of May that the doctors considered her sufficiently recovered to continue the journey. That was an anxious time for Sir Moses, the more so as he himself was ill and obliged to keep his bed for seventeen days.

May 15*th.*—We find them with their relatives at Pisa. Lady Montefiore continued to make satisfactory progress towards recovery, and Sir Moses was again able to enjoy the fine scenery of the country.

Saturday, he attended Divine worship, and the day following he gave a description in the Diary of the Synagogue, which, on account of the allusions therein made to his parents and god-father, appeared to me of sufficient historical importance to interest the reader.

"The Synagogue," he wrote, "was very well attended, both by males and females, and it is one of the handsomest little Synagogues I have ever seen. I wish I had seen it before I built one at Ramsgate. I would have gladly adopted the plan. It will accommodate three hundred persons, and has a splendid ark, containing the sacred scrolls of the Pentateuch. My god-father, Moses Haim Racah, of blessed memory, attended this Synagogue when residing at his country house at Pisa. He was a very liberal contributor to the Synagogue and charities at Pisa. I have often heard my dear mother, blessed be her soul, say that she and my honoured father had passed many happy days when staying on frequent visits with the best of friends, Moses Haim Racah and his amiable wife, my godmother. My mother frequently spoke of the kindness she ever experienced from them, being more the affection of parents both towards herself and my father. They were both young at the time, having been married only about a twelvemonth. I consider myself most fortunate in having been blessed on my coming into the world with such excellent friends as my godfather and godmother. My godfather continued a sincere friend to my dear parents to the end of his life. Peace to his soul!"

May 23*rd.*—They left Pisa for La Spezia, where they remained eight or nine days, Lady Montefiore being again in ill health.

May 31*st.*—They started for Genoa. On their arrival in that place their travelling companions became most anxious to return without delay to England, and wishing to go by sea to Marseilles to avoid a fatiguing journey across the Alps, took an affectionate farewell of Sir Moses and Lady Montefiore, who, in the hope of deriving some improvement by a longer stay, resolved to remain in Genoa for some time.

In this, however, they were disappointed. Dr Canham told Sir Moses that he was anxious for their return to England, not on his own account, but on that of Lady Montefiore, as he feared her health would not get better until she was back in England. Nevertheless he strongly advised very short journeys, not to exceed, if possible, four hours a day.

June 24th.—They arrived at Paris. Lady Montefiore continued very poorly and weak. Sir Moses himself was under great apprehension regarding his own health, feeling the symptoms of a very dangerous malady, from which he had suffered before. Their stay in the French capital was very brief. They left four days after their arrival. They arrived safely at Ramsgate on July 2nd. A few days later they were at Park Lane, after an absence of five months.

Here Sir Charles Locock and Dr Canham met in consultation respecting Lady Montefiore's illness, and Sir Moses had the happiness of hearing from Sir Charles that he saw no reason to despair of her ultimate recovery.

The entries referring to the month of July show that, notwithstanding the anxieties both of them had on their minds during their last journey, which would have made it desirable for them to have a few weeks' rest, they were immediately called upon to exercise their wonted activity in the performance of duties partly self-imposed, and, to a certain degree, obligatory, owing to the position they held in their own community, as well as in society in general.

The reception they had given in the preceding year to Toussoun Pasha, and the benefit which he derived from his stay in England, induced his father, the Viceroy of Egypt, to send him again to this country, and a telegram to this effect having reached them from Corfu, the necessary arrangements had at once to be made for his reception.

July 22nd.—They were much pained to hear that the Committee of the Holy Land Appeal Fund were obliged to come to a decision to discontinue the weaving establishment and the girls' school, each requiring at least £300 a year to keep them up.

To counterbalance, as it were, their disappointment in the success of two institutions in the Holy Land, for which they had so much exerted themselves, they had the satisfaction of witnessing in England the successful issue of their struggles for civil and religious liberty.

Baron Lionel de Rothschild took his seat (July 26) in the House of Commons, and Sir Moses, as President of the London Committee of Deputies of British Jews, signed the following resolutions, which had been unanimously adopted at a meeting held on that day at the Spanish and Portuguese Vestry Chambers :

"That this Board hails with the sincerest gratification the passing of the Bill affording to Her Majesty's subjects professing the Jewish religion the means of enjoying seats in the Legislature.

"That this Board offers its warmest thanks to those members of the Houses of Lords and Commons whose votes and influence have produced this great result.

"That the grateful acknowledgments of this Board are especially due to the electors of the city of London, whose noble, untiring, and enlightened labours have achieved a crowning victory in the cause of civil and religious liberty.

"To Baron Rothschild, M.P., and to all those valued friends whose efforts have for years been unceasingly devoted to the removal of Jewish disabilities, this Board is also desirous to testify its respect and gratitude.

"This Board assures its fellow-countrymen that it prizes most highly this act of right and justice ; and that the heart of every British Jew yearns as warmly and beats as vividly for the glory and prosperity of his native land as that of every other British subject.

"That the foregoing resolutions be advertised in the daily papers and in the Jewish press.   "MOSES MONTEFIORE, *President.*"

Two days later he went to meet the young Prince, Toussoun Pasha, on his arrival from Folkestone, and took him and his suite to Park Lane.   Amusements of every description were provided for him—excursions, dinners, and soirees, similar to those given in his honour on the occasion of the former visit of His Highness to England.

Sir Moses had now been associated with the London Committee of Deputies of the British Jews for nearly half a century, and for more than twenty years, with a few interruptions, had presided over its affairs.   Alderman Philips (now Sir Benjamin Philips), in the early part of the year 1857, at the first meeting of the Board, after Sir Moses had formally resigned the presidential seat, moved : " That an address should be presented to him, expressing the thanks of the Board for the faithful, zealous, and impartial manner in which he had fulfilled his duties." All parties unanimously assented to it, but a variety of circumstances had tended to prevent the presentation till now.

Monday, October 11th.—When, at the meeting of the Board of Deputies, Alderman Philips presented the address, he said, "that, in doing so, he deemed it a great honour to be the medium of communicating the sentiments of the Board to one whose uniform kindness and courtesy, and whose veneration for the religion of his forefathers, has won for him the esteem, the admiration, and, he might almost say, the love, not alone of the Jews of this happy land, but of those of the civilised world."

In reply to the address, Sir Moses said : " However inadequately I may express my deep sense of this valued evidence of your esteem and regard, I desire most earnestly to assure you of my sincere and cordial thanks for the tribute of appreciation conveyed to me in the very flattering address with which you have been pleased to honour me   I desire further to assure you that Lady Montefiore most heartily unites with me in grateful thanks for your congratulations on our safe return to England, and for the expression of your hope that the God of Israel may vouchsafe to us, in happy union for many years, His gracious protection and blessing.

"You remind me that for nearly half a century I have been associated with this body, and that for more than twenty years of that period I have, with few interruptions, presided over its affairs.   It is true that advanced age and impaired health might, some time since, have reasonably resulted in the severance of our connection in this latter relation, the continuance of which I must attribute, not to any merit of my own, but to your kind personal feeling towards me.   But sensible as I have been that the high and honourable office of your president might well have been entrusted to younger and abler hands, I feel that no one could have experienced from you more friendly support or more flattering indulgence than you have extended to me.

" With respect to the efforts which I have been privileged to make in foreign countries to advance the position of our co-religionists in the social and moral scale—and to which you have so gracefully and complimentarily alluded in referring to the temporary interruptions of my presidentship—they are, independently of the gratification I derive from your approval of them, a source of enduring, welcome remembrance, both to myself and to Lady Montefiore, who, accompanying me on all occasions, has most cheerfully encountered no inconsiderable amount of fatigue and hardship.   I rejoice greatly that, by the blessing of the Almighty, these efforts have not been fruitless.

" Grateful for all your acts of kindness, and particularly for this valued token of your commendation, I heartily pray God—and in this prayer Lady Montefiore sincerely joins—to bless you all with continued health and prosperity."

November 10th. — Sir Moses received a letter from the Honourable C. B. Phipps, stating that the Queen had commanded him to inform Sir Moses that Her Majesty would receive the son of the Viceroy of Egypt on the following Monday, at three o'clock, at Windsor Castle.

Accordingly, on the 15th November, Sir Moses proceeded with the Prince to the Castle.   On their arrival, they were asked if they had lunched, as Her Majesty had given orders for lunch to be prepared for them.   Sir Moses replied that he was thankful for Her Majesty's hospitality, but they had lunched already. They were then conducted into a beautiful drawing-room commanding a view of Windsor Park, and, after waiting there a few minutes, Colonel Biddulph entered, and led them along a gallery into a beautiful room, where they found assembled the Queen, the Prince Consort, and several children of the Royal family.   Sir Moses introduced Toussoun Pasha to Her Majesty. They were most graciously received by the Queen and the Prince.   Her Majesty thought the Pasha had grown tall and stout, and was looking well.   Her Majesty then brought forward the children to shake hands with the Pasha.   A little girl, apparently not above two or three years old, came forward and held out her little hand in the most elegant and graceful manner possible.   "The dear little angel," Sir Moses says, "looked pleased, and smiled when the young Prince stepped forward and took the little hand."   Her Majesty then introduced the other children to him, and all shook hands, the Queen remarking that one of the Princes was of his own age.   After some few inquiries of Sir Moses whether the Pasha had been long in England, and when he would leave, the Queen came and shook hands with the Pasha, and said to Sir Moses: "I wish him to tell his father everything that is kind on my part."   Sir Moses assured Her Majesty that her wish should be complied with.   He then thanked Her Majesty and the Prince, for the Pasha, for their kindness and condescension, and took leave, Colonel Biddulph conducting them to their carriage.

Sir Moses remarked in the entry he made that day in his Diary : "I never in my life witnessed a more lovely picture than the Queen, the Prince Consort, and the Royal children, beauty and goodness combined, a perfect picture of a noble family. May the God of our forefathers bestow on them all good, grant them length of days, continued content and happiness, and may His blessings ever be with them. Long and happy live the Queen."

Believing that a visit to St George's Chapel would be entertaining to Dr Etienne and the Pasha, they stopped there, and went over it.   On going out of the chapel Colonel Biddulph came to Sir Moses to enquire if a sight of the apartments in the

Castle would be agreeable, supposing they were not too much fatigued. Sir Moses did not hesitate to accept the offer, and Colonel Biddulph accompanied them back to the Castle, and shewed them some of the splendid rooms. Then having sent for Mr Richards to accompany them round the galleries, St George's Hall, and the beautiful armoury, he took his leave.

"I much regret," Sir Moses says, "my dear Judith was not with me. She could not have failed to have been pleased."

It was five o'clock when they took leave of Mr Richards.

November 18*th.*—His Highness, accompanied by Sir Moses and Lady Montefiore, arrived at Dover. After remaining the night at the Ship Hotel, the young Prince took an affectionate leave of them, and embarked in the morning for Calais, the Prince intending to reach Paris before midnight.

CHAPTER X.

1858.

LADY MONTEFIORE was still very unwell, and Sir Moses
himself was so ill at Dover that he could not leave his
couch in the morning after his arrival; but there was no time
for him now to allow himself to be treated like an invalid or
seek a few weeks' rest.

An important event which for the last five months agitated
the minds of Christians as well as Jews all over Europe and
America seriously called for immediate and energetic action, and
he considered it his duty to rouse himself, and step into the
breach.

I refer to the case of the abduction of the child Edgar
Mortara from the house of his parents at Bologna.

The first official information of this had been received by
means of a letter from the President of the Council of the
Israelite community of Turin, addressed to Sir Moses as President of the Board of Deputies. This letter was accompanied by
a memorial from twenty-one Sardinian congregations, adverting
briefly to the facts of this distressing case, detailing the measures
they had adopted in reference thereto, and earnestly appealing
to the Board of Deputies for its immediate co-operation.

The full details of the case are given in a memorial
addressed to the Pontifical Government on behalf of the
Mortara family, of which I give a short abstract.

"On the 24th of June 1858, in Bologna, the boy Edgar
Mortara, under seven years of age, was snatched away from his
Jewish parents under pretext of having been secretly baptised.
The distressed father repeatedly but vainly applied to the
authorities for an explanation of the circumstances which had

led to the abduction of his son. It was only after several weeks that he was able in an indirect way to learn that Anna Morisi, a former servant in his house, had, many months previously, told another servant girl that, at the instigation of a certain Lepori, a druggist, she had baptised the child Edgar when no one was present, and when he was about one year old and dangerously ill. It was further said that this took place on an occasion when another of Mortara's sons was dying, and Morisi was urged by the other girl to baptise him also, which, however, she declined to do."

Mortara on these statements made the following observations :—

"*1st.* That it is true that the child Edgar, when a little more than one year old, was taken ill, but only of a slight ailment very common among children, and the child's state could not have created any serious apprehensions in the mind of any one, therefore the condition did not exist on which it is permitted to baptise the children of infidels *invitis parentibus*, viz., the certainty of an inevitable death. And, indeed, it would be in contradiction to the maxims of the Church on paternal authority to suppose such a thing authorised before the approach of death, which removes a child from the authority of his parents. Supposing for one moment that the confidence entertained by the parents in the recovery of their child were not shared by the over-zealous servant, it could not be supposed or maintained that on the erroneous supposition of a person the law could be diverted from its true meaning and from the established rules for its application.

"*2nd.* The event, as narrated, was not legally examined into, nor was any witness called or confronted. How is it then that while nobody can be legally deprived of the smallest of his possessions without incontestible proofs, now on a simple and bare assertion of a servant girl it is sought to establish a fact, the consequence of which is to rob a father and mother of their child? And indeed there are some important authorities on canonical law, who find the sole deficiency of evidence a sufficient reason to declare the nullity of baptisms under similar circumstances.

"*3rd.* The girl Morisi has spoken on the subject after five years of absolute silence. Therefore the suspicion is not without foundation that she could not perfectly recollect having then observed and fulfilled all the requirements of the baptismal rite with that zealous precision required for the validity of this sacramental act, and particularly as she had not then arrived at the sixteenth year of her age, and was as simple, ignorant, and inexperienced as could be."

After these considerations of the legal aspect of the case, he proceeds to some general arguments on which the Mortara family found a hope that the authorities in whose hands the decision rests will order the restoration of their child.

The memorial then points out the aversion and contempt resulting from an imposed religion, and shows that ever since the Church adopted the solemn principle, " Love thy neighbour as thyself," it tacitly acknowledged free-will in all, and, at the same time, its own inability to punish, although it might lament, the religious beliefs of others. It next argues that baptism conferred upon an unwilling adult being null and void, the same law should apply to a minor *invitis parentibus*, and declares that there is no power on earth within the bounds of justice and humanity that could impose upon a child a creed different to that received from the paternal precepts as long as the will of the father is that of the son. There is nothing on earth that belongs more legitimately to a father than his children. The baptism of an adult while asleep is void, as the free consent so essential to the sacramental act is wanting; why then, in the present case, where the subject was also asleep, should he be judged differently?

Then follows a series of references to high clerical authorities from the year 1587 down to 1840, who have, one and all, decreed the illegality of forced baptism, and the necessity of restitution in cases of abduction.

A correspondence was immediately opened with the principal Hebrew communities, and with many persons of distinction professing various religious creeds, in Europe and America. In England especially, the Evangelical Society, through Sir Culling E. Eardly, took a leading part in their endeavour to serve the cause of justice. Copies of the memorial, from which I have given the above extract, together with copies of the " Bullarium Romanum " (vol. v., p. 60, xxvi.), against secret baptisms; a letter from " The Jurist," published in London, November 13th, 1858 ; an extract from the Annual Register of October 1774, referring to the restoration of a Jewish girl, aged nine, to her parents ; and a copy of depositions made at Bologna before the notary Verardini, were forwarded to them to guide them in their pleadings for humanity, and frequent meetings of a Committee appointed by the Board were convened by the President to consider the best means for securing the restoration of the child to his parents.

A report of the result of the deliberations of the said Committee has been made by Sir Moses to the Board of Deputies, a portion of which I copy for the information of the reader.

" The letter and memorial from Sardinia," Sir Moses says, "were without loss of time submitted to the Deputies at a meeting, and this Committee was thereupon appointed with power to adopt such proceedings as, in their judgment, they might consider expedient.

"'The Committee met on the day of their appointment, and at once determined to appeal for co-operation to the Central Consistory of the Israelites of France, and to the central Jewish authorities at Amsterdam. They further determined to memorialise the British Government, soliciting its powerful intervention, and feeling well assured of its humane and friendly sympathy. The Committee further resolved to transmit to the press copies of communications received from Turin, and they have every reason to feel grateful to the press, particularly in England, France, Germany, and the United States, for its able and humane assistance.

"'At a subsequent meeting the Committee determined to transmit a report of the case, as it had appeared in the *Times* newspaper, to every member of the Catholic clergy throughout the United Kingdom, and about 1800 of such reports were circulated accordingly.

"'The Committee, through the medium of the President, have also appealed for co-operation to the Jewish Congregational bodies in the principal cities and towns of Germany and the United States of America, and they rejoice to be able to report that their appeal has been zealously responded to, and that various bodies of their co-religionists are taking active measures to seek redress for the grievous wrong which has been committed.

"'It is well known,' the Board of Deputies announced, 'that the Committee of the Evangelical Alliance and other religious societies of the Protestant community have manifested great interest in this unhappy case. They have on various occasions conveyed to this Committee the expressions of their kind sympathy, and the Committee are assured that the humane and zealous interposition of these important bodies may be relied on.

"'Although, as will have been seen from the correspondence which has been published in the daily press, the British Government is unable to assist the case by a direct intervention, its views thereon are emphatically pronounced, and the Committee offer their grateful acknowledgments for the prompt attention and great kindness they have received from the Earl of Malmesbury and Mr Fitzgerald throughout the communications which have taken place between your Committee and the Foreign Office.

"'The Committee are strongly urged to appeal personally to the Emperor of the French by means of a deputation from your body, and from the Jewish congregations in the principal states of Europe and America, under the hope that His Imperial Majesty, conscious that the public opinion has declared itself indignantly against an outrage so disgraceful to the present age, will exercise his powerful influence with the Papal Government, so as to induce it to restore the young child, Edgar Mortara, to its bereaved parents, and to denounce the repetition of any similar practice.

"'The Committee, however, feel that they would not be justified in the adoption of so important a step without bringing the matter under the attention of the General Board, and have resolved to report thereto their proceedings to date, and to seek therefrom further instructions. They protest most strongly against baptism without the consent of the party baptised.

"'In this particular case the Committee have purposely abstained from entering into the full details of the abduction and of the subsequent events relating thereto. To do this would be to extend this report beyond reasonable limits. The Committee are in possession of important documents and voluminous correspondence, extracts from portions of which have from time to time appeared in the press. After a careful consideration of these documents, your Committee have strong grounds for believing that the alleged baptism never took place. If it did, it was administered by the menial and illiterate servant girl Morisi, when she was herself a child only fourteen years old, and under circumstances **which** appear to render it invalid, even by **the** Roman canonical **laws.** It is **quite** clear **that** the child, from its tender age (twelve months), **must have been** unconscious of the act ; that up **to** the date of its abduction it **had** been nurtured **in** the faith of its parents, and so far from there being any truth in the statement that Edgar Mortara rejoices in his adoption into the Catholic Faith (a statement which, considering the still tender age of the child, is manifestly absurd), it yearns incessantly for the restoration **to** its home,—while, alas ! if report speaks truly, its unhappy mother has **been** bereft of reason, and its father, prostrated in spirit, is about to emigrate from the **scene** of his recent afflictions.

" ' The case in itself **is one** deserving **of** the sincerest commiseration ; **but** when viewed with **reference to its bearings** on society at large, **it** appeals irresistibly to all ; and **the civilised world will** indeed be wanting **in** energy and wisdom if it permit the nineteenth century **to** be disgraced by the reten**tion of** the child in contravention of the laws of nature, morality, and religion, **and** most especially it behoves the Jewish community **to** exert itself to **the** utmost in so urgent a **cause, so** that if it fail it may have **at least** the consolation of knowing that it **has done** its duty, while if, under **the** blessing of the Almighty God, it succeed, **it** may rejoice not only because **the** sorrows of an afflicted family will thereby be alleviated, but also because **a** moral victory will have been achieved, the advantages of which will be recognised and prized by every **friend of** humanity, law, and order throughout the world.

" ' Moses Montefiore, *President.*'

" At a meeting of the Board, held on the **22nd of December** 1858, Sir Moses Montefiore, President, in the chair, the following resolutions were unanimously adopted :—

" ' That in the opinion **of this Board it is desirable to** memorialise the **head** of the Pontifical **Government on the** subject **of the** Mortara case.

" ' That Sir Moses Montefiore, Bart., President, **be** requested to present the same personally, if and when his health **and** engagements, and the health of Lady Montefiore, enable him to undertake **the** journey.

" ' That the **Committee on** the Mortara **case be empowered to** prepare **the** memorial, and to make such arrangements as they may deem expedient for a deputation from **this** Board, and other public Jewish bodies, to accompany Sir Moses Montefiore **on** his mission ; and to adopt such other measures on the subject as they **may** consider **necessary.'** "

Sir Moses, with his usual readiness to serve a good cause, consented to proceed to Rome, the Board having resolved that it was inexpedient to send a deputation to the Emperor of the French, and now commenced making the necessary preparation for his departure, as soon as Lady Montefiore's state of health would permit her to accompany him.

He had, however, a pleasing **duty of a** political nature to perform **before** leaving England, which he did **not** like to relinquish.

He was desirous to assist in the election **of** Baron Meyer de Rothschild, to fill the vacancy at Hythe occasioned by **the** retirement of Sir John William Ramsden ; and, accompanied by his nephew, Mr Arthur Cohen, Q.C., he proceeded on Tuesday, February 10, 1859, to the hustings.

Baron Meyer de Rothschild was accompanied from Folkestone and Sandgate by a vast cavalcade and two bands, and just before reaching the town the horses were taken from his carriage, and the candidate drawn by the inhabitants to the hustings, where he was received with reiterated plaudits. He was surrounded by a number of influential friends, conspicuous among them being Sir Moses Montefiore.

The usual formalities having been gone through, and the returning officer having declared Baron Meyer de Rothschild duly elected, the latter addressed the electors, after which Sir Moses congratulated them on their choice. They could not, he said, have a better member than Baron Rothschild. (Cheers.) " I thank God," he added, " that old as I am, I have lived to see this day, and to witness your choice. I sincerely thank you all. May God bless you."

The same day, on his way to Ramsgate, he received at Ashford a telegram announcing that Alderman Salomons had been elected for Greenwich by a majority of 889. " This intelligence," he said, " afforded me the sincerest pleasure, for the Jews owe a deep debt of gratitude to him for his strenuous exertion in the cause of civil liberty, regardless of labour and expense." " I truly hope," he continued, " that both the new members may long live to enjoy their honours."

Prayers having been offered up in all the London Synagogues for the success of his mission to Rome on behalf of Edgar Mortara, Sir Moses gave orders to hasten the preparations for the journey, and proceeded to the Foreign Office to present a copy of the memorial of the Board of Deputies to Lord Malmesbury. His Lordship received him most kindly, read the memorial, and promised to give him letters of introduction to the British Ambassadors and Consuls abroad ; " although Sir Moses should bear in mind, from a former conversation on the subject, that he (Lord Malmesbury) entertained doubts as to the result of the mission."

February 25th.—He received letters of introduction from Lord Malmesbury to the Embassies of Paris, Turin, Florence, Vienna, and to Mr Odo Russell (the late Lord Ampthill) in Rome ; and on March 3rd he and Lady Montefiore, accompanied by Dr Hodgkin and Mr Kursheedt, embarked at Dover for Calais.

The journey from London was most trying to Lady Montefiore in consequence of her impaired health, and they did not reach Rome till April 5th.

Sir Moses lost no time in calling upon Mr Russell, and leaving his letters of introduction from the Foreign Office and Lord Russell. Mr Russell remembered having seen Sir Moses when he was with Lord de Redcliffe at Constantinople, and said, " He would do all he could for him, but without any expectation of succeeding in doing more than obtaining for him an interview with His Holiness." " That day," he said, " was a council day, and the ministers did not receive." Sir Moses gave him a copy of the address, also a full statement of the Mortara case. Mr Russell repeated his promise to do all he could, but added, " What can a poor Attaché expect, when the French Ambassador with a French army with him has failed, after making every endeavour ? "

April 9.—Mr John Abel Smith having given Sir Moses' letters of introduction to Mr Pentland, the latter called, and said that he was perfectly acquainted with the case, and had spoken with the boy. In his opinion there was no hope of getting the boy, but every effort should be made to obtain a pledge that such a proceeding should not be sanctioned in future. He appeared to think that Sir Moses should see the French Ambassador, and obtain his support, he having taken so active a part in the matter by order of the Emperor. Sir Moses, however, did not approve of that. " I am," he said, " so much of an Englishman that I prefer the English representation, and would only act in accordance with the advice of Mr Russell."

Mr Pentland, whom Sir Moses took to be an Irishman, was a highly educated man of elegant and agreeable manners. He was very much with the Prince of Wales, and said, " His Royal Highness was most amiable and talented, and very popular with the Roman nobility and people."

April 11*th*.—Sir Moses received the following letter from Lord de Redcliffe :—

" MY DEAR SIR MOSES,—I return you herewith the Mortara memorial. The case appears to be so clear that, according to our notions, you ought to find no difficulty in obtaining justice ; but judging from what reaches me in conversation, I fear it will require all your ability, energy, and experience to open the smallest prospect of success. With every good wish, I beg you will believe me, sincerely yours, "S. DE REDCLIFFE."

"Everything I hear and see," Sir Moses said, "unfortunately confirms the opinion given me before my arrival. I have not heard from any person since I left London that there was the slightest hope of success for my mission, and now fear that I may even be denied the opportunity of presenting the address of the Board to the Sovereign Pontiff. Should I fail in this object, my next endeavours must be to obtain an introduction by Mr Russell to the Minister, Cardinal Antonelli."

CHAPTER XI.

1859.

MR RUSSELL, in a private note, wrote to him :—
"It is with deep regret that I have to inform you that all my
exertions in the interest of your cause have failed. Cardinal Antonelli declined
to enter upon the subject, saying, ' It was a closed question,' and His Eminence referred me to Monsignor Pacca, the papal chamberlain, or to Monsignor
Talbot, to obtain an audience for you of His Holiness, but His Eminence
added that he thought it would be difficult at this moment. I next applied
to Monsignor Talbot, who assured me that the only possible course was
that you should apply yourself, in writing to, or personally call on, Monsignor Pacca, who lives in the Vatican. Monsignor Talbot thought the
Pope would see you, but he also considered the question closed.

"I fear you were but too right in saying our only hope now rests with
that great God whose holy laws have in this melancholy case been violated
by the hand of man.

"I need not assure you that if there is anything in which I can serve you,
I beg you will command my services at all times."

Sir Moses immediately went to thank Mr Russell for his
kind and zealous exertions for the cause he had so much at
heart, and said that he deemed it his duty to follow up the
suggestions made in his letter.

On his return home he wrote his application, and took it
himself to Monsignor Pacca at the Vatican. As he was out, Sir
Moses left it with his servant, with but faint hopes of a favourable
answer.

He and Lady Montefiore then left cards on Lady de Redcliffe. Sir Moses saw his Lordship, who appeared to think he
should apply for an audience without naming the object he had
in view; but Sir Moses' opinion did not coincide with those of

Lord Redcliffe ("perhaps a wrong one," Sir Moses remarks). " It would not be becoming in me," he said, " to gain an audience but as the representative of the Board of Deputies of British Jews."

April 14th.—In accordance with an invitation which Sir Moses had the privilege of receiving, he rode to the Hôtel des Isles Britaniques at seven o'clock, and had the honour of dining with the Prince of Wales. I quote Sir Moses' own words on the subject from the Diary :—

"His Royal Highness," he writes, "received me most cordially, and said he had seen me at Windsor Castle. Within three minutes after my arrival the Prince handed down the Hon. Mrs Bruce, the only lady present at the dinner, but she did not sit next to His Royal Highness. He had Prince Torlonia on his right, Mrs Bruce was next to Prince Torlonia, and I sat exactly opposite His Royal Highness. On my right, the Rev. G. F. Tarver, the Prince's chaplain, and Major Teesdale, R.A.

"There were twelve persons at table, and, before dinner, Colonel Bruce introduced me to each, excepting Prince Torlonia, who came in only two minutes before we sat down.

"The conversation was on general topics. I think all spoke English except Torlonia, who spoke French with His Royal Highness. Dr Chambers, the Prince's physician, was present. We were at table about an hour and a half, then retired to the drawing-room. His Royal Highness requested each to be seated, and took a seat himself in the centre of the half circle formed by his party. He enquired if Toussoun Pasha was in England at present, and said the Viceroy had given a grand dinner to his brother.

"Soon after nine the party took leave. His Royal Highness shook hands with each. I could not have had a more gratifying evening.

"Dr Chambers told me that Mrs Chambers had a few friends and a little music upstairs, and would be happy if I would do them the honour to join them. He accompanied me to their apartments on the floor above His Royal Highness, and introduced me to Mrs Chambers. She said she remembered me by the kindness I had shewn her many years since by giving her some very thin biscuits,* of which she was very fond. Gradually

---

* Probably Passover biscuits, which Sir Moses was in the habit of sending sometimes to his friends who expressed a desire of having them.

the two drawing-rooms became very crowded. She introduced me to a considerable number of her visitors, mostly English travellers, and many from India. They all alluded to the object of my mission with feeling, and expressed an ardent desire for my success, but not one among them thought that there was a hope of it.

"The son-in-law of the late Joseph Hume, who had been in India, was there with his wife. I should think there must have been 150 persons present. Mrs Chambers and her sisters have beautiful voices, and sang delightfully. A gentleman belonging to the Royal Chapel at Rome, who is celebrated for his beautiful voice and for being an excellent musician, performed also. Dr Hodgkin, who was present, having left my dear wife weak and poorly, I got away as soon as I well could. A most lively and agreeable party."

The apprehension of failure in his mission, so strongly foretold by all who spoke to him that evening on the subject, threatened to become almost a certainty, owing to a serious accusation brought against the Jews in the Ghetto.

On Friday evening, April 15th, some officers of the police entered the Jewish quarter and searched a house adjoining the Synagogue, the room containing the cloaks, bells, &c., of the sacred scrolls of the Pentateuch, and afterwards the cellars under the Synagogue. They did not say at the time what was the object of their search, but a crowd had assembled outside the Synagogue, accusing the Jews of having stolen two children with the object of using their blood in making the Passover cakes, a woman exciting the crowd by declaring she had lost two of her children. The alarm continued for a considerable time, and it was late before the crowd left the Ghetto. Happily all was quiet the next morning, but the Jews still laboured under great anxiety, as this was the first instance of such a charge being made against them at Rome, and hitherto their Synagogues had been held sacred. Early in the morning a deputation waited upon the Governor of the city, but he had heard nothing of the matter. On enquiry of the head of the police it was ascertained that the report was spread by the malice of one of the police officers. The Governor assured the deputation of his protection, and said he would, if necessary, send a force into the Ghetto to protect the Jews.

Sir Moses on hearing of the outbreak at once offered to go to the Synagogue if the reports were repeated, but happily all remained quiet.

The next day (April 17th) he received the reassuring information that the lost child had been found, and had returned to the mother's house. It appeared that a woman had said that she had lost her child, and a neighbour advised her to go to a particular man, a barber, who told fortunes. She did so, whereupon this man informed her that her child had been stolen by the Jews, who had murdered it for the sake of using its blood with the Passover cakes. On receiving this account she went direct to the Ghetto, and created a great disturbance, calling upon the Jews to give up the child. She gave information to the office of police, and they sent to search for the child. The Governor had since put the barber and the woman in prison, but nevertheless there was a very uneasy feeling among the Jews the next night and day, as women and boys frequently cried out, " Take care of your children, or the Jews will murder them." It was a singular circumstance that until that year nothing of the kind had happened at Rome ; and it was not a little remarkable that the newspaper published at Rome on the 16th inst., yesterday, called *Il vevo amico del popolo*, contained a letter from Smyrna, giving an account of the assassination of a Frenchman in the Jewish quarter of that city by the Jews, as it was alleged, for the purpose of using the blood in the Passover cakes. The letter also alluded to the case of Father Tomaso at Damascus. It was a most mischievous article, and could not fail to excite a very bitter feeling against the Jews, frustrating every attempt made to rescue the poor boy Mortara, and to restore him to his parents.

Sir Moses felt much depressed in spirits ; Lady Montefiore was weak and ill. The Passover festivals commenced, and they were both anxious for the safety of the Hebrew community. A lady who had dined with them the previous night was so much alarmed as to dread returning home to the Ghetto. Two gentlemen, besides her husband and a lady, had to walk with her to see her safely home.

In a telegram Sir Moses sent to his friends on the 17th inst., he said, " Suspense and perplexity still prevent me from writing."

He invited several friends to dine with them, and be present at the recital of the history of the exodus from Egypt, in conformity with Biblical injunction, and attended the morning service each day in the Synagogue, no further disturbance having taken place in the vicinity.

Wednesday, April 20th.—On his return from Divine worship in the morning, Lord Stratford de Redcliffe paid them a visit. He had been with Cardinal Antonelli, and had spoken about Sir Moses. From what had passed he believed that his Eminence would see Sir Moses if the latter called on him ; and would also have no objection to his being presented to the Sovereign Pontiff, but the Cardinal would have public duties to perform after that day which would prevent his receiving anybody at all till after the holidays. His Lordship said "between four and five o'clock would be the best time to go to him." Sir Moses told his Lordship that he was prevented from riding that day, and the walk was too far for him, as he was already much fatigued with a walk to and from the Synagogue. His Lordship replied that he did not usually have his carriage out on a Sunday, but he should think it right to do so on such an occasion. Sir Moses mentioned that he would, with his permission, see Mr Odo Russell, and ask him to present him to his Eminence, when he was able to go to him, which he might do after seven this evening. His Lordship approved of this, and remained more than half an hour chatting. Sir Moses afterwards renewed the conversation about his mission. His Lordship said he believed the question of the Mortara case was considered as completely closed by his Eminence the Cardinal, and that it could not be re-opened after the discussion with the French Ambassador.

Sir Moses expressed himself truly thankful to Lord Stratford, for he was sure if it were in his power he would in every way promote the success of his mission, which, Sir Moses said, he had every reason to fear was quite hopeless.

After his Lordship had left, Mrs Chambers, the wife of Dr Chambers, and her sister Miss Maitland, paid Lady Montefiore a visit ; also several gentlemen, whom Sir Moses met at her evening party. "All concur," Sir Moses says, "in the general opinion of the great amiability of the Prince of Wales." As Mrs Chambers remembered the circumstance of Sir Moses having sent her many years since some Passover biscuits, he promised to send her some again, as he had brought with him a sufficient quantity from London. Many Christians like them very much.

I remember having once seen over the shop of a Passover biscuit baker in London an inscription on a shield to the effect that he had the distinguished honour of being appointed Passover biscuit baker to Her Royal Highness the Duchess of Gloucester.

The Jews in Rome, however, did not enjoy the Passover biscuits much that year, nor for that matter any other food.

The President of their community, Signor Samuel Alatri, paid Sir Moses a visit, and appeared much alarmed, apprehending another attack on his community. Sir Moses offered to sleep in the Ghetto, so little fear had he, but Signor Alatri preferred going to the French General.

Returning again to the Mortara case, Sir Moses writes :—

" Early this morning I sent a note to Mr Odo Russell, requesting to have an interview with him. He replied by note that he would call on me at half-past ten, which he did. I showed him Baron Rothschild's telegram, enquiring as to the progress in the Mortara affair. He said, in reply to it, I might make any use of his name that I thought might be of service to my cause, as he felt most anxious to do all in his power to help me. I then mentioned the conversation I had had with Lord Stratford de Redcliffe yesterday, pointing out that it was his Lordship's impression that Cardinal Antonelli would have no objection to see me if I called on him. I therefore asked Mr Russell's opinion as to whether I should call on his Eminence, and if so, whether he would be so good as to introduce me to him. Mr Russell said Lord Stratford was intimate with the Cardinal, and it would perhaps be better if his Lordship would introduce me, but he thought perhaps I should wait for the answer of Monsignor Pacca before seeing the Cardinal. I then asked him if he thought I should leave my card. This he approved, and said he would see Monsignor Pacca, and find out how the matter stood, and would also converse with Lord Stratford concerning Cardinal Antonelli. He thought the Sovereign Pontiff would see me after the holidays.

" At four I rode, with my dear wife, to the Vatican, where his Holiness resides. On the floor above are the apartments of Cardinal Antonelli. I had to ascend 190 steps, a most splendid marble staircase. The steps were easy to ascend, being very broad and low. The person in waiting took my card, and enquired if I wished to see his Eminence. This, I said, I hoped to do some other day. I then drove to the Palazzo Colonna and left my card for the French Ambassador, to whom we are all so much indebted for his most zealous endeavours on behalf of young Mortara."

In the evening Signor Tagliacozzo came in to report on two other attempts made by some of the Roman populace to cause trouble to the Hebrew community. In two different Synagogues, he said, arrangements had been made to hide a child there, with a view of raising the alarm outside the moment the door should be closed, and then falling upon the Jews and accusing them of intended murder. "By the mercy of heaven," he said, "these plans were frustrated, and in each case the lost child was found."

"The director of the police," he continued, "sent to the President of the Deputies of the Jews at Rome, and informed him of the discovery of the missing children. Meanwhile many of the Jews had been afraid to pursue their daily avocations in the city, several having been ill-treated by the ignorant people, who pelted them with stones, injuring two or three very severely. Signor Tagliacozzo observed that the Jews had had a miraculous escape, for on the beadle closing the doors of one of the Synagogues on Friday evening last he observed a child under a seat in one of the corners, as if asleep. He turned the child out, but could get no satisfactory explanation as to how he came into the Synagogue, or why he remained after all the people had left.

About half-an-hour after the beadle had locked up the Synagogue, the people in the Jewish quarter were alarmed by the noise of a concourse of women and children, and some men, with officers of the police, saying that the Jews had concealed in the Synagogue or house adjoining a Christian child, to sacrifice it and use its blood in their Passover cakes. The woman whose child was supposed to be stolen shrieked dreadfully, and led the officers of the justice, in the first instance, to the house, and then to the Synagogue, to the very spot where the child had been found. Had the beadle not seen the child, as no doubt was the expectation of those who hatched the plot, the lives of hundreds of innocent persons would have been sacrificed. In another Synagogue a child endeavoured to enter on a Friday evening, when all the service was over and the doors were being locked, but was fortunately also discovered by the beadle, and driven away.

Rome is not the only place in these States where endeavours have been made to excite hatred against the Jews on the old base and wicked charge of eating human blood. At Sinigallia, near Ancona, a woman went to the police, saying she had escaped being murdered by the Jews, and the ignorant populace threatened the poor Jews with vengeance, and the place was in great agitation. All this is scarcely to be believed, but I have heard, though I can scarcely give credit to it, that this charge against the Jews is impressed upon the children at the several colleges. I myself believe that the colleges are free from this crime, and shall be glad to find that the common sense of the case is explained to the children.

The reader may well imagine how painfully these unfortunate occurrences must have affected the mind of both Sir Moses and Lady Montefiore, and how disheartening it was to them to see the object of their mission becoming every day more hopeless. This, together with the very disquieting reports from England regarding the political state of Europe, and the feeble state of Lady Montefiore's health, made Sir Moses very anxious at receiving no reply from Monsignor Pacca. "I begin to think," he observed to his friends, "I shall get none."

Rome, April 27th.—Lady Montefiore was very unwell. Sir Moses continued in a state of great excitement. "I fear," he said, "there is little hope of an audience for me with the Sovereign Pontiff."

At about one o'clock Mr Odo Russell came. He drove Sir Moses to the Palazzo Colonna, the residence of the French Ambassador, the Duc de Grammont. The latter received them in a very friendly manner, and recounted to Sir Moses all he had done in the case of the boy Mortara, and said he was certain that all his efforts would be unavailing.

Rome, April 28th.—Mr Odo Russell accompanied Sir Moses on a visit to Cardinal Antonelli.

"His Eminence," Sir Moses writes in his Diary, "received us immediately. I told him the object of my coming to Rome, and of my disappointment at not being able to obtain an audience of the Pope to present to him the address of the Board of Deputies. Every endeavour I had made having failed, I had to request his Eminence to present it for me to the Sovereign Pontiff. I then gave him the address, and said, 'I would remain a week in Rome for an answer to it.' The Cardinal replied that 'it was impossible to do anything in the Mortara case, but that every precaution should be taken to prevent so unfortunate an occurrence for the future ; that a child once baptised was a Christian, and as the Catholic Church considered that those of all others could not be saved, the child would not be given up until the age of seventeen or eighteen, when it would be free to follow its own inclinations. In the meantime the parents should have free access to the child, it should be well educated and taken care of, but the law of the Church prevented its being given back to the parents. He alluded to an order that Jews should not have Catholic servants, as any conscientious woman might, from pious motives, seeing a child dangerously ill and apprehending its death, baptise it, she at the time believing that it could not be otherwise saved in the event of its death.' I said, 'As we were all the children of one God, it was deeply to be lamented that we could not dwell together in peace.' He again alluded to the laws of the Church.

"On my expressing a hope to receive a reply to the address from the Pope, he said: 'No reply had been given to similar memorials from Holland, Germany, and France.' He gave an assurance of goodwill towards the Israelites in the Papal States.

"The Cardinal was most courteous, made me sit by his side on the sofa, and very cordially shook me by the hand, both when Mr Odo Russell introduced me to him and on my withdrawing after our interview.

"On leaving the Vatican, Mr Russell rode with me to our house, and repeated to Lady Montefiore all that had passed, when we drew up a telegram, which he approved, and I forwarded it to London for the Board of Deputies, and to inform the Lord Mayor, the Chief Rabbi, Baron Rothschild, and Sir Culling Eardly."

Rome, April 29*th.*—Sir Moses called on Dr Chalmers, and met His Royal Highness the Prince of Wales on the staircase, with Colonel the Hon. R. Bruce and Major Teesdale. The Prince graciously stopped to shake hands with him. Sir Moses then called on Lord Stratford de Redcliffe, who thought Sir Moses should make yet another effort to see the Pope.

Rome, April 30*th.*—On his way home from the Synagogue he went to Mr Odo Russell, being anxious to see him, as he was extremely desirous, in accordance with Lord Redcliffe's advice, to make another effort to see the Sovereign Pontiff; but Mr Russell had just gone out. "The English," Sir Moses writes, "are all taking their departure. It is reported that hostilities have actually commenced between Piedmont and Austria; also that 14,000 Tuscan troops have gone over to Piedmont, and the Grand Duke fled to Bologna. The Prince of Wales, it is said, will leave on Monday next."

Rome, May 1*st.*—" Unpleasant reports," says the Diary, "are in circulation to-day regarding the state of the political world.

Some feeling, it is said, has been evinced in several Colleges. It is expected that the greatest part of the French troops will leave Rome. My companions are all very anxious that we should return to England."

Rome, May 5th.—Sir Moses gave the order to engage berths in the *Vesuvius* from Civita Vecchia, having to pay double fare from Naples to Marseilles in consequence of the great number of people anxious to embark. He called on Lord de Redcliffe, and remained with him for a full hour, conversing on the Mortara subject and the plans which might lead to the possibility of prevailing upon the Pope to restore the child to his parents.

Rome, May 6th.—Cards were left by him at the Vatican for Cardinal Antonelli, and farewell visits paid to his friends. In the evening, while attending Divine Service, he witnessed an attempt made by a Roman recruit to create a disturbance in the Synagogue. "The man," Sir Moses says, "was pushed out, and the doors locked till the end of the service." Nothing further occurred, but the city was full of disagreeable reports. "War, war, war," was the general cry. "I was quite knocked up," he continues, "and obliged to lie down for some time."

Rome, May 10th.—Sir Moses and Lady Montefiore left Rome. "I thank, bless, and praise the God of my fathers," Sir Moses said, "for bringing me and my dear wife in safety out of Rome; and may He bring us in improved health to old England and our relatives and friends."

On proceeding to the railway station they met Mr Odo Russell on his way to take leave of them. They stopped the carriage and had a few minutes' chat. "It is some satisfaction," Sir Moses writes in his Diary, "that all whom I had consulted in the Mortara case agreed in opinion that I could do nothing more, and that, in the present state of things, my remaining at Rome would in no way be useful or desirable." "This journey and mission," he says, "has been, on many accounts, a painful and sad trial of patience, and, I may truly add, of perseverance, but our God is in Heaven, and no doubt He has permitted that which will prove a disappointment to our friends, &c., and is a grief to us, for the best and wisest purposes. Blessed be His name!"

CHAPTER XII.

1859.

INTERVIEW WITH THE DUC DE GRAMMONT—ANOTHER UKASE
—INFLUENTIAL PROTEST IN THE MORTARA CASE—PERSE-
CUTION IN ROUMANIA—ATTITUDE OF THE FRENCH AND
TURKISH GOVERNMENTS TOWARDS THE JEWS.

MAY 20*th*.—Sir Moses and Lady Montefiore arrived in
Paris. Lady Montefiore's state of health being very
unsatisfactory, Sir Moses resolved to remain five or six days in
the French capital to allow her some rest.

May 24*th*.—He called at the British Embassy, where he saw
Viscount Chelsea, who recommended him to write to Count
Walewski to express his gratitude for the warm and generous
efforts of the Duc de Grammont in the Mortara case. This Sir
Moses did, and the next day the Minister of Foreign Affairs
wrote him a note to the effect that he would receive him on the
following Friday. Sir Moses accordingly called on his Excellency, and told him that his object was to thank the Emperor
and his Excellency for the very generous exertions they had
made for the restoration of the child Mortara to its parents, and
to express his gratitude towards the Duc de Grammont for the
very zealous manner in which he had exerted himself at Rome
to attain that object, and he (Sir Moses) believed that, although
his exertions had not been attended with the success so much
desired, the Duke had done much good, as his warm expostula-
tions would no doubt prevent, at least for some time, any
similar outrage against humanity. " Not only his co-religionists,"
Sir Moses observed, " but also the Christians in England, felt
deeply in this unfortunate case, and were equally affected by
the circumstance."

His Excellency said that not only the Emperor, but all the
people in France, felt keenly on the subject. The Emperor had

written to the Duc de Grammont in the strongest manner. His Excellency was sure that the Duc de Grammont had done his best.

Sir Moses then begged of his Excellency to use his influence at any future time when an opportunity occurred to obtain the restoration of the child to his parents, and this his Excellency promised to do, saying that he was happy to have made Sir Moses' acquaintance. The reception, Sir Moses remarks, was truly kind and friendly. The Count said he believed the boy was well treated, to which Sir Moses rejoined that he thought so; but this was little consolation to his parents for being robbed of their child.

Before leaving Paris Sir Moses and Lady Montefiore had the satisfaction of hearing some pleasing news regarding their co-religionists in Russia.

Mr Ginzberg, a gentleman from St Petersburg, informed them that the Emperor had issued an Ukase permitting Jewish youths to attend the public colleges, and to absent themselves from school on Sabbaths and festivals.

May 29th.—They bade adieu to their friends, and started for Lille, where they remained for the night.

Early in the morning the champion of the Mortara family showed himself again in his commercial character as the energetic President of the Imperial Continental Gas Association. He visited the station of the Association's works, and saw the splendid new gas-holder, of which the superintendent gave him a satisfactory report in all respects.

At the same time he learned the sad news of the death of one of the officers of the Association, Mr G. H. Palmer, whom he had so lately seen at Marseilles. He had died suddenly of heart disease.

Sir Moses was much shocked and distressed. "God preserve us all," he said, "from sudden death," and he began to think how he might render some service to the family of the deceased.

They left Lille for Calais, where they arrived in safety, and had great cause to be most thankful to Providence, for on reaching Calais they found that the truck on which they had been travelling in their carriage was nearly in flames, and smoking to such a degree as to require the immediate application of several buckets of water. It appeared that the great weight of their travelling carriage had forced its wheels nearly through the bottom, in fact, had done so to such an extent as to cause the iron at the bottom to press on its wheels. In a little while their carriage would have been on fire.

Tuesday, May 31*st.*—They crossed the Channel, arrived at Dover, and were able to walk on shore. The next day, June 1, they left Dover for London, where they met with a most hearty welcome from their relatives and numerous friends.

June 6th.—Sir Moses called on Lord John Russell and Mr John Abel Smith, also at the Foreign Office, to express his thanks for the letter of introduction to Mr Odo Russell, and his gratitude for that gentleman's very kind and active assistance.

Five weeks later, on Wednesday, 13th July, he attended a meeting of the Board of Deputies. The vice-president conducted the business until Sir Moses' letter accepting the office of President was read, when the former stepped forward and conducted him to the chair. The report of his mission to Rome was well received by the meeting, and the following resolutions were unanimously adopted :—

"1. That this Board recognises with grateful appreciation the pious, zealous, and philanthropic feelings which induced its President, Sir Moses Montefiore, Bart., notwithstanding his advanced age, to undertake, at a very great personal sacrifice, a mission to Rome to present to the Sovereign Pontiff the memorial from the late Board of Deputies on the subject of the abduction of the child, Edgar Mortara.

"2. That the Board regrets the refusal of the Sovereign Pontiff to receive the memorial from Sir Moses Montefiore personally, and sincerely deplores the determination of his Holiness, declining to institute further inquiry into the truth of the child's alleged baptism, and in enforcing its continued separation from its bereaved parents.

"3. That this Board desires to record its emphatic protest against the right or validity of clandestine baptism,—a practice which it believes is opposed to the wishes and intelligence of mankind.

"4. That this Board delights to express its esteem and gratitude to its venerable President for the eminent services rendered by him, not only in this unhappy case, but on former occasions, to the cause of humanity and civilisation ; and it is also mindful of its obligation to Lady Montefiore, her husband's constant companion in his travels and the sharer of his fatigues and anxieties.

"5. That this Board feels assured the sentiments embodied in the foregoing resolution will find a faithful echo in every Jewish heart, and will ensure the sympathy of every friend of human progress throughout the world.

"6. That these resolutions be advertised in the public press."

"All the efforts of Sir Moses Montefiore," the daily papers report, "having proved ineffectual in obtaining the restoration of the child Mortara to its parents, a committee of gentlemen in the city felt that some protest was demanded on behalf of British Christians, and the following protest, having been privately circulated, has been most extensively signed, and a copy of it has been forwarded to the French Ambassador :—

"'Whereas a Jewish child, Edgar Mortara, son of Momolo Mortara, late of Bologna, in Italy, was, on the 24th of June 1858, forcibly seized and taken from its parents, by order of the Cardinal Viale Prela, Archbishop of Bologna and Legate of Pope Pius IX. :

"'And whereas the ground of the seizure was, that the said child, Edgar Mortara, had been secretly baptised by a Roman Catholic maid-servant six years previously, being then of the age of twelve months :

"'And whereas the said child was, by the order of the said Cardinal Legate, conveyed by night, under an escort of gendarmes, to the Convent of San Pietro, in Vincoli, at Rome, and is there detained contrary to the wish, and notwithstanding the protestations of his parents :

"'And whereas the Government of France has in vain urged the Court of Rome to restore the said child to his parents :

"'And whereas Sir Moses Montefiore, Bart., at the request of the Deputies of the British Jews, made on the 22nd of December 1858, went to Rome in their name to present a memorial to the Pope, signed by the whole of the said Deputies, asking for the liberation of the said child Edgar Mortara ; and whereas the Pope refused even to see Sir Moses Montefiore ; and Cardinal Antonelli, Minister of State, has declared to Sir Moses Montefiore that the Roman Government will not release the child :

"'And whereas it is a dishonour to Christianity in the eyes of the Jews among all nations that the seizure and detention of the said child, Edgar Mortara, should be supposed to be consistent with the principles of the Christian religion :

"'Now we, the undersigned British Christians, do hereby protest, and declare that the proceedings of the Pope of Rome, in taking away the Jewish child, Edgar Mortara, from his parents, and educating him, contrary to his parents' will, in the Roman Catholic faith, are repulsive to the instincts of humanity, and in violation of parental rights and authority, as recognised in the laws and usages of all civilised nations, and, above all, in direct opposition to the spirit and precepts of the Christian religion.'"

More than two thousand names of persons of rank and influence were attached to the protest.

I now invite the attention of the reader to the subjects which occupied Sir Moses' mind during the remainder of the year.

It has been stated before that Sir Moses signed the contract with Mr William E. Smith of Ramsgate for building the Juda Touro Almshouses in Jerusalem. The special authorisation from the Turkish Government, as well as the approbation of the former Governor and of every member of the City Council, fully justified Sir Moses at that time in expecting to see the building proceed rapidly. But in this he was disappointed. On the 15th day of June Mr Smith reported that the Governor had ordered a suspension of the works, on the ground that the building would be too near the city fortifications. This was most unfortunate, as nearly all the stone had been prepared, the foundations excavated, the water-receivers almost completed, and all the doors, iron-work, and windows sent out from England. His first step was to address Arabic letters to Sureya Pasha, the Governor of Jerusalem. Subsequently Sir Moses called on the Turkish Ambassador in London, and applied also to the Sublime Porte for renewed instructions to the authorities in Jerusalem. But it was not until the end of December that he received a letter from the Turkish Minister, to the effect that the permission for the continuance of the building would be sent to Jerusalem.

In the meantime the delay of work greatly increased the expense, as the builder had to remain six months longer in Jerusalem than he had expected, and the principal working men had to be retained, not knowing when their services might again be required.

To those who have had some experience of building schemes in the East, such an interruption in the work would not be a matter of surprise. It is the general rule among the natives, in order to be able to proceed peaceably with any private or public building, to secure, in the first instance, the friendly approbation of all the officers connected with the Government; and in this case the superintendents of the works, being English-men, may have unintentionally neglected to do so; hence what had been right in the eyes of Kiamil Pasha, was considered wrong in the eyes of Sureya Pasha, the latter acting, as he said, on special orders received from the Sublime Porte.

July 6th.—Sir Moses having ascertained from Mr O. W. Galloway that the Viceroy was anxious for his son, Toussoun Pasha, to spend another summer with him, invited the Prince to London, and the invitation having been cordially accepted, Toussoun Pasha, attended by his physician, Dr Ettienne, Mrs G. Williams, his governess, and the Mamlook, arrived at Park Lane on July 9th. The young Prince looked very thin, but in excellent spirits. "God grant," Sir Moses said, "their stay with us may prove beneficial."

The Prince, as on the two former occasions, improved in health and gained strength during his stay in England under the hospitable roof of Sir Moses, and became every day more cheerful in his disposition,

In the same month (August 29th) Sir Charles B. Phipps, by command of the Queen, forwarded to Sir Moses a musical box as a present from Her Majesty to His Highness Toussoun Pasha before he left England.

Sir Moses wrote to Sir Charles, acknowledging the receipt of Her Majesty's gracious commands, and sent Said Pasha, the Viceroy, a copy of Sir Charles Phipps' letter.

His Highness, in return, conveyed to him his deep sense of gratitude for the care he and Lady Montefiore had taken of the young Prince, and entreated Sir Moses to take the first occasion to tender to Her Majesty the Queen his high appreciation of the honour conferred by Her Majesty on him by the gracious reception granted to his son.

The gracious attention of Her Majesty to the young Prince, and the gratitude of his father the Viceroy to the Queen, undoubtedly contributed, in a certain degree, towards the preservation of friendly relations between England and Egypt; and Sir Moses had the satisfaction of knowing that he became indirectly the acknowledged medium of fostering and promoting the blessings of peace and mutual interest between two countries.

He never sent a letter to the Pasha without showing it first at the Foreign Office, and awaiting the approval of the Minister; nor did he ever withhold the contents of any letter addressed to him by the Pasha. He took the original himself to the Minister of Foreign Affairs, and deposited with him a copy for the perusal of others in office interested in Egypt.

October 10th.— Subsequently the hour of parting drew near, and Toussoun Pasha had to take leave, and, in doing so, expressed himself affectionately towards both of them.

Lady Montefiore unfortunately continued to suffer from illness. She often had medical advice, but was at times very ailing. Sir Moses had little time to rest, but his presence at East Cliff inspired hope and cheerfulness in the heart of his suffering companion. Every day almost brought him letters, imploring his aid in cases of dire distress.

A month previously he had received some most painful communications from Galatz, in Roumania, respecting the unparalleled cruelties committed on the Jews there. Some of them had been murdered, others fearfully wounded, many deprived of all their property, and their Synagogues desecrated. Sir Moses forwarded all the letters on the subject to Lord John Russell, and, as President of the Board of Deputies of British Jews, requested the British Government to intercede for the Jews, by giving instructions to the British Consuls to render help and protection to the sufferers, as far as lay in their power; but it took a long time to extinguish the flames of persecution. Letters continued to arrive from villages and towns, imploring help.

A month or six weeks later a cry of distress reached him from Gibraltar. Owing to the war which was then expected to ensue between Spain and Morocco, the Jewish inhabitants of Tangier, fearing the repetition of the brutal usage which they had experienced when the wild Kabyle tribes came down to the coast in 1844, had fled from their homes in a state of utter destitution.

Nearly 2700 of these unhappy people had arrived at Gibraltar from Tangier, and it was but too probable that they would be followed by many thousands of others from different parts of Morocco.

Sir Moses convened a special meeting of the Board of Deputies of the British Jews. The Board formed itself into a committee of relief, and energetically appealed to its co-religionists, not only in this country, but throughout Europe and other parts of the world, for prompt assistance.

Sir Moses and Lady Montefiore gave £200 towards the immediate relief of the sufferers, and many benevolent persons of various denominations followed with generous contributions.

To Sir W. Codrington, the Governor of Gibraltar, who manifested much thoughtful humanity towards the unfortunate Jewish emigrants from Tangier, Sir Moses had the pleasing duty to convey a vote of thanks from the Board of Deputies.

Sir William, in acknowledging the receipt of Sir Moses' letter enclosing the resolution, said that he was only carrying out the intentions of Government in assisting refugees. "You will have heard," he observed, "that Government has since authorised me to give temporary assistance to those necessitous persons, by affording them a bread ration from the commissariat."

" The French Government," Sir William continued, " will receive into Algeria those who wish to go there. I hope that many will avail themselves, and that soon, of this permission, for it will be well for them to seek at once their future permanent abode, wherever it may be."

It appears that the intention of the French Government to receive into Algeria all who wished to go there, impelled another power to make a similar offer to those who wished to go to Palestine; for, a day before Sir William had written his letter to Sir Moses, Mr Kingsite called on the latter, and stated that the Turkish Ambassador wished him to inform Sir Moses that if the Jews were inclined to return to the Holy Land, and could advance money to the Turkish Government to effect the withdrawal of the existing coinage, they should have every liberty and land, with all possible protection. Sir Moses told Mr Kingsite he did not think that there was a single Jew in England who wished to return at present, nor did he believe that a loan for that purpose would be raised. Mr Kingsite was going to speak with a well-known house on the subject.

November 21st.—Sir Moses called on the Turkish Ambassador, who received him very courteously, heard all he had to say, and entered very fully into the whole affair of the Holy Land. He said all would go well, and he would write to the Governor of Jerusalem, and same time send him a copy of his letter which he had forwarded to him some time since. He expressed himself as being anxious to see a colony of Jews in Palestine.

Both the French and Turkish Governments, we see, were desirous of having Jewish colonies in their respective countries ; with the sole difference, that the French authorities were content with the poor of all classes, while the Turkish authorities only offered to extend their privileges and protection to the rich colonist.

During the last month of the year Sir Moses received a visit from the father of the unfortunate young Mortara. He gave him a note to Sir Culling Eardly, who promised to do all in his power for the restoration of the boy. A few days later Sir Moses convened a meeting of the Mortara Committee, when it was resolved to write to Sir Culling Eardly, that, having done all in their power in the Mortara case, they could not attempt to do more, but hoped he would persevere and be successful.

In his capacity of Deputy-Lieutenant of the county, Sir Moses, together with Captain Isaake, another Deputy-Lieutenant of the county, invited Colonel Stothard of Dover to come to Ramsgate and select the land for a battery to protect the harbour. On his arrival they went to Wellington Crescent, and selected for that purpose a plot, 200 feet in length and 50 in depth, in the centre of the garden in front of the Crescent.

Sir Moses, ever anxious to serve his country, expressed himself as much satisfied in having had the opportunity of assisting in so important a cause.

Lady Montefiore's state of health, to which I have already alluded, continued to be most unsatisfactory. Her condition frequently prevented Sir Moses from attending meetings or special appointments in the city.

CHAPTER XIII.

1860.

THE SULTAN PERMITS THE BUILDING OF THE JERUSALEM ALMSHOUSES—CONCESSION FOR A CARRIAGE-ROAD FROM JAFFA TO JERUSALEM—SIR MOSES CHAMPIONS THE PERSECUTED CHRISTIANS OF SYRIA—PUNISHMENT OF THE CULPRITS—DISQUIETING REPORTS FROM DAMASCUS.

THE year 1860 opens with the record of a satisfactory reply from the Turkish Government to Sir Moses' petition respecting the building of the Juda Touro Almshouses in Jerusalem, the interruption of which, by order of Sureya Pasha, had caused him much annoyance and expense. Musurus Pasha, the Turkish Ambassador in London, thus addresses him on the subject.

" I have the pleasure to inform you that I have just received a dispatch from His Excellency Fuad Pasha, the Minister of Foreign Affairs of the Sublime Porte, in reply to the communication that I addressed to His Excellency on the subject of the interference by the Imperial authorities at Jerusalem with the erection of the building lately commenced there by your orders for the benefit of your co-religionists. This dispatch states that although, according to the general regulations respecting fortified places in the Ottoman dominions, the erection of such buildings in such proximity to a fortress should not be permitted, yet, notwithstanding this, considering that an exceptional permission was previously granted to you of which you have already availed yourself to erect a building in the vicinity of the fortress above mentioned, His Imperial Majesty the Sultan has been pleased to order that the building last begun should be allowed to be finished, according to your wish, and the necessary orders have in consequence been sent to His Excellency the Governor of Jerusalem.

"Congratulating you on this desirable result being obtained, I have the honour to be, &c."

About the same time he received some intelligence from Count Pizzamano, the Austrian Consul in Jerusalem, respecting a subject which had often engaged his attention in former years, viz., the construction of a carriage road from Jaffa to Jerusalem. It appears that the Count had at last succeeded in obtaining a fifty years' concession from the Turkish Government for the purpose, and he now proposed forming a company with a capital of one million francs, on which he calculated he could offer the shareholders a dividend at the rate of ten per cent. per annum, leaving a surplus to be divided between the contractors and the Amortisation Fund.

The Count was not willing to dispose of any shares before hearing from Sir Moses; and asked him whether he would be inclined to associate himself in the undertaking, sharing profits and losses alike; or, should this not suit him, how many shares he would take himself, and how many he could place in England among his friends?

The concession which the Turkish Government granted to Count Pizzamano to facilitate traffic in the Holy Land may probably have had some connection with the conversation Sir Moses had with Musurus Pasha in London on the subject of Jewish colonisation, consequent upon the offer which the French Government had made to the Jews of Morocco. However gratifying the communication of Count Pizzamano may have been to Sir Moses, his advanced age, and the great anxiety occasioned by the very unsatisfactory state of Lady Montefiore's health, precluded the possibility of his then associating himself with the Count in his important undertaking.

April 3rd.—Sir Moses laid the foundation stone of the Spanish and Portuguese Branch Synagogue at Bryanston Street, near Cumberland Place, towards the building of which he and Lady Montefiore had contributed £500.

June 15th.—The Viceroy of Egypt sent him a portrait of his son, Toussoun Pasha, with a very complimentary letter.

July 3rd.—The entry of this day, regarding the Juda Toura Almshouses in Jerusalem, I give in Sir Moses' own words.

"Being anxious," he writes, "to make arrangements, with the advice of our esteemed Chief Rabbi and Dr Loewe, for the

Judah Turo Almhouses at Jerusalem.

See Vol. II., fa ;e 111.

guidance of Mr Kursheedt respecting the filling of the Almshouses in Jerusalem, as so much would depend on the choice of
individuals,—I wish them to be persons of excellent character,
men well learned in our Law, who devote much of their time to
study, and by whom a nice house, free of rent, in a pleasant
situation, would be considered a boon,—I therefore started at
seven o'clock with Mr Kursheedt for Brighton to consult Dr
Loewe."

Soon after the train started Sir Moses opened some letters
which had been brought to him to the station, and found that
they required his immediate attention in London. He left Mr
Kursheedt at Red Hill, and went back to town; and having
disposed of his business, he started again for Brighton, but the
train, being a slow one, arrived so late, and the return journey
had to be undertaken so soon after his arrival, that the meeting
was only productive of a fresh appointment for the following
Tuesday. Accordingly he returned to Brighton on that day.

"My dear Judith," the entry says, "had not a comfortable
night. I left her with great regret, but it was unavoidable,
having made an engagement with the Chief Rabbi and Dr
Loewe to meet them at Brighton. Mr Kursheedt accompanied me. We arrived there at twelve o'clock. Dr Loewe
was at the station, and went with us to Dr Adler's. We immediately commenced the consideration of the minutes prepared
by Dr Loewe. The result was, the building is to be called
'Mishkenót Shaananim' (the dwellings of those who are at
ease), to avoid hurting the feelings of the inmates by calling the
buildings almshouses. There are to be eight houses and a
Synagogue for the Portuguese; a similar number of houses with
a Synagogue for the German community; one house for the
weaver" (who was then the master at the weaving school
established by the Trustees of the Holy Land Appeal Fund);
"another for the Rev. Samuel Salant" (who, however, never
availed himself of the offer then made to him); "and one for a
Dispensary. The heads of the several congregations in Jerusalem" (at that time nineteen in number) "are to select the
persons for the houses they think the best, and Mr Kursheedt
will see them installed in accordance with Eastern custom.
Tokens of esteem are to be presented on that occasion to the
Officers of the Guard, the Officers of the Mosque of Omar,

Ahmed Agha Dizdar " (the former owner of the land on which the Almshouses were built), " and his son ; also presents to the poor of the Holy City, the Greek, Armenian, and Latin Convents, and the Guard of the Jaffa Gate. Offerings made by visitors who attend Divine Service in either of the two Synagogues, in memory of the benevolent founder, are to be appropriated to defray the expenses of keeping the sacred edifices clean, lighting them, and to paying a gate-keeper and well-keeper for water."

A number of regulations intended for the guidance of the inmates were then agreed to, but before half the business had been finished, Sir Moses was obliged to leave, and only reached Ramsgate late in the evening, after a fatiguing day's work.

July 11*th.*—Lady Montefiore had a restless night, and was very weak that day. Sir Moses, however, himself far from well, and scarcely recovered from the fatigue of the previous day's journey, was called upon to work for his fellow-beings in Syria, for " the Lebanon had opened its doors to the fire of destruction and dissolution."

The Druses, the daily papers reported, had destroyed 151 Christian villages and killed one thousand persons, and the Mahommedans had massacred Christians at Damascus. About 3300, it is said, have been slain.

Lady Montefiore reading to Sir Moses the debates of the House of Lords referring to Lord Stratford de Redcliffe's speech on the massacre of the Christians in Syria, in which he stated that twenty thousand Christians, women and children fugitives, were then wandering and starving on the mountains of Syria, he determined, with the willing and cheerful consent of his wife, to go to town.

There he addressed a letter to the Editor of the *Times*, and suggested the formation of a committee to collect subscriptions for a fund for their relief.

After having done so he immediately drove to Printing-house Square, though fearing, as it was after midnight, that there was no probability of its appearing the next day in the *Times*. " I must be content," he said ; " I have done all in my power to prevent any loss of time in affording assistance to the unfortunate and destitute fugitives in Syria. I left my dear Judith with great reluctance. I was poorly, my legs swollen, and I had travelled five hundred miles, and this night's journey added a hundred miles to it. I have not spared any exertions this week to fulfil my duty."

Happily his endeavours to serve the good cause were crowned with success. The *Times*, on the 12th July, under the heading of " The Civil War in Syria," published his letter, of which the following is a copy :—

" Sir,—I have noticed with the deepest sympathy the statement made last evening in the House of Lords that, owing to the recent outbreak in Syria, there are twenty thousand of the Christian inhabitants, including women and children, wandering over its mountains exposed to the utmost peril. Being intimately acquainted with the nature of that country and the condition of its people, I appreciate, I am sorry to say, but too painfully the vast amount of misery that must have been endured, and which is still prevalent.

" I believe that private benevolence may do something towards the alleviation of the distress of the unhappy multitude now defenceless, home-less, and destitute.

" I well know, from experience, the philanthropy of my fellow-countrymen, and I venture to think that the public would gladly, and without delay, con-tribute to the raising of a fund to be applied as circumstances may require, and under judicious management, for the relief of these unfortunate objects of persecution.

" I would suggest, therefore, that a small, active, and influential com-mittee be at once formed, with the view of raising subscriptions and of placing themselves in communication with the British Consul-General at Beyrout, and the other British Consular authorities throughout Syria, so that assist-ance may be rendered by the remittance of money and the transmission of necessary supplies ; and I take the liberty of enclosing my cheque for £200 towards the proposed fund.

" Your recent eloquent and judicious advocacy of the cause of the Syrian Christians has encouraged me to address you, and will, I trust, be a sufficient excuse for my so doing.—I have the honour to be, Sir, yours faithfully,

" MOSES MONTEFIORE."

" EAST CLIFF LODGE, RAMSGATE, *July* 11*th*."

July 27th.—Sir Culling E. Eardly and Sir James Fergusson apprised Mr N. Moore, Consul-General at Beyrout, of the for-mation of the British Syrian Relief Committee. Lord Palmer-ston, Lord Stratford de Redcliffe, Lord John Russell, Lord Overstone, the Earl of Shaftesbury, Sir Moses Montefiore, Mr A. P. Kennard, Baron Rothschild, and many others were con-tributors to the fund.

" We have already," the honorary secretaries write, " by the kindness of Lord Wodehouse, Under Secretary of State, sent you a telegraphic message through the Foreign Office, authorising you to draw upon us for £1000."

The Committee included the Marquis of Lansdowne, Sir Moses Montefiore, the Lord Mayor of London, the Earl of

Malmesbury, Lord Stanley, M.P., Baron Rothschild, the Bishop of London, Sir Charles Napier, M.P., Mr Austen Layard, &c.

August 1st.—We find Lord Stratford de Redcliffe acting as President, and Sir Moses Montefiore as Chairman, of the Executive Committee of the British Syrian Relief Fund.

Sir Moses, when in England, attended almost all the meetings, and continued to be one of the most active members until the year before his death, when he and Mr H. W. Freeland were the only trustees of the fund. The amount left with their bankers at that time was £180. The Committee in London was assisted by a Committee in Beyrout, under the Presidency of Mr N. Moore, the British Consul-General. They also had the co-operation of Mr Consul Brant in Damascus. Much good was accomplished. By the end of August £7500 had already been remitted for distribution among the sufferers.

Circulars were issued to the leading Jews of Europe, accompanied by copies of an address of the Chief Rabbi to the Jewish community at large, and the result was a generous contribution to the Fund.

The English and French Governments intervened, and a convention was signed at Paris, twelve thousand men to be sent by France.

Fuad Pasha, in the same month, proceeded to Damascus, and severely punished the Mohammedans implicated in the massacres; 160 of all ranks, including the Governor, were executed.

General Hautpoul, at the head of four thousand French soldiers, landed at Beyrout; and there was every reason to hope that peace would soon be restored, and that all feeling of animosity among the various nationalities would cease.

August 8th.—Sir Moses presided at a meeting of the Morocco Committee, and agreed to send a commissioner to Morocco, who was to visit several of the principal towns on the coast, and to report on the state of the Jews and their wants, so that the money the Committee had on hand might be applied to the best advantage of the Israelites in that country.

August 9th.—Having received distressing accounts from Persia regarding the unfortunate state of the Jews in that country, he addressed Lord John Russell on the subject, and in his capacity as President of the Board of Deputies of the

British Jews, sent him a copy of the communications from Hamadan, and entreated the kind offices of the British Government to protect the Jews of that city.

August 14*th.*—He received a requisition to call a meeting of the Board of Deputies to consider the best means to be taken to effect the removal of the inscription on the marble slab in the church of the Capuchins at Damascus, accusing the Jews of the assassination of Father Tomaso.

The moment, it was believed, would be most favourable for another attempt in this direction.

Sir Moses having endeavoured for so many years to obtain the removal of the same, he was very willing to assist, and to determine on the best means to be adopted to accomplish the object in view.

August 28*th.*—At a Court of the Irish Bank Sir Moses advocated the cause of an orphan child of one of the oldest clerks in the Bank, who had held his situation thirty-five years, and who had died a fortnight since, his widow following him a few days afterwards. They left an only child, a daughter, who had an admirable character, and was very clever, and Sir Moses appealed to the Board to deal liberally, and give her some substantial support.

August 29*th.*—In accordance with an arrangement for carrying out the instructions regarding the Touro Almshouses, Mr Kursheedt took leave of Sir Moses, the latter repeating to him all the conversation they had on that subject at Brighton in the presence of the Chief Rabbi, with the request that he would endeavour to do his best in the interest of the Trust.

September 1*st.*—The Turkish Ambassador in London made a communication to Sir Moses regarding the persecution of the Jews at Bagdad, which by the intercession of the Turkish Government had happily ceased.

Sir Moses was highly pleased, and would have gone to town on purpose to thank his Excellency for the good tidings, but the state of Lady Montefiore's health caused him much anxiety, and prevented him from doing so.

She passed night after night in a state of restlessness and pain, and her medical advisers in Ramsgate and London strongly urged that she should pass the winter in a warmer climate.

Accordingly, September 20th, Sir Moses wrote to Dr

Hodgkin, inviting him to accompany them to some place on the Mediterranean recommended by him and Sir Charles Locock. Dr Hodgkin accepted his invitation. He felt it a duty, he says, as well as a satisfaction, to comply with the wishes of so kind a friend.

October 14th.—Sir Moses received a letter from the Spiritual Head of the Hebrew community of Damascus, entreating him to intercede on their behalf with the British Government, the Turkish Ambassador, and the Consuls at Beyrout. The Jews in their city, he wrote, were exposed to great danger from false accusations. Sir Moses went to town, communicated with the Chief Rabbi and the Secretary of the Board of Deputies, and addressed a letter to Lord John Russell, enclosing, for his Lordship's perusal, a translation of the letter he had received from Damascus. He took it himself to Downing Street. Lord Wodehouse was not there, but he saw Mr Hammond (now Lord Hammond), and acquainted him with the perilous position of the Jews of Damascus. Mr Hammond promised to send the letter to Lord John Russell, and added that it would be satisfactory to Sir Moses to know that they had later accounts from Damascus, which did not say one word about these accusations against the Jews. Lord John Russell had gone to Richmond, and should have Sir Moses' letter sent to him at once.

CHAPTER XIV.

1860.

APPEAL FROM THE JEWS OF DAMASCUS — LORD JOHN RUSSELL'S ACTION—THE MORTARA CASE AGAIN—SERIOUS ILLNESS OF LADY MONTEFIORE.

HAVING given the reader a copy of the letter Sir Moses wrote to the *Times*, pleading the cause of his Christian brethren when persecuted by the Druses and Mohammedans, he will probably read with equal interest a copy of the letter he addressed to Lord John Russell, pleading the cause of his Jewish brethren, accompanied by a translation of the original Hebrew letter from the representatives of the Jewish community.

" EAST CLIFF LODGE, RAMSGATE, *October* 16*th*.

" MY LORD,—With painful reluctance I submit to your Lordship the accompanying translation of a letter from the heads of the Jewish community at Damascus.

" There can be no doubt whatever that the Jewish body of that city is guiltless of any participation in the recent outbreak, and I venture to believe that your Lordship requires no argument to satisfy your mind on this point.

" May I entreat your Lordship, as heretofore, to exercise the powerful influence of Her Majesty's Government to protect and save the Jews of Damascus from the perils to which they are so imminently exposed? As the affair is urgent, I venture personally to attend your Lordship with this letter and its enclosure.—I have the honour to be, my Lord, your Lordship's faithful and obedient servant,   " MOSES MONTEFIORE."

" *To* The Right Hon. LORD JOHN RUSSELL, &c."

Copy of enclosure.

" *To* Sir MOSES MONTEFIORE, Bt., our Benefactor and Deliverer, whom may God long preserve, &c.

" We had the honour to address you a letter in the course of last month, in which we spoke of the enmity of the Christians towards the Jews here in Damascus, which has risen up in addition to all former hatred.

" Now a great, bitter, and intense jealousy fills their hearts, by reason that they have been murdered, plundered, and maltreated, whereas against all the children of Israel not a dog moved his tongue. Our hearts were then moved as the sea, least, by reason of this bitter hatred and jealousy, false accusations should be brought against us. We therefore besought you to aid us by obtaining instructions from the English Government to the Consuls, Generals, and Commanders who come to Syria; also from the Turkish

Government to His Highness Fuad Pasha that he should stand by us, and not be ready to receive malicious reports against the Jews, for His Highness is a just and upright man.

"Now we have to inform you that since the commencement of the month of Ellul (August) the Christians have been plotting and preparing false and malicious accusations against us ; many of us have been thrown into prison, and falsely accused of having participated in the massacre. The Christians are believed in their statements, when they say, 'So and so killed some one.' That person is thereupon immediately brought before the tribunal. Testimony of honourable men among the Turks is not received when they declare that the accused was in their house during the tumult. Even the evidence of Christians is not believed when they bear witness to the Jews having been hidden with themselves, and their not having parted from each other during the whole outbreak. Even should the accused himself testify anything in favour of an accused Israelite, it is not attended to.

"A woman accused a certain Jew, who she thought had killed her husband ; she was asked to swear according to her own faith that the accused was the man. She refused to swear, and asked the Jew to swear by the law of Moses that he had not done it so that he might go free, but the tribunal would not listen thereto. Even the testimony of our Chief Rabbi has been rejected.

"The Jews still remain in prison, and one has since died in his dungeon from the effects of terror.

"Oh, Sir ! consider only for a moment the fearful consequences of innocent Jews being thrown into prison with murderers, when all the testimony and proof that they may bring forward will not aid in their deliverance.

"We know not, therefore, what is to become of the people of Israel when the Christians see that there is no hope for Israel ; that false accusations against them are listened to ; but that to the voice of Israel there is none to give ear or reply, none to pity or compassionate.

"Indeed those who rose against the Christians and killed them are not judged according to the ordinary laws of the land, nor is evidence taken in the usual manner ; but there has been established what is termed an 'extraordinary tribunal.' Now it appears that it is intended to judge the Jews also by this tribunal, and to condemn them to death upon the mere word of the Christians. This is indeed a great and bitter calamity. How is it possible to compare the condition of the Jews to that of those who rose up against the Christians ? Were not the Jews themselves during that terrible time in the greatest fear and danger ? Surely there was but a step betwixt us and death. Most of the Jews hid themselves in the houses of respectable Turks, in cellars and in caves, in company with Christians.

"Is it possible to suppose that one who was in momentary fear for his own life should rise up to kill another ? Reason and common sense testify against it. God forbid that such a thought should enter the mind of Her Most Gracious Majesty the Queen of England or her Government—a queen whose justice and mercy is as that of the kingdom of heaven, and for whose prosperity, honour, and glory we the congregation of Damascus have prayed these twenty years.

"We have gratefully to acknowledge the great mercy, kindness, and benevolence Her Most Gracious Majesty showed us in former troubles. May she long reign in peace, happiness, and prosperity.

"In this trouble also do we lay our supplications before Her Majesty, beseeching her to have pity and compassion upon poor afflicted Israel in Damascus, who only desire her aid and support and all powerful influence, that the imprisoned Jews may have a fair trial before the ordinary tribunal in accordance with the well-known custom of the country, for Israel both young and old are wholly guiltless in this matter, and free from the crime of shedding blood,

"Truly this is a time of great trouble and distress, for every Jew dwelling in Damascus is in continual dread of being accused, for there is none to say unto the Christians, 'Why do ye thus?' It has been openly declared by some of them that they will grant Israel neither peace nor rest.

"Already they have begun to conspire against the best, the most honourable and esteemed of our community, viz., the well-known Jacob Abulaffia and Solomon Farchi, son of the late Isaac Hyam Farchi (of whose hospitality you partook on your visit to Damascus), a youth fourteen years of age, and only son of his father's house.

"A certain Christian declared that his father was killed between the two houses of the above-named parties. Were not the Lord on our side what would become of us? The accused being under French protection, the French and Greek Consuls prevented this case being brought before the 'Extraordinary Tribunal,' but had it heard before the two Consuls. The Lord brought his innocence to light. May God save those who uphold His Law from such fearful machinations!

"And on what was the whole accusation based? If a man had been found slain in the highway at the time of the rising of the mob, when all the streets of the Christians, as well as the streets of the Jews and Turks, which are near each other, were filled with the slain, was it in the power of man to prevent a murder from being committed before his own house? Would the ruffians have had any regard? Who should tell them not to murder all who stood in their way? Were the lives of the Jews themselves then secure?

"Wherefore we beseech you to have compassion upon us, to put forth your right hand to save us, to answer us, as the Most Holy—blessed be He —shall direct and prepare the way for you. 'Behold it is a time of trouble unto Jacob, oh, that he be saved out of it!' Our hope is in you, that salvation may come through your means, to obtain the influence of the English Government, as well as that of the French and Turkish, with His Highness Fuad Pasha, who is an upright judge; also that instructions may be sent to the English Consul in Damascus, so that the Jews may not be confounded with those who rose up in rebellion.

"You are our Father; hasten to help us. As you have been our former deliverer, so save us now, and compassionately be the means of frustrating their evil devices, so that it may be said of our troubles, and the troubles of all Israel, 'It is enough,' and redeem us with an everlasting redemption. Amen.

"Attached are the signatures of the Rabbins, the elders, and the most worthy of the congregation of Damascus, who anxiously await your answer.

<table>
<tr><td>"Hyam Romano.</td><td>Nahum Lusano.</td></tr>
<tr><td>David Harpy.</td><td>Isaac Kalon.</td></tr>
<tr><td>Menahem Farchi.</td><td>Raphael Halevi.</td></tr>
<tr><td>Jacob Halevi.</td><td>Isaac Maimon.</td></tr>
<tr><td>Jacob Peretz.</td><td>Aaron Jacob."</td></tr>
</table>

"Damascus, *7th Tishri* 5621 (1860, *September 23rd*)."

"Foreign Office, *October 24th*, 1860.

"Sir,—I am directed by Lord John Russell to acknowledge the receipt of your letter of the 16th inst., enclosing a petition from the Jews at Damascus, praying for protection against the hostile proceedings of the Christians, by whom they have been falsely accused of having taken part in the late massacres.

"I am to state to you in reply that Her Majesty's Ambassador at Constantinople has been instructed by telegraph to take immediate steps for the protection of the Jews, and that written instructions to the same effect will be sent to Sir Henry Bulwer, as well as to Her Majesty's Consular Agents at Beyrout and Damascus.—I am, Sir, your most obedient, humble servant,

"C. HAMMOND."

"Sir MOSES MONTEFIORE, Bart., &c."

"EAST CLIFF LODGE, RAMSGATE, *October* 26*th*.

"MY LORD,—I cannot adequately convey to your Lordship the gratification afforded to me by your Lordship's esteemed communication of the 24th inst., informing me of the prompt and efficient measures taken by your Lordship for the protection of the Jews of Damascus.

"I feel assured that the energetic manner in which your Lordship has thrown the shield of the British Government over the Jewish community of that city will, under Providence, be the means of saving the lives of many innocent persons.

"The knowledge of this fact must afford your Lordship the highest satisfaction, and it is indeed a source of pride and triumph when, as in this case, the influence of the British Government is successfully exerted in the cause of humanity and justice.

"Believe me, my Lord, I am deeply impressed with your Lordship's kindness, which cannot fail to elicit the warmest sentiments of admiration and gratitude from the hearts of the whole Jewish body.—I have the honour to be, my Lord, your Lordship's faithful and obedient servant,

"MOSES MONTEFIORE."

"*To* The Right Hon. LORD JOHN RUSSELL, &c."

The following letter from Mr Brant bears testimony, if any were needed, to the groundlessness of the charges against the Jews :—

"DAMASCUS, *October* 16*th*.

"SIR,—In your letter of this day's date you ask me to state what I know of the behaviour of the Jewish community during the late outbreak against Christians.

"I know that many of the principal members took refuge in the houses of Mussulmans for fear of being massacred if they remained in their own. I do not know that any one of your nation has been proved to have been concerned in injuring the Christians. Some have been accused of doing so, and were detained in prison, but I begged his Excellency Fuad Pasha to have them fairly tried, and, if found innocent, to order their release, which, I believe, has been, or is on the point of being done.

"I am not aware that any Jew has behaved ill in this calamity, and the accusations I have heard seemed to be the result of prejudice and a malicious disposition, and not to be grounded on any established proof.—I have the honour to be, with respect, Sir, your obedient, humble servant,

"JAMES BRANT."

"*To* JACOB SCREZ, Chief Rabbi of the Jewish Congregation at Damascus."

"I certify the above to be a true copy of the original letter.

"WILLIAM H. WRENCH, *Acting Consul.*"

"DAMASCUS, *October* 19*th*."

Sir Moses also had letters prepared on the subject, which were to be forwarded to the Turkish Ambassador and Sir Culling Eardly, with copies of the Damascus letter, and a few days later Sir Culling sent him the copy of a letter he had written to Lord John Russell. It was an admirable and affecting appeal for his Lordship's intervention.

October 25th.—He received a most satisfactory reply to the letter he had addressed to Lord John Russell respecting the persecution of the Jews in Damascus. His Lordship had telegraphed to Constantinople, had sent instructions to Her Britannic Majesty's Ambassador at that place, and to the Consular Agents at Beyrout and Damascus, to take immediate steps for the protection of the Jews.

The next day Mr G. Kursheedt, who had gone to Jerusalem with instructions respecting the Juda Touro Almshouses, returned in safety from the Holy Land, and gave Sir Moses an account of the state of his co-religionists in Jerusalem. It was by no means unfavourable.

October 31st.—Sir Moses convened a meeting of Deputies of British Jews for the following Monday evening, to bring before them Sir Culling E. Eardly's letters respecting the boy Mortara, and it would rest with the Deputies, Sir Moses remarked, to say what part they would take with Sir Culling in his efforts to get young Mortara away from Rome.

November 7th.—Lady Montefiore passed a restless night. She had been very weak during the day, and somewhat feverish. The doctor came and saw her. He told Sir Moses they were making no progress, and he must determine at once to leave England within ten days, or make arrangements at Park Lane for the winter. "It would not do," he said, "for Sir Moses to be going to and from London every week."

Sir Moses was now in a state of great uneasiness. "Lady Montefiore," he says, "appears to me falling away." He hoped to leave England Thursday, the 15th, but, finding that Lady Montefiore had become worse, he determined at once to try the effect of a change to their house at Park Lane.

Sir Moses apprised Dr Hodgkin of the change in his plans, which would postpone their leaving England perhaps for a month or more.

The same day Sir Moses and Lady Montefiore left East Cliff for Park Lane. Soon after their arrival at the latter place, Sir Moses was told of the serious illness of Alderman Wire, his former Under Sheriff.

November 9*th.*—On sending to enquire after his health, he was greatly shocked and pained by the answer: " He expired this morning." Sir Moses most sincerely lamented his decease. A month later, he suffered another loss. " I heard with deep regret," he writes, " of the death of Sir George Carroll. He survived but a very short time the death of poor Alderman Wire. We acted with great harmony and friendship together during the whole time of our serving together the office of Sheriff; indeed we have been on terms of friendship, since I first knew him, more than fifty years ago."

Lady Montefiore continued very ill, requiring the consultations of Dr Hodgkin and Dr Rees.

December 15*th.*—The entry is, " I cannot make up my mind to leave England, and from day to day postpone positively fixing the time for our departure. At any rate," he says, " it now cannot be before the end of this month. May the God of Israel in His mercy direct us!"

December 17*th.*—The Rev. D. Cardall called on him from Sir Culling Eardly, saying he had received on the previous night a telegram from Paris, stating that the deputation from the " Alliance Israelite " would arrive in London on the following Wednesday evening; and Sir C. Eardly wished to know if a deputation from the Board of Deputies of the British Jews would join him and the gentlemen from Paris on Friday to wait on the Lord Mayor, to have a public meeting at the Mansion-House regarding the child " Mortara." Sir Moses told Mr Cardall that he would endeavour to have a meeting of the Deputies the next afternoon, and would let him know their decision.

It appears that the idea of the Board's acting conjointly with Sir Culling Eardly and his party with regard to a public meeting was not favourably entertained by some Deputies, who were apprehensive that strong language might be used against certain persons differing in religious views with Sir Culling, of which they could not approve. They had no objection of signing a temperately worded Memorial, jointly with the Christians, to the Emperor of the French, to pray for his influence with the Pope for the restoration of the child to his parents.

At the meeting which was held on the following day, a resolution was adopted to the effect, " That until the Board shall have had an opportunity of conferring with the deputation from the Alliance Israelite, for which purpose a meeting has been specially convened on Thursday next, it is unable to resolve upon any course of proceeding with reference to the Mortara case.

A preliminary meeting of Jews and Christians, however, was held at the Mansion House, on Friday, December 21st, to receive a deputation of the Universal Israelite Alliance from Paris. In consequence of the absence, on official business, of the Lord Mayor, Sir Culling Eardly took the chair. The subject having been introduced by the chairman, the meeting was addressed by Messieurs S. Carvalho (Ingénieur des Ponts et Chaussées), S. Cahen (Professeur à l'Ecole Normale), and N. Leven (Avocat à la Cour Impériale de Paris), constituting the deputation from France; by Messrs Isaacs (Member of the Board of Deputies of British Jews) and Hart (Member of the Board of Delegates of American Jews) ; and by Signor Fernandez, on the part of the Jews of Italy. It was stated that the Board of Deputies of the British Jews had met on the previous night to receive the French Deputies, but that, owing to the absence from illness of the President, Sir Moses Montefiore, the decision on the subject of Mortara had been deferred for a few days. After a long conversation, characterised by harmony of feeling, it was unanimously resolved—" That we, Christians and Jews of England, France, Italy, and America, having heard the views entertained by the Universal Israelite Alliance, concerning new efforts to be made for the restoration of the child Edgar Mortara to his parents, take this, the earliest, opportunity of putting upon record our united conviction that the cause is one which, at the right time, and in the use of right means, it is our duty to resume."

Sir Culling Eardly, addressing the editor of the *Times*, under date of the 25th of December, writes : " Be so kind as to announce that arrangements are made for housing several thousands of the homeless fugitives of Syria in the Government buildings of St Jean d'Acre. Through the kind initiative of Lord Stratford de Redcliffe, President of the Committee, the rapid appeal to the Porte of Lord John Russell, and the zealous agency of Sir Henry Bulwer, this has been effected.

" Statesmen will not pass, nor their countrymen wish them a less ' Happy Christmas,' because they have been instrumental in gaining a shelter for the destitute at this inclement season.

" Let such kindness stir us all up to fresh efforts to feed, clothe, heal, and employ the sufferers ! "

Sir Moses had every reason to be pleased with the result of the labours in which he was permitted to take so prominent a part, and he considered himself justified in entertaining the hope that, in the future, the communities of various religious creeds in Syria would live peaceably together.

The state of Lady Montefiore's health became with every day more unsatisfactory, and preyed very much on the mind of Sir Moses.

CHAPTER XV.

1861.

DURING the first part of the year 1861 Sir Moses continued to give attention to various pursuits of a financial, communal, and political character, and devoted much time to the interests of the Syrian Relief Fund. A report of Fuad Pasha, Governor of Damascus, on the discontinuance of persecutions in that place, forwarded to him by the Foreign Office, contributed greatly to increase his gratitude to the British Government for their intercession, and later on a revival of the scheme for the construction of a railway from Jaffa to Jerusalem prompted him again to take a prominent part in the exertions of a Committee appointed for that purpose.

When Count Pizzamano originally asked Sir Moses to co-operate with him in his plans for making a high road between those two places, the latter feared that being no longer in the vigour of life, he would be unable to devote himself to a scheme which required much assiduity to ensure a successful issue, but circumstances were now different ; and, impressed with the idea that a great benefit might accrue from it to the people in Palestine, as well as to the sufferers in Syria, he set to work with a view of meeting in this respect the wishes of the Syrian Relief Committee.

February 17th.—Sir Culling Eardly called on him, and was anxious for Sir Moses to accompany him to Lord Palmerston respecting the growing of cotton in Syria. Sir Moses complied with his wish, and they went there together. The point to which they most directed the attention of Lord

Palmerston was, protection of life and property, and they suggested that about one thousand British marines should be stationed at St Jean d'Acre. Their simple presence would be sufficient for the purpose. But Lord Palmerston said, "How could we send troops when we are requiring the French to leave?" He agreed that the people employed might appoint a police of their own, and related an anecdote of an Englishman having fired a shot and struck a man one thousand yards distant, and this so completely intimidated a large body of men that they all ran away. Lord Palmerston's opinion respecting a division of the Druses and Christians agreed with that of Sir Moses, though it was contrary to the opinions of Lord Stratford de Redcliffe and Sir Culling Eardly. He said the Turkish Government were strong enough to secure the tranquillity of the country. Fuad Pasha had sufficient men, but the foreign troops must leave the country before perfect tranquillity could be restored. The Turkish Government were extremely poor at that time. The army had not been paid for eighteen months, except the soldiers in Syria, who were more fortunate, having only six months pay due to them. The army was badly clothed and fed; the customs revenue was pledged for the next three months, and there was no money in the treasury.

Sir Culling Eardly repeated to him, that Manchester would give the Syrian Committee seeds and plants for the cultivation of cotton in Syria, but they would give no capital unless there was a guarantee against persecution. The result of their long interview was his Lordship's determination to have the French troops withdrawn from Syria, and not to have any British force introduced there.

After leaving Lord Palmerston they drove to Lord Stratford de Redcliffe, and informed him of what had just passed. Lord Stratford thought that the Porte had a sufficient force to keep order in Syria, and that the presence of the French did not promote the tranquillity of the country.

February 18*th.*—There was a consultation between Dr Hodgkin and Sir Charles Locock respecting the state of Lady Montefiore's health. As the spring season was generally severe in England, Sir Charles advised, but did not order, her to go to Hyères, on the coast of France. He thought the mild climate would be advantageous, and would mitigate the pain occasioned by her complaint. "I must not make any further delay," Sir Moses says, "but hope with the blessing of heaven, to leave England on Tuesday, the 26th of February, for Hyères; it is only a few hours distant from London."

February 24th.—Being the Fast of Esther, Sir Moses attended divine service in the ancient Synagogue at Bevis Marks, and distributed numerous gifts among the pupils attending the Portuguese schools and their masters.

After his return to Park Lane, Sir Culling Eardly called on him respecting the Mortara case. "In a few days," he said, "Victor Emanuel will be declared King of Italy, and immediately acknowledged in England." Sir Culling desired to be prepared with a requisition to the Lord Mayor for a public meeting, to be held at the Mansion House, to take measures for the restoration of the child Mortara to its parents. He proposed to send a deputation to the Emperor of the French and to the King of Sardinia. He had no doubt that Lord John Russell would give his support to such a movement.

Sir Culling further said to Sir Moses, that the French troops would leave Rome very shortly, and that city would have a garrison of six thousand Sardinian soldiers. When that took place, he was sure Mortara would be released without any action on his part; but Sir Culling wished the English to have the merit of obtaining the boy's freedom.

Sir Moses promised soon to convene a meeting of the Mortara Committee.

February 27th.—He attended a meeting of the Executive Committee of the British Syrian Relief Fund, Lord Stratford de Redcliffe in the chair. Colonel Burnaby, attached to Her Majesty's Commission in Syria, and a member of the Beyrout Committee, gave a most unfavourable account of the state of the East. The Druses were in the deepest distress, and it did not appear likely that for the moment anything could be done for the cultivation of cotton.

March 16th.—"We have learned with deep and sincere regret," Sir Moses writes, "the death of Her Royal Highness the Duchess of Kent, from whom we had received great kindness during her residence at Ramsgate with our gracious Queen. I heartily grieve for her loss."

April 25th.—Sir Moses and Lady Montefiore went to Ramsgate in an invalid carriage, in hopes that the change of air would prove beneficial to Lady Montefiore; but on the 20th of May they were again in town. "Restless nights and great weakness" had often been reported to her medical attendants whilst she was at East Cliff Lodge, and Sir Moses was very anxious about her.

June 6th.—He was much gratified by a letter from Damascus, to the effect that one of his co-religionists, Mordecai Ashkenazi, so long in prison on the charge of murder, committed during the outbreak the previous year, had been acquitted after a long trial before the Extraordinary Tribunal, and the verdict approved by Fuad Pasha. Sir Moses at once wrote letters to his friends and the Board of Deputies, suggesting the propriety of their acquainting Lord John Russell and the Turkish Ambassador with the news.

Lady Montefiore, being desirous of attending divine service in her own Synagogue at Ramsgate, on the anniversary of its dedication, as well as that of their marriage, she left town with Sir Moses for East Cliff, where they arrived safely. A few days later they returned to town; and being most anxious to visit again a place where, in early life, they had spent many happy hours, they drove to Smithem Bottom.

"On our arrival," Sir Moses says, "my dear Judith and myself said our afternoon prayers; and I read to her, before we took dinner, a chapter in the Pentateuch intended to be read next Sabbath in the Synagogue." "Smithem Bottom," he continues, "appears to me to be the same quiet place it was half-a-century ago. It was ever to me a caution against ambition, and has led me to esteem independence far beyond riches.

"At this place man appeared to want but little. With peace and content, and the quietness of the place, which afforded us the opportunity of keeping the Sabbaths undisturbed by the fluctuations which were at that period daily taking place in London from the vicissitudes of the war, endeared Smithem Bottom to my dear Judith and myself far beyond every other place we have ever seen, excepting Jerusalem and East Cliff. At all these places we have been able to enjoy the comfort and happiness of our holy religion.

"Fifty years have made a great change in the inhabitants of the place. At least, when I reflect on the withdrawal from this world of so many dear friends, who had partaken with me of the happiness of its old host and hostess! How many friends are now in heaven who had passed happy hours with us! However, we cannot be sufficiently thankful to God for His bountiful mercy and goodness. May He guard and protect us, even beyond death. We cannot expect to be able to revisit Smithem Bottom very often, but truly grateful are we for having been permitted to see it once more."

The sentiments expressed here by Sir Moses appear to have been due to the presentiment of an event which he apprehended might soon deprive him of the happiness of coming to this place again with Lady Montefiore. But he would not permit his cheerful temper, in her presence, to be depressed; and both returned to Park Lane highly pleased with their visit.

Lady Montefiore passed a good night, and Sir Moses, finding that she did not feel too fatigued, resolved to leave Park Lane for Ramsgate.

He gave orders accordingly to have all the necessary preparations made, so as to be able to leave Park Lane for the season on the 21st June.

June 22nd.—We find them at East Cliff Lodge, a number of friends and relatives, together with some emissaries from foreign countries, for several months affording them pleasure and occupation.

July 25th.—A special messenger arrived from Jerusalem with despatches from the heads of the Hebrew congregations. The English Consul had sent certain notices to be made public to the Jews in Jerusalem and Hebron, the tenor of which, the messenger feared, was to weaken, and, if possible, destroy the influence and power of the Spiritual Heads over their congregation. Sir Moses lost no time in attending to the request of his brethren. He addressed a letter to the Consul; and, on the 17th of December, was in possession of a satisfactory explanation from the British Consul in Jerusalem and the British Consul at Damascus. Soon after fresh complaints were made by the representatives of the Hebrew community, in consequence of which Sir Moses convened a meeting of the Board of Deputies, where it was resolved to address Lord John Russell on the subject.

December 15th.—In the early days of December of this year, public interest was absorbed in the illness of the Prince Consort. Sir Moses' Diaries testify to the grief and anxiety with which he received the more and more gloomy reports of the progress of the fatal malady which were given to the world. On the day after the Prince's death he writes: "It was whispered that most unhappy intelligence had been received at Ramsgate regarding the Prince Consort, and I could not rest without going myself to Ramsgate. Alas, I found on my arrival the unhappy news but too true. We have lost a great and good Prince; our beloved and gracious Queen the best of husbands; her children the best of fathers. He was amiable, benevolent, and most liberal as regards religious freedom to all. We have lost a great friend. It is to England and to Englishmen a great and sudden calamity. May the Almighty, in His mercy, comfort and support our beloved Sovereign; grant her length of days, with peace, and guard her from all misfortunes.

December 17*th.*—Sir Moses had the satisfaction of being informed at the Foreign Office that a letter had been sent to the British Consul at Jerusalem ordering the withdrawal of the notices of the British Consul.

On the same occasion he was also informed that the prayer of the Jews in Moldavia had been considered by the British Government, and that Mr Green, the British Consul in Bucharest, would no doubt attend to Lord John Russell's instructions in their favour.

December 23*rd.*—He and Lady Montefiore attended a special service at their Synagogue, the reading desk being covered with black cloth—"The only symbol of mourning," Sir Moses says, "we ever had in our Synagogue."

"The loss of his late Royal Highness the Prince Consort," he continues, "is felt by every one as a great domestic loss. He was respected and beloved by all the nation, and all Her Majesty's subjects participate in her grief.

"I can never forget the courtesy evinced by the lamented Prince when I had the honour of being both at Osborne and Windsor."

December 31*st.*—Lady Montefiore had a most restless night, and her state of health appeared so unfavourable to Sir Moses that he could not make up his mind to leave her, though he felt a great desire to attend a meeting at the Alliance Marine, where he had to propose to the shareholders some important measures for the benefit of the company.

Lady Montefiore, ever anxious to see him accomplish his intentions, advised him to go, and he, though with much pain and great hesitation, went to town. In the evening, in reply to a telegram he sent to Ramsgate, he had the happiness of being informed that Lady Montefiore was much better and more comfortable, and would be happy to see him on the morrow.

In token of gratitude to heaven for this good news, and the accomplishment of the object he had in view by attending the meetings, he terminated the civil year by making generous presents to several persons in need of help, and giving to one of them £500 to enable him to establish himself in business.

Lady Montefiore's great weakness continued to cause great anxiety at the beginning of 1862. Frequent consultations of her medical attendants often alarmed Sir Moses, and deep sorrow clouded his mind. Nevertheless, at her frequent and urgent requests, not to discontinue attending to his usual pursuits on her account, he went to town whenever he thought his presence there might help some good cause.

January 14*th.*—Sir Moses attended a large meeting in the Egyptian Hall at the Mansion House, to propose a Memorial to the late Prince Consort. Lord Stratford de Redcliffe was present. A committee was appointed to carry the proposal into effect. Sir Moses gave, in his and Lady Montefiore's name, £52, 10s. as a contribution towards the amount required. Subsequently he attended a meeting of the Board of Deputies, where Alderman Phillips presented a letter of apology from Messrs Chambers, the editors and publishers of " Chambers's Journal," for having published, on the 14th of September 1861, a tale entitled " The Mystery of Metz," calculated to leave on the mind of the reader a most erroneous impression regarding the religious ceremonials of the Jewish people, thus bringing an unpleasant matter to a happy conclusion.*

February 24*th.*—General Chesney and Sir John M'Neil called on him at the Alliance, and requested him to be the chairman of the proposed railway between Jaffa and Jerusalem, which he

---

* The *Daily News*, Thursday, 31st October 1861, published an interesting letter on the subject, addressed to the Editor by T. Theodores of Manchester.

declined. He consented, however, to his name being added to the scheme as a patron.

February 25*th.*—Attended a meeting of the Syrian Improvement Committee, Lord Clanricarde, Sir Culling Eardly, Mr Freeland, and several other members being present. They agreed to give £300 towards the building of an hospital at Beyrout, by the order of St John, under the Prussian Government, and £50 for the translation into Arabic of some useful instructions, to be inserted in the newspaper published at Beyrout. Lord Clanricarde and Mr Freeland were to inquire into the practicability of making an artesian well at Jerusalem. The fund still left that day at the disposal of the Committee was about £2700.

CHAPTER XVI.

1862.

THE JAFFA AND JERUSALEM RAILWAY—LORD DUFFERIN—
SIR MOSES AND LADY MONTEFIORE'S GOLDEN WEDDING—
DEATH OF LADY MONTEFIORE.

TWENTY-FOUR years having now passed since Sir Moses made the entry in his diary on the desirability of having a railway between Jaffa and Jerusalem, without his having witnessed any further attempt to accomplish so important an undertaking, the reader will find it interesting to learn his suggestions.

March 10*th.*—Sir John M'Neil and General Chesney came to him at the Alliance. He expressed his feelings regarding the prospectus, in which his name had been printed as a director. They said it was a mistake. In the end he promised to meet them at the Athenæum on the morrow. Lord Dufferin would be there, and Sir Moses promised he would endeavour to find some city man as a director. He immediately wrote to some of his friends on the subject, but did not succeed in persuading them to become directors of the proposed railway.

In the course of the afternoon Sir Moses went to the Athenæum, where he met Sir John M'Neil, General Chesney, and General Sabine. They were soon joined by Lord Dufferin. Sir Moses says: " I held that the concession for the Jaffa railway should be obtained with a guarantee of five or six per cent. on the outlay; that two or three influential persons should be selected as directors, and that the Turkish Ambassador should be an *ex-officio* director, as his presence at the board would sanction the contracts, and thereby secure, without dispute, the guarantee return on the outlay. I mentioned several persons it would be desirable to get as directors. Lord Dufferin told the gentlemen present that he wished to speak with Sir Moses alone, and they then took their leave. His

Lordship said that he was happy to have the opportunity of seeing him, and that at Damascus he had heard how much he had done for the people there. He said the outbreak was very near reaching the Jewish quarter. He had received great attention from the Jews, and had dined with some of them. He expressed his satisfaction at the course Sir Moses had recommended, but said he could not act without the addition of some wealthy city people.

"His Lordship," Sir Moses observes, "is a most elegant and agreeable young man."

"Lord Dufferin," he adds, in a postscript, "said to me he had asked Lord John Russell to be a patron, but he would not consent. Lord Dufferin spoke of Lord Stratford de Redcliffe and Lord Clarendon; but I said I thought it would be quite unnecessary to have any patrons, if his Lordship was the chairman of the company."

After leaving the Athenæum, Sir Moses called on Sir Culling Eardly and told him that he had been with Lord Dufferin, and had great hopes that the scheme would be carried out. Early in May he sent a letter to the representatives of his ancient congregation, resigning his office as one of their Deputies, an honour which he had enjoyed for thirty-seven years. He was urgently requested to withdraw his resignation, but would not do so, as he felt it out of his power to fulfil the duties to his own satisfaction.

During the same month he received a letter from the Viceroy of Egypt, who was then staying at the Palace of the Tuileries at Paris as the guest of the Emperor. His Highness thanked Sir Moses, who had offered him his house in Park Lane, and regretted that it reached him too late, as he had already engaged a house at Richmond. He added, however, that he was none the less grateful for Sir Moses' offer.

June 28th was the fiftieth anniversary of the wedding of Sir Moses and Lady Montefiore. Relatives, friends, and many representatives of congregations hastened to offer them their felicitations, and letters and addresses from all parts of the world. To mark the solemnity of the day, Sir Moses attended a special service in his own Synagogue, and on his return wrote the last verse in a Hebrew scroll of the Pentateuch, which he presented to a congregation in need of one for their Synagogue, and too poor to buy one. Lady Montefiore, although very weak and ailing, left her bed in the hope of being present whilst Sir Moses was writing; but the doctor, who came soon after, found her too weak to leave her room.

"The absence of my dear Judith," Sir Moses writes, "was a severe drawback to the happiness I had in being permitted, by the mercy of God, to write the concluding words of the Pentateuch scroll. May He, in His merciful goodness, allow me to have the happiness to complete the next sacred scroll which is now being written for me at Wilna, in my dear wife's presence. May she be in better health; may she enjoy renewed strength to participate in the joy which this act affords me."

The next day Mr Manser of Dumpton, his nearest neighbour, came to present him and Lady Montefiore with a most friendly address of congratulation, signed by the ministers and inhabitants of St Peter's and Broadstairs. Dr Canham brought them an address from the bench of magistrates, most kind and complimentary; and several other friends, unable to offer their congratulations personally, sent letters.

July 2nd.—A telegram arrived, informing him that the Viceroy of Egypt had ordered his son, Toussoun Pasha, to come to England again; and Sir Moses at once wrote to Tulfica Pasha to ask the Viceroy to allow the Prince to be his guest. A few days later he received an invitation to dine with the Viceroy on board His Highness's yacht; but Lady Montefiore and himself being unwell, he was unable to accept it.

July 20th.—Sir Moses went to Woolwich to pay his respects to the Viceroy. The latter was much pleased to see him, thanking him for the invitation he had given to Prince Toussoun Pasha and the offer of the house made to himself. In the course of conversation, referring to the French and English languages, the Pasha said he understood English very well; he had not been in England so long for nothing. His Highness said, Lord Palmerston had held out two of his fingers to him, by way of shaking hands, and Lord John Russell, one.

He appeared to be in excellent spirits, and asked Sir Moses if he had seen his yacht, and told him to go and see the cabins. Sir Moses found them truly magnificent. The richness of the furniture was almost beyond description. Sir Moses says, "They are far too richly furnished for my taste. On my taking leave of his Highness," he adds, "I wished him long life, and hoped he might see the prosperity of Egypt increased a thousand fold.' "Of what consequence," said the Pasha, "could that be to me? I do not expect to live more than ten years." "When I left, Sir Moses continues, "he shook me heartily by the hand. I sincerely wish him health, long life, and contentment. I would not sail in the yacht to Egypt for ten thousand pounds."

September 8th.—In accordance with the decision of the doctors, after several consultations, Lady Montefiore was to pass the winter at Nice, and she was strongly advised not to postpone her departure after the 19th October.

Dr Hodgkin still feared that she was too weak to undertake the journey, but he would meet Sir Charles Locock, when they would come to a final decision.

That morning all preparations were completed to leave Ramsgate for London.

Lady Montefiore left her bed with considerable reluctance, although she felt she was unable to travel on that day. Sir Moses sent for her doctor, and as the latter was of opinion that they might venture, Sir Moses did not hesitate to undertake the journey. After a most careful journey in an invalid's carriage, they arrived in town and drove to Park Lane, where Lady Montefiore was with equal care carried from the carriage to the hall, and from there to the back drawing-room. She immediately went to bed, and after taking a cup of tea, felt very comfortable, "and certainly," Sir Moses said, "not more fatigued than one could have expected."

September 10th.—Sir Charles Locock met Dr Hodgkin at Park Lane in conference, and passed more than half-an-hour with Lady Montefiore and Sir Moses. The result was, that Sir Charles found Lady Montefiore better than when he last saw her, and more able to bear the fatigue of their proposed journey, and felt no hesitation in giving his opinion in favour of their going to Mentone. Dr Hodgkin was content not to oppose Sir Charles Locock's opinion, but did so, Sir Moses says, evidently under restraint.

September 16th.—Lady Montefiore accompanied Sir Moses in their brougham to make several calls, he took her to see the new carpets for East Cliff, and went to Ludgate Hill to select a new silk dress for her.

September 17th.—She had a better night, the entry in the Diary states, and in the course of the afternoon took a drive with Sir Moses round the Exhibition.

September 19th.—Lady Montefiore had an undisturbed night, and Sir Moses left Park Lane at half-past nine, attended various meetings in the city, and about half-past one he returned with the intention of going with Lady Montefiore to see the National Exhibition. But unfortunately he found her very unwell, and still in bed. The carriage had been ordered to convey them to see the Exhibition, but Sir Moses went instead to Dr Hodgkin, requesting him to call at once. Dr Hodgkin found Lady Montefiore seriously ill, and the next day told Sir Moses he was very uneasy, and would like to have a consultation with Sir Charles Locock, who, unfortunately, had gone to Brighton and could not come. The next day her state was more favourable, but after a restless night became again so serious, that another doctor was called in, who, to Sir Moses' great grief, could give him no better account. Most of the members of the family were there. Mr Sebag (now Mr Sebag Montefiore) remained all night, and together with Sir Moses, read with her the prayers for the sick.

September 23rd.—Lady Montefiore had a very restless night. Sir Moses attended Divine Service in the Portuguese Synagogue early in the morning, and had a special prayer offered up for her recovery. He distributed generous gifts among the poor, and subsequently returned to Park Lane.

Dr Hamilton Rowe came and had a long consultation with Dr Hodgkin; they found Lady Montefiore in the same state as last night, and ordered some strong remedies. Dr Rowe told Sir Moses that he was not entirely without hopes. In the afternoon Sir Moses attended again Divine Service in the German Synagogue. He distributed more charitable gifts among the poor, and joined the community in offering up special prayers for his wife. In the evening on his return to Park Lane, he wrote the last verse in a Pentateuch scroll written for him and Lady Montefiore at Wilna, in Russia, by a distinguished scribe. The ceremony was performed in a room (their private oratory) adjoining their chamber, with the door open, so that Lady Montefiore might hear the prayers offered up on the occasion. Several of his relatives and friends were present and joined in supplications to the Almighty to alleviate her sufferings and to restore her to health. " She was as patient as an angel," Sir Moses says, " under her sufferings. All our friends have shewn their sympathy for my dear wife." Innumerable calls and enquiries have been made during the day.

September 24th.—Dr Rowe and Dr Hodgkin declared that a very favourable change had taken place, but still the utmost quietness must be observed. They cautioned him against being too sanguine, as Lady Montefiore was very weak and no longer young.

The time was now fast approaching for one of the best daughters of Israel to return home to her Heavenly Father.

On the day when the doctors still left a spark of hope for her recovery, Lady Montefiore remained silent, apparently preparing her spirit for flight. Many a sigh of deep sorrow might have been heard around her couch, many eyes were dimmed by tears of grief, but no sigh, no tear was to be noticed on the countenance of the dying lady; with a heavenly smile she greeted those who came to see her, endeavouring at the same time to incline her head towards them. Relatives and friends were anxious to remain with her, but she motioned to them to leave her and to go to prayers, as it was the eve of the Hebrew New Year, one of the most solemn festivals. The Sabbath lamp was lighted, shedding its subdued light around, and in the adjoining oratory the hymns for the festival were softly and solemnly chanted to the ancient melodies.

At the conclusion of the service Sir Moses came back, laid his hands affectionately on the head of Lady Montefiore, and invoked Heaven's blessing upon her, which she reciprocated by placing her hand upon his head, in token of blessing. Sir Moses then descended to the dining-room, where the relatives were assembled, to pronounce the grace before meals, but he had scarcely pronounced the blessing when he was called up by Dr Hodgkin, who had been watching by the bed of the invalid, and who informed him that the end was very near. All present immediately followed Sir Moses, the solemn prayers for the dying were recited, and the pure spirit of Judith, the noble, the good, and the truly pious, took flight Heavenwards.

CHAPTER XVII.

1862.

ON the following Saturday night her mortal remains were
taken to Ramsgate, accompanied by Sir Moses and his
near relatives, the officers of the Synagogue, and Dr Hodgkin,
her physician.   In the morning the Chief Rabbi of the German
congregation, and the Rev. B. Abraham of the Spanish and
Portuguese congregation, the ministers of all the Synagogues in
London and in the country, together with a considerable number
of gentlemen, representatives of schools and charitable institutions, assembled in the house of mourning, and at two o'clock
in the afternoon the mournful cortege left East Cliff Lodge.
Hundreds of the inhabitants of Ramsgate and the neighbouring
places assembled near the Synagogue, where the place of burial
is situated, to manifest their feelings of sorrow and regret;
nearly all the vessels in the harbour had their flags half-mast
high; in most of the churches the ministers in their sermons
feelingly dwelt on the great loss which the poor had sustained
by the death of Lady Montefiore.

The body having been taken into the Synagogue, the Chief
Rabbi addressed outside a large assembly of various denominations, describing to them the noble qualities of the deceased,
the services she had rendered to humanity by the encouragement she had given to the promotion of every good cause, and
by the manner in which she had associated herself with her
husband in all his philanthropic missions. Subsequently the
coffin was carried to the spot selected by both Sir Moses and

Lady Montefiore, many years before her death, for their final resting-place.

There the Rev. B. Abrahams, of the Spanish and Portuguese congregation, delivered another oration, dwelling on the manifold virtues of the departed, and reminding his hearers of the innumerable good deeds of her whom they now deeply deplored.

At the conclusion the body was lowered into the grave, and in commemoration of her devotion to the interest of the Holy Land, Terra Santa was copiously thrown upon the coffin. The orphan children of the Spanish and Portuguese schools of London intoned hymns and psalms to the ancient solemn and mournful melodies, after which the mourners and all present entered the Synagogue, where the afternoon service was performed. During the night workmen were engaged in building a brick vault for the coffin, and all that time several members of the community recited psalms and prayers near the spot and in the house of mourning. After the grave was closed, the nearest relatives and friends returned with Sir Moses to East Cliff, and remained with him during the first seven days, endeavouring to comfort and console him, joining with him in prayers, and assisting him in receiving the numerous visits of condolence.

Although Sir Moses and Lady Montefiore had both decided upon their last resting-place, Sir Moses still appeared earnestly to entertain the idea of having her body taken to Jerusalem. He had a letter written to that effect to the representatives of the Holy City, requesting them to send a number of respectable persons, students of the Holy Law, to England for the purpose of taking charge of it, and interring it in the Valley of Jehoshaphat. Upon re-consideration of the matter, however, the idea was abandoned.

Lady Montefiore, Sir Moses said, made no will, but among her papers was found an unfinished letter to him in her handwriting, in which she most touchingly expressed the wish that a token of her esteem should be handed to relatives whom she named, to friends, and to charitable and educational institutions, when it should please the Almighty to call her away from this world. In compliance with her wishes, Sir Moses sent upwards of 360 very liberal souvenirs and parting gifts to relatives, friends, Synagogues, and charitable and educational institutions in England and abroad. He then invited a number

Synagogue and Mausoleum at Ramsgate.

See Vol. II., page 141.

of distinguished Hebrew poets to prepare an epitaph to be engraved on the marble slab which covers the grave of Lady Montefiore. This was followed by the following lines in English :—

"Angels saw thy glorious works, and called thee to join them in singing the praises of the Most High in Heaven, where God is thy strength.

"Ask mercy for thy husband, and also for thy brethren, and pray that the light of Zion may again shine, when in its splendour thou shalt re-appear in radiance."

"SACRED TO THE MEMORY OF JUDITH, LADY MONTEFIORE, THE BELOVED WIFE OF SIR MOSES MONTEFIORE, BART., AND DAUGHTER OF JOSHUA LEVI COHEN, ESQUIRE, WHO DEPARTED THIS LIFE ON THE EVE OF THE FIRST DAY OF THE NEW YEAR, 5623 A.M.

In the course of a few months an edifice, surmounted by a cupola, was erected, after the model of the Tomb of Rachel on the road to Beth-Lékhém. Tablets, containing prayers and psalms to be recited by those who visit the tomb, were placed on the walls, and a lamp suspended from the centre of the cupola, bearing a Hebrew inscription, the translation of which is, "The spirit of man is the light of the Lord" (Prov. xx. 27). A seat was placed in the corner, intended for Sir Moses, who often used to visit the mausoleum, and remain there in prayer and meditation.

The Tabernacle festivals which for half a century had always been spent so happily by Sir Moses at East Cliff were this year shrouded in the gloom of sorrow and affliction. There was no other way to rouse him than by reminding him of his useful pursuits, which soon prompted him to follow in the path which his angel wife had so often traced out for him, and in the continuance of his service in the cause of all that is good, noble, and holy. It had been the ardent wish of Lady Montefiore that Sir Moses should pay another visit to the Holy Land, in order to secure from the Turkish Government some concessions which were greatly needed for the proper working and expansion of the institutions that had been established for the benefit of our poor brethren. Although suffering in mind and very weak in health, Sir Moses determined to fulfil the desire Lady Montefiore had so often expressed before her lamented death, and prepared for the journey. He began by addressing the following letter to Musurus Pasha, the Turkish Ambassador in London :—

"I need not assure your Excellency," he writes through an amanuensis, his state of health not permitting him to write the letter with his own hand, "that I feel sincerely grateful for your kind offices, and I flatter myself, at the same time, that it may interest your Excellency to learn that a considerable number of almshouses, and other buildings, and especially a large windmill, which, in consequence of the concession, were erected in Jerusalem, are offering shelter, social advantages, and employment to a great number of the poorer inhabitants.

"Being anxious to extend the scope of their benefits, as far as it may be in my power, I propose once more to re-visit the Holy Land, and expect to leave England in a few days, to make a short stay for the restoration of my health in the south of France, *en route* for Constantinople.

"With a deep sense of the advantage of the aid and support which your Excellency has on all occasions so readily accorded to me on my visits to the East, may I request the favour of your kindly giving me, at your early convenience, letters to His Highness the Grand Vizier, and His Excellency the Minister of Foreign Affairs to the Ottoman Government, to use their good offices in furtherance of my desire to obtain from His Imperial Majesty the Sultan 'Abd-ool-Azeez a confirmation, and a letter to the Governor of Jerusalem, to afford me the necessary assistance and facilities towards the accomplishment of my objects."

The readers of these Memoirs will probably remember the difficulties encountered in Jerusalem in connection with the building of the Juda Touro Almshouses, notwithstanding the special permission for that purpose granted by the late Sultan 'Abd-ool-Medjid, and will perceive for this reason that it was a most judicious step on the part of Sir Moses, to secure the confirmation of the said permission by an edict from the new Sultan.

Musurus Pasha readily and kindly complied with Sir Moses' request, and forwarded to him the letters required.

In the month of May 1863, we find him at Constantinople, where the British Ambassador and the Turkish Ministers received him with marked attention, supporting with their advice in all matters. The Sultan accorded him an audience, whereat he confirmed all the privileges granted to his Israelite subjects, and the concessions which had been given to Sir Moses personally with regard to the purchase of land and the building of houses in Jerusalem. Vizierial letters were ordered to be forwarded to the Governor of the Holy City, and Sir Moses had the satisfaction of seeing the object of his visit to Constantinople fully accomplished.

During his stay at the Ottoman capital he visited the charitable and educational institutions of his community, and distributed generous gifts to the poor of all religious denominations, in memory of Lady Montefiore, as he had done in all places in

Italy where he happened to stop on his way to Constantinople. At Rhodes, where the inhabitants suffered severely from an earthquake, he also gave donations in his own and his departed wife's name.

Prayers for the preservation of his health and long life were offered up by rich and poor, irrespective of their religious creed. But his deep sorrow had affected his health so much, that serious symptoms began to appear, and his physician strongly disapproved of Sir Moses continuing his journey to Jerusalem.

His friends joined with the physician in dissuading him from proceeding further, calling his attention to the many changes which had occurred during the last few months in Eastern politics. Said Pasha, the Viceroy of Egypt, and friend of Sir Moses, was dead, and Ismael Pasha had assumed the reins of the Egyptian Government. This new Viceroy did a great deal for Egypt, by introducing financial and other reforms. The papers reported that he had made a very promising speech to a deputation of merchants. He was not inclined to support the Suez Canal, but it was thought that he would have to yield to French influence, and to pressure from the Emperor of the French.

The Sultan had visited Egypt, and signed a firman guaranteeing eight per cent. for the railway to be established along the banks of the Orontes, which it was supposed would have a most favourable influence on the traffic in the Holy Land. These events were accompanied by other political events in Turkey, where Fuad Pasha, the former Governor of Damascus, had been raised to the high office of Seraskier. All this, the friends of Sir Moses said, did not make the time propitious for the objects Sir Moses had in view in going to Jerusalem, and so he was reluctantly persuaded to give up the journey and return to London, where he arrived early in July, after going first to Ramsgate.

There is the following entry in his Diary :—

" I have returned home in safety, and somewhat better in health, after a long journey and an absence of more than six months, but am still very depressed in mind."

He drove immediately to his wife's grave, and prayed to God to give him strength to bear his irreparable loss with resignation, and to grant him the happiness of joining his angel wife in

Heaven, when it should please God to call him from this world.

He intended going to London, but still had not sufficient fortitude to sleep at Park Lane. Mr and Mrs Benjamin Cohen having heard of this, immediately requested him to stay with them in their house at Richmond, and he was pleased to accept the hospitality of his kind relatives.

During his stay with Mr and Mrs Cohen, his health and spirits improved so much that he soon felt able to go to London, and during the time he remained there to attend, as before, the meetings of the financial and communal institutions of which he was President. After he returned to Ramsgate, his time was fully taken up in answering his numerous correspondents in all parts of the world.

To his young friend, Toussoun Pasha, he sent an affectionate letter, conveying to him his sympathy and condolence on the death of his father; and, in return, the young Egyptian Prince wrote to him, expressing his deep grief at the death of Lady Montefiore, and his gratitude for the kind sentiments Sir Moses manifested to him on the mournful occasion of the early and unexpected death of his father.

The young Prince himself did not live long. He died at an early age of consumption—so it was said.

October 20*th.*—This being the eve of the seventy-ninth anniversary of his birthday (corresponding in that year with the Hebrew date, the 8th of Heshvan), he sent £79 to the secretary of the Spanish and Portuguese community for distribution among seventy-nine families. He also sent similar sums to other congregations in the Holy Land.

In recording in his Diary the events of the day, the memory of his wife appears to have been ever present with him, and in moments of hesitation, or when undecided what course of action to pursue, he would frequently say, "What would my dear Judith have advised?"

He was at this time overwhelmed with letters and work, and it would appear from various entries that nothing would have been more welcome to him than a recommendation from his friends to withdraw from all his financial engagements, as well as his communal work, at home and abroad, and simply enjoy rest, contemplating the pleasures of the past, and hoping for a blissful future. But the necessity of energy and action in any good or holy cause soon roused him from such moments of depression. We read in his Diary on October 21st:—" Before I was dressed this morning, I received a packet, marked private, from A——. The writer says: ' My dear Sir,—I am unwilling to bring you up to town in order that you may read this duplicate. I therefore send it you to Ramsgate.' The papers which accompaned this were from —— of Tangiers, and told of the warm and generous efforts of Her Majesty's Government on behalf of the two unfortunate Jews now in prison at Saffi. But the situation of the poor men appeared to me so dangerous that I determined to go at once to London to get the Board of Deputies to take some active steps to secure their release from prison."

These dispatches refer to an unfortunate occurrence at Saffi, in Morocco, concerning which the Jews of Gibraltar and Tangiers had addressed Sir Moses and the Board of Deputies of the British Jews.

A Spaniard in Saffi, in the service of the Spanish Vice-Consul, had died suddenly, and suspicions of his having been poisoned were aroused in the mind of the Vice-Consul, who insisted upon the Moorish authorities investigating the case, and inflicting punishment on the guilty person. No steps were taken to ascertain whether there were any facts to prove that the death of the Spaniard was due to violence ; but, according to the custom in Morocco, those parties upon whom it was sought to fix suspicion were examined under severe torture, and the application of the bastinado. A Jewish lad, about fourteen years of age, who resided in the family of the deceased, was the first person so examined (the Jews being the most unprotected portion of the population). After persisting for a long time in the assertion of his innocence, he at length yielded to the protracted agony, and declared that poison had been administered. Again, under the influence of torture, ten or eleven other persons, whose names were suggested to him, were denounced by the lad as participators in the crime.

Most of these were arrested, but one of them only was submitted to examination under torture. Though this measure was pushed to a fearful extremity, no confessions of guilt could be wrung from him. The lad also, when released from torture, uniformly asserted his innocence.

However, as he had confessed his guilt, and the man had been denounced, both were condemned to death, doubtless to prove the readiness of the Morocco Government to comply with the demands of its recent conqueror.

The lad was accordingly executed at Saffi, the execution naturally producing great dismay amongst the Jewish population; but the man was conveyed in a Spanish vessel to Tangiers, to be executed there. Nothing is known of the reason which led to the adoption of this course, but it seems probable that it was taken in order that the knowledge of the circumstance might spread more rapidly and extensively through the Moorish dominion. This public execution could not fail to impress the people with a striking idea of the strength of the Spanish influence at the Court of the Sultan.

The alarm felt by the Israelites at Tangiers was extreme, and as has already been said, was forthwith communicated to Gibraltar.

Nine or ten individuals lay at Saffi, menaced with a fate similar to that of their two brethren.

Sir Moses immediately sent a telegram to the President and Secretary of the Board of Deputies of the British Jews, appointing a meeting with them in London. At the time mentioned, these gentlemen came to him, and he read them the dispatches he had received. It was then agreed to call a meeting of Deputies for the earliest day possible. A letter was also drawn up for the Foreign Office.

On the following Tuesday, a meeting of the Board of Deputies was held, and Sir Moses was invited to proceed to Saffi, an offer which he readily accepted.

November 12*th.*—He went to the Foreign Office for his letters of introduction, and also called at the Mansion House to see the Lord Mayor and several of the Aldermen, who took a great interest in his Mission.

November 14*th.*—Prayers were offered up for him in all the Synagogues in London and the country.

November 16*th.*—We find Sir Moses at Dover, accompanied by Mr Haim Guedalla, Mr Sampson Samuel, the Secretary and

Solicitor of the Board of Deputies, and Dr Hodgkin, proceeding to the Lord Warden Hotel, with the intention of remaining there over night, in order to be ready to leave the next morning for Calais. Many friends being anxious to express their good wishes, they came in the evening to see him, and remained till a late hour. Even then he did not retire, but continued writing and making arrangements, until he was entreated by his physician to take some rest.

THE MISSION TO MOROCCO—TANGIER—LIBERATION OF TWO
PRISONERS—DEPUTATION OF MOORS—SIR MOSES SUCCESS-
FULLY INTERCEDES FOR THEM—DEATH OF SIR MOSES'
SISTER, MRS GOLDSMID—OPPRESSIVE REGULATIONS RE-
SPECTING THE JEWS IN MOROCCO—FAVOURABLE EDICT
OF THE SULTAN.

I SHALL now give the reader a *resumé* of the Mission of
Morocco, using for the more important episodes Sir Moses'
own words as contained in his letters to the President of the
Board of Deputies.

"You will recollect," he writes to that gentleman, "that we left Dover on
Tuesday morning, the 17th ult., and reached Madrid within six days of our
departure from London. I mention this in order that the Board may understand that, to the best of our ability, we used every effort to proceed with all
possible celerity towards the hoped-for accomplishment of the objects of the
Mission. Considering that some important matters calculated to lead to a
prosperous issue might receive attention at Madrid, I deemed it expedient
with this view to make some stay in that city. I waited on his Excellency,
Sir J. F. Crampton, our Ambassador at the Court of Madrid, on Thursday,
the 26th ult., and experienced from him a most kind and friendly welcome.
On the same day, his Excellency introduced me to the Marquis of Miraflores,
the Prime Minister of Spain, who gave me the encouraging assurance that I
need be under no apprehension of any further steps being taken for the present against the unfortunate prisoners at Saffi, the proceedings against whom,
he stated most emphatically, had not been influenced by any prejudice or ill-
will, on account of their religious persuasion ; and the Marquis consented to
solicit Her Majesty the Queen of Spain to grant me the honour of a private
audience ; he also, at my request, promised to give me a letter of introduction
to Don Francisco Merry y Colon, the Spanish Minister at Tangier.
"On Monday, the 28th ult., in the afternoon, I had the honour (upon the
introduction of his Excellency Sir J. F. Crampton) to be presented to Her
Majesty, and to the King Consort, at a private audience. I have reported to
you, in a former letter, how gracious a reception was accorded to me, but I
may add that I shall never cease to bear in mind the gratification I experienced on that interesting occasion. I was received by their Majesties
with the utmost courtesy and kindness, and was joyfully impressed with the
assurances of the King Consort of their respect for all religions.
"During my stay at Madrid, I had the advantage of introductions to his

Grace the Duke of Tetuan, General Prim, several of the foreign ambassadors, and other distinguished persons, by several of whom I was favoured with letters of introduction for Tangier.

"Having, under the blessing of God, succeeded in effecting, at Madrid, the objects contemplated, I left that city with my companions very early the following morning (Tuesday, Dec. 1), *en route* for Seville, as I was desirous of handing to Don Antonio Merry (the Russian and Prussian Consul at Seville, and the father of the Spanish Minister at Tangier) a letter of introduction. We travelled by railway to Santa Cruz de Mudela. On Wednesday, the 2nd December, we left Santa Cruz, and proceeded by diligence to Andujar, at which place we arrived the same evening. I was too exhausted to proceed further that night, although my fellow travellers, Dr Hodgkin and Mr Guedalla, in their kind anxiety to secure for me a fitting resting-place at Cordova, continued their journey till midnight by the same diligence, so that they might make the necessary arrangements.

"We arrived at Seville on Sunday, the 6th inst. The following day I delivered to Don Antonio Merry the letter of introduction to him with which I had been favoured, and he very kindly gave me a letter to his son, Don Francisco Merry y Colon, the Spanish Minister at Tangier.

"On Tuesday, the 8th inst., we left Seville by railway, and reached Cadiz late the same night, where, after some delay, I ascertained that a French steam frigate, the *Gorgone*, under the command of Captain Celliér de Starnor, was lying off the port, and would proceed the same night direct to Tangier.

"I lost no time in transmitting a request to Captain Starnor to allow me and my companions to embark in his beautiful ship. This request was at once most politely acceded to, and we were gladdened at 5 A.M. the next morning, Friday, the 11th inst., with the tidings that we had anchored off Tangier.

"We found, on our arrival at Tangier, that, owing to the care and kindness of Mr Moses Pariente, the President, Mr Moses Nahon, Vice-President, and the other members of the Executive Committee of the Hebrew Congregation here, an excellent house had been prepared for our reception ; and we were greeted with a most enthusiastic welcome by these respected gentlemen, and by the whole Jewish population. And here I may be permitted to say, before reverting to the more immediate purport of my Report, that I cannot sufficiently express my grateful appreciation of the demonstrations of regard, and evidences of good-will and kind-heartedness we were daily experiencing during my stay here, nor omit rendering a just tribute of praise to the intellectual and educational advancement distinguishing the gentlemen of our faith, and their families, resident at Tangier, with whom I have had the good fortune to be placed in contact since my arrival.

"Here also I have had the gratification to receive deputations from our co-religionists of Gibraltar, Tetuan, Alcassar, Larache, Arzila, and Mequinez. I have also received addresses from the Jews of Fez, Azemor, and Mogador.

"On Sunday, the 13th inst., I had the pleasure to wait on Sir John Hay Drummond Hay, K.C.B., the British Minister, and of conversing with him, and also Consul-General Reade, on the subject of the Mission. On the same day (accompanied by Mr Samuel), I placed in the hands of Don Francisco Merry y Colon, the Spanish Minister, the letter given to me by his father, also the letter of introduction entrusted to me at Madrid, by the Marquis of Miraflores, and several other letters, which I had obtained at Madrid.

"I am happy to say that I was most courteously received by the Spanish Minister, who gave me his willing consent for the immediate release of the two men, Shalom Elcaim and Jacob Benharrosh confined at Tangier ; and he also promised to place in my hands a letter to the Moorish Government, intimating the desire of the Spanish Government that the proceedings against the two unfortunate prisoners at Saffi, 'Saida and Mouklouf,' should be stopped. Within an hour of this interview with the Spanish Minister, we had the gratification of seeing the liberated prisoners, Shalom Elcaim and Jacob Benharrosh, at our residence.

"Although my interview with the Spanish Minister took place late on the afternoon of Sunday, yet, early in the forenoon of the following day (Monday, the 14th instant), I had the gratification to receive from him a note, expressing his satisfaction in complying with my request, and containing the promised letter. Immediately on the receipt of the letter I applied to Sir John H. D. Hay to introduce me, with Mr Samuel, to Sid Mohammed Bargash, Minister for Foreign Affairs at Tangier. Sir John accompanied us to the Minister, to whom I presented the letter from the Spanish Minister, and who expressed his pleasure at its contents, and promised to forward it instantly by special courier to his Sovereign at Morocco. He stated, however, that he feared a month would elapse ere a reply could be received.

"A letter to the Sultan was also transmitted at the same time from the British Minister, representing the desire of our own Government to the same effect as that of Spain.

"With the view to obtain the earliest possible release of the prisoners, I requested that the order for their liberation might be forwarded direct to Saffi.

"On the 16th instant we paid a visit of respect to the Rev. Mordecai Bengio, the Chief Rabbi, and also on the same day had the pleasure of being introduced by the British Minister, at their respective residences, to the Ministers of the several Powers at Tangier (France, Spain, United States, Italy, Portugal, &c.), to several of whom I had letters.

"On my return from visiting the Moorish Minister I found awaiting for me a deputation of upwards of fifty Moors, with their chiefs, from a distant part of the country, urging my intercession for the release from prison of one of their tribe, who had been in confinement for two years and a half, on suspicion of having murdered two Jews. As this unfortunate being had endured the horrors of a Moorish prison for so long a period on mere suspicion, and without having been brought to trial, I considered that his was a case in which I might with propriety intercede ; and I am happy to say that such intercession was successful, that within a few hours his chains were struck off, and he was brought to me by his tribe to return thanks for his deliverance, and the chiefs gave me their solemn pledge that they would be answerable for the safety of all Jews travelling by day in their country.

"I am induced to place great reliance on this pledge, because it is evident these men were unable to extend it for the safety of those who should incautiously travel by night.

"I am thankful to say that from the religious authorities here of the Catholics and the Moors I have also received evidence of respect and goodwill.

"I know the Sultan is most kindly disposed towards his Jewish subjects, and we may reasonably hope from this pleasing fact, and the kind assurances I received from all the Representatives of Foreign Powers in Tangier, that the Jews of Morocco may look forward to a brighter future.

"It remains for me only to add that, although in effect the objects of the Mission have, under God's blessing, been happily attained, still I do not consider that its work will have been fully done, nor that I ought to leave this vicinity until the actual liberation of the prisoners. I feel certain that the Sultan will, immediately on receipt of the despatches, give directions to that effect.

"I intimated in my telegram of the 15th instant that I contemplated a visit to the Sultan at Morocco. This will be with the object of thanking His Sheriffian Majesty for his gracious compliance with the request of the British and Spanish Governments, for his favourable disposition towards his Jewish subjects, and to entreat that His Sheriffian Majesty will extend to them his favour and protection, and direct the removal of the degrading grievances under which the Jews of the interior are still suffering. With objects so important, I shall not hesitate, before my return home, to encounter this long, fatiguing, and hazardous journey."

Sir Moses had no doubt of the innocence of the two unfortunate men who had been executed. "True," he says, "alas! we cannot recall the dead to life, but it is consolatory to reflect that, out of the unhappy events which gave rise to the Mission, good will follow; and it will indeed be a subject of rejoicing to us all to learn of the future welfare and prosperity of the vast Jewish population (nearly half a million of souls) in the Moorish Empire."

Tangier, December 21st.—Sir Moses sent to the President *pro tem.* a copy of a draft of the instructions which Don Francisco Merry y Colon, the Spanish Consul at Tangier, had directed to the Consuls, to the effect that Her Majesty the Queen of Spain had been greatly pained to hear that the Spanish Consuls in Morocco were accused of ill-treating the Jews; that it was her wish the Consuls should aid and protect the Jews, and avail themselves of every opportunity to prevent acts of cruelty on the part of the Moorish authorities, and the infliction of the lash or tortures to extract confessions.

From Tangier Sir Moses went to Gibraltar, and it was during his stay there that the sad intelligence reached him of the death, at Nice, of his sister, Mrs Goldsmid. He would have at once returned to England had he not felt it a duty to continue his journey in the sacred cause of suffering humanity; but the party lost the valuable co-operation of Mr Guedella, the son-in-law of Mrs Goldsmid, as he had to start at once for Nice. In a further report to the Board of Deputies Sir Moses says:

"Through the kindness of Earl Russell and the Naval Authorities here and at Malta, H.M. ship the *Magicienne*, Captain Armytage, R.N., has been sent from Malta to convey me to Saffi. She is now in port, and her departure is fixed for to-morrow evening.

"We embarked on board the *Magicienne*, Captain Armytage, on Tuesday evening, the 5th instant, and left the Port of Gibraltar early the following morning. We arrived off Saffi the following Saturday, the 9th instant, but it was not safe to land; we learned, however, that the Saffi prisoners had been set at liberty on the preceding Wednesday, the 6th instant.

"Not being able to land at Saffi, we proceeded onwards to Mogador, and arrived here the following morning, the 10th instant.

"The Sultan's escort was awaiting us at Saffi, but had to follow us here. The preparations for the journey to the City of Morocco are, however, as yet very incomplete, and probably we may have to wait here till Monday or Tuesday next, if not later. This, I can assure you, is a great trial of patience.

"On Friday night, the 8th instant, while at sea, part of the rudder of the ship broke, and on the following night we had a very heavy gale.

"The whole of our party, consisting, in addition to myself, of Dr Hodgkin, Mr Samuel, Captain Armytage, two of his officers, and Mr Consul Reade, with servants, &c., are being most hospitably entertained by Mr Abraham Corcos, one of the most opulent of the Jewish merchants at this port. The whole of his house is placed at our disposal."

On Tuesday, January 26th, Sir Moses wrote to the Board of Deputies :

"My last letter, dated the 14th instant, was addressed to you from Mogador. We experienced considerable difficulty in effecting the preliminary arrangements for our departure from Mogador, as a journey through a desert country, for so large a party, needed great care and foresight.

"At length we were enabled to fix on Sunday, the 17th instant, for the day of our departure. The bustle of preparation lasted from an early hour in the morning till between one and two in the afternoon. The Governor and his officers accompanied us to the gates of the city and for about an hour on our way; and our hospitable host, Mr Abraham Corcos, the Chief Rabbi, the Second Rabbi, and several other members of the Mogador Jewish Community, travelled with us the first day's journey, and stayed with us during our first night's encampment.

"Were I to attempt even an outline of each day's events, I should greatly exceed the limits of an official letter. Suffice it therefore to say, that we happily accomplished our journey from Mogador to this city in eight days, resting on the Sabbath. During this period we were subjected to a broiling sun by day, and cold and occasionally heavy dews and high winds by night. Nevertheless we have borne our fatigues well. Fortunately we escaped rain; otherwise, apart from every other inconvenience, we might have been detained for days in staying to pass rivers ; as it was, happily no such impediment arose. We were met at a short distance from Morocco (at which place we arrived yesterday at about 1 P.M.) by a guard of honour, and we were all located in a palace of the Sultan, in the midst of a garden ; and I can assure you that the change, after sleeping under canvas for so many nights, is most acceptable. The Jews here are not allowed to walk the streets except barefooted. It will be, indeed, a happy event for them, if I can induce the Sultan to do away with these degradingly distinctive marks, and also to place all his subjects, irrespective of faith, on an equal footing. Whether there is the remotest possibility of success in this, I am at present utterly unable to say. I am assured by every one, that the moral effect of my visit to Morocco will prove of advantage to my Moroquin co-religionists."

On the 17th February, Sir Moses informed the President *pro tem.* of the Board of Deputies, by telegram from Gibraltar, that he had succeeded in obtaining an Imperial Edict from His Sheriffian Majesty, and forwarded a translation by post to London. I therefore invite the reader's attention to the following translation of the address presented on that occasion to the Sultan, as well as of the latter's reply.

Edict of the Emperor of Morocco.

See Vol. II., page 153.

The Address to the Sultan.

To His Sheriffian Majesty THE SULTAN OF MOROCCO.

MAY IT PLEASE YOUR MAJESTY,—I come supported by the sanction and approval of the Government of Her Majesty the Queen of Great Britain, and on behalf of my co-religionists in England, my native country, as well as on the part of those in every part of the world, to entreat Your Majesty to continue the manifestation of Your Majesty's grace and favour to my brethren in your Majesty's Empire.

That it may please Your Majesty to give the most positive orders that the Jews and Christians dwelling in all parts of Your Majesty's dominions shall be perfectly protected, and that no person shall molest them in any manner whatsoever in anything which concerns their safety and tranquillity ; and that they may be placed in the enjoyment of the same advantages as all other subjects of Your Majesty, as well as those enjoyed by the Christians living at the ports of your Majesty's Empire : such rights were granted, through me, by His Imperial Majesty Abd-ool-Medjid, the late Sultan of Turkey, by his Firman, given to me at Constantinople, and dated 12th Ramazan, 1256, and, in the month of May last, confirmed by His Imperial Majesty Abdul Aziz, the present Sultan of Turkey.

Permit me to express to Your Majesty my grateful appreciation of the hospitable welcome with which Your Majesty has honoured me, and to offer to Your Majesty my heartfelt wishes for Your Majesty's health and happiness, and for the prosperity of Your Majesty's dominions.

Translation of the Imperial Edict.

In the Name of God, the Merciful and Gracious.   There is no power but in God, the High and Mighty.

(L. S.)

BE it known by this our Royal Edict—may God exalt and bless its purport and elevate the same to the high heavens, as he does the sun and moon !—that it is our command, that all Jews residing within our dominions, be the condition in which the Almighty God has placed them whatever it may, shall be treated by our Governors, Administrators, and all other subjects, in manner conformable with the evenly-balanced scales of Justice, and that in the administration of the Courts of Law they (the Jews) shall occupy a position of perfect equality with all other people ; so that not even a fractional portion of the smallest imaginable particle of injustice shall reach any of them, nor shall they be subjected to anything of an objectionable nature. Neither they (the Authorities) nor any one else shall do them (the Jews) wrong, whether to their persons or to their property.   Nor shall any tradesman among them, or artizan, be compelled to work against his will.   The work of every one shall be duly recompensed, for injustice here is injustice in Heaven, and we cannot countenance it in any matter affecting either their (the Jews) rights or the rights of others, our own dignity being itself opposed to such a course.   All persons in our regard have an equal claim to justice ; and if any person should wrong or injure one of them (the Jews), we will, with the help of God, punish him.

The commands hereinbefore set forth had been given and made known before now ; but we repeat them, and add force to them, in order that they may be more clearly understood, and more strictly carried into effect, as well as serve for a warning to such as may be evilly-disposed towards them (the Jews), and that the Jews shall thus enjoy for the future more security than heretofore, whilst the fear to injure them shall be greatly increased.

This Decree, blessed by God, is promulgated on the 26th of Shaban, 1280 (15 February 1864).   Peace !

CHAPTER XIX.

1864.

THE next letter Sir Moses addressed to the President *pro
tem.* of the Board of Deputies was dated Gibraltar,
February 24th.

"On Wednesday, the 27th ultimo, I was visited by deputations from the
several learned Jewish bodies in the city of Morocco. I should estimate the
number of my visitors to have amounted to between three and four hundred.
I fear, from their appearance, that they are in very poor circumstances ; yet
one cannot but admire their devotion to the study of our Holy Law.

"On Sunday, the 31st ultimo, I received an official intimation that the
Sultan would give our party a public reception on the following day.

"On Monday, the 1st instant, long before dawn, we could distinguish the
sounds of martial music, indicating the muster of the troops in and about
the environs of the Sultan's palace. At the early hour of 7 A.M., I had the
honour to receive a visit from Sid Taib El Yamany, the good and intelligent
Oozier, or Chief Minister of His Sheriffian Majesty, Sidi Mohamed Ben
Abderahman Ben Hisham, the present Sultan of Morocco. He expressed
the pleasure of the Sultan to receive us at his Court, and his Majesty's desire
to make our visit to his capital an agreeable one. Shortly after the departure
of the Oozier, the Royal Vice-Chamberlain, with a *cortége* of cavalry, arrived
at our palace to convey us to the audience.

"You may recollect that our party, in addition to myself, consisted of Mr
Thomas Fellowes Reade, Consul to Her Britannic Majesty at Tangier;
Captain William Armytage, of H.M.S. the *Magicienne*, two of his officers;
Dr James Gibson Thomas Forbes and Lieutenant Francis Durrant ; my
fellow-travellers, Dr Thomas Hodgkin, and Mr Sampson Samuel; and Mr
Moses Nahon, of Tangier, who had volunteered to accompany us to Morocco,
and to whom we are all deeply indebted.

"I have not stated in my previous letters that Senor José Daniel Colaco,
the Portuguese Minister at Tangier, kindly placed at my disposal his chaise-
a-porteurs to enable me to perform the journey over the rough and stony
plains of the interior of Morocco. To this were harnessed two mules, one
behind and one in front of the vehicle. I believe I should not have been
equal to the fatigue of travelling on horseback, and even as it was, this mode
of transit was very trying and fatiguing.

"A quarter of an hour's ride brought us to the gates opening upon an
avenue leading to the court-yard, or open space, before the palace.

" This avenue, which is of very considerable length, was lined on both sides by infantry troops of great variety of hue and accoutrements. They were standing in closely serried rank, and we must have passed several hundreds before emerging into the open plain. There a magnificent sight opened upon us; we beheld in every direction masses of troops, consisting of cavalry and foot soldiers. I should estimate the total number assembled on this occasion at not less than six thousand.

" We went forward some little distance into the plain, and saw approaching us the Oozier, the Grand Chamberlain, and other dignitaries of the Court. I descended from my vehicle, and my companions alighted from their steeds to meet them. We were cordially welcomed. We arranged ourselves in a line to await the appearance of the Sultan. This was preceded by a string of led white horses, and the Sultan's carriage covered with green cloth. His Majesty's approach was announced by a flourish of trumpets; he was mounted on a superb white charger, the spirited movements of which were controlled by him with consummate skill. The colour of the charger indicated that we were welcomed with the highest distinction.

" The countenance of His Majesty is expressive of great intelligence and benevolence.

" The Sultan expressed his pleasure in seeing me at his Court; he said my name was well known to him, as well as my desire to improve the condition of my brethren; he hoped that my sojourn in his capital would be agreeable; he dwelt with great emphasis on his long-existing amicable relations with our country; he also said it was gratifying to him to see two of the officers in its service at his Court.

" I had the honour, at this audience, to place in the hands of His Majesty my Memorial, on behalf of the Jewish and Christian subjects of his empire.

" After the interview we were escorted back to our garden palace with the same honours as had been paid to us on our way to the Court, my chair having a white horse led before it, as well on my going, as on my returning, which is a high and distinguished mark of honour.

" The Oozier had invited us to his palace for the evening of the same day; we were entertained with true oriental hospitality.

" In the course of the evening's conversation, we elicited from the Oozier, the assurance of the Sultan's desire, as well as his own, to protect the Jews of Morocco. He took notes of some particular grievances which we brought to his knowledge, and promised to institute the necessary enquiries, with a view to their being redressed. Other measures were discussed, such as the enlargement of the crowded Jewish quarters in Mogador, and the grant of a house for a hospital at Tangier, all of which the Oozier assured us should receive his favourable consideration.

" Arrangements had been made that the *Magicienne* should meet us at Saffi on the 8th instant, by which time we had expected we should be able to reach that port on our return from the Capital; but I had determined to await a response, favourable or otherwise, to my Memorial to the Sultan; nor was it considered desirable that we should proceed to Saffi. The surf there at all times runs very high, and great danger might have been incurred in attempting to pass through it, even if such attempt were deemed practicable.

" Under these circumstances, Captain Armytage resolved that he and Mr Durrant should leave Morocco on Thursday, the 4th instant, to meet his ship at Saffi at the time appointed, and to proceed therewith to Mazagan and await our arrival there.

" All our party accompanied him and Mr Durrant on Wednesday morning, the 3rd instant, on their farewell visit to the Oozier. I availed myself of this opportunity to represent to the Minister my anxiety to receive an early communication from the Sultan. The Oozier assured me that it would be such as would be satisfactory to me.

"On Friday, the 5th instant, the Imperial Edict, under the sign-manual of the Sultan, was placed in my hands.

"On the following day we received an intimation that His Majesty would receive us on Sunday morning, the 7th instant.

"Soon after 7 A.M., on that day, the Vice-Chamberlain arrived at our palace, with the same state as on the former occasion, and we were conducted, with like honour, to the palace; there was a similar display of troops, and this time the Emperor received us in a kiosk in the palace-gardens; he was seated on a mahogany sofa covered with green cloth. His Majesty renewed his friendly and courteous assurance of welcome, and expressed his hope that we had been happy and comfortable during our stay at his capital, and he renewed his assurance that it was his intention and desire to protect his Jewish subjects.

"He directed us to be conducted through his royal gardens by the chief of that department; they are very extensive, abounding in magnificent vineries, orange, olive, and other trees; there are two lakes of ornamental water, on one of which is a pleasure boat, with paddle wheels moved by mechanism. You may form some idea of the vast extent of the gardens, from the fact that it took us several hours to pass through some of the principal avenues.

"Immediately after quitting the royal gardens, we visited the Jewish quarter. The crowd was enormous, our reception enthusiastic. The narrow streets or lanes, through which we had the greatest difficulty to make our way, were all but choked up with our numerous friends; from every window, from the city wall, in fact wherever the eye rested, we beheld groups of our brothers and sisters all uniting to bid us welcome.

"We first went to one of the many Synagogues—the oldest and the largest, (though, I regret to say, a very humble structure). Here were assembled the Chief Rabbis and others to meet us; from thence we paid visits of respect to Mr Corcos, a relative of Mr Abraham Corcos, of Mogador, and Mr Nahon, a relative of Mr Moses Nahon, of Tangier, two of our most respected co-religionists in the City of Morocco.

"The same evening we were again entertained by the Oozier.

"On Monday, the 8th inst., about noon, we bade adieu to the city of Morocco, being escorted to some distance by a Guard of Honour of horse and foot soldiers, some of whom accompanied us until our arrival at Mazagan. The Sultan had provided me with a magnificent pavilion tent; in fact, our horses, mules, provisions, &c., &c., were all furnished at his expense. Mr Corcos, Mr Nahon, and several others of the principal Jews of Morocco travelled with us during our first day's journey, and encamped with us overnight. . . .

"On Thursday, the 11th inst., we were met on our way to our night's encampment by the son of the Governor of the District, accompanied by some fine cavalry soldiers. He brought us an invitation from his father to encamp for the night at his city, and pressed his request so earnestly that we could not in reason refuse compliance. This, however, involved considerable addition to our day's travel. We did not reach our destination until nightfall, having accomplished on that day a distance of about twenty-seven miles. The Governor, in addition to the usual mona, supplied us with a magnificent repast of cous-cous and other delicacies, which were pronounced by Mr Reade to be very savoury.

"We were all very much exhausted by our day's hard work. During the day I had been met by a deputation of about a hundred of our co-religionists from Saffi.

" In compliance with an urgent invitation from the Governor of another district, we consented to stay during Sabbath at his Palace, this being within a day's easy journey to Mazagan.

" We were met, on our approach to the town, or rather walled village, consisting almost entirely of tents and huts, by some of its Jewish inhabitants, the females bearing banners composed of silk handkerchiefs, embroidered muslin sashes, and other articles of female finery. I was informed that the Governor is very kind to the Jewish families. He appropriated one of his residences to myself and friends. We remained in this place from the Friday afternoon till the following Sunday morning, the 14th instant.

" The Governor presented me with a horse, and at the earnest entreaty of one of my co-religionists of Saffi I was obliged to accept a like gift from him.

" Here also I had the pleasure to see one of the liberated Saffi prisoners, who satisfied me that there had not existed the slightest cause for his imprisonment.

" When within about an hour's distance of Mazagan we were met by Mr Octavus Stokes, the British Consul at that port, the principal Christian and Jewish merchants, and by a procession of numerous co-religionists, the females carrying a profusion of banners, and vociferating their huzzas Moorish fashion, the shrill tones of which were intended to demonstrate an enthusiastic welcome.

" We caught soon after a glimpse of the sea, and then were gladdened with the sight of the *Magicienne* lying off the port, awaiting to re-conduct us to Gibraltar.

" As Captain Armytage was under the necessity of returning without delay, we were unable to make any stay at Mazagan, but as a house had been prepared by our Jewish friend for our reception, it was arranged that we should stay there over night, and embark early the next morning. Great preparations had been made for our evening repast—one bullock, two sheep, and I know not how many turkeys and fowls, with a profusion of other good things, had been supplied by our co-religionists.

" On reaching Mazagan I forthwith proceeded to the Synagogue to offer my grateful thanks to God for the prosperous issue of my mission, and for His gracious mercy in permitting the members of our perilous expedition to return thus far on our homeward travels in health and safety. It had taken us seven days, exclusive of the Sabbath, to travel from Morocco to Mazagan, the distance being about 120 miles."

In a letter, dated East Cliff Lodge, Ramsgate, 5th of April 1864, addressed to the President *pro tem.*, he gives the conclusion of the narrative of his mission :—

" My letter to you of the 11th ultimo informed you of my desire to place in the hands of Her Majesty the Queen of Spain a copy of the Sultan's Firman. I have now the gratification to tell you that on Friday, the 18th ultimo, I had the honour (accompanied by His Excellency Sir John F. Crampton) to have a second audience of Her Majesty, the King Consort being present. I presented to Her Majesty a copy of the Imperial Edict of the Sultan of Morocco, with a translation in Spanish, which were most graciously received by Her Majesty.

" On Sunday morning, the 20th ultimo, I left Madrid, and travelled by railway and carriage road for twenty-five hours continuously, so that I might arrive in time at Bayonne to attend the service of Purim at the Synagogue, which I was thus able to attend on Monday evening, the 21st, and Tuesday morning, the 22nd ultimo. I reached Paris on Thursday, the 24th, and on the following Thursday, the 31st ultimo, through the kind offices of His Excellency Lord Cowley, I had the honour of a private audience of His Imperial Majesty the Emperor of the French, at the Palace of the Tuileries, and placed in the hands of His Imperial Majesty a copy of the Sultan's Edict, with a translation in French; these were accepted in the most gracious manner. Doctor Hodgkin was present on the occasion. I left Paris yesterday."

Scarcely had Sir Moses arrived in England, when hearty welcomes reached him, not only from this country, but from all parts of the civilized world.

Two thousand addresses, alphabetically arranged, in the Lecture Hall of Judith, Lady Montefiore and Theological College, manifest in eloquent terms the appreciation of the services rendered by a man nearly eighty years of age.

At a public meeting, held at the London Tavern, on Wednesday, the 13th April—Mr Alderman Salamon in the chair—the following resolutions were unanimously adopted, on the motion of Sir Anthony de Rothschild, seconded by Mr Gladstone :—

That Moses Montefiore, by his philanthropic zeal in undertaking, at an advanced age, a laborious journey for the purpose of remonstrating against the cruelties inflicted on the Jews at Tangiers and Saffi, and by his successful representations to the Emperor of Morocco on behalf of all non-Mahometan subjects of that Empire, has rendered an important service to the cause of humanity, and that Sir Moses Montefiore has thus added to the many claims which he has already established on the gratitude and admiration of the Jewish community, and of his fellow citizens at large.

It was moved by Sir Francis H. Goldsmid, and seconded by Mr Wolverley Attwood,—

That an address expressive of these sentiments be presented, on behalf of this meeting, to Sir Moses Montefiore.

It was moved by Mr John Abel Smith, seconded by Mr Sergeant (now Sir John) Simon,—

That this meeting desires to express its deep obligation to Earl Russell (Her Majesty's Secretary of State for Foreign Affairs) for the readiness with which he afforded to Sir Moses Montefiore the countenance and support of the Government, and to offer its earnest thanks to Sir John Hay Drummond Hay (Her Majesty's Consul-General in Morocco), to Mr Consul

Reade, and to all those who personally aided in carrying into effect the objects, and thus contributed to the success of the journey.

It was moved by Mr Goschen, and seconded by Mr Jacob Waley,

That this meeting, bearing in mind the gracious reception accorded by His Majesty the Emperor of Morocco to the representations of Sir Moses Montefiore, Bart., wishes to record its high appreciation of the desire shown by that enlightened Sovereign to extend his protection and ensure justice to all classes of his subjects, without reference to religious creed, and that this meeting would be gratified if Her Majesty's Secretary of State for Foreign Affairs would communicate this resolution to His Majesty through the British Consul-General in Morocco.

It was moved by Mr A. Cohen, and seconded by Mr Henry Isaac, that this meeting contemplating with deep satisfaction the social and political equality now happily enjoyed by all the subjects of Her Majesty, feels pride and gratification in remarking how the example thus set has contributed to induce other countries to adopt the same beneficent principles.

SAMPSON LUCAS,	
SAUL ISAAC,	
ERNEST HART,	*Hon. Secs.*
JULIAN GOLDSMID,	

Meetings of a similar kind were held by all the Hebrew congregations and many public institutions in the British realm. Resolutions were adopted, and copies of the same conveyed to Sir Moses by their respective deputations ; but he did not consider that he had yet completed the work of the Mission.

He thought it desirable to address a letter to the Minister of State in Morocco urging him to see that full effect was given by the Governors and Pashas of provinces to the edict of the Sultan, and, in accordance with his own views on the subject, he sent a letter in the Moorish language to the Minister, of which I here give an exact translation :—

"GROSVENOR GATE, PARK LANE, LONDON,
"*June* 1, 1864.

" TO THE ILLUSTRIOUS OOZIER SID TAIB EL YAMINY, Minister of State, Morocco, &c., &c., &c.

" May it please your Excellency,—My heart is deeply impressed with thankfulness to your Excellency for the kind letter which your Excellency has so courteously transmitted to me in reply to that which I had the honour to address to your Excellency on the 23rd February last.

"Since my return to Europe I had the honour, while at Madrid, to place in the hands of her Catholic Majesty the Queen of Spain, a copy of the Imperial Edict of your august Sovereign, with a translation in the Spanish language; and while at Paris, to place in the hands of his Imperial Majesty the Emperor of the French a like copy, with a translation in the French language; also on my arrival in London I had the gratification to present to the Government of my beloved Sovereign a like copy, with an English translation.

"The Imperial Edict of his Sheriffian Majesty has obtained a world-wide celebrity, and has everywhere received the eulogies to which it is so eminently entitled.

"The friends of humanity and civilization throughout the world entertain the earnest hope and belief that your gracious Sovereign, and that you, illustrious Sir, will cause that edict to be known and respected by all the governors and officials in the empire of Morocco.

"There is too much reason to fear that there exists a disposition on the part of some of these governors and officials to ignore or disregard the benign commands of the Sultan, and that they are acting in direct contravention of the Sheriffian Majesty's high and exalted intentions, that his Jewish and other non-Mahomedan subjects shall be permitted to enjoy the benefits so humanely secured to them by his Sheriffian Majesty's glorious edict.

"These are indeed sad tidings. Oh, let not these oppressors be allowed to persevere in their wrongdoing. I entreat the immediate and effectual interposition of his Sheriffian Majesty and of your Excellency. The Imperial Edict went forth as a beam of light to my co-religionists in Morocco. Suffer not, I implore you, its brightness to be dimmed, its effulgence to be extinguished. It imparted joy and promise. Permit not that joy to be destroyed, that promise to remain unfruitful.

"Hundreds of thousands of human beings in Morocco raised their voices in praise and thankfulness to God for the benign desire of his Sheriffian Majesty and of your Excellency to ameliorate their condition, and to remove from them oppression and suffering. Let it not be that their fond hopes are a vain shadow; that their cheering anticipations of a brighter future are a delusive dream.

"How great and how sacred are the prerogatives of Majesty! It directs its people's welfare, and their path is bedecked with flowers; it forbears to punish their oppressors, and that path is beset with thorns.

"I know full well, and have personally experienced the kindness of your august Sovereign and of your Excellency, and therefore I rely with firm faith on the generous promises which I have received, that the Imperial Edict should be promulgated throughout the Moorish empire, and its provisions strictly enforced.

"Happy, most happy are the nations dwelling in peace and security! Glorious, most glorious are the rulers to whose wisdom and humanity, inspired by Almighty God, the people look up for the perpetuity of these blessings.

"Condescend, illustrious Sir, to consider these my humble words spoken in the fulness of my heart and with most truthful earnestness.

"Deign to convey my assurances of respect to your august Sovereign, and to receive with favour my wishes for his and your health and welfare, and for the prosperity of the Moorish empire,—I have the honour to remain, your Excellency's faithful and obedient servant,

"(Signed)   MOSES MONTEFIORE."

Two months later the Minister sends a most satisfactory reply, of which I also subjoin a translation :—

"Praise be to the only God.
There is no strength and no power
but in God the Most High.
From him who is the servant of God, the Secretary of State,
and the Noble Commander, whose name from God is
SID TAIB EL YAMINY,
to the beloved, wise, and most benevolent
SIR MOSES MONTEFIORE, Bart.

"After rendering praise to God the Most High, we beg to inform you that we have received your letter describing the gracious reception accorded to you by the different monarchs, their appreciation of the object which has been accomplished, and the advantages derived therefrom. All mankind will give thanks to you for the readiness and devotion to the good cause which you manifested by bringing the present under the special notice of the great Powers.

"With regard to your statement respecting the affairs of the Jewish subjects of our Lord, whom God may preserve in strength, we have to observe that they are his subjects, and he—may God preserve him and perpetuate his glory and greatness—does not like that they should be pursued by acts of injustice and torment in their unfortunate position ; because God the Most High forbids injustice towards people professing our religion, and He likewise forbids injustice toward people professing any other religion.

"Our Lord—may God grant him support—has already commanded the inhabitants of all the other provinces in his Empire, that his Jewish subjects should be treated with kindness and strict justice, so that no wrong whatever be done to any of them. He also rebuked them (the inhabitants of all the other provinces of his Empire), by the power and strength of God, for the injustice they have done. We have not forgotten your polite attention, and the kindness evinced in your letter ; we shall never fail to watch rigorously the proceedings of the officials in the provinces of our Lord, whom may God preserve.

"Completed in the month of Mohharam, in the year 1281 of the Hidjrah."

Sir Moses sent an address to the Spiritual Chiefs and Elders of the Morocco Jews, counselling them to inculcate in their poorer and less educated brethren, the necessity of uniform obedience and respect to the Moorish authorities. The danger that the Jews might lose some of the benefits conferred by the recent edict of the Emperor, by exciting the hostility of the Moorish authorities by too independent a tone in demanding the equal treatment with Mohammedans ordered by the Sultan, was mentioned in letters from Barbary, and Sir Moses, whose intercession had already done so much for the Morocco Jews, wisely counselled patience under petty injuries and submission to the authorities, as the best means of preventing the just and generous intentions of the Sultan from being defeated by the fanaticism of his Mohammedan subjects.

II.   L.

CHAPTER XX.

1864.

SIR MOSES RECEIVES THE THANKS OF THE CITY OF LONDON—
THE PROJECTED SURVEY OF JERUSALEM—BAD NEWS FROM
ROME, HAMADAN, AND JAFFA—ENDOWMENT OF JUDITH
COLLEGE, RAMSGATE—DEATH OF LORD PALMERSTON.

THURSDAY, October 6th.—We meet **Sir Moses** in the Guildhall, surrounded by the most influential merchants and bankers of the City of London, standing before the Lord Mayor, and receiving from him the resolution of thanks voted by the Corporation.

The Lord Mayor, addressing Sir Moses, who remained standing on the dais during the ceremony, said :

"Sir Moses Montefiore, this Court, as representing the citizens of London, has from time immemorial voted the freedom of this City to distinguished naval commanders and to renowned soldiers, who have prized the honour exceedingly. It has also voted the freedom to statesmen, to patriots, to philanthropists, and to those who have devoted their time, their energies, and their money to alleviate the sufferings of humanity. (Cheers.) To you, Sir Moses Montefiore, a distinguished member of the Hebrew community, this great city has voted a resolution of thanks, expressive of their approval of the consistent course you have pursued for a long series of years, of the sacrifices you have made, of the time you have spent, and of the wearisome journeys you have endured, in order not only to alleviate the sufferings of your co-religionists, but at the same time to alleviate the sufferings and miseries of people of all creeds and denominations. (Cheers.) It gives me great pleasure, Sir Moses Montefiore, to be the medium of presenting to you this resolution, and of congratulating you upon being enrolled among those whom this city has thought worthy to receive the tribute of their respect and admiration. (Cheers.) This city has at all times been most anxious on all occasions to evince its sympathy with suffering humanity, irrespective of creed, of colour, and of country, and I beg to shake you by the hand.' (Cheers.)

Sir Moses Montefiore replied :

"Lord Mayor and Gentlemen of the Corporation, I am so deeply impressed by the high compliment you have just been pleased to offer me that I fear my emotion will incapacitate me from conveying to you in adequate terms my thanks and gratitude.

"Vividly recalling how many, distinguished by their brilliant achievements, in war, in science, in art, and by general service to mankind, have enjoyed in your hall the cordial reception with which you have this day greeted me, my heart glows with feelings of delight that you have estimated so favourably my humble endeavours in the cause of humanity.

"The Imperial edict which, through the Divine blessing, I had the happiness to obtain from His Sheriffian Majesty the Sultan of Morocco, securing to the Jews and Christians in his dominions the same rights and privileges which are enjoyed by other classes of his subjects, constitutes a bright epoch in the history of that Empire, and must assuredly tend to advance its prosperity.

"Permit me to present for your acceptance a copy of this important edict, and beg for it a record in the minutes of your Court.

"Mindful of my long and valued association with the Corporation of the City of London, and of the high and responsible office to which I was elected by the confidence of my fellow-citizens in the first year of the reign of our beloved Queen, and remembering how nobly and how successfully your ancient Corporation has toiled for religious freedom, I am the more gratified by the distinguished honour I have this day received—an honour I shall ever bear in grateful remembrance.

"My Lord Mayor and Gentlemen, I thank you most heartily for your kindness, and I offer you my earnest wishes for the continued prosperity of this great Corporation, and for your individual welfare."

Sir Moses, accompanied by the mover of the resolution, Mr Alderman (now Sir) Benjamin Phillips, then retired from the hall amidst the cheers and applause of the numbers who had assembled to witness the gratifying scene.

A copy of the resolution, beautifully emblazoned with the city arms, as well as those of the Lord Mayor and Sir Moses, and surrounded by paintings representing the Missions of Sir Moses, may be seen in the Lecture Hall of the College. It is greatly admired by visitors for its elegant execution.

"Nothing," Sir Moses observes in his Diary, "could have exceeded the courtesy of the Lord Mayor, Aldermen, and Common Council. I was delighted with the Lord Mayor's address, and I am happy to say they were pleased with my reply."

A copy of the edict of His Sheriffian Majesty and Sir Moses' speech had been entered in the minutes of the Court, and a copy sent to each of the members.

Sir Moses then attended the afternoon and evening service at the Spanish and Portuguese Synagogue, receiving congratulations from all present.

In the Court Circular, dated Windsor Castle, June 20th, we find a notice:

"His Highness Mustapha Pasha, the Turkish Ambassador, and Sir Moses Montefiore arrived at the Castle to-day from London.

"Sir Moses Montefiore had an audience of Her Majesty."

We may infer, from the gracious receptions which Her Majesty on several former occasions had given to Sir Moses, that, in the present instance, she did not fail to manifest her approbation of his Mission to Morocco.

September 25th.—We meet him at his favourite retreat, Smithembottom.

"I have great cause," he says, "for thankfulness. Since I was here in November last, I hope that, by Divine blessing, I have been of some use to my fellow-creatures, both Jews and Christians, and, I believe I may add, 'Moors.' To God alone, who helped and sustained me, be honour and glory. I believe that my dear Judith would have approved my conduct, and, sure I am, had it pleased an all-wise Providence to have spared her, she would have shared my fatigue and dangers, but it was otherwise ordained, and I can only submit with humble spirit to the decree of Heaven. My angel guide of so many happy years being no longer with me on earth in mortal form, I sincerely pray the God of Israel to be my guide, and to permit her heavenly spirit to comfort me, and keep me in the right path, so that I may become deserving of the happiness to rejoin her in Heaven when it shall please God to call me from the world."

"A visit to Smithembottom," he remarks in his Diary, "is now to me very similar to that of the solemn 'Day of Atonement,' with the exception of fasting. I hope hours spent in serious reflection on the past incidents of a long life tend to make me better, and constitute a great moral lesson."

Sir Moses now contemplated establishing a college for the study of theology and Biblical literature in Jerusalem. "I have," he says, "with, I hope, the Divine blessing, resolved on establishing in the Holy Land, in memory of my ever-lamented and blessed wife, a college (Beth Hamedrásh), with ten members, to erect ten houses with gardens for their dwelling, with a certain yearly allowance to them, and to purchase and send them a good Hebrew library for their use." He hoped to go there and purchase the land, and to lay the foundation-stone. This idea, however, he soon relinquished for a similar institution in Ramsgate, to which I shall have an opportunity further on in this work to direct the attention of the reader.

December 7th.—He received from Mr (now) Lord Hammond, of the Foreign Office, by permission of Lord Russell, despatches from Sir John Drummond Hay, and a letter from him, addressed to Sir Moses, also despatches for his perusal from Athens and Corfu, all of which were most satisfactory. "It was, indeed," Sir Moses says, "truly kind of Earl Russell and Mr Hammond to favour me with the perusal of them."

Earl Russell, as well as all his successors at the Foreign Office, have repeatedly afforded him opportunities to read despatches received from their Ambassadors and Consuls at Foreign Courts, whenever they contained any important communication regarding the Jews.

Sir Moses was enabled to attend his meetings in the city, notwithstanding the great fatigue he had undergone during his journey, and was as ready and eager as ever with his suggestions for improvements in any measure of financial importance.

On the recurrence of the anniversary of his birthday, which this year was the eightieth, he sent his usual gifts to communal schools and charities in England, as well as to those in the Holy Land, conveying to the latter his hope to pay them another visit soon.

Some readers who have attentively perused the narrative of Sir Moses' Mission to Morocco, will perhaps say that since the issuing of the Sultan's edict twenty-three years ago, His Sheriffian Majesty's commands contained therein do not seem to have been very strictly adhered to. The Moors say, and apparently with good reason, "To promise is not the same as to perform." Their observation seems just, when we find that, notwithstanding the promises made by the Sultan to Sir Moses, he continued to receive complaints from almost every Hebrew community of the oppression and ill-treatment to which they had been subjected. Still one must bear in mind, that even in European countries rights and privileges granted by a sovereign would be many a time, intentionally or unintentionally, withdrawn from loyal subjects by those appointed to carry out the will of the reigning monarch, were it not for the numerous votaries of the cause of justice who are ever ready to bring before the court those who thus wilfully violate the rights of others. But such is not the case in Morocco. Even the lovers of justice cannot always succeed in making known to the Sultan the acts of cruelty committed by the local governors or military officers. As this would necessitate long and tedious journeys before reaching the Palace, and should they reach it in safety, there is yet another difficulty to encounter in procuring evidence, witnesses being in general very reluctant to testify against any man in power. Thus it happens that injustice is practised by some of the local governors with impunity; but there is every reason to believe that the Sultan himself, as far as lay in his power, strictly adhered to the words of the edict.

The Sultan gave his word in the presence of the representative of the English Government, and would not, if reminded of it by Her Majesty's Government, withdraw his promise.

East Cliff, February 6th.—Sir Moses, being anxious to see if anything could be done through the medium of the English officers of engineers then at Jerusalem, with regard to the water supply there, he proceeded to London. "In spite of old age and weakness," he says, "I would willingly undergo any fatigue and risk to benefit Jerusalem." He called at Adam Street for a copy of the resolution on the subject passed by the Committee of the Syrian Relief Fund during his absence, went to the Athenæum to see Mr John Freeland, and called on Sir John Macneil.

February 9th.—He went to Southampton on a visit to the Ordnance Survey Office, where he had a long interview with Sir Henry James with reference to the survey of Jerusalem, then being carried out by a party of engineers belonging to that department—a work in which, as may readily be imagined, Sir Moses took the deepest interest. Sir Henry presented him with a beautiful photograph of the wailing wall at Jerusalem, with which Sir Moses expressed himself highly gratified.

February 15th.—He attended a meeting of the Syrian Improvement Fund Committee, Mr Layard, Mr Hodgkin, and several other members being present, when £100 was voted for the use of Captain Wilson and the engineers at Jerusalem towards the expenses of excavations, &c., for the purpose of finding a mode of providing Jerusalem with a better supply of water.

February 16th.—Count P. de Strezelski wrote a letter, by desire of Miss Coutts (now Baroness Burdett-Coutts), to learn whether they could venture on some steps to improve the lamentable and humiliating state of the Jewish community at Rome. In spite of the snow, Sir Moses went to see the Count, and told him that he believed no good could be achieved by agitation ; but perhaps a mild and very quiet application, personally made at Rome on behalf of the Jews, might be successful. "I would," Sir Moses says, "if this plan was favourably received, go at my own personal expense to Rome."

The Count, wishing to have Miss Coutts' advice, and Sir Moses being himself desirous of expressing to her his thanks for her kind and benevolent solicitude for the welfare of his co-religionists, they drove to Piccadilly, but as Miss Coutts was not at home, the Count promised to see her in the evening, and report to Sir Moses by letter to Ramsgate.

Sir Moses then called on the President and Secretary of the Board of Deputies in reference to the same subject. Both agreed with them as to the impossibility of moving the Pope by public agitation, and would not express any hope that good could in any way be obtained for the Jewish inhabitants at Rome. However, Sir Moses says, "I am ready at all risk to try it, if the mode I suggest shall meet with the approval of Earl Russell, and I have his powerful support in my Mission. No time should be lost."

March 25th.—An alarming letter reached him from the Hebrew community at Hamadan (the ancient city of Shooshan) in Persia. They were suffering terribly from persecutions by the Persians, and appealed to him for his intercession with the Shah in their behalf. "The weather has been very rough and cold, with rain, wind, and sleet," he writes. "I could not sleep last night for thinking of our poor suffering brethren in Persia." Early in the morning he commenced making inquiries regarding travelling in Persia, and left East Cliff for London to take the letter he had received to the Chief Rabbi, who, he found, had already received a similar one.

In order to gather further information regarding Persian affairs, he went to see the lady whose son he had placed at the Bluecoat School, and who was well acquainted with Teheran. "I found her," he says, "a very intelligent woman, about forty years of age. She first went to Persia when she was thirteen years old, and married there. She lived in Persia twenty-six years, and had been to England three times during that period.

She went from Liverpool to Constantinople by sea, was then about ten days on the Black Sea, and afterwards journeyed one thousand miles on horseback to Teheran. She described the climate as being good, but very hot in summer—too hot to travel by day."

March 28th.—He called on Mr Layard (now Sir Austen H. Layard), presenting him with his (Sir Austen's) bust, which Sir Moses had ordered of Mr Wiener, a distinguished sculptor of Brussels. Sir Austen received it with great pleasure. Sir Moses spoke of the letter from Hamadan, and offered to go there to obtain a firman from the Shah, if Sir Austen would give him letters. Sir Austen said he should have every assistance, and as many letters as he wished, if he went, and that he would write to Mr Alison, our representative at the Court at Teheran. Sir Moses then gave him the translation of the Hamadan letter, which Sir Austen read with great attention. Sir Moses said he intended to start on the 1st of May, upon which Sir Austen informed him that Mr Alison should be instructed to afford him every assistance and information as to the best mode of reaching the capital.

" But could not some plan be found to save you from so long and dangerous a journey?" asked Sir Austen. He proposed that Sir Moses should write in his own name to the Shah, and state what he had obtained from the Sultan at Constantinople and the Sultan of Morocco in favour of their Jewish subjects, and to send him copies of the firman and edict, with a petition for a similar edict from him. Sir Austen said he would forward Sir Moses' letter to the British Minister at Teheran to present it to the Shah, which he thought would answer the purpose, and save him great fatigue and risk.

Sir Austen presented him with a most beautiful copy of his large work, containing an account of his researches in connection with the excavations at Babylon. Sir Moses asked for one of his smaller works instead, but Sir Austen said, " You have had your way, and now I must have mine." After mature consideration, and acting upon the advice of Sir Austen, Sir Moses gave up the idea of a journey to Persia, but wrote an address to the Shah, praying for a firman in favour of his brethren, and Lord Russell was good enough to forward it to its destination through Mr Alison, the British Minister at Teheran.

Having abandoned the scheme of building a Theological College in Jerusalem, he was determined to have one near his Synagogue in Ramsgate, in memory of his wife, and made an agreement with this object with a local builder. " May God in His mercy and goodness," he prays, " grant that the inhabitants of the intended College may devote themselves to the study of His Holy Laws, and may they find peace and happiness in their dwellings." On Saturday evening, the 24th of June, the eve of the new moon of **Tamuz**, 5625 A.M., he laid the foundation stone of the College, in the presence of his relatives and friends. In the same month he made the first remittance of £50 to the inmates of the Juda Touro Almshouses in Jerusalem. In the succeeding years he considerably increased these remittances, and continued forwarding them up to his death. To Mr Hyde Clarke of Smyrna he sent a similar sum, to be distributed by that gentleman among the indigent sick at that place; and to Jerusalem he forwarded a case of medicines for the Dispensary.

August the 27th.—Sir Moses had scarcely despatched his appeal to the Shah on behalf of his brethren at Hamadan, in Persia, when a heartrending cry came from the Holy Land, an unusual combination of misfortunes having befallen them. " No rain had fallen for many months, the harvest was spoilt, locusts covered the ground for miles around, the cholera had broken out in all its fury, famine and plague reigned supreme in the Holy Cities.

" The fatal disease commenced its ravages on the coast of Egypt, and raged furiously in Alexandria; with intense virulence it advanced to the city of Jaffa, and devastated it. The corpses of the dead lay in the streets unburied, the living fled on every side, and the once bustling seaport town was stricken with terror and awed into silence. All the towns and villages between Jaffa and Jerusalem were affected. The gates of the latter were closed, so that none could come out or go in. The city was in a state of siege, and the inspectors of quarantine surrounded it.

" The representatives of all the congregations combined to do all in their power to alleviate the distress, but their funds were exhausted, the plague showed no signs of abating, and they sent forth their piteous cry for help to their brethren abroad."

The Chief Rabbi and Sir Moses at once invited the attention

of the London Committee of Deputies of the British Jews to the distressing condition of the Jews in Palestine, asking their powerful aid, and suggesting that they should issue an appeal to all the congregations in the British Empire. To this the Board of Deputies readily agreed, and immediately published an appeal in all the leading papers. The result was most satisfactory. The contributions to the appeal fund amounted to a large sum, and, knowing the willingness of Sir Moses to assist personally in the administration of the same, the Board invited him to proceed to Jerusalem for that purpose.

Sir Moses, without hesitation, disregarding his advanced age and feeble state of his health, accepted the invitation, and promised to proceed to the Holy City as soon as the necessary preparations for such a journey would permit.

Before giving the reader a full account of this fresh journey to the Holy Land, I have still to bring to his notice some entries in his Diary of the current year.

October 19th.—"The *Times* of to-day," he writes, "gave me the mournful intelligence of the death of that great and good man, Lord Palmerston. I most sincerely grieve at his loss. I have had very many interviews with his Lordship, and he was on every occasion most kind and friendly. He was ever ready to attend to any representation I had to make on behalf of the Board of Deputies. On my return from Morocco, the last time I spoke to him, he was kindness itself. Peace to his honest soul. May he rest in Heaven."

November 1st.—Sir Moses endowed the Judith College; and on the 15th of the same month he considered the constitution of the same, which he subsequently submitted to his friends to ascertain their views on the subject.

December 31st.—Notwithstanding the severity of the weather, he frequently went to town and attended the meetings of companies and associations.

CHAPTER XXI.

1866.

JANUARY 26th, 1866.—Sir Moses had the satisfaction of hearing from the Foreign Office that the grievances of which the Jews of Persia complained, and which were happily now about to be removed, where unknown to the Shah. Sir A. H. Layard thus addresses him on the subject:

"FOREIGN OFFICE, *January 26th*, 1866.

"DEAR SIR,—I have much pleasure in informing you, by direction of the Earl of Clarendon, that it appears, from a report which has this day been received from Her Majesty's Minister in Persia, that in consequence of his representations with respect to your petition to the Shah, His Majesty has addressed an autograph letter to the Sipeh-salar, in which he signifies to his Prime Minister that it has come to his knowledge that his Jewish subjects suffer from oppression ; and that being contrary to his wishes, the Sipeh-salar is strictly enjoined to see that the Jews are henceforward treated with justice and kindness."

When this communication became known, Sir Moses received many letters of congratulation on his success ; but the appreciation of his exertions only prompted him to expedite as much as possible his preparations for his next journey to Jerusalem.

February 17th.—He attended Divine service, at eight o'clock in the morning, at the Spanish and Portuguese Synagogue. The Lord Mayor, Sir Benjamin Philips, was present, and opened the Ark containing the Sacred Scrolls of the Penta- teuch, when a special prayer was offered up for a prosperous journey for Sir Moses. In the afternoon he attended Divine service at the great Synagogue of the German Congregation, where the Chief Rabbi offered up a special prayer, which was also done in all the other Synagogues.

February 18th.—He went for a day's retirement to Smithembottom. "I find," he says, "I am gradually getting weaker, but I am indeed most grateful for the many blessings I have so long enjoyed."

February 26th.—Sir Moses left Ramsgate for Dover, where he met Mr and Mrs Sebag (now Sebag Montefiore), Dr Hodgkin, and the writer, who were to be his companions on this journey.

I shall now give the reader an account of the Mission, but for the more important facts I shall use his own words as addressed to the Board of Deputies.

On Tuesday morning, the 27th February, we left England, travelling *viâ* Paris and Marseilles to Alexandria. On arriving at this world-famous city, we repaired to the Synagogue, the Kenees Eleeyahoo, which is built on the spot where it is said the celebrated Temple of Alexandria, or Onias, once stood (modern authors maintain that the "Temple of Onias" was at a place known by the name of "Tel-el-yahood"), and there offered thanks to our Heavenly Father for having guided us safely to the shores of Egypt. On stepping into the boat at Alexandria Sir Moses hurt his foot. This necessitated a stay of a few days, which he devoted to the arrangement of all the documents which might be required for use in the Holy Land, and also to receiving information brought to him by Haham Joseph Burla and other persons from Jerusalem. On Sunday, the 18th of March, we left Alexandria, and arrived at Jaffa the next day about 1.30 P.M. On landing Sir Moses was received by his Excellency the Governor of the town, by the Judge, the Commander of the Troops, and the representatives of the various religious denominations. Numerous deputations called to congratulate him on his safe arrival. Mr Consul Moore, who came purposely to welcome him, most kindly made all the necessary arrangements for the journey to the Holy City. In order to ascertain the cause of the destitution which there prevailed, and to devise proper plans for removing it, Sir Moses caused certain statistical forms and documents to be prepared, in which returns were to be made of the number of synagogues, colleges, schools, charities, and institutions belonging to our co-religionists in the Holy Land, as well as the ages, property, occupations, and families of its inhabitants. A similar method was adopted by Sir Moses in 1838.

For the purpose of having the blanks in these papers properly filled up, they were distributed amongst the representatives of the several congregations in the Holy Land, then present at Jaffa, and messengers were despatched with like papers to the authorities of distant congregations.

It was Sir Moses' intention to proceed to Jerusalem after only one day's sojourn at Jaffa, but this intention was frustrated by the illness of Dr Hodgkin. "Being most reluctant to leave him," Sir Moses writes, "I remained with him up to the latest moment, until it became absolutely necessary to depart for Jerusalem, in order to arrive there in time for the Passover holidays. At this time I received descriptions of the sufferings and fearful loss of life occasioned to our unfortunate brethren by the recent outbreak of the cholera. Very frequently these afflicting narratives were interrupted by the appearance upon our windows of the new and still green locusts, which we were informed were the much dreaded forerunners of another bad season. Many a morning, before sunrise, we heard the rattling of the drum to awaken the inhabitants of Jaffa to the fulfilment of their duty, each to collect a measure of locusts before daybreak, so that the threatening enemy might be destroyed, for the appearance of these locusts is the more dreaded on account of the belief that it always brings in its train some epidemic disease, the woeful consequences of which had so recently been experienced.

"While at Jaffa I had frequently expressed my strong desire either to remain there with my lamented friend, to take him with me to Jerusalem, or to relinquish my journey thither, and return with him to Europe ; but all my friends assured me that it would be most imprudent for Dr Hodgkin to travel at that time, and that the best and only advisable course was to let him remain in the house of Mr Kyát, the British Consular Agent, under the most kind and watchful attendance of that gentleman and of his family, with whom he had been staying since our arrival at Jaffa. Advice so earnestly urged, I could not but follow. Accordingly, on Sunday, the 25th of March, having previously secured the professional services of Dr Sozzi, the physician of the Lazaretto, and left my own English servant, and likewise engaged another, to be constantly in attendance on my esteemed friend, I reluctantly quitted Jaffa for Jerusalem, after paying a farewell visit to my friend, in the full hope of being soon rejoined by him, and having for this purpose left for his convenience the Takhteerawán,* which the Governor of Jerusalem had kindly sent to Jaffa for my own use. This hope, however, was not destined to be realised. Unfortunately the state of health of my lamented friend had not been, previously to his departure from England, as satisfactory as his friends could have wished ; and, indeed, he left home to accompany me on my journey, in the hope and belief that the voyage and change of air would prove beneficial to him. I have at least much consolation in reflecting that all that could be done was made available for the preservation of his valuable life.

"It has pleased the Almighty to take him from us, and that he should not again behold his loving consort and beloved relatives ; he breathed his last in a land endeared to him by hallowed reminiscences. To one so guileless, so pious, so amiable in private life, so respected in his public career, and so desirous to assist with all his heart in the amelioration of the condition of the human race, death could not have had any terror.

"I trust I may be pardoned for this heartfelt but inadequate tribute to the memory of my late friend. His long and intimate association with me, and with my late dearly beloved wife, his companionship in our travels, and the vivid recollection of his many virtues, make me anxious to blend his name, and the record of his virtues, with the narrative of these events.

"On leaving Jaffa, I was escorted on my way by the dignitaries of the town, accompanied by a large number of persons, cavasses, and soldiers. They proceeded a few hours' ride, until we reached the village of Ramlah. On approaching this village, we were met by its governor with troops, and, thus escorted, entered Ramlah, and took up our abode there at the Russian Hospice, where we found all the comforts a traveller could desire. On Monday, the 26th of March, we continued our journey as far as Aboo Goosh, supposed to be the Kiryát Yeárim of Scripture, where Abinádáb dwelt, in whose house, on the top of the hill, the Ark of the Lord had been placed, when taken from the Philistines of Beth Shémásh. The present chief, Mahommed Effendi Aboo Goosh, a man of great authority and importance,

---

* A Sedan chair.

sent his brother to invite us to his house, and subsequently came himself to request the acceptance of his hospitality, a request with which I readily complied. The house of our host was situate on the summit of the hill, and the road to it was so rough and precipitous that I thought many a time my Takhteerawán would break to pieces. The fatigue, however, which I endured was amply compensated by the cordial hospitality with which I was welcomed.

"Many deputations from Jerusalem and Hebron had arrived during the night, and on our leaving the village of Aboo Goosh, at an early morning hour, there could be seen from the neighbouring hills a considerable number of persons directing their course towards us, and not far from the Village Colonia I had the pleasure of again meeting our excellent Consul, Mr Noel Moore, who came from Jerusalem to welcome me. I was told, as we proceeded, of the great sufferings which the people of Jerusalem had endured during the prevalence of the epidemic, and was assured in glowing words of the benefit which the people anticipated from my visit, expecting, as they did, to receive direct relief from me. This clearly proved the difficulty and delicate nature of the task that lay before me, for my principal object in visiting Jerusalem was not so much to afford pecuniary aid to the people, as to ascertain what could be done for them, so as to remove the more permanent causes of their trouble.

"Every moment brought new comers, until a few hours' journey from the Holy City, the road and the adjacent hills became covered with a concourse of people of all the different denominations. His Highness, Izzet Pasha, the Governor of Jerusalem, sent forty horsemen and cavasses, headed by their officer. My old friend, Akhmed Agha Dizdar, formerly the Governor of Jerusalem under Mohammad Ali, also came with his grandson and a number of his followers, the Rev. Haïm David Házán, the Háhám Bashi, mounted on a beautiful Arab steed, accompanied by the members of his ecclesiastical court—the spiritual heads of the German congregation—the Rev. Samuel Salant, the Rev. Meyer Auerbach, and all the members of their ecclesiastical court. I believe, I may say without exaggeration, there were to be seen all our brethren from Jerusalem who were capable of leaving the city, headed by the representatives of their synagogues, colleges, and schools, all hailing my approach with the exclamation,* 'Bárookh Hábá,' 'Blessed be he who cometh.' By the roadside stood hundreds of children, singing Hebrew hymns, which had been specially composed for the occasion, and in which were recited the sufferings of Zion, and the hope in Israel's future. I particularly noticed forty boys from the Simon Edlen von Lämels school, whose healthy and neat appearance, and beautifully harmonious voices, added greatly to the impressiveness of a scene not easily to be forgotten. In truth, what I then beheld, not without deep emotion, firmly convinced me that a sincere interest in the welfare of the Holy Land does not, and will not fail to arouse in the hearts of its inhabitants an enthusiastic acknowledgment.

"We alighted for a short time to recite the customary prayers at the site where the pilgrim or traveller first obtains a glimpse of the Holy City, and afterwards proceeded to tents prepared for our reception by the Háhám Báshi. Here refreshments were provided, and congratulatory hymns chanted, but I would not tarry, being anxious without delay to enter within the walls of Jerusalem; and again we were met by crowds of persons crossing from the Hebron road, who joined in procession towards the Jaffa Gate. On our arrival at the gate, we halted to listen to the prayer of one of the chief officers of the synagogue, in which he invoked God's blessing on the mes-

* בָּרוּךְ הַבָּא

senger from a distant land, a prayer to which the vast concourse of persons responded with a heart-stirring 'Amen !'

"My first duty on entering Jerusalem was to repair to the synagogue 'Kenees Istambooli,' there to render thanks to my Heavenly Father for having permitted me to see Jerusalem this the sixth time ; then after prayers and thanksgiving from all present, we proceeded, amid shouts of joy from the people, to the estate known as 'Kérém Moshe Vĕ Yĕhoodit,' situate on the Hill of Gichon.

"I had previously made known my willingness to receive communications from every individual desirous of addressing me, either on his own behalf or on that of the people in general. I had also appointed stated times for the reception of all who might wish to address me personally, and every available moment was employed in collecting from all sources information that might be useful.

"A guard of honour from the Governor, as well as the cavasses of the English Consul and of the Háhám Báshi, were stationed day and night around our dwelling.

"The first day of our arrival was devoted to the distribution of the remittances, which had been entrusted to me by several friends of Jerusalem, with a special request to dispense the same to the poor.

"I also despatched letters and messages to persons who might be able to furnish useful information, and thus amidst a numerous assembly of visitors joining in the evening prayers, the first day's visit to Jerusalem terminated."

CHAPTER XXII.

1866.

SIR MOSES continues his narrative as follows :—

"Wednesday morning, the 28th of March, at 10 A.M., having been appointed for my first visit to his Excellency, Izzet Pasha, I proceeded to his palace, accompanied by Mr Consul Moore, Mr Sebag, and Dr Loewe, and was received by his Excellency with the greatest kindness and respect. In the course of my conversation with the Governor, the scarcity of water in the city was the subject more particularly adverted to, and his Excellency described the works he had benevolently originated and superintended, with the view of insuring a sufficient supply of that indispensable element. This important topic will be more particularly referred to in a subsequent part of this report. I will now only mention that the scheme which the Governor had designed, and had already begun to carry out, was to turn the three water reservoirs, generally known as the Pools of Solomon, into two reservoirs, and to increase the force of the fall of the waters from Urtas, in the vicinity of Etham into these pools, by which means it was expected that within a few weeks a plentiful supply of water would be secured to the city. The Governor, however, seemed to intimate that there were difficulties in the way, arising from the want of sufficient pecuniary means, and I thereupon considered that having regard to the extensive and permanent advantages, sanitary and otherwise, which would result from an adequate supply of water to the Holy City, I should be carrying out the intentions and wishes of the generous contributors to the Holy Land Relief Fund, and of your Honourable Board, by devoting a portion of the fund to this object. I placed, therefore, at the disposal of the Governor the aforementioned sum of £200 in the name of the donors to the Relief Fund, adding thereto £100 as my own individual contribution.

"The Governor likewise mentioned to me the desirability of the removal beyond the city gates of persons unhappily afflicted with leprosy, and that to provide a proper place for their reception would probably involve an expense of £1500. Although sensible of the beneficial consequences likely to result from the proposed plan, I did not consider myself justified in devoting to it any portion of the Relief Fund which had been entrusted to me, and therefore contented myself with contributing from my own private purse, £100, to serve as a nucleus for further subscriptions towards the required sum.

"During the conversation with his Excellency the Governor, I was much pleased with the friendly sentiments he expressed towards our English Consul in Jerusalem. 'Not only,' said he, 'do I entertain the highest regard for Mr Moore in his capacity as representative of the English Government, but I consider him a valued friend, an enlightened statesman, and an accomplished scholar, in every respect deserving the regard and attachment of all who have the pleasure of his acquaintance.'

"On Thursday, March 29th, hearing of the sufferings of the poor, and their inability to provide all the necessaries of life during the approaching festival, I forwarded £100 to the Háhám Báshi, for the poor of the Portuguese and Morocco communities, and I also transmitted the like sum to the representatives of the German congregation, for a similar purpose.

"During the first and second days of the Passover, I visited the Touro almshouses. I satisfied myself that the inmates were fully deserving of the advantages they were enjoying. These almshouses are situated in the most healthy part of the suburbs of the Holy City ; scrupulous attention is paid to the preservation of order and cleanliness, and the inmates are cheerful and happy, devoting a portion of their time to religious observances and study ; but nevertheless, not neglecting the following of industrial pursuits. I conversed with most of the inmates, who were mechanics, and found there was no hesitation or reluctance in doing the hardest work with the object of earning a sum, however small, towards their maintenance. The inmates apply themselves to a variety of trades.

"The evidences of the industrial activity of the Israelites afforded me much satisfaction. I was also gratified to observe the healthy appearance of themselves and their children, more especially as most of them are unable to incur the expense of providing themselves and their families with animal food, except on the Sabbath. These almshouses are so highly esteemed that even many inhabitants of the city seek permission for a short sojourn there, for the recovery of their health ; and I even found that some of the back offices, only intended for lumber rooms, had been actually, though without my knowledge, appropriated as dwellings for several families.

"On Sunday, the 1st of April, the Governor of Jerusalem, accompanied by his officers, honoured me by returning my visit. On this occasion the condition of Jerusalem was fully and freely discussed ; it was estimated that at least fifteen per cent. of the poorer population had been cut off by the cholera, the fearful ravages of which were mainly attributable to the confined and unhealthy dwellings of the poor,-the insufficiency of water, and the impoverished state of the inhabitants.

"The Governor during this visit kindly gave me permission to erect an awning for the 'wailing place' near the western wall of the Temple, so as to afford shelter and protection from rain and heat to pious persons visiting this sacred spot.

"Monday, April 2nd, was the day which had been fixed for the reception of the representatives and spiritual heads of the several Congregations, and invitations had been previously sent to secure as full and complete a representation as possible. At the appointed time I had the satisfaction of finding that the invitation had been cordially responded to on all sides, and of seeing myself surrounded, in the presence of Dr Loewe and Mr and Mrs Sebag, by several hundreds of the most respectable of the inhabitants of Jerusalem. There was the Háhám Báshi, with the members of his Ecclesiastical Court ; the Revs. Meyer Fanadjil and Benveniste, together with some of the most influential members of the Portuguese or Sephardim Congregation ; the Rev. Samuel Salant and Meyer Auerbach of the Perooshim and Warsaw Congregations, and the Chief Rabbis of all the various communities almost without exception, as well as the representatives of all charitable institutions and colleges, with their officers.

II.   M

" Having bid them a hearty welcome and expressed the delight I felt at being amongst them for the sixth time, I proceeded to observe that the object of my present visit was not so much that of rendering them momentary relief by the distribution of money amongst their poor, as to ascertain from them the most effectual measures which could be adopted by their friends in other parts of the world, whither my words might reach, in the hope of removing the real and more permanent causes of poverty amongst my brethren in the Holy Land. I concluded by assuring them of the ardent love I entertained for the holy territory and its pious inhabitants, and by entreating them to assist me freely and fully with all such advice and information as might directly or indirectly further the object and purpose of my mission.

" The Háhám Báshi was the first who, according to my request, proceeded to enlighten me with his views. The reverend gentleman said that, in his opinion, an increase in the number of proper dwellings for the poor, and occupation in agricultural pursuits, would be the safest remedy for securing the salubrity of the place and the comfort of its inhabitants. The gentlemen in his retinue, the Revs. Fanadjil and Benveniste, were of the same opinion ; but, added the latter, the cause of their (the Sephardim's) great poverty was to a great extent the consequence of the heavy burden of debt which the Congregations had incurred, and were obliged to incur from time to time,—a burden which weighed most heavily on them. The Rev. Samuel Salant was next addressed, and he entirely endorsed the opinion of the Háhám Báshi. After attentively listening to all the speakers, I gathered that there was a general consensus of opinion that increased accommodation for the poor, providing them with remunerative occupation, the granting of facilities for leaving the Holy Land to those who were desirous of emigrating, the establishment of building and loan societies, and permission to open butchers' shops, were some of the most essential means that could be devised to alleviate the then distressful condition of the inhabitants.

" The representatives subsequently showed me documentary evidence to prove that, if a remittance of, say, £100, or 12,025 Egyptian piastres, is forwarded to Jerusalem (which is not a frequent occurrence), the average amount to which each recipient becomes entitled is about 4 piastres, or 8d sterling !

Tuesday, April 3rd.-- I appointed for the reception of a deputation from Safed, representing sixty families, numbering three hundred souls, all of whom most earnestly prayed to be afforded the means of devoting themselves to agriculture.

" The documents which they brought with them were accompanied by certificates from Mr J. Miklasiewicz, the Austrian Consul at Safed, who testifies to the sincerity of the wish expressed by these three hundred people ; whereas in a publication of the Rev. Dr Macleod, to which I shall have soon more particularly to refer, the gentleman, who professed last year to be the Austrian Consul in the same city, is reported to have accused its Jewish inhabitants of ' being idle, lazy, and suspicious.' Of the other grave accusations contained in the same periodical, I shall speak at length in the sequel, and will now but point to the pregnant fact that the name of the Rev. Dr Macleod's informer, who professed to be the Austrian Consul at Safed, is stated by that rev. gentleman to be Mieroslowski, whereas I have clearly ascertained that no one bearing that name has filled the Consular Office in that city. In fact, one of two conclusions seems inevitable : either an almost miraculous change has within the period of one year come over the character of the Jews at Safed, or the Rev. Dr Macleod has been deceived by the story of an artful impostor ; nor is it, perhaps, difficult to decide which of these two conclusions is the more probable. I need scarcely say that the certificate transmitted to me by the **actual Austrian** Consul at Safed was a source of the highest gratification to **me, and I am sure** it will be so to yourself **and all** our brethren, who **may have read the statement which** Mieroslowski, **or** some one assumed **to be holding the office of Austrian Consul,** is said to have made in **reference to the Jews at Safed.**

"**Applications for** employment in agricultural pursuits were **also about** this **time handed to me** from the people of Tiberias and the Bokea : **the** latter **suffered terribly** during the last war **or** contest between Joseph Kareen and **Daoud Pasha ; their** cattle, the produce of their fields, and all the property **they had in their** houses, and **even** their wives, having been forcibly **taken away from them.** I assisted them with a small amount, and promised **to make their case** known to my friends.

" **On Wednesday,** April 4th, believing that **I should be rendering a service** to the poor in **the** Holy Land by providing **them with necessary funds for** emigration from Jerusalem and its neighbourhood, **I requested that the parties** mentioned at the general meeting by some of the **representatives of the con**gregations should be brought before me, and **on this** occasion **I witnessed a** scene which seems not unworthy of narration. **At the** appointed **hour a young** widow was introduced to me, apparently twenty **or** twenty-two years of **age. Her** husband had died **recently** from the cholera, leaving her with **three children,** the eldest five **or six years, and the** youngest **three** or four months **old. The** history of her **own life was simply as** follows :—**She** herself was left **an** orphan when of tender **age, and was adopted as a foster** daughter by a person who at present **officiates** gratuitously as **a reader in a** small synagogue. **He** happened **to** have another orphan in **the house, a boy,** and when both grew to what is called in the East a mature age, **it seemed to** him that a most suitable union might be formed between those **two** orphans, and accordingly they were married under **the roof** of this charitable man. After their marriage they maintained themselves respectably, and lived happily together until the husband fell under the fatal scourge of the **cholera.** The foster-father then **provided a** home for **the** destitute widow **and her children. This consisted of one** small room, **which** I had previously **visited, when I was delighted with** its cleanliness, as **well as** with the interesting **appearance of the children.** Having, **among other** matters, conferred **with my co-religionists on the sub**ject **of facilities for** emigration in **fitting** instances, **I thought this a most deserving case,** and offered the widow **my** aid in **providing for the departure of herself and** family from Jerusalem to join **her relatives or friends in** Germany, **who were** believed to be in comfortable circumstances. **To my** surprise, she declined to avail **herself** of my assistance, though in the **most** grateful terms. As a faithful representation of her feelings, and that of many other dwellers on the **sacred** soil, I will here, as nearly as possible, transcribe her words. She said : ' **God** has granted me the high privilege to breathe the hallowed atmosphere **of the** land of our forefathers, Abraham, Isaac, and Jacob. He has caused **His grace and** mercy to descend upon me by bringing me, when an infant, unto **this sacred** spot, **whence** the radiant glory of His divine law emanated. He has permitted me to tread on that hallowed ground on which our prophets and **our** teachers lived, and taught me the words of lasting truth. Am I now to leave it, and take my children **away** from Zion, where we truly believe and daily expect " Truth and **Peace** " again to rule ? No ; I would rather starve together with my children, **whilst kissing the dust in** the Holy City of Jerusalem, than live in plenty elsewhere.'

"**Applications were** made to me by various persons for the necessary **means to enable them to** leave the Holy City ; but, **on** making inquiry, I found that **in all** these cases the applicants had merely temporary objects in view, without any intention to remain **away** permanently, and I, therefore, did not deem it my duty to do more than **aid** them with a trifle, in order to relieve them from their immediate distress.

" Thursday, the 5th of April, was devoted to the examination of documents having reference to several plots of ground in the suburbs of Jerusalem, offered to me for purchase, either for building purposes or for cultivation. I requested Dr Loewe and Mr Sebag, to make a personal survey of these properties, and to ascertain particulars as to their extent, value, and price, with which request they kindly complied. I had also caused memoranda to be made as to valuable houses, within the Holy City, offered for sale. The notes having reference to these negotiations have been carefully preserved, so as to be made available for future guidance.

" But soon I was to sustain a heavy affliction. After having left Jaffa I constantly received telegrams about the state of Dr Hodgkin's health ; and when I was informed that the symptoms had become more alarming, I begged my friend Captain Henry Moore to proceed to Jaffa in the company of the physician of Jerusalem, Dr Chaplin. They at once complied with my request, and remained at Jaffa with my lamented friend until the period of his decease, the melancholy tidings of which I received during the night of the 5th of April. Having already referred to this sad event, I shall not again dwell thereon, except to say, that it overwhelmed me with sorrow and cast a gloom over me which I vainly sought to dispel.

" On Friday, the 6th of April, I attended the afternoon service in the Sephardim Synagogue belonging to the Almshouses and conversed with the inmates, eliciting from them much useful information.

" On Saturday, the 7th of April, in the course of the day, some youths were introduced to me for the purpose of being examined in the various subjects of their studies. When their father, who accompanied them, was asked why he had not placed them to learn some useful trade, he replied :— ' Before we provide our children with the means of attending to their temporal wants, we deem it our duty to promote their spiritual welfare. They must first learn the Word of God, to serve them as a guide and beacon of hope in all their worldly vicissitudes.' He also brought others of his children who were already engaged in learning trades.

" There are two Synagogues attached to the Touro Almshouses, one of them for the Sephardim, which I had already visited, the other for the Ashkenasim ; to-day I visited the latter. On my way thither, a young woman passed us with a large book in her hand, and, on my inquiring what it was, she informed me it was a Hebrew Psalm Book, with several Commentaries of ancient authors printed in Hebrew-German characters. I requested her to read one of the Psalms with the Commentary, this she did with great fluency and without hesitation. I have often had occasion to admire the ability of many females in our community of Jerusalem, not only in respect of their household duties and in needlework of every description, but also in Hebrew lore. I was on one occasion addressed by the mother of two or three children who solicited aid, and, to my surprise, she spoke to Dr Loewe and myself in the Hebrew language with elegance and facility. Subsequently I ascertained that she was a Portuguese, the widow of a German Rabbi, who had recently died and left her in straitened circumstances.

" Intermarriages between Sephardim and Ashkenasim, are, I am happy to say, no longer of rare occurrence in the Holy Land.

" In the evening, a short time after prayers, a large concourse of persons proceeding from the Jaffa gate, with lights and music, approached my residence, desiring to illuminate it ; but in my then state of mind, I was indisposed to any such joyous demonstration. Mr Selig Hausdorf, who headed the procession, assured me that their object was to show the grateful appreciation in which they held the generous benefactors I represented.

" Although I could not consent to the intended illumination, I willingly received my kind visitors. They recited to us psalms and poetical compositions ; and I afterwards obtained, in conversation with them, much useful information relating to the wants and condition of their community.

CHAPTER XXIII.

1866.

VISIT TO THE MOUNT OF OLIVES—SITE OF THE HOLY TEMPLE —DR NORMAN MACLEOD'S CHARGE—SIR MOSES' INQUIRIES —DR MACLEOD'S RETRACTATION.

"ON Sunday morning, April 8th, wishing to examine some documents uninterrupted by visitors," says Sir Moses, "I determined to leave home therewith, and to direct my steps to the Mount of Olives. I left my residence at an early hour, in the company of Dr Loewe. Proceeding towards the Damascus gate, we passed the Grotto of Jeremiah, the Tombs of the Kings, and went thence towards the Báb-el'-Asbát. We then crossed the Valley of Kidron, and finally reached the Mount of Olives, to the highest point of which we ascended. From thence we had a most beautiful view of the Dead Sea, and of the wild scenery of the heights of Moab, and having rested there for a short period, we descended on foot, and stopped at a large tree. From this spot we obtained a fine view of the Mosque of Omar—the hallowed spot formerly occupied by the Holy Temple—and remained here two hours, engaged in the examination of the documents and plans I had brought with me. We then continued to descend the mountain till we reached the Valley of Jehoshaphat. Here we were met by Khasin, the sheikh of the village of Siluan, who described to me the sufferings of the Jews during the visitation of the cholera, and showed me the newly constructed graves, a most affecting sight, whilst another sheikh spoke to us of the many noble instances in which the Jews had heroically assisted one another during the period of calamity.

"That sheikh, as well as another such dignitary, who happens to have some landed property near the burial-ground, still expects presents from the Jews who visit the cemetery. Formerly they committed great outrages on the dead whenever their demands were not satisfactorily responded to ; but at present, thanks to the protection of the Turkish Government, these bararities have been put an end to. I continued my wanderings in the Valley of Jehoshaphat for some time, listening now and then attentively to communications from the Arab sheikhs, and towards evening returned with much useful information to my own dwelling. In the evening the messengers whom I had despatched to Safed after my arrival in the Holy City returned, bringing letters from the Rev. Samuel Helir and Samuel Abu, to say that they would cheerfully comply with my wish, and come to Jerusalem as soon as possible. My object in seeking an interview with these gentlemen was to obtain an explanation from them respecting a statement of the Austrian Consul at Safed, which has been widely circulated through the medium of a monthy magazine entitled *Good Words*, edited by the Rev. Norman Macleod, D.D., one of Her Majesty's Chaplains.

"That statement was not less than a direct accusation brought against the spiritual heads of the Safed Congregation for having inflicted the punishment of death on a Spanish Jewess the day before the Rev. Dr Macleod had arrived in that place.

"I had already heard a most satisfactory refutation of that foul accusation from several trustworthy persons of Safed, but I would not rest until I had received all the particulars from the spiritual heads of the congregation themselves, and was anxiously awaiting their arrival.

"On Monday, the 9th of April, I paid return visits to the Consular authorities and to the Háhám Báshi. I also called upon the Protestant Bishop, the Rev. Dr Gobat, whose unvarying courtesy, enlightened views, profound learning, and warm zeal for the welfare of the inhabitants of the Holy City, no one who has enjoyed the honour of his acquaintance can fail to appreciate.

"The new Synagogue, called the ' Khoorbát Rabbi Yehooda Hakhássid,' is a noble edifice. Whilst resting at the Mount of Olives I could see its cupola overtopping all other buildings in the Jewish quarter. Great praise is due to the perseverance and skilful management of the Building Committee. They had to collect the funds for the erection of the Synagogue in very small sums and at long intervals ; yet, notwithstanding the many obstacles with which they had to contend, they at length, by their energy and patience, happily succeeded in accomplishing their labours.

"It was very gratifying to me to know that I had been the bearer of the firman from the late Sultan Abd-ool-Megid, granting permission for the erection of this synagogue, and that I had had intrusted to me considerable remittances to be applied for that pious purpose. On the present occasion I was permitted to be the bearer of a silver ornament for a sacred scroll of the Pentateuch, an offering from Mr Aaron Silverman, of Birmingham ; and I had the gratification, with my own hands, to append it to a scroll of the law in the holy edifice.

"The synagogue of the Volhynian congregation will also, when completed, be a fine structure. In connection with this synagogue, there will be a hall for vestry meetings, rooms for a college and library, the secretary's office, and a public bath.

"The before-mentioned dispensary, established by me in the Holy City about twenty-five years since, was of great service during the cholera, and afforded the needful remedies to many hundreds of persons. It is well regulated ; there is a register containing entries of all prescriptions, with the signature of the physician under whose order they had been dispensed ; and every drawer, case, barrel, and bottle is distinctly labelled with the name of its contents, as in Europe. I was greatly pleased to learn that a youth, a native of Jerusalem, had been recently apprenticed in the Dispensary, and that he was acquitting himself of his onerous duties to the entire satisfaction of the community.

"The house recently erected by the Institution of Bikoor Kholim is as yet in an unfinished state. Great praise is due to the members of that institution ; they attend the poor in sickness, and provide for their requirements, endeavouring to soothe their sufferings with the most affectionate solicitude.

"The many experienced persons with whom I had consulted, being unanimously of opinion that no greater boon could be bestowed on the poor than the erection of additional dwellings, a suitable site had been selected for that purpose contiguous to the Touro almshouses, and I had appointed Monday, the 9th of April, for laying the foundation stone of the dwellings, which I propose shall be erected with the surplus proceeds of the Holy Land Relief Fund, placed by the Board at my disposal.

"The fixed hour for laying the foundation stone now arrived, and the ground became full with thousands of people of all creeds, anxious to witness the ceremony.

"Dr Loewe repaired to the spot where the stone was to be laid, to arrange all that was necessary for the occasion, and soon afterwards I proceeded, in the company of Mr and Mrs Sebag, and many of our friends, to the enclosure intended for the new buildings. On my arrival I was received by all the representatives of the community who had previously assembled there, and the air resounded with the words, 'Blessed be he who cometh in the name of God.' After a short pause, Dr Loewe, to whom the conduct of the religious ceremony had been entrusted, commenced reciting the service. He then read the inscription of the scroll to be deposited in the cavity of the foundation stone, which was afterwards signed by myself, Mr and Mrs Sebag, and others of my friends present. I then deposited the scroll in the cavity, and proceeded to lay the stone with the customary formalities. Dr Loewe offered up a prayer composed by him for the occasion, imploring the blessings of heaven on the future edifice, and on those who should generously aid in providing the poor with suitable dwellings. He also offered up special prayers for His Imperial Majesty the Sultan Abd-ool-áziz and the Turkish Government, for our gracious Queen, the Prince and Princess of Wales, the Governor of Jerusalem, and the Consuls.

"I deem it a pleasing duty to record that many of the people expressed great pleasure on hearing the prayer offered up for England's beloved Queen, and the Jerusalem Jews, on hearing Her Majesty's name, exclaimed, 'It well behoves us to pray for the English Government. Are we not under a heavy debt of gratitude for the powerful aid which they have given unto us in Damascus and Morocco.'

"In commemoration of the interesting proceedings of this day, I forwarded £100 to be distributed amongst the poor of the Sephardim, and £100 amongst the poor of the Ashkenasim.

"How deeply the feeling of charity is implanted in the hearts of the poor of our community in the Holy Land towards each other has often been noticed, but some striking evidence of this was afforded us in the course of this morning, and I cannot refrain from mentioning one or two instances.

"Two young orphans entered the room; their pleasing and healthy appearance attracted my notice. 'Who takes care of you? and in whose house do you live?' I asked. They replied, 'We are under the care of and reside with Jacob Aaron Kalisher.' I inquired who he was, assuming him to be in easy circumstances, but I was informed that far from this he was actually very poor, that his business of a whitewasher was only lucrative at Passover time, when every Jewish inhabitant has his dwelling thoroughly cleansed and whitewashed, but that during the remainder of the year there was very little work for him. Being desirous of seeing this benevolent man, I sent for him. He came, and his appearance, notwithstanding his poverty, was not by any means careworn; on the contrary he seemed cheerful and happy, and as though possessed of independent means.

"'Are these two orphans under your care, and do you support them;' He replied, smiling, 'Yes.' 'Have you any children of your own?' 'Yes, seven.' 'Why, then, have you burdened yourself with the maintenance of these two orphans in addition?' He replied, 'Their parents were my next neighbours, and when I saw them left fatherless and motherless, it appeared to me that it was my duty to protect them, and that they should share my home with my own children. Thank God, they are well and happy, sharing our food when I and my children have any, and when we have none enduring hunger alike with ourselves.' Subsequently a widow, in almost destitute circumstances, was introduced to me. She, likewise, had taken two orphan children under her care. Then another poor man was introduced, who had also taken upon himself the support of several helpless orphans.

"Assuredly these noble characteristics distinguishing the poorest of our community in Jerusalem, will entitle them to our admiration, sympathy, and assistance.

"After the persons just mentioned had left, our cavasses next announced the arrival of the pupils belonging to the Simon Edlen von Lämels institution. They were forty in number, accompanied by their master. I was much pleased with their appearance and demeanour, which would do credit to any European institution. They sang some beautiful hymns, and gave me a full account of their course of study. I presented to each of them a small sum, exhorting them to cling faithfully to their religion, to be grateful to their noble benefactress, and emulous to give her satisfaction by their progress and good conduct.

"Thursday, April 12th, was fixed by me as the day for the enquiry into the accusation which is reported to have been brought against the Jews of Safed by an Austrian Consul of that city, an account of which was published in the monthly magazine, *Good Words*, part xii., December 1, 1865. The representatives of the Safed congregation had, as I have already mentioned, come from Safed to Jerusalem, and on this day I invited them to lay before me fully the facts connected with the matters referred to in the accusation.

"I accordingly commenced by reading to these gentlemen the whole of the account given by the alleged Austrian Consul concerning the Jews of Palestine in general, and of those in Safed in particular, and I called their attention to the note at the bottom of page 915, which runs as follows :—'One terrible story was to the effect that the punishment of death had been inflicted on a Spanish Jewess the day before we (the Rev. Dr Macleod and his party) reached Safed, for a crime in which one of the Rabbis who tried and condemned her was himself notoriously implicated. We begged the Consul to make further enquiries on the subject. This he did, assuring us that all he heard was confirmed by an intelligent Jew, who, though he hated the proceedings, feared to speak. Such is the reign of terror.'

"Thereupon the Rev. Samuel Abu and Samuel Helir, who were the representatives of the German and Portuguese congregations of Safed, made to me the following statement :—

"'A Damascus woman, divorced from her husband, came to settle in Safed, where, after a six months' residence, she was married to a person of the name of Masood Tabool, a goldsmith by trade, with whom she went to live in a house opposite to the Synagogue.

"'This dwelling being in a locality frequented by the Jews, morning and evening, her conduct was necessarily open to public observation, and as her mode of life was only consistent with the bad reputation she had brought with her from Damascus, she herself seems to have become apprehensive of evil consequences, and removed to the house of a person called Bekhor Namias.

"'On Sabbath morning, during Divine Service in the Synagogue, the wife of Bekhor Namias, who had not left home, observed a Turk of the name of Abdallah Greri, enter the woman's private apartment (an act which, in the East, and particularly in the Holy Land, is deemed to be utterly inconsistent with every sense of decency and morality), and there he remained some time. Mrs Namias, not doubting the immoral object of so unusual a visit in her own house, hastened to the Synagogue and gave information to the heads of the congregation of what she had witnessed. No doubt existing as to the woman's guilt, a number of persons, enraged at her immoral conduct, severely chastised her, in accordance with the not uncommon mode of dealing with immoral persons in the East.

"'It being against the laws of the Jews that a husband should continue to live with an adulterous wife, Massood obtained a divorce, and the divorced wife is now living in Damascus in the house of her own father.

"'There has been no trial, no punishment of death, nor was the Rabbi in the slightest degree implicated.

"'Indeed, no Jewish authority in the Holy Land, nor in any part of the world, has ever passed sentence of death since the close of the great Sanhedrin in Jerusalem.'

"This statement having been made to me by these two reverend gentlemen, with whom I have had the pleasure of being in correspondence for nearly thirty years, on charitable and congregational matters, and who were and still are the heads of the congregations of Safed, corroborated by two other gentlemen, Aboo Charaz and Isaac Friedman, strongly recommended by Mr Miklasiewicz, the Austrian Consul himself, as worthy representatives of sixty families, and testified by the Rev. Mordecai Halevi Ashkenazi, well known to me as the former messenger to England from the congregations of Safed and Tiberias, I have not the least doubt about the falsehood of the accusation brought against our brethren.

"To me and to your Honourable Board, it must afford sincere gratification that the cruel slander which has been so widely circulated by the *Good Words* of the Rev. Dr Macleod, has been thus proved to be utterly devoid of truth, and I am confident that a gentleman of the high character of Dr Macleod will sincerely regret to have inflicted so serious an injury on an innocent community."

I may be permitted, perhaps, to interrupt the reader in the perusal of Sir Moses' report, by stating that on his return from the Holy Land, he sent a copy of the information he obtained in Jerusalem, respecting the Safed affair, to the Rev. Dr N. Macleod, and had the pleasure of receiving an acknowledgment from him, which, I think, will be read with much satisfaction. The letter addressed to Sir Moses on the subject is as follows:—

"ADELAIDE PLACE, GLASGOW, *October* 19*th*, 1866.

"MY DEAR SIR,—I thank you very cordially for your courteous letter, and for the copy of your Report which you were so good as to send to me. I have read all your Report with the greatest attention, and dissent altogether from what is personal to myself.

"I shall have very great satisfaction, indeed, in publishing, possibly in *Goods Words*, but certainly in the cheap edition of my 'Eastward,' and in both, if you wish it, your contradiction of the story regarding the Safed woman. I have no doubt whatever, that my informant was imposed upon.

"But I have as little doubt that my informant was the Austrian Consul, though I may (how I cannot tell) have made a mistake about his unpronounceable name, by trusting possibly to my memory, and not having rightly taken it up at the time. Nevertheless, he was the Consul. We were living in his house; the official arms were, as I have stated, hung up at the end of his room; he read to us several official documents which he had sent to his Government, and narrated the story in the presence of our party. We rejected it as too shocking to be true, and insisted that he should make further enquiries, and only when he professed to have done so, and again assured us of the fact, did I feel justified, as travellers, in recording the fact and noting the evidence on which it was received.

"Forgive me for saying that I think you should have asked the present Consul whether he had ever lodged our party (we having paid him), or given any such information? If not, who was Austrian Consul at the time? or who represented him in his official residence? And if the present Consul did give us this information, on what evidence was it founded? I do not object to the *ex parte* statement of the Rabbis. But, in justice to myself and the Consul, his statement most certainly should have been obtained, and opportunity given him to verify or to contradict all his stories. I may also state that he described the fights for charity-money to have been sometimes continued for days, and to the effusion of blood; this may also be false. But other parties besides those implicated should, when possible, be heard.

"But I have no wish to make this a controversy. I shall give your contradiction to the story. I have received an affidavit to the same effect, made before Consul Rogers of Damascus, and a letter from him, expressing his disbelief in it, which I may also publish. In any case, I shall act justly. —With deepest respect, and sincerest goodwill, I remain, yours faithfully,

"N. MACLEOD."

With regard to the desirability of making further inquiries of the Consul himself, and of hearing the evidence from other persons besides those implicated, it must be observed that Sir Moses had this time not been able to go to Safed. Had he been there, he would undoubtedly have made the inquiries suggested by the Rev. Doctor. On the other hand, it must be borne in mind that Sir Moses did not appear in the Holy Land as a judge, with the power of cross-examining the Austrian Consul, and therefore could not have made such inquiries until the latter had come forward and offered voluntarily to assist in clearing up the matter.

All Sir Moses wanted to ascertain from the representatives of the Safed Hebrew Congregation was, whether the accusation brought against them had any foundation in truth? And if not, that it should be refuted by undoubted evidence.

He had long known the character of the representatives as spotless, and was in the habit of placing the utmost confidence in them on all important occasions. This, and the circumstance that the woman who was said to have been executed by order of the Rabbis was still living at Damascus—a fact which has been testified by the Consul of that place and several other persons who had seen her there—ought to be admitted as the most striking evidence in favour of the representatives of the community.

CHAPTER XXIV.

1866.

DEPARTURE FROM THE HOLY CITY—RETURN TO ENGLAND—
VISIT TO BARON BRUNNOW AND LORD CLARENDON—
FRIGHTFUL OUTBREAK AGAINST THE JEWS IN PERSIA—
FRESH COMPLAINTS FROM MOLDAVIA.

CONTINUING the narrative of his travels, Sir Moses says :—

"On Friday, the 13th of April, being desirous of leaving some pecuniary relief from myself for each of the synagogues, colleges, schools, and various charitable institutions, with their respective representatives themselves, I had previously made an arrangement to see them on that day, but a restless night and a constitution enfeebled, partly by the incessant work, and partly by the grief I acutely felt at the loss of my late friend Dr Hodgkin, compelled me to alter my plan, and instead of personal interviews I had to satisfy myself with addressing these gentlemen by letters, forty-two of which were despatched to the authorities and their accredited secretaries, accompanied by my humble offerings for the benefit of all the charitable institutions in Jerusalem.

"It was late in the afternoon, and the place was still crowded, but I considered now the object of my visit to Jerusalem realised, and retired to my own room to prepare for Sabbath.

"On Saturday, April 14th, after the morning service, I took a walk round the garden, and was much pleased with the improvement of the place since my last visit to Jerusalem.

"I regret, however, not being able to report the same of the land of Jaffa, which has been unfortunately let to persons who, being unable to resist the threatened attacks of the neighbouring Arabs, deserted the place altogether. The consequence is that the houses are completely demolished and the trees destroyed. I am at present, however, in communication with the Chief Háhám of the Morocco Congregation in Jerusalem in reference to this matter. If sufficient funds can be obtained for the purpose, I hope to see four or five families established at that now deserted place, who will apply themselves sedulously to the cultivation of the land, which is of considerable value, and ought to be immediately secured by a fence to mark its boundaries.

"As soon as the evening prayers were over, I gave orders for our departure. The whole of Saturday night was spent in communicating with a number of people who brought letters, or had some verbal communication to make, but as the morning dawn appeared, I wound my way towards the Jaffa Road, and took my departure from the Holy City, more deeply than ever impressed with its sacred reminiscences and its perennial beauty, and more fervently than ever offering prayers for its future welfare. 'As a seal I set thee on my heart, as a seal on my arm, if ever I forget thee, O Jerusalem, may my right hand forget her cunning.'

"We arrived, after a long day's journey, at Ramlah, where again we took up our abode in the Russian Hospice. All the way from Jerusalem to Jaffa we were followed by agriculturists from the Bokea, who were anxious to lay their case before me in hopes that I would at once afford them relief. I could, however, do no more than assure them that all should be done to make their situation known, and to arouse sympathy in their favour.

"On the following day, Monday, about noon, we left Ramlah for Jaffa, and on approaching the avenue at the entrance of that city were again met by the Governor, Judge, and Commander of the troops, with a numerous retinue. But I would not proceed into Jaffa until I had first visited the place which enclosed the mortal remains of my dear friend, Dr Hodgkin. That spot is at present surrounded by a strong railing, but will, I trust, soon be covered by a granite column, for which I gave orders on my return to England, as a mark of my respect and esteem. We embarked the same evening on board the *Rosetta*, and on Wednesday, the 18th of April, arrived at Alexandria. The same night we went on board the *Tanjore*, which, by the blessing of heaven, brought us, after a most pleasant voyage, on Wednesday evening, the 25th of April, to Marseilles."

Before proceeding to notice the entries in his Diary after his arrival in England, we have to record two incidents in connection with his homeward journey, which he in his narrative left unnoticed.

Sir Moses' state of health, during the last few days of his sojourn in Jerusalem, manifested symptoms of great weakness, and it appeared most desirable to his travelling companions that he should leave the place as soon as possible. There were, however, none of the large steamers in the Jaffa harbour, and it was only with some difficulty that a few berths could be secured on board a small one. Unfortunately, the accommodation there was far from being comfortable. We had on board 1500 sheep, a dozen horses, and many oxen. There was no railing round the deck, where we had our places, except a rope or chain passing through iron stancheons. The sea was very rough and boisterous; the ship rolled terribly; and every now and then the towering waves, as they rushed on deck, swept some of the sheep, horses, and oxen overboard. Sir Moses could not go down into his cabin, and remained the whole night sitting on deck. The old man of eighty-one did not utter a single murmur; he bore the exposure to the raging elements, and endured the anxiety, which was felt by every one on board, with calmness and resignation. By the mercy of heaven we arrived safely at Alexandria, and we at once went on board the *Tanjore*, Captain Brooks. There Sir Moses found comfort and rest after the dangers he had braved. The sea was calm, the company agreeable. Theatrical performances, dances, and concerts beguiled the otherwise long and tedious hours on board ship, and it was on occasion of one of these concerts that Sir Moses experienced a most agreeable surprise. One of the band, handing round the programmes of the concert to the passengers, brought one to Sir Moses, which contained, amongst others, the following pieces :—

Hymn,	-	" Yigdál Elokim Kháy,"	- *Unknown.*
Hymn,	-	"Adón Olám,"	- *Unknown.*

These are two hymns in the Jewish Prayer-book. Sir Moses hardly expected to find them in a programme of music on board the P. and O. Company's steamship *Tanjore.* He therefore thought that possibly some Hebrew scholar among the passengers might have written the words in Hebrew for the amusement of the travellers, some of whom were Oriental scholars from India. But, when after a valse the ancient Hebrew hymn was intoned to a well-known melody, which may be heard on Sabbath and festivals in the Spanish and Portuguese Synagogue in London, he was much affected, and softly sang the words to himself.

He considered it a mark of great attention on the part of those who had arranged the programme, and expressed himself in grateful terms for the pleasant surprise.

May 9th.—Sir Moses arrived at Ramsgate. Next day he proceeded to Brighton, thence to Lewes to pay a visit of condolence to Dr Hodgkin's brother. On the 14th he was again at the Alliance, and on the 17th he called on Baron Brunnow.

" He received me," Sir Moses says, "most kindly. Though much engaged, he heard my report of the Russian Hospice, and expressed a desire that I would write him and he would send my letter to the Emperor, who, he said, was always pleased to hear that his efforts for the happiness of others had been successful. I then called at the Foreign Office, and was received by Lord Clarendon ; thanked him for his letters of introduction to the British Consul at Syria, and for the letters he had procured for me from the Turkish Government through Lord Lyons. I gave him an account of my visit to Jerusalem, the kindness I had received from Mr Moore, the distinguished manner in which I had been received by the Governor of Jerusalem, and the anxiety his Excellency has evinced for the improvement of the condition of the Jews in Jerusalem. I informed his Lordship that great improvements had already been made there, and on my arrival at Jerusalem I found that the land was much better cultivated, and that there were many more buildings than on the occasion of my last visit. Lord Clarendon said that if I sent him in writing all that I had said, he would take the opportunity of thanking the Turkish authorities, in the name of the English Government, for their reception of me. I then spoke of the great kindness and attention I had received from Mr Moore, of the friendship he evinced during my trouble (the loss of my friend, Dr Hodgkin), of the esteem in which Mr Moore was held by persons of all classes without distinction of faith. Lord Clarendon asked me to write this to him also, and said, ' It is seed that shall produce fruit.' Nothing could have been more kind than his Lordship's reception of me."

June 3rd.—He went to his favourite retreat, Smithembottom, for a few hours' reflection on the past and the future, but not until he considered he had discharged all the duties in connection with his last mission.

July 24th.—A granite pillar was bought by him for the tomb of his lamented friend, Dr Hodgkin, and sent to Jaffa at his expense.

August 13th.—On calling at the Foreign Office he had the satisfaction of being permitted to peruse two despatches, dated Teheran, 10th and 11th of June, from Mr Alison. The latter had been most active in his powerful appeal to the Persian Government in favour of the Jews, but a few months later dispatches were again given to him to read which caused him acute sorrow. " I called at the Foreign Office," he says, in his entry of the 1st of November, "and gave Mr (now Lord) Hammond a copy of my report. He said he had written to me yesterday, but I had not yet received his letter."

An opportunity was then afforded to him to read several dispatches from Mr Alison at Teheran, giving an account of another frightful outbreak against the Jews at Benfarouch. Many of them were killed and had their houses plundered and destroyed. In fact, the whole of the Jewish population of that place were homeless and starving, and crying aloud for mercy. The Shah's officer was beaten, and the head of the Moslem population declared that he was king there, and that not a Jew

should remain alive in the place. The authority of the Shah
had disappeared, and the ministers of England, France, Russia,
and Turkey had declined to make any further remonstrances
to his government. "Heaven protect the poor Jews." I begged
Mr Hammond to advise me what I could do for them. He
said, "Nothing; that I must wait with patience, and he would
let me know when they had further dispatches." I offered to go
to Persia, but he said, "It was not possible, I could do no
good."

In a letter Sir Moses addressed to me in reference to the
outbreak against the Jews at Balfaroosh, he writes: "Lord
Clarendon has sent Mr Alison a telegram to express to the Shah
the full assurance felt by Her Majesty's Government that the
persons who have committed the outrage in question will be
severely punished, and that the Jews at Balfaroosh and elsewhere throughout Persia will be protected from ill-treatment and
persecution." "Alas," he continues, "I am not yet finished
with one effort in favour of our brethren when a new misfortune
occurs."

November 5th.—He went to the Isle of Thanet Union at
Ramsgate; visited all the rooms, and the infirmary, &c.; distributed parcels containing tea and sugar, in addition to gifts in
money among 340 persons present. The inmates were always
pleased to see him, as he made it a rule to speak a few kind
words to them.

He was in the habit of visiting the Union and other charitable
institutions in Ramsgate regularly every year, when his health
permitted him to do so, and always remembered the inmates on
the Queen's Birthday and on other festive occasions.

December 4th.—Sir Moses went to Dover to meet the Rev.
Dr Artom, the spiritual head of the Spanish and Portuguese
congregation, on his arrival after election. A few days later he
had the pleasure of receiving a kind note with an offer of £100
from Miss Burdett Coutts towards the fund to be raised for the
supply of water and the improvement of the dwellings of the
Israelites in Jerusalem. Subsequently he devoted much time to
making arrangements regarding his land at Jaffa.

When Sir Moses, a few months earlier, in a moment of weari-
ness, almost overwhelmed by the frequent appeals to his sym-
pathizing heart from his oppressed and suffering brethren in

foreign lands, said, " Alas, I am not yet finished with one effort when a new misfortune occurs," he little thought that he would so soon have again to set out on a mission, and so give up the comforts of home.   But the unexpected often happens, and Sir Moses did not think that he would be exempted from the usual lot of mankind ; especially as so many thousands of his fellow beings placed their confidence in him, knowing that he would hasten to their help as long as one spark of hope was left to remove their grievances.

In the first few months of this year he pursued his occupations in their usual order in the city, and when at Ramsgate, where he generally enjoyed the company of relatives and friends, his favourite theme was the improvement of the college buildings by the enlargement of the lecture hall.   But even this pleasure soon became clouded by the news of the death of his brother-in-law, Mr Benjamin Cohen, the father of Mr Arthur Cohen, Q.C. Both he and Lady Montefiore were greatly attached to him. He was a man of exceptional goodness of heart, most agreeable in manners ; endearing himself to all who associated with him.

Soon after this mournful event he received by the kindness of Lord Stanley, from the Foreign Office, various extracts from reports referring to Hamadan, dated February 22, 1867. " The Jews," Mr Alison's agent writes, " are this year much more ill-treated than last year.   Many of the Jews have run away from this province."

Mr R. T. Thomson in his notes on " The Jews of Oroomiah," writes, on February 1, 1867, " There are two hundred families of Jews residing in the town of Oroomiah.   The revenue which they pay to the Persian Government annually is fixed at four hundred tomans, but their master Rejjeb Ali Khan, son of Fazzan Agha, takes six hundred tomans besides sundry fines and other small exactions.   It was agreed about twenty years ago that they should pay ten tomans annually, in lieu of forced labour.   This sum is regularly exacted, and the forced labour likewise, which consists of clearing snow from the houses of the Master and his friends, removing rubbish, and clearing their courtyards.

If a Jew dies, and has no son to succeed to his property, the will of the deceased is set aside, and the Master takes possession of his property.

" Rejjeb Ali Khan, who returned from Tabreez to Oroomiah last summer, demanded, while I was at the latter town, 120 tomans, the greater part of which he had then collected, and he absolutely refused to reckon this sum as part of the regular taxes. A deputation from the Jews left for Tabreez last summer to petition the authorities there, but the son of the Master heard of their departure, and they had been seized and brought back to Oroomiah.

" As an example of the unfair manner in which these taxes are imposed, the case of one Jew may be cited, who during last year paid twelve tomans as his share, though there are only four persons living in his house, and also that of his brother, who lives by himself and has no shop, and yet had to pay six tomans."

Lord Stanley approved of Mr Alison's exertions in favour of the Jews and Nestorians, and desired him to take every suitable opportunity of strongly pressing upon the Shah and his Ministers the interest felt by Her Majesty's Government in both these classes of his subjects, and their earnest hope that the Shah would extend to them his protection, redress any wrongs which they may suffer, and make his Moslem subjects clearly understand that any act of violence and wrong on Jews or Christians would not only entail upon them personal punishment, but the payment of pecuniary compensation to the sufferers.

Notwithstanding the representations of the British Government, however, complaints of oppression continued to arrive from various places in Persia, appealing for help, and the anxiety of Sir Moses became considerably increased by the cry of anguish which reached him from Moldavia.

" On the 4th of May last," the supplicants say in their letter to him, " a decree was issued by the Minister to expel all the Jews from the villages of Moldavia as coming under the category of vagabonds. Scarcely was the edict made known, when the Minister himself arrived here ; in another moment the enemies of Israel filled the streets and public places, seized every Jew, without distinction, that came in their way, crying out, ' He is a vagabond ;' bound him hand and foot with chains, beat him unmercifully ; drove out alike old and young, chased them out of the city, and delivered them over to the mercy of the soldiery to drive them beyond the frontier.

" A cry of anguish from the women, and like lamentations from the men, went up to Heaven. Old men and children, women with children at the breast, cry aloud, but there are none to pity, none to look with compassion. They have been driven from all the villages, made to leave their possessions, their goods and chattels, in the hands of their enemies, and have escaped only with their lives.

" The heads of the congregation here have entreated the Minister to withdraw the decree, but in vain have they supplicated.   Non-Israelites have also sought justice for the Jews, but they have pleaded to a deaf ear.   He seeks only their expulsion.

"In three days the prisons were overcrowded with our brethren.   Their persecutions for a while abated, still we were in fear and trembling lest every moment they should be renewed with fresh vigour, for the decree has not yet been recalled.

"A great evil threatens us, the hatred increases every day and every hour—there is none to stay the hand.   We therefore make known to you these our troubles and distresses, beseeching you with burning tears to aid us all in your power, and to defend the cause of the oppressed Israelites who are driven from the land of Moldavia.

"May the Creator of heaven and earth, the God of Israel, help us.

"Trouble upon trouble !   During the last three days soldiers have been going about the streets molesting the Jews, and with their swords they in-jured a woman with child.   Her cries brought persons to her rescue, and those who endeavoured to take the weapons from the soldiers were seized, thrown into prison, and charged with attempting to murder the soldiery. We have no one to look to for help except our Father in Heaven and His servant Moses.   The chief matters we dare not venture to write, out of dread and apprehension, for we are as sheep in the hands of the slaughterers."

Sir Moses received numerous petitions to the same effect from Galatz and Berlad, which he forwarded to the London Committee of Deputies of the British Jews.   The British Government took every opportunity to help them, yet no redress could be obtained, and the cries of the sufferers continued.

CHAPTER XXV.

1867.

SIR MOSES ACCEPTS A MISSION TO THE DANUBIAN PRINCI-
PALITIES — ACTION OF THE BRITISH, RUSSIAN, AND
PRUSSIAN GOVERNMENTS—PRINCE BISMARCK'S OPINION—
DEATH OF SIR MOSES' BROTHER, HORATIO.

SIR MOSES then addressed the following letter to the President *pro tem.* of the Board of Deputies of British Jews :

" GROSVENOR GATE, PARK LANE,
" *30th June* 5627 (1867).

" MY DEAR SIR,—It is with deep regret that I have to place in your hands further despatches received from Jassy, from which it would appear that the position of our unfortunate co-religionists in Moldavia still continues most distressing.   You will be pleased to submit these communications to the Board of Deputies without delay.

" The several memorials which I have received from Moldavia solicit so frequently and so urgently my personal presence there, that if, in the opinion of your Board and that of our community, it should be considered that my presence in Moldavia might prove of utility to those who in their misery apply to us for sympathy and aid, I should feel it an imperative duty, at whatever personal risk and sacrifice, to respond to the appeal thus piteously made.

" There can be no doubt that, as the delegate of our community, any representations that I might be entrusted to make as its organ would acquire great force and significance, while I should be encouraged by the consciousness that I should be acting, not only in accordance with my own sense of duty, but also as the exponent of the earnest wishes of your Board and of the Jews at large, that so unhappy a state of things as is now existing in Moldavia as affecting the Jews of that Principality, may, under the blessing of the Almighty, speedily cease."

The President *pro tem.* immediately convened a meeting, at which the Deputies expressed their deep sympathy with the sufferings of the Moldavian Jews, and entreated Sir Moses to undertake a Mission to the Principality, in the hope that his presence there would be as successful in relieving the grievances of our unfortunate brethren in that country as it had been in his previous Missions to Damascus, Russia, Morocco, and the Holy Land.

Sir Moses, in accepting the Mission thus urged upon him, had every possible support from the British Government. The Russian Government also manifested their sympathy with the sufferers, and expressed their approval of his going to Bucharest.

Baron Brunnow sent him a copy of a despatch to that effect, which he had received on the subject from Prince Gortchakoff, dated Tsarkoé Séla, 12th July 1867, which I subjoin in the original French :—

Copie d'une dépêche de S. Exc. Mr. le Chancelier Prince Gortchacow à l'Ambassadeur de Russie à Londres, en date de Tsarkaé-Sélo, le 12 Juillet 1867 :

"MR. LE BARON,—Dès la réception de la dépêche de Votre Exc., sub 155 je me suis empressé d'informer notre Consul-Général à Bucarest de la résolution de Sir Moses Montefiore de se rendre à Bucarest pour y plaider la cause de ses coreligionnaires. D'ordre de Notre Auguste Maitre, j'ai invité le Baron d'Offenberg à prêter à cette mission d'humanité tout le concours qui pourra dépendre de lui.—Recevez, &c.,

(Signé)   "GORTCHACOW."

The Prussian Government, as will be seen in the copy of a letter from Lord Loftus to Lord Stanley, as forwarded to Sir Moses through Lord Egerton, also supported the cause. Lord Egerton transmitted for his information a copy of a despatch which he had received from Her Majesty's Ambassador at Berlin, in which the latter reported a conversation he had had with Count Bismarck on the subject of the persecution of the Jews in the Danubian Principalities :—

" In obedience to the instructions of your Lordship's despatch, No. 20 of the 31st ultimo, the Ambassador writes : 'I have brought under the notice of Count Bismarck the subject of the ill-treatment to which the Jews have been subjected in the Danubian Principalities, and I requested His Excellency to furnish the Prussian agent at Bucharest with the necessary instructions to enable him to co-operate with Her Majesty's Consul-General in behalf of an unoffending and peaceable class of inhabitants, whom it behoved every civilized government to protect from acts of violence.

" Count Bismarck said that the Prussian Government would readily co-operate with Her Majesty's Government in this humane work.

" Last year, on a similar occasion, instructions of a like nature had been given to the Consul at Bucharest, and he would again renew them.

" His Excellency observed that the difficulties of Prince Charles were great. He was anxious to establish order and a legalised state of things. But he was not always able to carry out his wishes.

" He felt confident that the ill-treatment to which the Jews had been exposed was most repugnant to the feelings of Prince Charles, and that His Highness would do his utmost for their protection.—I have, &c.,

(Signed)   " AUGUSTUS LOFTUS."

On July the 20th he received letters of introduction from the Foreign Office to Mr (now Sir John) Green, and was informed at the same time that the British Government had written to Paris, Vienna, and St Petersburg about his journey to Moldavia.

July 27th.—Prayers were offered up in the Synagogues of the united congregations of the British Empire for the success of Sir Moses' Mission to Jassy, and two days later we find him at Dover, at the Lord Warden Hotel, surrounded by his travelling companions—Mr Arthur Cohen, Q.C., M.P.; Captain (now General) Henry Moore, of the Bombay Staff Corps; Mr James S. Daniel of Ramsgate, his medical attendant; and the writer. The following morning he crossed over to Calais, and in the evening he and his party arrived at Paris, where they stayed at the Hotel Meurice.

August 3rd.—Sir Moses received a letter from Mr Fane, the British Ambassador, appointing the following day for an audience with the Emperor at the Tuileries, of which the following is an account in Sir Moses' own words :—

"This day, Sunday, the 7th of August," he writes in his Diary, "I had the honour and happiness of an audience with His Imperial Majesty the Emperor Napoleon III. His Majesty received me most courteously, shook me by the hand, and said he was glad to see me again. I expressed my sincere thanks for the honour of the audience, tendered to His Majesty the expressions of the heartfelt gratitude of my co-religionists of England for His Majesty's powerful intercession on behalf of their brethren in Moldavia, and prayed His Majesty to continue his gracious efforts, so as to allow me to enjoy the invaluable benefit of His Majesty's support. The Emperor said I should have his support, enquired when I purposed leaving, and said Bucharest was a long journey. He again shook me by the hand on my taking leave. It was impossible for any person to have evinced more kindness than was shown me by His Majesty. After leaving the Palace I left a card at the British Embassy for the Hon. Mr Fane. He called on me at the Hotel Meurice, and I told him all that had passed at my audience with the Emperor. He was much pleased, and said that he should write home, and that what I had said was the same language as that of the Marquis of Moustier, the Foreign Minister."

We left Paris on the 6th of August, and travelled through Strasburg, Stuttgart (where Sir Moses was greeted by Dr Von Mayer, the Chief Rabbi), Donauwörth, and Ratisbon, and reached Vienna on the 14th, stopping at the Hotel Munsch.

" Accompanied by Arthur Cohen and Dr Loewe I paid a visit to Lord Bloomfield, the British Minister at the Court. He was very courteous, but said the Emperor would leave Vienna this evening. Lord Bloomfield rode with me to the Minister of Foreign Affairs, but he was out. I afterwards called on the Russian Minister ; he was at Ostend. Being greatly fatigued and very weak, on my return to the hotel I soon retired to rest.

" *Vienna, August* 15*th.*—This morning my kind nephew, Arthur Cohen, and my friend, Dr Loewe, communicated to me the intelligence they had received yesterday of the loss I had unhappily sustained by the demise of my dear brother Horatio. He was relieved from all suffering and called to eternal glory not many minutes before I took my fast on Sunday night (August 10th—Ab. 10th, the anniversary of the destruction of the Temple of Jerusalem). He was a very charitable man, a good husband and father. We entertained the most affectionate regard for each other.

" *Vienna, August* 16*th.*—Last night I received a telegram from Mrs Arthur Cohen to the effect that Dr Jenner had said it was dangerous for Arthur to go to Bucharest, and that consequently she could not give her consent to his going with me. I regret this decision on his account as well as my own. I thus lose the companionship of a very amiable and talented relative and friend at a time I stand most in need of his assistance.

" I am losing my strength, and am anxious to get on my voyage to Bucharest.

" The British Ambassador, Lord Bloomfield, paid me a long visit, and the Austrian Minister left his card."

Sunday, August 18*th.*—We left Vienna on board an Austrian steamer for Pesth, and proceeded to Bucharest, where we arrived on Thursday, the 22nd inst., taking up our quarters at the Hotel Otettelichano. Sir Moses at once called on Mr Green. The latter returned his visit the next day, and went with him to the Prince. On his return from the palace he received a visit from the prefect of the place.

Saturday, August 24*th.*—Sir Moses invited several members of the Hebrew community to be present at divine service, which on that day was held in his drawing-room, the distance of their place of worship and the overpowering heat of the day preventing him from walking there and joining the congregation.

Subsequently the Foreign Minister, also the two private Secretaries of the Prince, Monsieur Friedlander and Monsieur Picot, called, and when these had left, deputations from various Hebrew educational institutions and charitable societies came to pay their respects, and to thank him for the great fatigue he had undergone on their behalf.

Tuesday, August 27th.—" I suffer greatly," Sir Moses says, " by this climate, the heat of the weather deprives me of strength. Nevertheless, the hope of success cheers me. The reports constantly made to me of the serious aspect of affairs in this country, and at the intended outbreak against my co-religionists, are very alarming, more particularly as they are repeated to me by Mr Green, Her Britannic Majesty's Consul, as well as by many other Christians." Mr Hertz, the Director of the bank, came to inform Mr Green that money had been distributed among the mob to attack us, and to slaughter the Jews.

Still Sir Moses did not lose heart, but directed his attention to the petition he was about presenting to the Prince, of which the following is an exact copy :—

" BUCHAREST, 27th August 1867.

" TO HIS SERENE HIGHNESS PRINCE CHARLES I., Reigning Prince of Roumania.

" May it please your Serene Highness,—Statements having been circulated in England and elsewhere that my co-religionists in Roumania were no longer in the enjoyment of that tranquillity and safety to which they had, thanks to the Almighty and to the honour of this nation, been accustomed for several generations, I bethought me that as on other occasions and in other lands I had succeeded in restoring confidence among my co-religionists, so in Roumania on the present occasion I might do good by my presence among them. But before carrying out this resolution, I obtained the sanction of it from Her Britannic Majesty's Government, and through Her Majesty's Government, the approval of the Governments of Austria, France, Italy, Prussia, and Russia. I now, on behalf of my co-religionists in England, my native country, as well as on the behalf of those in every part of the world, with all humility entreat your Serene Highness to be pleased, through the Government of your Serene Highness, to warn all evil disposed persons not to molest the Jews in any manner, and to give positive orders that the Jews dwelling in all parts of the United Principalitica shall enjoy perfect protection in all which concerns the safety of their persons and their property. Permit me also to express to your Serene Highness my grateful appreciation of the enlightened sentiments of religious toleration of which your Serene Highness has always given proofs in matters concerning Jewish subjects of your Serene Highness, and in offering your Serene Highness my humble thanks for the personal honour conferred on me by listening to the manifestation of my anxiety with respect to the welfare of my co-religionists. Allow me to tender my heartfelt wishes for the health and happiness of your Serene Highness, and for the prosperity of the United Principalitica.—I have the honour to be, with the profoundest respect, the most obedient, humble servant of your Serene Highness,

(Signed) "MOSES MONTEFIORE."

Wednesday, August 28*th.*—A copy of the journal *Natinuea* was this day sent to Sir Moses, containing a harangue addressed by the editor to the people of Roumania. I give a full copy of it, that the reader may form an idea of the dangerous position in which Sir Moses found himself, and appreciate the courage and perseverance he manifested in the task before him :—

"Two weeks ago we announced to our readers the arrival of a wealthy Israelite from London, Sir Moses Montefiore, and now this personage, who is in possession of the keys to all the doors of the Cabinets of Europe, actually arrived yesterday in our capital. We understand that M. Crémieux is to follow (if he has not arrived already). Need we tell our Roumanian brethren what these people want in our beautiful country? Is it possible that the Roumanians should be so simple, so foolish, so led away by the friends of the Hebrews, so betrayed by those who secretly sell the soil of our ancestors? Can our brethren be indeed so indifferent to their natural interests, so blinded by some Jewish journals written in the Roumanian language, as not to penetrate into the real intentions of these persons amongst us? What they strive at just at a time when anarchy prevails in the land, and the ministers are ignorant of their mission, and resign just at a moment when the Hebrews enter the land? No! No! No! Ye Roumanians ; ye descendants of those who knew how to preserve this beautiful land in all storms, who knew how to defend and rescue it from the claws of the Goths, the Huns, Turks, Poles, Hungarians, Germans, &c.; ye descendants of these noble ancestors, you know as well as we what these Hebrews want here, and who has brought them here. You will indeed still have in your veins sufficient of the blood of your ancestors not to permit that the land should fall into the hands of the Hebrews ! There will yet be found in Roumania patriotic voices, whose echo will carry the cry of despair of this poor and betrayed nation into the Cabinets which are occupied with the future of Roumania, and which are engaged in rescuing this land from the hands of the enemies of civilization, that have no other design than money—money—and again money ! and thus the ruin of the simple Roumanian people.

"We have watched the steps of the enemies, who mean to surprise us, and to transform our land into a Palestine ; we have watched all their steps and traces, and followed them without intermission, and to-day we call to all Roumanians : sleep not ! and more especially it is the commercial classes, who daily suffer grievous wrong, and are brought near their ruin—and indeed only through these bloodsuckers, the Hebrews—to those we call, sleep not, assemble, consult—hasten, all ye commercial men of Roumania, to the common consultation as to what is to be done, in order that we may not awake one fine morning and see the crown lands, to the value of hundreds of millions, bought by the Hebrews, as is to be expected from the measures taken by the present Government.

" The unfortunate **Roumanian** peasants, who have defended and preserved this sacred soil with rivers **of** their blood, and have maintained it by their language, religion, and sweat, in what cries and lamentations would they burst forth when seized by the claws of the Hebrews, as the innocent bird cries out when caught by the teeth of the poisonous serpent of India. 'Awake ye Romans,' was lately **sung** in the Halls of the Athenæum, on the field of literature and nationality. Awake ye Roumanians! let **us** all awake and assemble on that field upon which **the** sentiment **of all** political, social, national, and patriotic duty **calls, the duty not to allow** the naturalization of the Hebrews, of those outcasts, **which even our Redeemer** Jesus Christ has cursed, that they should possess no country, no **home ;** were **we** to allow their naturalization, then all Crown domains now **exposed to** sale, to the ruination **of** the country, this sacred treasure **of our fathers** would fall into the hands of the Hebrew bankers! . . . and then! . . . Roumania would become a Palestine, and the free Roumanian, the Christian Roumanian would become the slave of those outcasts ! . . . and Roumania will be the land of the Hebrews and not of the Roumanian.

" **Merchants and Brethren of Bucharest! Merchants and Roumanian Brethren of the Mountains !** (Wallachia). **Do you not see in what net our** brethren beyond the **Milkor (Moldavia) have been** caught ? Do **you not hear** the cries and lamentations **of those brethren who** have been sold to the Jews, by the protection **of some Ciokois ?** . . . **Shall you** suffer political privileges to be given to the Hebrews, **so that** nothing will be left in your hands **wherewith to carry on your commerce ;** neither the **meat,** nor the egg, nor the fruit of the **tree, nor the berry of the** vine, nor the fruit of your garden, nor the onion, **nor the maize,** . . . **not** even the drop of wine which the Christian stands in **need of for** preparing the Lord's Supper—as is done in Moldavia ? Shall you suffer any longer the groans of your brethren beyond the Milkor (Moldavia), and their sighs under the lacerating **claws** of the Hebrews, without raising your powerful voice—powerful, **for** it is the voice of God ! without **demanding** that the rights and the soil of Roumania remain intact ? No ! Oh no ! You will not suffer that ! The God of our Fathers will be with us, will assist us in cutting the thread of those **machinations by which our land is to** be bartered away to the Hebrews ! . . . May God be with us !

" **Citizens** of the Capital ! and **especially ye merchants and brethren of** Bucharest, ye who in common **with us have** welcomed our brethren of the literary society, **it is** incumbent upon **you to take the initiative, and through** your example to **call** out all Roumanians **for a common action, as a welcome** to the noble Israelite, Montefiore ; that **Hebrew—whom** even our Minister of State, Mr Stefan Golesku, **is said to have received at the gates of the** capital with great splendour.

" Let this action consist in **our signing this** day **three** petitions : **one to** His Serene Highness, the **Prince, a second to the** House of Deputies, and a third **to the Senate, in which we demand the fulfilment of** the following four points :—(1) That of the Crown **domains** nothing be sold, but vineyards and small fields situate at **a** distance, **which prove** only injurious to the State ; (2) All Hebrews **who have come** into the land since 1848 provided with passports, and who **have no** industrial occupation, shall **be sent by the Government** to the land from whence they have come ; (3) All **Hebrew proprietors** of **factories, where Roumanian** workmen are employed, as **also those who carry on a trade, as tinmen,** tailors, &c., all men of the higher sciences—shall **be tolerated in the land ;** provided, however, that they enter upon the path of **civilisation, for which the** Government will take the necessary measures. As to **the privileges of these Jews,** they will be limited to those prescribed by the **civil law ; (4) Henceforth no Hebrew shall** have permission to enter the land **for the purpose of settling in it.**

"This is the policy and wish of the journal *Natiunea*, in respect of the Hebrews, and we believe it is the wish of all true patriots of Roumania, who have at heart the welfare of their country.

"The signature of the above petitions takes place from to-day at the office of this Journal; let all Roumanians hasten to sign them! For the facility of citizens, lists for signature will be laid out before the Theatre and in St George's Place.

"We hope the communities of the united and indivisible Roumania will send, within a few days, thousands of signatures to the office of the *Natiunea*, a committee will then be formed to send the petitions to their respective places.

"To work! to work! ye Roumanian Brethren! and may God be with us!"

CHAPTER XXVI.

1867.

THE *Natiunea* having given notice to the Prefecture of its
intention of publicly securing signatures to the above
petitions, the following reply was received :—

"In reply to your notice, No. 3915, without date, I hasten to inform you
that in Roumania, no lists for signatures may be laid out in the streets and
public places, except on the occasion of the plebiscite, and I do not believe
that it is permitted to a private gentleman to open such plebiscites. The
right, however, of petition and meeting in houses is granted to every
Roumanian. If Government were to allow any one to place subscription
tables in public places or streets it might easily occur that adversaries, entertaining opinions differing from those expressed in the lists, might come
forward, and the police might hardly suffice to maintain public order. The
leading article of your last Journal has already found many adversaries, and
these could avail themselves of the opportunity to disturb the public peace,
which the Government could by no means suffer, more especially as your
ideas rest upon no sound basis, and the Government feels itself, without
your assistance, sufficiently powerful to protect the right of the land."

The editor of the Journal *Speranta* called to say that he was
told in the Public Garden, "we should run away, as the people
were now going to kill Sir Moses."

Reverting to the Diary I find the following entry :—"I feel
very weak and poorly to-day, the air is excessively hot, and I
am vexed with sinister reports and intended outbreaks against
the Jews.

"About two o'clock I received, as did likewise Dr Loewe,
Captain Moore, and Mr Daniel, the honour of a card of invitation
from His Serene Highness the Prince, to dine to-day at the
Palace.

"We arrived at the Palace a few minutes before half-past

five. Mr Green soon arrived, and he presented my companions to His Serene Highness.

"Prince Charles (now His Majesty, the King), was most courteous and kind to us. We dined in the Palace, contrary to His Highness' custom. He generally dined, he told me, in his garden, but was fearful I might take cold. I sat on the Prince's right; he was exceedingly courteous, and spoke on many subjects. He had been in Morocco, in the year 1862, during the Spanish war, in Gibraltar, and twice in England. We had an excellent entertainment, and his military band played some beautiful pieces in the garden during dinner.

"The Prince and all the party went into the garden afterwards, and I had the honour of smoking a cigar with him. Coffee, cigars, and liqueurs were handed round. We returned much pleased.

"*Thursday, August 29th.*—This morning the chief officer of police, and Monsieur Soveser, Chef de division au Ministère de L'intérieur, called, and arranged with Sir Moses to accompany him to-morrow to see the Christian charitable institutions in the city, in accordance with the wish he expressed yesterday to His Highness. He then rode to Mr Green's, and had the great benefit of half-an-hour's conversation with him. 'I hope,' Sir Moses says, 'I satisfied him that the object of my visit to Roumania was limited entirely to obtain from the Prince and his Government their assurance that the Jews should enjoy security of their persons and their property, and be treated kindly and with justice.'"

On his return to the hotel an extraordinary scene of tumult and uproar presented itself.

Notwithstanding the reply of the Prefecture to the Notice No. 3915 given by the editor of the *Natiunea*, informing him that in Roumania no lists for signature may be laid out in the streets and public places, except on the occasion of the Plébiscite, a table was placed, with the lists in question for signatures, in front of the windows of the apartments occupied by Sir Moses, and thousands of people crowded round the table, many of them approaching towards the windows in the most threatening attitude. Some persons from the hotel then suddenly entered the room occupied by Sir Moses, terror-stricken at what they had seen and heard in the streets, calling his attention to the

Sir Moses addressing the threatening populace from the Hotel at Bucharest.   *See Vol. II., page 205.*

crowds at his window, and saying, "They want to take your life."

Most persons in Sir Moses' position would have manifested great fear and excitement, but this was not the case with him. He went to the window facing the enraged populace, opened both wings, and placed himself right in front of it, and I had the privilege of being permitted to place myself at his side.

"Fire away," he said, "if you like. I came here in the name of justice and humanity to plead the cause of innocent sufferers." They stared at him first for a few minutes. Then the shouting and tumult increased, but still he did not move.

Ultimately the crowd, threatening and shouting, dispersed. In the evening Mr Halfon, the banker, called. With tears in his eyes, he cried, "We shall all be massacred."

Monsieur A. Halfon, the President of the Comité de l'Alliance Israélite de Bucharest had strongly advised Sir Moses not to come to Moldavia at all, as by doing so he might hurt the feelings of the Prince, the Government, and the Roumanian population. Sir Moses, however, having before him the appeal of the Hebrew communities in Moldavia, who strongly and repeatedly supplicated him to plead their cause before the Prince personally, did not consider himself justified in following the advice of Mons. Halfon, especially as Mr Green had made a statement to the effect that it was the opinion of some persons in Bucharest "that the wealthy class among the Hebrew community, having no cause whatever to complain, would not like to join the middle and poorer classes, who publicly complain of the grievances they have to endure."

At the foot of the page I give an exact copy of Monsieur A. Halfon's letter.*

* Under date of August the 6th, 1867, he addressed him as follows:—

TRES VÉNÉRABLE BARONNET,—J'ai pris la liberté de vous adresser aujourd'hui le telegramme suivant:

"Informé de votre projet de venir ici, je vous prie d'arrêter votre depart jusqu'à reception de ma lettre de ce jour," et je m'empresse de porter à votre connaisance les raisons pour lesquelles j'ai pensé devoir arrêter votre voyage.

1°. Et tout d'abord pour ne point vous soumettre, à votre age, que le bon Dieu vous prolonge pour bien d'années encore, aux fatigues d'un pareil voyage.

2°. Pour ne point blesser l'amour propre et la subtibilité de notre Prince, de notre gouvernement et de la population roumaine.

Le Prince autant que ses Ministres nous font toutes les promesses pour le bien de nos correligionaires.

Quand aux pérsecutions dont nos frères furent victimes, il nous reste à ésperer

The tears of the banker, and the threatened massacre of the Jews, did not affect in any way the indomitable courage of Sir Moses. "Are you afraid?" said he to M. Halfon; "I have no fear whatever, and will at once order an open carriage, take a drive through the principal streets and thoroughfares, go even outside the town, and drive near some public garden. Every one shall see me; it is a holy cause; that of justice and humanity. I trust in God; He will protect me."

One of the attendants entering the room, Sir Moses gave the order for an open carriage, with two lights in front, so that his person might be seen by everybody. Within ten minutes' time the carriage was ready at the door. I had the honour of being invited to take a drive with him and sit by his side. Monsieur Halfon, dreading the consequence of what he deemed so rash an act, returned to his house. The people in the hotel, as well as all those who had been watching the house from day to day, as if they expected some extraordinary event to occur, placed themselves along the street in two rows, right and left. Hundreds of new-comers did the same; but we continued our drive without taking any particular notice of them. We had been driving for nearly two hours, and all went on peaceably enough; but there was one carriage, as we drove along outside the town, which appeared purposely to follow us in every turn we made. Not feeling quite so calm and easy as Sir Moses, I suggested we should halt and inquire the object of the gentleman in the rear carriage following us. Sir Moses consented to our doing so. We were a good distance from the town, on the public road. No lamps were to be seen except the two in front of our carriage. It was rather an exciting moment. Upon asking that gentleman, in the Roumanian language, whether there was any particular reason for his following so closely to our carriage,

qu'elles ne se représenteront de plus, vu que les appuis de nos frères à Paris, Londres, et Vienne n'ont pas manqué de produire par les journeaux l'effet desiré.

Notre opinion est donc de ne point vous déranger pour venir dans nos contrées.

Veuillez très-respectable Baronnet continuer à nous aider de loin et d'accord avec le très-honorable Monsieur Crémieux; ce serait beaucoup mieux, nous le pensons, pour notre cause.

Voici l'humble opinion du Comité de l'Alliance Israélite d'ici et de votre devoué que a l'honneur, très vénérable philantrope, de vous presenter ses civilités les plus respectueuses.

Le Président du Comité de l'Alliance Israélite de Bucarest.

A. HALFON.

he jumped out quickly, and, with an air of determination, proceeded towards Sir Moses, which made me feel even more uncomfortable than before, apprehending as I did the sight of a revolver or a dagger. But happily, to my great relief, he commenced addressing Sir Moses, not in Roumanian, but in German.

His object in following Sir Moses, he said, was to find an opportunity, in a convenient, secluded place, to request him to intercede in his behalf with his Serene Highness Prince Charles, that he would grant him the continuance of the privilege to light the town with oil-lamps!

It was late when we returned to the hotel, where we found a woman of ladylike appearance and manner of address waiting to see Sir Moses. She would not give her name for political reasons, and was very pressing in her request to have an interview with Sir Moses on a political subject. A military officer also came to have some private conversation with him, likewise on a political subject. He was unknown to the persons in the hotel, nor could his name be ascertained. Sir Moses would not see either of them, and it was with great difficulty they could be persuaded to leave the hotel.

Friday, August 30th. — "I am," Sir Moses says, "most anxious, weak, out of health, and vexed to the heart. No one can imagine the extreme pain of my situation. Political factions strive to create confusion by my presence in this place."

In the evening, however, he had the satisfaction of receiving from the Prince a reply to his petition, which cheered him up again. His Highness thus addressed him :

"Monsieur le Baronnet,—J'ai reçu votre lettre du 27 Août dernier et j'en ai pris connaissance avec un vif intérêt. Comme j'ai eu l'occasion de vous le dire de vive voix, les vœux que vous formez pour vos coreligionnaires sont déjà accomplis Les Israélites sont l'objet de toute ma sollicitude et de toute celle de mon gouvernement et je suis bien aise que vous soyez venu en Roumanie pour vous convaincre que la persécution religieuse dont la malveillance a fait tant de bruit n'existe point. S'il est arrivé que des Israélites fussent inquiétés, ce sont là des faits isolés, dont mon gouvernement n'entend pas assumer la responsabilité. Je tiendrai toujours à l'honneur de faire respecter la liberté religieuse et je veillerai sans cesse à l'exécution des lois qui protègent les Israélites comme tous les autres Roumains dans leur personne et dans leurs biens.—Veuillez recevoir, Monsieur le Baronnet, l'assurance de ma considération très distinguée,   "Charles."
  "Sir Moses Montefiore, Bart."
  "Cotroceni, le 18/30 Août 1867."

Saturday, August 31st.—Sir Moses attended Divine service

in his drawing-room, the minister of the Spanish and Portuguese community officiating. At the conclusion, Sir Moses showed the letter of the Prince to all present, and it caused great satisfaction.

In the course of the day he paid a visit to Mr Green, and in the evening the Prince's Secretary called, remaining with us nearly two hours. Speaking to him of the disturbances of last Thursday, and the threatening attitude of the populace, he said, only a few days previously two persons had been murdered in the public street in daylight, and the friends of peace and order on hearing it expressed great satisfaction that none of our party had hitherto been molested. We then showed him the letters we had received from persons who gave their full names and addresses, suggesting even that we should make enquiries as to the correctness of their statement to the effect that it was intended, and had been arranged, to make an attack on the life of Sir Moses; upon which the Prince's Secretary observed, " Threatening letters of the kind are sometimes sent to the Prince himself, even pointing out the place where an attack is to be made on him ; but His Highness shows no fear, and proceeds even to the very spot at the hour named for the attack.

Sunday, September 1st.—We all went to the Palace to take leave of the Prince. His Highness repeated to Sir Moses all that he had stated in his letter, and regretted the unfortunate occurrence which had taken place in front of his hotel. In the room in which we assembled before we were conducted to the presence of the Prince, we were told that when the populace a year or two ago had attacked a Jewish place of worship, His Highness, from his private purse, paid all the damage done. His Highness expressed himself most graciously to Sir Moses, and the latter reiterated his gratitude to him in his own name and in that of the Board of Deputies of the London Committee of British Jews for the gracious reception His Highness had accorded him and the gentlemen who accompanied him on his Mission.

On leaving the Palace Sir Moses called on the Consuls, all of whom evinced great satisfaction with the Prince's letter, and returned home to indite a letter to Mr Green, of which the following is a copy :—

" BUCHAREST, 30th *August* 1867.

" MY DEAR SIR,— It is with sincere satisfaction I beg to hand you enclosed a copy of the reply I have had the honour to receive from His Serene

Highness Prince Charles to my petition of the 27th instant in reference to my Mission to this country on behalf of my co-religionists.

"May I now beg the favour of you to communicate its contents to Lord Stanley, with my grateful thanks to his Lordship and Her Majesty's Government for the powerful aid they so kindly granted me?

"As the object of coming to this country was not to make enquiry regarding past unfortunate events, but to obtain for my brethren dwelling in Roumania security for the future, and fully relying on the honoured words of His Serene Highness Prince Charles, 'Les Israélites sont l'objet de toute ma sollicitude et de toute celle de mon Gouvernment,' . . . 'je tiendrai toujours à l'honneur de faire respecter la liberté religieuse et je veillerai sans cesse à l'exécution des lois qui protègent les Israelites comme tous les autres Roumains dans leur personne et dans leur biens,' I consider my object happily accomplished, and feel confident that his Lordship will be pleased with the result.

"I deeply regret that the state of my health, with other considerations, prevents my going to see my co-religionists at Jassy, otherwise I would at once have proceeded to that city.

"Allow me to take this opportunity to tender you my heartfelt thanks for your valuable advice and assistance which have so materially contributed to the satisfactory issue of my humble labours in the cause of humanity. —Believe me, my dear Sir, with great esteem, yours very faithfully."

Sir Moses informed the Board of Deputies in London by telegram of all that had occurred. Subsequently he paid visits to the representatives of the Hebrew community at Bucharest in order to ascertain what foundation there was for the pretended dread expressed by the editor of the *Natinuea* that Bucharest would be converted into a second Jerusalem. He also inquired about the Synagogues, charitable institutions, and schools. He was told that they had a large number of places of worship, colleges for Hebrew and theological subjects, hospitals and societies for the sick, loan societies for the poor, irrespective of creed, societies for providing shelter for travellers and fuel and clothing for the poor, and a large number of schools for boys and girls, rich and poor.

"To a person unacquainted with the spirit which pervades Jewish institutions," he says, "the expression of dread that 'Bucharest' might be converted into 'a second Jerusalem' in the face of so considerable a number of houses of prayer, colleges, and charitable institutions, cannot be a matter of surprise ; but he who knows the principles—heavenly principles revealed on Sinai which breathed the 'breath of life' into every act of benevolence performed, into every sentiment of truth expressed in institutions similar to those I have now seen, and of which you have given me the particulars—would entertain no such feeling of uneasiness. On the contrary, he would rejoice if, in the sense of peace, loyalty, and humanity in general, Bucharest were to make itself deserving, in the language of the non-Roumanian visitors, of the appellation of 'a second Jerusalem,' and the reason of it is obvious: the more Synagogues, the more prayers are offered up for the preservation of the life of the reigning monarch and the prosperity of the country; the more colleges for religious instruction, the more efficient the promulgation of the law of God: 'Thou shalt love thy neighbour as thyself' (Lev. xix. 18); the more charitable institutions, the more aid, comfort, and consolation for the poor and suffering. 'Jerusalem' is the emblem of peace, as the word 'Shalom' indicates, and Bucharest, nay, the whole country under the sway of His Serene Highness, the reigning Prince, would become renowned as an abode of peace for all his loyal subjects, without distinction of creed or nationality."

The street was now thronged with thousands of his co-religionists, and many houses presented the appearance of an impromptu illumination.

CHAPTER XXVII.

1867.

IT had been Sir Moses' intention, when setting out on his
Mission, to proceed direct to Jassy, but he was advised to
go to Bucharest first, and to place the petition in the hands of
Prince Charles. Having now accomplished this, and received
from His Highness the assurance that justice should be done,
and help rendered to those who stood so much in need of it, he
prepared to go to Jassy and other places, in order to make
known to the Governors, Judges, and high functionaries, the
promises made by the Prince, and the gracious sentiments
expressed by him towards the Jews, but the excited state of
the country precluded the realisation of that wish.

On the day after the uproar in front of the Hotel Otetteliano,
being in a state of great anxiety, I went, without the knowledge
of Sir Moses, to Mr Green, showing him the threatening letters
I had received, and describing to him minutely all that had
happened. Whilst expressing deep regret and sympathy, he
did not hold out any prospect of seeing the excitement of the
populace abate as soon as he would have wished, nor could he
suggest any means by which at that moment the cause of the
agitation might be removed.

As for Sir Moses going to Jassy, he said that was quite out
of the question. Were he to insist on doing so, he (Mr Green),
as the English Consul General, might perhaps accompany him
himself, and Prince Charles and his government would undoubtedly do all in their power to protect him. Nevertheless,
he thought there was no guarantee for his personal safety nor
for that of his co-religionists.

Mr Green, after my interview with him, expressed to Sir

Moses personally the same views on the subject, and the latter, not because he apprehended any danger to his own life, but to avoid giving cause for any dangerous outbreak against those whom he came to help, was reluctantly compelled to relinquish the idea of proceeding to Jassy.

The same evening Sir Moses had the honour of receiving His Highness' portrait, accompanied by a flattering letter. This mark of gracious attention on the part of the Prince greatly pleased Sir Moses.

The portrait may be seen now in the Lecture Hall of Judith, Lady Montefiore's Theological College, most suitably placed above a tableau representing a number of His Highness' Roumanian subjects,—pupils assembled at a public school at Botuschau, Roumania, celebrating the one hundredth anniversary of Sir Moses' birthday.

We left Bucharest for Giurgevo in the evening, escorted by cavalry as a guard of honour. We had had similar protection at Bucharest, ever since the gathering of the populace took place, and soldiers and commissioners of police were posted in the hotel, some of them even near the apartments of Sir Moses. One of the soldiers was pointed out to us as being an Israelite, and a fine handsome fellow he was. The presence of these men did not prevent certain suspicious looking persons from entering the apartments of Sir Moses, unexpectedly, at very inconvenient moments. How that happened could not be explained.

We arrived at Giurgevo by eleven o'clock A.M. A large number of deputations were announced to Sir Moses, and he began to receive them, but the day was oppressively hot, and accompanied by a sandstorm, which made itself unpleasantly felt even in the room, so that Sir Moses was obliged to desist and take some rest. The next day he visited the German and Portuguese Synagogues, also several Jewish and Christian schools, leaving souvenirs for the pupils and teachers, and gifts for the charitable institutions. Two commissioners of police and a guard of honour remained with us night and day until our departure on the 24th September, when we went on board the *Danube* steamer, on our return to England. We cast anchor at Rustschuk, and remained there over night, Sir Moses having in this place also to receive many deputations, who brought information respecting their schools and charitable institutions.

Friday, September 6th.—We continued our journey to Thurn Severin, thence we steered our course to Sistova and Nicopolis. The situation of the town is very picturesque, Nicopolis resting partly on the brow of a range of cliffs and partly in the bed of a narrow valley. Sir Moses intended remaining there to rest on the Sabbath, but as it was still early in the day, he continued on board till we reached Drenkova, where, as soon as the boat stopped, he went on shore.

Sir Moses, as the reader will remember from what I stated on this subject before, was a great admirer of the beauties of nature. On his setting out on this journey from Pesth, he expressed great delight with the scenery at several places on the Danube, and he considered it a great compensation for the trouble, fatigue, and anxiety he had to endure in the course of the present Mission to be enabled to enjoy so grand a sight. As we went further up the stream, the scenery became still more beautiful. Near a place called " Palanka," the Hungarian Mountains in the Upper Banat almost touch the Servian Chain on the opposite bank, causing the bed of the river to contract to such an extent as to turn the latter into a torrent, which increases in impetuosity till the boat nears the famous rock of Baby Kaly. At this spot the roaring of the waters, the upheaved rocks, the flights of eagles ever hovering in the air in all directions, strike the ordinary traveller with awe. Sir Moses was the first to express his fervent devotion to the Creator of the Universe, and his rapturous delight at the sight presented by the wild grandeur of the country. "Emblems on earth," he calls them, "of rigorous justice, blended with calm mercy in the realms of heaven."

When our boat passed through the whirlpools, not far from the famous cavern " Piscabara," we were exposed to great danger. The bed of the Danube is here formed of numerous masses of perpendicular rocks, between which it is necessary to steer with the utmost caution. There was only one narrow channel through which vessels could pass, and then only one at the time, and had ours been met by another coming in an opposite direction, they would both have been carried away by the violence of the stream, and dashed to pieces by the water rebounding from rock to rock.

Every one on board anxiously watched the soundings of the

pilot in silence. Whilst Sir Moses was looking down the narrow channel as the vessel glided along, the Captain accosted him with the words, "There is not more than a foot and a half of water now in the channel," to which Sir Moses calmly, in the words of Isaiah, replied, "It is the Eternal God, who maketh a way in the sea and a path in the mighty waters. When thou passest through the waters, I will be with thee, said the Lord, and through the rivers, they shall not overflow thee." He added, "I admire the mighty works of the Creator, but no fear of danger enters my heart."

His attention was called to the remains of the road cut by Trajan on the Servian side of the river, along the side of the rock, and to a tablet commemorating the conquest of Dacia by the Roman Emperor. It is in the form of a tablet, held by two genii, on each side of which is a dolphin, while in the centre is the Roman eagle. The words

> "Imp. Caes. D. Nervae, filius Nerva Trajanus.
> Germ. Pont. — imus,"

may still be seen.

On reaching New Orsova, we saw the ruins of the bridge built by the same Emperor, after his victory over the Dacian King Decebatus. The remains of the arches are still visible at low water, and the towers on each side of the river apparently still in the same position. The bridge, we were informed, consisted of twenty-two stone piles, with wooden arches, the river being shallow, the current gentle, and the whole width not more than 443 feet. Thereupon Sir Moses observed:

"I have seen the spot where the ancient city of Tyre lies under water, the tops of its public buildings one might almost imagine to be still visible. I also visited the land where the gigantic palaces, the figures of the mighty Pharaohs, and the houses of assembly for idolatrous worship are in utter ruins. All that is false," he says. "All institutions intended for keeping the people in darkness, shutting out from them the light of God, encouraging and upholding the practice of injustice, teaching oppression of the poor, innocent, and helpless, have been ordained by Him, who is the Father of us all, to disappear entirely from the surface of the earth. I look upon the Roman remains in this locality as only one of a thousand other striking evidences of the fulfilment of the Word of God vouchsafed unto us by his prophets."

All on board flocked around him, listening in reverential silence to the words he spoke in his pleasing and impressive tone ; and, over-topping them all by his lofty figure, he had the appearance, as he stood among them, of an ancient patriarch addressing his loving children.

The " Iron Gate," or " Demirkapi," as the spot is called by the Turks, was another object to which his attention was directed, and called forth his admiration ; but it is too well known to need any further description here.

The place selected by Sir Moses for resting on the Sabbath was charming. The view presented by the river and the adjacent rocks was grand and imposing, and delighted him all day long. He now felt greatly relieved from the fatigue and anxiety which, during the last few weeks, had so enfeebled his health.

In the evening, about nine o'clock (September 7th), we went on board the *Szechenyi* steamboat, and arrived the following Monday at Pesth and Buda. On Tuesday we left Pesth for Vienna, where we arrived the same day. Sir Moses called on Lord Bloomfield, on the Russian Ambassador, on the Austrian Minister of Foreign Affairs, Herr von Beust, and again received deputations from various communities. On Thursday he bade farewell to his friends, and proceeded *via* Salzburg, Munich, Strassburg, and Paris to Dover and Ramsgate, where he arrived on Friday, the 20th, and went at once to Synagogue to render thanks to heaven for his safe return.

Among the numerous letters which awaited him at East Cliff was one from the representatives of the Portuguese and German congregations at Bucharest, in which the following passages, translated from the original Hebrew, show the gratitude of his brethren, and the high appreciation of his presence among them in a time of great trouble.

" In all generations," they say, " thorns and thistles have grown up in the vineyard of the Lord, but the Almighty delivered us from them ; also, in our generation, and in our land, our enemies have embittered our lives and resolved upon the extermination of our remnant, fear and dread surrounded us, our lives were in constant peril ; this was our portion and our lot.

" In our affliction we have called on our brethren to have compassion on us, but none of them took it to heart, until it came to your ears, Father of Israel. As your prototype Moses, son of Amrám, you stood by us in the time of our troubles, and for the benefit of all our brethren you pleaded our cause before princes, and, as rain from Heaven causes the plants to grow, so your words entered the hearts of princes and caused beautiful fruits of salvation to flourish.

"Be our lot whatever it may, we rejoice in the consoling hope that Israel has not been forsaken. We have our shield amongst us, and we may rest in safety, for 'when Moses held up his hand, Israel prevailed.'

"It is with the sincerest pleasure that we now come to express our heart-felt gratitude, and to narrate some of your good deeds, as it is written, 'Withhold not good from them to whom it is due.'

"When you heard that our enemies rose up against us, you left the care and comfort of your habitation, the city wherein your heart delights to dwell. You came to behold our troubles, and we have seen your face as though we had seen the face of a godly man, for the seed which you have sown will, with the assistance of God, bring forth delightful fruit; therefore we say of you as was said of Cæsar, 'He came, saw, and conquered.'

"We beg likewise to thank you most sincerely for the money which you left for the helpless and needy, and the support of the hospital. May the words be applied to you, 'He that giveth unto the poor shall not lack.' We call aloud, 'Happy London, Sir Moses dwelleth amongst you.'

"We cannot sufficiently express all the good which you have done for us, but we all give praise and glory to the godly man who, in his eighty-fourth year, has come to see our encampment in this wilderness. May the Almighty lengthen your days, and may your strength be as your days.—Signed by

"J. L. WEINBERG.   M. G. POPICZ.   LEON B. LÖBEL.
"M. MOSCOWICZ.   B. L. WISNER.   EM. BUCHNER.
"D. M. COHENISEN.   A. E. GASTER.

"*Representatives of the German Congregation.*

"JOSEPH HALFON.   ELIAS JOS. COHEN. JONA JOSEPH.
"*Representatives of the Portuguese Congregation.*"

Monsieur Halfon, the banker, to whom, before leaving Bucharest, Sir Moses had sent £200 for distribution among Christian and Jewish poor, also addressed a letter to him, conveying the thanks of the Mayor of Bucharest, and those of the Hebrew community, for his kind donations. "Since your departure," Mr Halfon writes, "no representation or complaint has reached me from any person. I am convinced of its being a happy prelude of the fruits of your philanthropic voyage."

The sentiments expressed in these letters afforded Sir Moses particular satisfaction, inasmuch as he was mindful of Monsieur Halfon's former advice to him not to come to Moldavia at all. Now he hears from the representatives of both the German and Portuguese communities of that place, and of the President of the Alliance himself, that his presence amongst them was not only desirable but most urgent.

The difference of opinion on the subject which manifested itself previously to Sir Moses' arrival may perhaps be explained by what had been stated in the British Consul's letter to Lord

Stanley, to the effect that the more wealthy class of the Jews in Roumania had apparently not much reason to complain of ill-treatment.

Sir Moses now made his reports to Lord Stanley, Baron Brunnow, and the London Committee of Deputies of the British Jews. The latter, six days later (26th September), at a special meeting, adopted a resolution, that "The Board can well appreciate the amount of peril and the great anxieties to which its venerated colleague must have been subjected in seeking the accomplishment of his arduous undertaking—doubtless the blessing of Providence, his perseverance, his untiring energy, and his wise discretion, have on this, as on previous occasions, enabled him to succeed; and the Board expresses its ardent hope that this honoured champion of Israel may be long spared to enjoy the esteem and love of his co-religionists, and the friends of humanity throughout the world."

September 27th.—It being near the time for the celebration of solemn festivals in the Hebrew community, Sir Moses invited to East Cliff a number of relatives and friends, who spent many happy days with him. On his return to London he attended the meetings of his companies and various communal institutions.

Thursday, October 10th.—The Deputy of Ramsgate having received a numerously signed requisition to call a public meeting for the purpose of requesting Sir Moses to sit for his portrait to be placed in the Town Hall, proceeded to East Cliff to make the request. Sir Moses consented, and at a meeting of the Committee, Mr S. A. Hart, R.A., was appointed to paint the portrait. It was to be a very large picture, nine feet long. A resolution was also passed to the effect that an address should be presented to Sir Moses on the 21st November.

In appreciation of the attention paid to him by his Ramsgate friends, he invited the Deputy, two of the Committee, and the clergymen of St Laurence and St Peter's to dine with him and his friends from London, including Mr Hart, the artist, on the day fixed for the presentation of the address, and at the same time sent £100 to the treasurer of the charity schools of Ramsgate to be divided amongst the children.

December 12th.—He had an interview with Mr Jackson, Her Majesty's Consul-General in Syria, on the desirability of appointing an English Consul at Haifa for the better protection of the Jews, and he addressed Lord Stanley on the subject. Hearing that Mr and Mrs Eldridge had seen a very neat and light carriage, which pleased them greatly, he considered it a great pleasure to be permitted to present them with the same as a token of appreciation of the Consul's kindness, and the protection afforded to Sir Moses' co-religionists.

The Diary of this day has an entry referring to a narrow escape he had from personal danger. On his way through Smithfield to Fitzroy Square in a cab, his footman being on the box with the driver, a butcher's cart drawn by a runaway horse ran into them. The terrified driver sprang from the box, leaving them to their fate; but fortunately the furious animal turned aside at the very moment when it appeared impossible for them to escape. "Another mark," he says, "of God's goodness and providential protection."

He attended a special meeting of the Middlesex Magistrates to consider what steps should be taken in consequence of the late outrage at the House of Detention, a collection being afterwards made for the relief of the sufferers.

CHAPTER XXVIII.

1868.

DURING the latter part of December 1867 and nearly the
whole of January 1868 he was confined to his chamber at
Ramsgate by a severe attack of bronchitis, and was just about
to start by the advice of his medical attendant for Tunbridge
Wells or Reigate for the improvement of his health, when,
unfortunately, a report of a serious outrage caused him to
abandon the idea.

"I passed a restless night," he says, "and was very weak
this morning, but my letters were brought to my bedside about
nine o'clock this morning. Among them a letter from the
Foreign Office, with a copy of a despatch from Mr Green, Her
Majesty's Consul-General at Bucharest, dated 15th January,
giving an account of a serious outbreak against the Jews at
Berlad in Moldavia."

After the assurance given to him by the Prince and his
Ministers, and the powerful support which had been promised
by the British Government and all the Great Powers, he was not
at all prepared to hear so soon of another outbreak in Moldavia,
and the communication he now received caused him great pain.

He immediately wrote to the Foreign Office to ask an
audience of Lord Stanley on the subject, and next day started
for London, where he at once proceeded to the Foreign Office to
see Mr Hammond, taking with him all the letters which had
reached him in the morning from Moldavia. Being informed
that the Jews there had not applied to the English Consul for
advice and protection, he at once sent a telegram to the Chief

Rabbi of Berlad, urging him to appeal to the British Consul at Bucharest.

Tuesday, January 28*th.* — He called on Lord Stanley, accompanied by the President of the London Committee of Deputies of the British Jews. His Lordship received them most courteously, and said he had done all he could, and would continue to do so.

Wednesday, January 29*th.* — Sir Moses addressed a letter to Prince Charles, and despatched it, by Lord Stanley's permission, through the Foreign Office. Monsieur Stefan Golisue, Minister for Foreign Affairs, sent a reply, of which the following, with the exception of a few sentences, is a translation :—

"BUCHAREST, 7/19*th February* 1868.

"SIR,—His Serene Highness Prince Charles I. has shown me the letter which you have addressed to him, in favour of the Jewish population of Roumania, in consequence of the troubles which happened at Berlad. In requesting me to answer it, His Highness has also charged me to thank you, sir, for your good wishes, and for the kind sentiments you were pleased to express. In conformity with the declaration contained in the speech from the throne, and true to the sentiments of equity which this declaration attests — sentiments which you, sir, are good enough to acknowledge and to praise, His Highness is determined not to permit that any class of his subjects, whatever may be their religion, shall ever be molested with impunity on account of their creed, or for any other cause.

"Our august Sovereign also desires me to assure you, that those of your co-religionists who have suffered in the troubles of Berlad will be indemnified for all losses legally certified to have been caused by these most regrettable occurrences, into which a most searching enquiry will be made, in order to find out their real authors.

"Although I deplore as much as you, sir, these sad occurrences, it is still my duty to caution you against the exaggerated accounts of the same, given by several public organs. I am able to assure you that, although most regrettable, they are far from having the gravity which has been incorrectly attributed to them.—With the assurance of my highest regard, I have the honour to be, sir, your very obedient servant,   "STEFAN GOLISUE."

Sir Moses published this letter in the *Times*, and, with a view of further impressing upon the Roumanian Government the necessity of putting a stop to the reported outrages, addressed the Minister for Foreign Affairs in a suitable letter, at the same time enclosing him a copy of the *Times*.

No stronger words, it will be seen, could be used than those given in the Minister's letter regarding the good intentions of the Roumanian Government. Unfortunately, however, in the very same month, and again three months afterwards, reports of violence and organised measures of oppression in Moldavia reached England, France, and Germany.

In a telegram from the Jewish community of Jassy, dated March 26th, information is given to the effect that "thirty-one Radical Deputies, including the President, have presented to the Chamber the following Bill, which has been at once sent to the Sections:

"*1st.* The Jews shall not reside in the country. For residence in the town, they must first obtain a special licence.

"*2nd.* The transgressors shall be treated as vagabonds, and expelled by the municipalities.

"*3rd.* The Jews shall not buy nor sell houses.

"*4th.* The Jews shall not farm lands, forests, vineyards, enclosures, pastures, mills, distilleries, public-houses, and inns.

"*5th.* The Jews shall not contract for any undertakings, nor be partners with Christians for such objects.

"*6th.* The Jews shall not exercise any commerce without a licence from the municipality; the transgressors shall be punished with fines, and their suits shall not be entertained by the authorities.

"*7th.* The Jews shall not sell beverages and eatables, except to their co-religionists.

"The Jewish committees shall be suppressed, and the laws contrary to this act abrogated."

The news referring to Monsieur Bratiano's circular had already been received by Her Majesty's Government long before it had been carried out at Jassy, and no time was lost in transmitting proper instructions to the Consul-General of Her Majesty's Government at Bucharest.

Before long the unfortunate occurrence at Galatz brought one more cry of anguish and prayer for supplication. On July 14th, ten Israelites, after being brought to Galatz from Jassy a few days before, ill-treated, and employed at the vilest and most degrading labour, were, by order of the Prefect, together with an eleventh fellow-sufferer and co-religionist, carried to the opposite side of the Danube, and there abandoned in the swamps and morasses, exposed to the wind and weather, without food or shelter. These people were then daily carried backwards and forwards—to one shore by the Turkish soldiers, and to the other by the Roumanians. Three days later one of the unfortunates was already missing, having undoubtedly met his death in the swamps. On Sunday morning the ten were again brought over by the Turks, but the Roumanian soldiers prevented them with their bayonets from landing, and two (an old man and a young man) were carried away by the stream and drowned. Seeing this, the officer on duty allowed the remaining eight to come on board, but no further. Of those saved, one was suffering from illness, and another had become insane.

The Austrian Consul, Monsieur Kremer, on hearing of it, took up the matter, and immediately sent two boats from the Austrian ship of war to the place to fetch the eight left alive, and to search for the bodies of the dead. Of the bodies, but one (that of the old man) was found. On the approach of the Austrian boats, the eight unfortunate sufferers were taken to the guard-house, and afterwards set at liberty.

The British Government sent instructions to Mr Green, but the Roumanian authorities laid the whole blame upon the Turks. Lord Stanley continued sending the despatches from the Consul-General to Sir Moses almost as soon as they arrived, for which favour Sir Moses always expressed his deep gratitude ; but the state of his co-religionists in Roumania caused him much anxiety.

A gleam of hope, however, regarding the condition of the Jews in another part of the world, came to gladden his heart.

A communication was made to him from Saffi in Morocco, referring to the Jews at Abdá, the substance of which I copy from the *Times* of Tuesday, February 18th, 1868 :—

"Letters received at Gibraltar from Saffi bring tidings that Hádj Dris, the commissioner, who was sent by the Sultan to that port to make an investigation into the circumstances of the murder and robbery of several Jews in the province of Abdá, has caused a letter from the Sultan to be read in public to the two Governors of Abdá, expressing His Majesty's severe displeasure on account of the atrocities. The Sultan desires that the Jews should be guarded from harm, and well treated, and reminds his officers that the Prophet ordered the Mahommedans to protect them. His Majesty adds, 'Whosoever shall kill a Jew we shall put him to death." 7500 Spanish dollars have been given as compensation to the Jews, and the Moors who were suspected of having committed the crimes, but against whom there was not evidence to justify their being put to death, have been sent in chains to Morocco, to be there imprisoned during the Sultan's pleasure. The Consular officers at Saffi were requested to attend a meeting of the Moorish authorities and principal Jews of the town, when this satisfaction was offered to the Jews and cheerfully accepted by them. It said, that the British, French, and other Governments had made sundry representations and remonstrances to the Sultan on the subject of atrocities, which led to these proceedings. The Sultan has afforded another proof of his intention to give practical effect to his promise to Sir Moses Montefiore, that equal justice should be administrated to his Mahommedan and Jewish subjects. He has offered a reward of 100 Spanish dollars for the apprehension, dead or alive, of the murderer

of the Austrian interpreter at **Tetuan, and ordered that** any Moor **sheltering**
or giving food to the murderer shall **be** treated **as an** accomplice."

"If a monarch, ruling **over an** Empire so far away from Europe, the land
of civilization, acts so energetically in the cause of justice and humanity, **and**
expresses publicly his severe displeasure to the officers in charge of the **ad**-
ministration of the law of **the** country, how much more," says Sir Moses,
"is there every **reason to hope** that His Serene Highness, Prince Charles,
himself a most enlightened ruler among **the** Potentates of Europe, **who** has
repeatedly expressed his disapproval of **acts of** injustice, **will** not **rest** in his
humane exertions until, even more effectively **than the** Sultan of Morocco is
always able to do, he will have secured to **all who dwell** under **his sway,**
irrespective of their religious convictions, **full protection and the rights**
and privileges to which every loyal **subject is fully entitled."**

Sir Moses having done his utmost for the welfare of his
brethren in the East, with what conspicuous success has already
been seen, he now turned his attention to the affairs of the
Hebrew community in England.

Monday, May 11*th.*—He writes : " I feel rather better ; have
more energy, and very anxious to be, if possible, useful to my
co-religionists.   Therefore am reluctant to refuse the proffered
appointment of President of the Board of Deputies of the British
Jews, as perhaps it may be the means of promoting the general
unity of all the Jews in England."   "I think," he adds, "our
Members of Parliament should be *ex officio* members of the
Board, as the best medium of expressing the sentiments of the
Board in the House of Commons.   To-day I went over the
House of my dear Judith College, and was pleased with it.   I
wish Dr Loewe would come and at once set it afloat."

It appears to have been the great object of his desire to secure
the strict adherence to the Statutes, enrolled by him in Chancery,
on the 26th of February 1866, for the regulation of the College ;
for, on his referring again in his Diary, four months later, to that
institution, in an entry dated East Cliff, Thursday, July 16th,
1868, he writes : "After deep consideration, and with the sincere
desire that it may be the means of securing more entirely the
fulfilment of my wishes respecting the conduct of the persons
selected to fill the buildings of my dear, dear Judith College, and
the strict performance of their duties, I have added Dr Loewe to
the Trust of the property, in the room of my lamented friend
Benjamin Cohen."

He now occupied himself with the selection of the various
objects necessary for the internal fittings of the College, such as
book-cases, desks, and forms, made after a model he had seen at

the great Exhibition of 1851. Kind relatives and friends sent him costly presents, such as a beautiful velvet curtain, embroidered with gold, for the Ark, and a mantle for the scroll of the Holy Law, from his sisters, Mrs Gompertz and Mrs Cohen; handsome embroidered covers for the pulpit from his nieces, Mrs Sebag-Montefiore and Mrs H. Guedalla; a splendid picture representing the vision of Ezekiel, painted and presented by Mr Hart, R.A., and many other suitable objects, all of which gave Sir Moses great pleasure. He himself deposited in the College whatever he thought interesting to the student of Jewish history, out of his own large collection of valuable objects. His ardent desire to promote the study of Hebrew and theological literature, and his great exertions to ameliorate the lot of his brethren wherever they were persecuted, earned for him the high esteem even of those not belonging to his own faith. As an instance, I will only state that in this year steps were taken by one of the highest and most esteemed in the land to raise Sir Moses to the peerage.

The late Earl of Shaftesbury, a man of unshaken belief in Scripture, in Christian dogma, and in prayer, entertained sentiments of the highest respect for Sir Moses.

Mr Edwin Hodder, the author of " The Life and Work of the Seventh Earl of Shaftesbury," referring to the desire of his Lordship to see Sir Moses raised to the Peerage, thus writes (vol. iii. p. 234):

"To Mr Gladstone, the new Premier, Lord Shaftesbury preferred a similar request to one he had made without effect to Mr Disraeli when he was Prime Minister. It was as follows:—

LORD SHAFTESBURY *to* THE RIGHT HON. W. E. GLADSTONE.

"*December 22nd, 1868.*

"DEAR GLADSTONE,—The new arrangements you have made in respect of certain young peers in the House of Lords will prove, I doubt not, very beneficial.

"But I have an impulse, which I cannot restrain, an impulse both from opinion and feeling, to suggest another movement; and I make it far less on the presumption of tendering advice than of disburdening myself of a strong desire. The Jewish question has now been settled. The Jews can sit in both Houses of Parliament. I myself resisted their admission, not because I was adverse to the descendants of Abraham, of whom our blessed Lord came according to the flesh, very far from it, but because I objected to the mode in which that admission was to be effected.

" All that is passed away, and let us now avail ourselves of the opportunity to show regard to God's ancient people.

"There is a noble member of the house of Israel, Sir Moses Montefiore, a man dignified by patriotism, charity, and self-sacrifice, on whom Her Majesty might graciously bestow the honours of the Peerage.

"It would be a glorious day for the House of Lords when that grand old Hebrew were enrolled on the lists of the hereditary legislators of England.—Truly yours, "SHAFTESBURY."

Mr Disraeli (Mr Hodder writes) had replied in a "gushing" letter, expressing his great willingness to do anything, but stating that he was, for obvious reasons, less than any other Prime Minister in a position to grant the request.

Mr Gladstone replied that the case should be carefully "considered," and made enquiry as to what Sir Moses Montefiore's fortune was supposed to be, and whether he had children, but there he allowed the matter to rest.

It was a great disappointment, the same author writes, to Lord Shaftesbury, who had the highest admiration for the character of the great Hebrew philanthropist. The admiration was mutual, and lasted to the end of their lives.

On one occasion, he relates, Sir Moses sent to Lord Shaftesbury a cheque for £95 to be used for the Field Lane Ragged School, or any other purpose he might think proper. It seems a curious amount. It was sent on the day that his wife would, had she lived, have attained her 95th year.

The last letter Lord Shaftesbury ever received from Sir Moses Montefiore was written with his own hand in his hundredth year, and was as follows :—

SIR MOSES MONTEFIORE *to* LORD SHAFTESBURY.

"EAST CLIFF LODGE,
"RAMSGATE, *July 9th,* 1884.

"MY DEAR LORD SHAFTESBURY,—Your able appeal in this day's *Times* on behalf of the fund to provide the means of giving the poor children of the Ragged Schools a day's enjoyment in the country has this moment been read to me, and, sympathising as I do with the desirable object, I enclose, with very much pleasure, cheque for £15, with the hope that the appeal may be both liberally and cheerfully responded to.

"Believe me, my dear Lord Shaftesbury, that I am delighted with the opportunity thus afforded me of evincing my heartfelt appreciation of the noble and benevolent works in which you have for a very long period taken so benevolent an interest.

"May God help you and prosper your labours. Hoping you are in the enjoyment of good health.—I am, my dear Lord Shaftesbury, very truly yours,

"MOSES MONTEFIORE."

Lord Shaftesbury sent the letter and cheque to Mr Kirk, the Secretary of the Ragged School Union, with the following note :—

"*July* 12*th*, 1884.

"DEAR KIRK,—You may keep the letter as a record of a man in his hundredth year, who can feel and write like one of five-and-twenty. Do not suppose that I have omitted to thank him. That grand old Hebrew is better than many Christians.—Yours,   "SHAFTESBURY."

Having during the last two months often complained to his medical attendant of being weak and unwell, the latter advised a change of climate. Accordingly, on the 6th of November, accompanied by Mrs Gompertz, his sister, Mrs Helbert, his sister-in-law, and Dr Canham, his physician, he left England on a visit to the south of France and Italy.

CHAPTER XXIX

1869.

THE PRINCE OF WALES AND SIR MOSES—CONSECRATION OF JUDITH COLLEGE—NAPOLEON III. A PRISONER OF WAR—SERIOUS CHARGES AGAINST THE JEWS OF DAMASCUS IN THE *TIMES* NEWSPAPER—SIR MOSES' ANSWER—DEATH OF SIR MOSES' SISTER, MRS GOMPERTZ.

ON January 1, 1869, Sir Moses was in Rome, and on March 4th at San Remo. There Sir Moses and Mrs Gompertz were preserved from a serious accident. They had been traversing the sides of very steep mountains, and after entering French territory commenced a long drive down the hills. Sir Moses had cautioned the driver to go "piano, piano," more than once, as he felt very nervous, but when they had nearly reached the level road, not far from the French Custom-house, a great rut in the road broke the hind wheel of their carriage, and they were thrown with a great jerk on the side. At first Sir Moses thought they were in a ditch, but "Heaven did not expose them," he says, "to such a misfortune." The coachman pulled up, and they were soon released from a perilous situation.

A few minutes after the accident a very neat open carriage arrived at the spot. The occupant, a lady, alighted, and most kindly and courteously obliged Sir Moses and his sister to enter her carriage. "She was only taking a drive," she said, "and they must go to Mentone in it ; " which they did, and were most thankful to her for her kindness to them.

That lady was a Mrs Coste. "I shall never forget her kindness," Sir Moses observes.

It may truly be said that the frequent rescues from perilous positions with which Providence favoured Sir Moses recalls part of a verse in which Solomon says (Prov. xxiv. 16), "A just man falleth seven times, and rises up again."

Sir Moses returned home on March the 10th, the change of

climate appearing to have much improved his health, and he was again able to attend to his occupations.

Having noticed in the daily papers a report of great distress among the peasants in Russia, he called (April 14th) on Baron Brunnow, requesting him to forward a letter from him to Prince Obelesko, the Governor of Kowno, in Russian Poland, with £100 for the sufferers of all religious denominations. His Excellency most cheerfully expressed his willingness to accede to his request to distribute this sum. The Governor of Kowno, in acknowledging the receipt of this donation, conveyed to Sir Moses the special thanks of the Emperor himself in most gracious terms.

May 31st.—This being the day appointed for the annual inspection of St Bartholomew's Hospital by the Governors, the Prince of Wales, as President of the Hospital, and the Princess of Wales, accompanied by the Crown Prince of Denmark, paid a visit to the Institution, and took part in the ceremony. The Governors mustered in unusual number on the occasion.

The *Times,* giving a full account of the ceremony, and the reception of the Royal party, notices that "during their tour of the wards the Prince recognized the venerable Sir Moses Montefiore among the company, and paused to present him to the Princess."

August 29th.—Three gentlemen, selected from a number of applicants for admission into Judith, Lady Montefiore's Theological College, were this day introduced to him.

Each of them had filled the office of spiritual head of a congregation for several years. Their learning, as well as their unblemished character, was vouched for by high authorities.

Sir Moses received them with much cordiality, assuring them that it would be a cause of much happiness to him if he were to see them happy in the College.

He told them that the College was intended :—

(1.) As a memorial of his sincere devotion to the law of God as revealed on Sinai and expounded by the revered sages of the Mishna and the Talmud.

(2.) As a token of his love and pure affection to his departed consort, Judith Lady Montefiore, of blessed memory, whose zeal and ardent attachment to the religion of her forefathers adorned all her actions in life.

It had for its objects :—

(1.) To promote the study of the Holy Law.

(2.) To provide for the accommodation of ten persons distinguished for their learning in the Holy Law, as well as for their high moral and religious character.

" It is my distinct wish," he continued, " that admission as members of the College should be given to all Israelites, from whatever part of the globe they may happen to come, provided their learning and moral and religious character qualify them for the College.

" Only in case of there being among the candidates British-born subjects and foreigners, both alike qualified by their learning and character, should preference be given to the British-born subject.

" Students having completed their classical studies in a college or university in England, or in any other country, who desire to qualify for any of the high offices in the Synagogue and the community, are admitted to all the lectures free of charge after having passed an examination in Hebrew and Theological subjects to the satisfaction of the Principal and Director of the College."

Saturday Evening, September 4th.—The new members were invited to witness the completion of a sacred scroll of the Pentateuch, which was effected by Sir Moses, who, in the presence of his relatives and friends, wrote the last verse of the Book of Deuteronomy.

On Monday, September 6th, corresponding to the first day of the year 5630 A.M., the consecration of the College took place, in the presence of all the members of the community, the readers of the Synagogue, and of relatives and friends of Sir Moses specially invited for the occasion.

A procession was formed, headed by Sir Moses bearing the sacred scroll of the Pentateuch. After him came the members of the College and the readers of the Synagogue, carrying books containing the Scriptures and Commentaries thereon, whilst the rear was brought up by the general company, and all proceeded towards the College door. As Sir Moses approached he exclaimed, in the words of the Royal Psalmist, "Open unto me the gates of righteousness, I will go in and praise the Lord," upon which the doors were immediately opened from within, and all present entered, ascending the staircase leading to the Lecture Hall.

Sir Moses, and those who carried the volumes of the Scriptures, made seven circuits round the hall, chanting impressively seven psalms. At the conclusion of the last Sir Moses ascended the pulpit, and expressed his great happiness to see the day on which his ardent wishes had been realised. He also dwelt on the noble character and exalted virtues of her in whose memory the College had been established.

After him, the Principal of the College addressed the assembly, concluding with a special prayer for the prosperity of the new institution.

Sir Moses then declared the College open, and from that day to the end of his life there was no break in the prescribed order of duties. The members attended regularly, lectures were delivered on every Sabbath, and on special occasions during the week addresses on literary or historical subjects were given to the general public. Often when the state of his health permitted he would himself attend the lectures, his presence always attracting a large number of visitors.

About the end of December he was present at the laying of the first stone of the Orphans' Home at Broadstairs, by Mrs Tait, the esteemed wife of Dr Tait, late Archbishop of Canterbury, on the land given by Mrs Tait for that purpose, adjoining the Archbishop's residence. The weather was most unfavourable; there was, nevertheless, a numerous attendance of nearly all of the most distinguished families in the Isle of Thanet.

The Archbishop had been very ill, and he was for this reason not able to be present at the ceremony. Sir Moses drove to Stone House to enquire, and on hearing from Mrs Tait that his Grace was progressing favourably, left his card and an envelope, enclosing two cheques for the Orphanage,—£50 from himself, and £50 in memory of his beloved wife.

During the month of January 1870 Sir Moses was frequently confined to his room by indisposition, and daily visited by his medical attendant. This, however, did not prevent him from having the daily papers read to him. It was a habit with him to read himself, or to have read to him, two of the leading journals every day whilst at dinner when no special guest happened to be present.

Wednesday, January 26th.—The *Times* gave an account of a dinner to the Archbishop of Syra and Tenos in the Jerusalem Chamber at Westminster Abbey.

The Dean, in proposing the toast of the evening, "The health of the Archbishop of Syra and Tenos," introduced two sentences, which appeared to be of peculiar interest to Sir Moses.

"We are seated," the Dean says, "in the chamber of Jerusalem. What happier name or place to receive the representative of those far-off Eastern Churches of which Jerusalem is the mother and mistress?"

"It is useful even for Englishmen to be reminded, by the presence of our guest, that there is a land more dear to us from our childhood even than England; that there is a city more sacred even than Rome, or Geneva, or Westminster: that land is the land of the East, and that city is Jerusalem."

Sir Moses, though in a state of great weakness of body, on hearing the above read to him, roused as by an electric flash, raised himself from his couch, and, addressing the person who had just been reading to him, exclaimed with great emotion: "And what ought Israel to think of Jerusalem? How ought we to receive the representatives of our communities in the Holy City when they come to visit us? What ought our attachment to be to the land of our forefathers? Ought it not indeed to be at least as intense as that of the venerable Dean of Westminster? I wish every one of my young friends of the rising generation would read the words of the Dean, and be reminded, even as Englishmen, of the words of the Royal Psalmist, 'If I forget thee, O Jerusalem, let my right hand forget its cunning. If I do not remember thee, let my tongue cleave to the roof of my mouth; if I prefer not Jerusalem above my chief joys' (Ps. cxxxvii, v. 5 and 6)."

A few weeks later he received a communication from Jerusalem, reporting another season of famine, drought, and ravages by locusts, and he lost no time in sending a copy of the letters he had received to the daily papers, stating that he would take charge of any donations in aid of the sufferers.

His appeal was most successful, and he had the happiness of becoming the medium of rendering early help to thousands of suffering families.

The month of July was devoted to a short trip to Belgium,

where he visited the chief stations of the Gas Company, of which he was President.

This was a most eventful year. Queen Isabella of Spain, dethroned in 1868, resigned her crown in favour of her son, Alfonso, Prince of Asturias; but the Spanish people elected the second son of King Victor Emanuel, Prince Amadeo, in preference; and the Franco-German war broke out, in consequence of the candidature of the Prince of Hohenzollern for the Spanish throne.

August 3rd.—Sir Moses attended the Board meetings of the Alliance Marine, and Alliance Life and Fire Insurance Company, and of the Imperial Continental Gas Association. "The political horizon," he says, "is most threatening, our shares dreadfully depressed." The bank unexpectedly raised the rate of interest to six per cent.

August 12th.—He entertained the greatest fears for the Emperor Napoleon. On September 3rd he read the despatch referring to the capitulation of General Wimpffen at Sedan. "I am deeply grieved for the Emperor of the French. I believe him to have been a sincere friend of England, and a lover of peace. He was basely betrayed into the war to secure his succession."

September 8th.—Sir Moses received an invitation to the consecration of the new Synagogue of the British Jews. It was signed by the late Mr Simon Waley, Warden. Feeling a sincere and deep anxiety for the unity of the Jews, he sent to Mr Waley, and expressed his wish to see unity happily restored before the day of consecration, with his hope that he and his brother, with Dr Adler, the Chief Rabbi, might accomplish the object he had so much at heart.

But Sir Moses was not permitted to indulge long in the pleasures of promoting communal and charitable objects at home, his attention being most unexpectedly drawn to a matter of serious consequence abroad, which required his immediate exertions.

As the hundred-headed Hydra is that terrible monster, "Hatred of race," even in the present enlightened age, it requires the labour of a modern Hercules to destroy it. This is unfortunately shown by the insertion of a letter in the *Times* on October 31st, 1870, addressed to the editor by Mr E. H. Palmer, of St John's College, Cambridge, and Mr C. F. Tyrwhitt Drake.

" The massacre of Christians at Damascus ten years ago," these gentlemen write, " created an excitement over the whole of Europe, but with Tien-tsin and Sedan to engross the public attention, such a trifle as a fresh outbreak in Syria has been quite overlooked.

" The events to which we allude occurred shortly after we had left the country, but we have received full details from both native Christians and Mahommedan correspondents in Syria.

" On August 26th it was rumoured in Damascus that a general massacre of the Franks by the Moslem inhabitants was contemplated, and affairs actually assumed so serious an aspect that most of the Christians precipitately fled from the town. Open menaces were uttered, the fanatical part of the population became clamorous, and evidently bent on mischief, and indeed the danger seemed imminent since the authorities took no step to suppress the popular agitation, when, thanks to the energetic conduct of Her Britannic Majesty's Consul, upon whom the management of the affair devolved, as the other European representatives retired from the scene of action, who seems to have himself addressed the Turkish soldiery, and insisted on proper steps being taken by the Government, the riots were quelled, and a most serious calamity averted.

" One of the causes which appears most to have excited the fanaticism of the mob was the presence, in the streets of Damascus, of crosses chalked up on the most conspicuous places. On subsequent inquiry by the Government, this was discovered to be the work of the Jews, the same people who, during the former massacre, distinguished themselves by standing at the doors of their houses, and voluntarily offering lemonade to refresh the Mahommedans, hot and weary with the slaughter of the Christians, and who, in many well authenticated instances, offered aid and concealment to the terror-stricken Christians, and then brought in the Turks to murder them.

" Some three hundred of these Jews are under the protection of various European Consulates, and can thus with impunity laugh at the authority of the Turks, and wreak their hatred on the co-religionists of their protectors. —We are, Sir, yours obediently,   " E. H. PALMER, St John's College.
       " C. F. TYRWHITT DRAKE."

" *October 27th.*"

Sir Moses at once sent the following letter :

To the EDITOR of the " Times."

" SIR,—I read with pain and surprise the letter which appeared in your paper of yesterday, bearing the signatures of Mr E. H. Palmer and Mr C. F. Tyrwhitt Drake.

" I am astonished, and I regret that gentlemen so intelligent as I assume Mr Palmer and Mr Drake to be, should be so ready to give credence to any absurd rumours that may be propagated against my co-religionists. I am in possession of authentic information which proves that these gentlemen have been entirely misled by their correspondents in Syria, and that the charges against the Jews, to which they have given currency in your influential columns, are devoid of truth.

" As regards the outbreak that occurred at Damascus ten years ago, it is enough to state that I have been an active member of the Syrian Relief Fund from its establishment in 1860, and I can confidently assert that until now I have never heard of the cruel accusations brought against the Jews of Damascus in the letter of your correspondents.

" I am sure, Sir, that you will sympathize with me when I express my sincere regret that at this late period of my life, notwithstanding the spread of education and the principles of religious toleration, I should still have to refute such idle charges, and I am confident that you will not be disinclined to insert in your paper this my reply.—I am, Sir, yours faithfully,

" MOSES MONTEFIORE."

" ' *The Times,' November 2nd,* 1870."

Messrs Palmer and Drake then wished to know what was his authentic information. To this Sir Moses replied by another letter in the *Times,* dated November 9th.

Subsequently three other gentlemen addressed the Editor of the *Times,* one under the signature of S. H. S., the other a Christian clergyman and a native of Syria, the Rev. Dr Anton Tien, K.C.M., Cumberland Terrace, Gravesend ; and the third, also a native of Syria, Mr Selim Bustros, a Christian merchant, residing at Liverpool.

The letters are as follows :

To the EDITOR of the " Times."

" SIR,—I have watched with great interest the correspondence in your columns about the Damascus Jews.

" I was in Constantinople at the time of the Syrian Massacre in 1860, and translated for the British and American Governments the Arabic documents relating to that subject ; in none of these did I find anything to implicate the Jews, nor in the letters of my noble friend, Abdel Rader, when he made his own simple statement of the affair, and the course adopted by him for the protection of the Christians.—Yours faithfully,   " A. TIEN."

" *November* 14*th,* 1870."

To the EDITOR *of the " Times."*

"SIR,—Having the advantage of possessing accurate knowledge of all the details concerning the outbreaks in Damascus, 1860, being there at the time, I can fully corroborate all that Sir Moses Montefiore has written you in exculpation of the Jews.   No greater mistake could be made than to suppose that the Jews were in any way responsible for the troubles of that country; but even if they were, what object is to be gained by reviving a matter that is so long out of date, unless it be to excite hostility against them?

"I am a Christian native of Syria, and without egotism may say that my name is well known throughout that country, therefore I have no other object in addressing you these lines, than to remove the false impression that is likely to be made on the minds of your readers less acquainted with the facts of the matter than myself, by the perusal of the communications made to you by your correspondent, Mr Drake.

"Syria is, happily, now free from the spirit of fanaticism, and a perfect unity of sentiment pervades all classes of the community.—I remain, Sir, yours obediently,   "SELIM BUSTROS."

"LIVERPOOL, *November* 11th, 1870."

Sir Moses concluded his December work by distributing £100 among the poor of Ramsgate, who, he had just been informed, were in great distress.

January 8th, 1871.—The Hon. Benjamin Franklin Peixotto, who had just been appointed American Consul in Roumania, was now in England, on his way to Bucharest. He came to see Sir Moses, and acquainted him with his proposed mode of action in matters concerning the Israelites in Wallachia. "He is a very agreeable and highly educated gentleman," the entry of that day records, "and should he act as he speaks, I hope he will be successful in the object of his appointment."

In the course of the conversation which Sir Moses had with the Consul, the Juda Touro Almshouses in Jerusalem were mentioned, and this little incident alone was sufficient inducement for Sir Moses on the following day to send £100 for distribution among the inmates in commemoration of the visit of the Consul, a countryman of the benevolent founder of the Almshouses.

During the following three months Sir Moses suffered great anxiety on account of the illness of his sister, Mrs Gompertz. In order to be near her, Sir Moses went to London, but was taken ill himself. Her death in March affected him greatly, but with pious resignation he submits to the will of God, only adding, " she was a devoted daughter, wife, and mother, a loving sister, and a friend to all in need! May we all benefit by her bright example. It is a sad loss to me."

April 7th.—Sir Moses received the news of an outbreak

against the Jews of Odessa, but fortunately the disturbance was quelled by the troops, and there was therefore no further occasion for him to intercede on their behalf. In reply to the telegram he received on that subject, he expressed his confidence that His Imperial Majesty's Government would secure the safety of the Jews and punish the evil-doers.

"I should like," he says, "to go to St Petersburg to thank the Emperor for the prompt measure that had been taken by the Government at Odessa to put an end to the outbreak against the Jews."

June 22nd.—Sir Moses received Her Majesty's command to be present at a concert at Buckingham Palace, but the state of his health would not allow him to come up to London.

CHAPTER XXX

1871.

JULY 22nd.—A despatch reached him from Captain Henry Jones, Her Britannic Majesty's Consul-General at Tabriz, Persia, of which the following is a copy :—

"BRITISH CONSULATE-GENERAL, TABRIZ, PERSIA,
June 5, 1871.

"SIR,—Knowing your sympathy for the sufferings of your co-religionists everywhere, I take the liberty to address you on behalf of the Jews of Shiraz, who are at present reduced to great want and misery through the famine which is now devastating Persia. They number, I learn, about three hundred families, and have always suffered great oppression at the hands of their Mussulman masters ; you may conceive how abject and degraded is their position when you hear that their protector is the public executioner.

"My informant assures me that unless relief comes very speedily, sickness and starvation will shortly annihilate the entire community. Their sufferings must indeed be extreme when they have impressed their Mussulman fellow-subjects, usually so callous and indifferent to the distress of others.

"The Persian Government will do nothing. Were they even to relieve the sufferings of the Mussulman population their means would be exhausted. The few Europeans dwelling in Persia have already given what they could in aid of the starving Christians of Isfahan, and as these wretched Jews know not where to look for help, and have no one to plead their cause, I consider it my duty to bring their case to your notice, trusting it may be in your power, in some degree, to relieve them.

"There are several colonies of Jews in Persia, at Uroomia, Hamadan, Yezd, I believe, and elsewhere, all oppressed and trodden down, as are all their co-religionists in these regions. None, however, are enduring the frightful amount of suffering which is borne by the Jews of Shiraz.

"In the event of their co-religionists in England taking steps to alleviate this great misery, I would recommend their communicating by telegram (as speedily as possible) with Her Majesty's representatives at Teheran, who will appoint some trustworthy agent at Shiraz to distribute their bounty among the most necessitous of the sufferers there.—I have the honour to be, Sir, your most obedient servant,

(Signed)   "HENRY M. JONES, *Consul-General.*

"Sir MOSES MONTEFIORE, Bart., &c., &c."

Sir Moses, without delay, addressed to Captain Jones a reply, of which the following is a copy:—

"GROSVENOR GATE, PARK LANE, LONDON,
July 2, 1871.

"SIR,—I have the honour to acknowledge the receipt of your esteemed letter dated the 5th ult., in which, prompted by a noble feeling of humanity, you have brought to my notice the present unfortunate state of my brethren in Shiraz, caused by the famine now prevailing in Persia.

" I lost no time in laying your communication before the Board of Deputies of British Jews in London, in hopes that they would, as far as may be in their power, endeavour to alleviate the sufferings of the above city.   In the meantime, however, I request you will allow me to hand you, per enclosed three ' lettres de crédit circulaires,' one hundred pounds sterling as a humble offering of myself.   £50 of this sum I should entreat you to give to the Jews, £25 to the Christians, and £25 to the Mussulmans in Shiraz.

" With regard to the great oppressions to which the Jews generally have been subjected in Persia, I beg leave to state that by the kind intercession of Her Britannic Majesty's Ambassador in Teheran I was permitted in the year 1866 to lay my humble petition on behalf of the Jews before His Majesty the Shah Nazr-ed-din, and had at that time the high gratification of being informed, through Her Majesty's Government, that the Shah had given immediate orders to the Sipeh Sálár to the effect that every possible care should henceforth be taken of the Jews, so that no injustice whatever be done any more to them.   It is for this reason a matter of deep regret to me, and as I have no doubt to every friend of humanity, to hear that the high officer under whose special care the Jews had then been placed should have ceased to act in accordance with the strict orders of His Majesty the Shah.

" Being anxious to impress on the minds of my brethren in Shiraz the gratitude they owe to you for having made known their state of misery to the Jews in England, I have addressed the enclosed letter to the spiritual head of their community, and will deem it a great favour if you will kindly have it forwarded to the proper authorities.

" I need not assure you how fully I appreciate your advocacy on behalf of my brethren.   Every lover of justice will admit you have rendered a great service to the poor and oppressed ; the consciousness alone of so noble an act is no doubt the highest gratification to you.—I have the honour to be, Sir, with great esteem, your most obedient servant,

(Signed)   " MOSES MONTEFIORE.

" Captain H. M. JONES, Her Britannic Majesty's
        Consul-General, Tabriz."

Sir Moses lost no time in communicating the sad intelligence to the Board of the London Committee of Deputies of the British Jews, who resolved :—" That the President be requested to forward a copy of his letter to the Board, with extracts from the letter of Captain Jones, and a copy of his letter in reply, to the President of every Jewish congregation in the United Kingdom, and to urge on such President, in the name of the Board, to take the speediest steps in order to obtain subscriptions from the congregation over which he presides and from individual congregants in aid of the sufferers, and that this Board desires to record its high appreciation of the benevolent feelings of which Captain Jones' communication affords such gratifying evidence."

Sir Moses readily complied with the request of the Board, and a very considerable amount was collected.

With reference to the kindness evinced on this occasion by the British Government, he makes an entry in his Diary under the date of July 28th as follows :—

" With feelings of gratitude to the God of my forefathers for all the mercies to the children of His Covenant, and for His blessings on my anxious efforts to relieve the sufferers by famine and sickness in Persia, I received this forenoon a letter from Mr Odo Russell, informing me that Lord Granville had the pleasure to comply with my request to forward to Her Majesty's Minister, Mr Alison, at Teheran my letter and enclosed £250. His Lord-ship's benevolence and kindness will cause the distribution of the money at least one month sooner than otherwise it could have been done, and consequently be the saving of much time. God bless him and the British Government ! "

July 29th.—Sir Moses attended the morning service in his Synagogue, breakfasted with some friends at the College, and at 2 P.M. attended a lecture delivered by the Principal in the Lecture Hall. On his return to East Cliff he had the satisfaction of finding a telegram from Her Majesty's Minister at Teheran, to the effect that Sir Moses' telegram of the 21st July had been received, and £250 sent to Shiraz as desired.

He commissioned Michael Angelo Pittatore, a distinguished artist, to paint the likeness of Mr Almosnino, the able secretary during a period of fifty years of the Spanish and Portuguese Congregation in London, and that of his wife, the esteemed and indefatigable president of the infant school of that congregation. He also commissioned the artist to paint the portrait of the writer of these Memoirs, the first Principal of the College founded in memory of Lady Montefiore, and presented the picture to that institution.

In October, on the approach of the Tabernacle holidays, Sir Moses had his Tabernacle erected in accordance with his annual custom. In former times he used to have it in a picturesque part of his park, but as he and Lady Montefiore advanced in years he found it necessary to choose a more sheltered spot, and he therefore had it erected in the quadrangle of East Cliff Lodge. Those of my readers who have never seen a tabernacle, as it is called in England, may be interested in a description of one.

It is in the form of a good-sized garden-house, with a movable roof and ceiling of lattice-work, thickly covered with fresh evergreens. The walls of the one constructed under the direction of Sir Moses were hung with tasteful draperies, the windows and door had beautiful curtains, and on the walls were large mirrors and appropriate pictures and scripture texts in gilt frames. A thick carpet was laid down on the floor; flowers and garlands were also distributed wherever practicable. From the centre of the roof a silver lamp with seven branches was suspended; the table underneath was laid out with handsome bouquets and flowering plants in beautiful pots; whilst there was no lack of choice refreshments in gold, silver, and crystal vessels. During this festival a number of relatives and friends dined with him in the Tabernacle every day, and his Christian neighbours and acquaintances considered it a great treat to get an invitation to the dinner.

On the date of this entry I noticed among those present at dinner, Mrs Warre, a lady from Ramsgate held in great esteem by Sir Moses on account of her charitable disposition; Mrs Max Müller, a niece of Mrs Warre, and her husband, Professor Max Müller.

"When I was sitting in the Palace, at the table with the Emperor of Germany," said Professor Max Müller, "my mind was engrossed with the idea that I was in the presence of the Emperor Charlemagne. Now," he said, "sitting in the Tabernacle at the table with Sir Moses Montefiore, I can fancy myself in the presence of the Patriarch Abraham, sitting in his tent, where his hospitality was accepted by angels, and gladdened the heart of all comers."

This observation was sufficient inducement for Sir Moses to speak on subjects connected with the locality of the tent of Abraham: the Holy Land, the Sacred Scriptures, and men of learning in ancient history and literature. Professor Max Müller, on his turn, spoke of Chevalier Bunsen, the author of " Egypt's Place in Universal History; " also of Professor Bernays of the University of Bonn (son of the late Rev. Isaak Bernays, Spiritual Head of the Hebrew community at Hamburg). " My friend,

Professor Bernays," he said, "is a strict observer of the dietary laws of the Pentateuch, and I greatly esteemed him for his learning and nobility of character. He used to come and stay with me, on which occasions he was in the habit of bringing with him his own cooking apparatus."

Sir Moses thereupon remarked, it was now admitted by medical men of great eminence that the dietary laws of the Pentateuch contributed greatly to the health and long life of those who observed them.

This, to the best of my recollection, is the substance of the conversation which passed between Sir Moses and Professor Max Müller.

Grace, in Hebrew, having been offered up after the repast, the company withdrew to take a walk in the garden, whilst Professor and Mrs Max Müller, after taking leave of Sir Moses, repaired to Lady Montefiore's Theological College.

They remained there for some time, inspected the books, manuscripts, and testimonials in the Library and Lecture Hall, and apparently were much pleased with what they saw. The Professor signed his name in the visitors' book in Sanscrit, giving literal translation of "Oxford" in the word "Gaoghat;" and a few days after his visit to the College he addressed Sir Moses in a letter, of which the following is a copy:

"Parks End, Oxford, 10*th October* 1871.

"Dear Sir Moses Montefiore,—Coming from Oxford, the city of colleges, I was so much struck with the new College of which you have laid the foundations at Ramsgate, and particularly with the excellent library which Dr Loewe has collected for you, that I should feel honoured if you would allow me to contribute a small mite to your library treasures.

"As I learnt from Dr Loewe that some of my publications would be welcome to the students of your College, I have taken the liberty to send you by railway two volumes of my lectures on the Science of Language, and those volumes of my essays under the title of 'Chips from a German Workshop.'

"I do not expect that you would find time to look at these books, but it would give me pleasure if you would glance at pp. 372 *seq.* of the first volume of my essays, where is an essay on Semite Monotheism. I have tried to vindicate the character of Abraham as the true founder of Monotheism against the theories of Renan and others.

"Allow me to thank you in my wife's name and my own for the kindness with which you received us under your hospitable 'tent.' I can assure you that it was to both of us a most interesting day, and that it will long keep its place in our memory.

"My wife wishes to be k'ndly remembered to you, and I remain, with sincere respect, yours truly,   "Max Muller."

December 10*th.*—" There has been for nearly a week past but one topic of conversation, the illness of His Highness the Prince of Wales, and upon every face there is written a look of concern and sorrow, as the illness of the Prince has gone to the heart of every one."   Sir Moses sent a telegram to the Háhám Báshi at Jerusalem, to have prayers offered up in all the Synagogues there, and in the holy cities of Hebron, Tiberias, and Safed, for his recovery, and for the health and happiness of the Queen, and all the other members of the Royal family.   " I hope," he writes in his Diary, " this will be done to-night in all parts of the Holy Land, and may the God of Israel hearken to their prayers.   Amen, amen."

To this telegram he received the following reply :—

" ' My help cometh from the Lord, who made Heaven and earth.   Seek the peace of the City, for in the peace thereof shall ye have peace.'   Jerusalem, 2nd day of Tebet 5632 (December 18th, 1871).

" May peaceful salutations, like the dew of Heaven, descend on Sir Moses Montefiore, Bart., the zealous promoter of peace.   Amen.

" We beg to inform you that your telegram, dated the 28th of Kislev (Sunday, 10th December), reached us just about the time for the afternoon prayers.   We immediately made its contents known to our brethren belonging to the several Ashkenázim congregations in the Holy City, and despatched special messengers to the Sephárdim and Ashkenázim congregations dwelling in the Holy Cities of Hebron, Tiberias, and Safed.   We then, conjointly with our learned and pious colleagues, assembled in the great Synagogue, gave orders to light up the candelabra in all the Synagogues in the Holy City, opened the portals of the Holy Ark, and offered up a most fervent prayer for the speedy and perfect recovery of His Royal Highness Albert Edward, Prince of Wales, invoking the Holy One (blessed be His name !) to make him live, to grant him health, to strengthen him, and to renew his youth.   We also sent a congregation of pious and learned men to pray the whole night at the tomb of our mother, Rachel (may her merit protect us !), while, at the same time, we ordered a congregation of equally pious and learned men to call upon our God at the western wall of the ancient Temple, from which spot, we are told by our ancestors, the Divine glory never departed.   And when we had concluded our heartfelt prayers for His Royal Highness the Prince of Wales, we implored God to cause His blessings to descend on Her Majesty, the mighty and most virtuous Queen Victoria (may her glory be exalted !), on Her Royal Highness the Princess of Wales, and on every member of the Royal family.   Oh ! that our prayers may have been favourably received in Heaven, and that we may yet hear the good tidings, the Lord hath strengthened the Prince of Wales upon his bed of sickness, and has completely restored him to health !   With sincere wishes for your own lasting happiness, crowned by the blessing of peace,—We remain, esteemed Sir Moses, yours faithfully,

" ABRAHAM ASKENASI.   HÁHÁM BÁSHI."

December 14*th.*—Sir Moses writes : " Accounts of the Prince of Wales are more favourable ; the bulletin of the afternoon confirms our hope for his recovery. It is impossible to describe the deep anxiety felt by all classes in England, indeed, in all parts of the world, for the Prince, the Princess, and our gracious Queen, and all pray most ardently for the Prince's recovery."

December 15th.—"With every hour telegrams happily continue to be more favourable."

"The Eternal God," Sir Moses writes, "listened to the prayers of many millions of Her Majesty's loyal subjects in all her vast dominions. The precious life of the Prince of Wales is saved! May it be preserved for very many years!"

December 27th.—A telegram from the Secretary of the Relief Committee at Ispahan reached him, acknowledging the receipt of one of his letters, with remittance, and adding that of the 1700 Jews of the community in Ispahan, 1200 were starving, and reporting further heartrending details.

"This is work," Sir Moses says, "for next year, but I hope, *D.V.*, to be able to accomplish it."

CHAPTER XXXI

1872.

PETITION TO THE SHAH—OUTRAGES IN SMYRNA—SECOND MISSION TO RUSSIA—VISIT TO STOCKHOLM—INTERVIEW WITH THE CZAR ALEXANDER II.

FROM January to July 1872 Sir Moses, as President of the Board of Deputies of the British Jews, was engaged in an extensive correspondence with many congregations and individuals in England, as well as in other parts of the world, and subscriptions to the fund for the relief of the famine-stricken Jews in Persia continued to flow in. The Board was most active. The sum of £10,850 had already been remitted, and distributed among the sufferers in Teheran, Shiraz, Ispahan, Bushire, Uroomia, Hamadan, Yeza, Demarend, Gilpaigon, Kashan, and Bagdad; but cries for more help, and appeals for rescue from the hands of oppressing governors and officials continued daily to arrive, and it was deemed expedient to petition the Shah in the matter.

Sir Moses, without delay, addressed a letter to His Majesty, of which I subjoin a copy.

To His Most Gracious Majesty NAZER-EDDIN SHAH, the Mighty Ruler of Persia, exalted Glory and lasting Peace.

"May it please your Majesty,—Relying on the magnanimous and most noble principles of justice and mercy which adorn the life of your Majesty, I ventured to lay at the foot of your Majesty's throne, on the 22nd day of Ramadan, 1282 A.H., by Charles Alison, Esq., Her Britannic Majesty's Minister in Teheran, an humble petition on behalf of my co-religionists residing under your Majesty's benign and glorious sway in Persia, and had the happiness of receiving from Her Britannic Majesty's Government a communication to the effect that, in consequence of the representations which Her Britannic Majesty's Minister in Teheran had made, your Majesty had most graciously written an autograph letter to the Siphesálár, informing him that the Jews should henceforth be treated with justice and kindness.

"Emboldened by the gracious reception your Majesty has given to my most humble prayer, I crave now your Majesty's permission to tender the offerings of most heartfelt gratitude of many thousands of my brethren dwelling in Her Britannic Majesty's dominions, and to entreat your Majesty further to extend your Majesty's powerful protection towards the Israelites residing in your Majesty's vast realm, especially at the present moment, when the papers throughout Europe spread the report that my brethren are greatly oppressed by a number of officers, who do not understand the noble and humane intentions of your Majesty—officers who, it is said, give to an apostate from the religion of his forefathers (against the will of your Majesty, whose sole glory consists in securing perfect happiness and justice to all your Majesty's subjects, without regard to their faith and social conditions)—the right of claiming and taking possession of all the property that may have been left at the demise of any of their relatives still adhering to their ancient religion, causing thereby the greatest possible distress to those of my brethren, who prefer death to apostacy from their religion.

"All friends of humanity and civilisation look up with a feeling of the utmost anxiety to the vigilant eye of the Mighty Ruler of Persia, and are longing to hear that your Majesty, as on a former occasion, received graciously the most humble prayer of an Israelite, who, whilst invoking the Creator of the Universe, the Father of all, that the glorious reign of your Majesty may be exalted by justice and mercy, the guardian angels of your Majesty's throne, begs leave to subscribe himself with reiterated expressions of the most profound gratitude, your Majesty's most humble and most obedient servant,   (Signed)   "MOSES MONTEFIORE."

Sir Moses wrote to Lord Granville at the same time, entreating him to recommend his petition to the Shah's gracious consideration; and on January 30th Lord Enfield, by direction of Earl Granville, informed Sir Moses that his Lordship would comply with his wish.

February 18*th.* — He received another letter from Her Majesty's Minister at Teheran to the effect that the Jews at Bushire, Shiraz, Ispahan, Teheran, Hamadan, and Oroomia were suffering greatly from famine, relief being most urgent. He was very anxious to go himself to Persia.

February 22*nd.*—We read the following entry in his Diary :— "I went to the Foreign Office, and found that Mr Hammond had been confined to his house for the last two months with the gout. I drove to his residence, where he received me most kindly. I returned the despatches Lord Granville had kindly sent for my perusal, and then I spoke of my desire to go to Persia to endeavour to ameliorate the condition of the Jews. He said the journey was too difficult for me, and would not permit it. Lord Granville would willingly afford me all the assistance I required. 'After the 1st of April,' Mr Hammond continued, 'the Red Sea was closed, the season was already too far advanced, travelling in Persia was most difficult.' He was against my going at my time of life; he thought I must be eighty. I was obliged to own to being in my eighty-eighth year. He was indeed most kind and friendly. When I said I was going by way of Egypt, he said jestingly that the British Consul had great power, and he would put me in prison, and in Egypt there was no Magna Charta. I ought not to go. And what did my nephew, Mr Joseph Meyer Montefiore, say to it? he asked. I replied that my nephew said it was evident I wished to be buried in Persia. It is impossible for any friend to have spoken more kindly than Mr Hammond. He promised to send my letter to Lord Granville."

February 23rd.—His Lordship wrote Sir Moses a most kind note, almost forbidding his going to Persia, but in the most flattering terms. He intimated that Sir Moses could have the letters he desired.

February 27th.—Sir Moses was very weak and too unwell to leave the house to attend Divine service, held in all places of worship, to render thanks for the recovery of H.R.H. the Prince of Wales. He had, however, the happiness, he writes, of seeing the grand procession pass his house. " Long may they live," he observes ; "it was a glorious sight, and the hearts of all England glow with delight."

May 15th.—A telegram from the Hebrew community of Smyrna, and from Mr Cumberbatch, Her Majesty's Consul in that city, informed him of very serious outrages committed by foreign Greeks upon the Jews of Smyrna, and upon others on the Island of Marmora, and implored the help of the Board of Deputies, but most fortunately the British Government had already most humanely interposed. The Turkish Government followed their example, and punishment was vigorously meted out to the guilty, perfect tranquillity being restored throughout the island.

Sir Moses was much pleased with the promptitude and energy exhibited by the Sublime Porte, and in his own name and that of the Board, conveyed to Earl Granville and Mr Consul Cumberbatch the deep gratitude he felt for the action they had promptly and readily taken.

Every preparation for the journey to Persia had now been made. The writer, who was to have accompanied him, had already gone to Ramsgate to arrange with him all matters connected with the journey, and then proceeded with him to London to make the necessary purchases.

Sir Moses, however, on arriving at Park Lane, felt greatly fatigued. He retired early to rest, but had a very bad night, and complained of indisposition.

Being informed in the morning that, according to the latest accounts, the interior of Persia was actually overrun with bands of marauders, he was reluctantly induced to abandon his projected journey, at the earnest solicitations of persons occupying high official positions in this country, who assured him that such a journey would be perilous, even to a young man, and could be undertaken by him only at the risk of his life.

His active philanthropy, however, could not let him rest. If the journey to Persia was to be deferred, a journey to Russia, he thought, might be undertaken without risk of life, and might render good service to the cause of his brethren in that country.

Five or six months prior to this date he had received letters from several Hebrew congregations in Russia, requesting him to proceed to St Petersburg and offer the Czar his own congratulations, and those of his brethren in England, on the occasion of the bi-centenary of the birth of Peter the Great. Sir Moses readily consented, and on the 20th of June he informed the Board of Deputies, that, if they should determine to vote an address of congratulation to the Emperor of Russia, he would have great pleasure in presenting it to the Czar in person.

The Board at first hesitated to encourage the President at his advanced age to undertake such a long and fatiguing journey, but ultimately resolved to accept his offer. As soon as Sir Moses became acquainted with their decision he commenced making his preparations.

On Wednesday, July 10th, Count Brunnow, the Russian Ambassador, paid him a visit at Park Lane, and subsequently sent him letters for St Petersburg and Stockholm. On the 11th, accompanied by his medical friend, Mr James S. Daniel, of Ramsgate, and myself, he left London for Hull.

The full particulars of this Mission are given by Sir Moses in his Report to the London Committee of Deputies of the British Jews, and I copy them from the original manuscript :—

"On Friday, the 12th July," he writes, "we embarked at Hull in the steam-packet *Orlando*, for Gothenburg, thence to proceed *via* Sweden and Finland to St Petersburg.

" Before leaving the port, a special messenger from London brought me a letter from a gentleman of high authority, informing me that the cholera had broken out, and was at that time raging in St Petersburg. Grave as this intelligence was, I resolved that no fear should impede my onward course. Placing my firm reliance in the Almighty to protect me and my companions during our intended journey, and to vouchsafe the realisation of my heartfelt wishes for the success of my Mission, I cheerfully prepared for the Sabbath.

" On Monday morning, the 15th July, we arrived at Gothenburg, where we were enabled, after some difficulty, to take the train for Stockholm, which place we reached at about six o'clock that evening. I lost no time in calling on his Excellency, Monsieur de Giers, the Russian Ambassador, in order to deliver to him the letter from Count de Brunnow. I also called on the English Ambassador, but both these gentlemen being at their summer residences, some distance from the town, I was unable to see them that day. The following morning I again called on Monsieur de Giers, and he received me with the utmost courtesy and attention. To facilitate and expedite my journey, he put me in communication with Monsieur Moeurius, the Russian Consul-General at Stockholm, and being anxious to reach my destination with the least possible delay, I requested that gentleman to telegraph to General Nordenstam, at Helsingfors, to engage a special train to take me on to St Petersburg, and the Ambassador himself telegraphed to that city to secure apartments for me at the Hotel Klée. Her Majesty's Consul, Mr G. R. Perry, also in the absence of the Ambassador, assisted me in my arrangements.

" During my short stay at Stockholm I had the gratification of receiving the most satisfactory accounts of our brethren in that city The Chief Rabbi, Dr L. Lewysohn and the representatives of the community, Dr Lamm, Consul Davidson, and Mr Wolner, favoured me with full particulars of all their communal institutions. Their Synagogue, which is one of the finest in Europe, and their schools are well attended. Many non-Israelites resort to this place of worship, to listen to the eloquent preaching of the minister, and the study of Hebrew and the Talmud was diligently cultivated by the learned Gentiles in Sweden.

" Here again the journals of that city gave an alarming account of the unsatisfactory state of the public health in St Petersburg ; but after due consideration we decided to resume the journey. Towards evening we went on board the *Dagmar* steamship, which brought us on Thursday, the 18th July, at about 6 P.M., to Helsingfors, whence we immediately departed by special train, travelling the whole night, and at an early hour on Friday morning we entered the railway terminus at St Petersburg, where the carriages and attendants of the hotel were awaiting our arrival.

" At the earliest possible moment I called at the British Embassy to present the letter from Earl Granville to Lord Augustus Loftus, but his Excellency being away from St Petersburg, Mr Egerton opened the letter, and told me he would communicate with the Russian Minister for Foreign Affairs, and that Lord Augustus Loftus was expected to arrive soon from Finland.

" I then called on Monsieur de Westmann to deliver the letter from Count Brunnow. His Excellency received me with marked kindness and urbanity, and after some conversation he observed, ' We were acquainted with the object of your visit to our city before your arrival. The Emperor will receive you, and we shall endeavour to render everything as easy and agreeable to you as possible. His Imperial Majesty is at present absent from St Petersburg, but I shall seek his orders regarding the day and place, when and where he will receive you.'

" I need scarcely say how grateful I felt to our Heavenly Father for having thus, only a few hours after my arrival in St Petersburg, enabled me to receive from the Russian Minister such kind and assuring expressions, and deeply sensible of the goodness of the Almighty, who had succoured and protected me and my companions, I prepared with gladness for the Holy Sabbath.

"Monsieur de Westmann afterwards requested me to send him a copy of the address which it was my intention to present to the Emperor, it being probable that His Majesty would ask for it on the following day, when his Excellency would receive his commands as to my audience. I at once forwarded the desired copy by the hands of Dr Loewe, and I had subsequently the satisfaction of hearing the Minister's perfect approval of the address.

"During the day I was favoured with visits from the Rev. Dr Newmann, Chief Rabbi, the Rev. Isaac Baser, and the representatives of several congregations in St Petersburg and other towns. I took occasion to read the papers and documents which had been left with me for my attentive perusal. In the afternoon several of our brethren came to the hotel, and joined us in our Sabbath prayers. I noticed among them two who had been with me on a similar occasion twenty-six years ago. At that time they were serving in the army; they are now enjoying all the advantages of free citizenship.

"The following day I received a letter from Monsieur de Westmann, informing me that the Emperor would come to St Petersburg on the 24th July, on which day he would receive me in the Winter Palace at eleven o'clock in the morning. His Excellency instructed me that I was to enter by the gateway known as 'Le perron de Sa Majesté Imperiale l'Imperatrice,' and requested that Dr Loewe should be with him on Monday morning at eleven o'clock. Dr Loewe accordingly called at the Bureau of the Minister at the appointed time, when his Excellency expressed in the kindest terms his solicitude for my health. He also took Dr Loewe into an adjoining saloon, pointing out to him most minutely the gateway through which I should have to enter the Palace.

"Having been informed of the arrival of Lord Augustus Loftus, I called on his Excellency, and had a long and most interesting conversation with him on all subjects connected with my visit to St Petersburg, which afforded me the most gratifying evidence of his Lordship's wise and sound judgment on all matters affecting the welfare of our brethren, not only within the dominions of the Czar, but in every part of the world.

"On Wednesday at the appointed hour I proceeded to the Winter Palace, accompanied by Dr Loewe. We ascended in a lift to the great ante-room of the Emperor, into which we were immediately ushered. There we found his Excellency Monsieur de Westmann, the Imperial Lord Chamberlain, the Imperial Grand Maître des Cérémonies, and several other distinguished personages, who entered into conversation with me on various subjects of importance to our co-religionists. After an interval thus agreeably passed, his Excellency the Minister for Foreign Affairs was summoned before the Czar, and soon afterwards I was conducted into the presence of His Imperial Majesty, to whom, in the name of your Board and its several constituent congregations, I presented the address, of which the following is a copy :—

"'To His Imperial Majesty ALEXANDER THE SECOND, Czar of all the Russias.

"'May it please your Imperial Majesty,—Impressed by the deep sense of gratitude for the numerous acts of grace which your Imperial Majesty has been pleased to extend to our brethren who have the happiness to dwell under your Imperial Majesty's exalted rule, and prompted by the ardent desire to join the numerous hosts—friends of enlightenment and civilisation —who hasten to tender their felicitation on Russia's great day of gladness and joy, we, the London Committee of Deputies of British Jews, on behalf of ourselves and the several congregations we respectively represent, humbly approach your Imperial Majesty to lay **at the** foot of your Imperial Throne the tribute of our sincere and heartfelt congratulations on the occasion of the two hundredth **anniversary** of the birth of **your** Imperial Majesty's **august** ancestor, the Emperor **Peter** the Great.

"'Glorious and renowned were the deeds **of the** beatified Monarch. He was "the father of his people," and the author **of all that** was right and just in the vast Empire which he ruled; but **all the good** he effected would have vanished had not Eternal Providence **ordained** his spirit, the spirit of wisdom, justice, and humanity, to descend on **his august** offspring; and it is **in** this heavenly mercy that we, your Imperial **Majesty's** humble servants, **discern a** special cause for felicitation.

"'Already, in **the** year 1846, Sir Moses Montefiore, Bart., **the** President of **our** Board, had **the** distinguished honour to receive personally from your Imperial Majesty's august father, **the** Emperor Nicolas, the expression of his ardent desire for the happiness **and** welfare **of** all classes of his Imperial Majesty's subjects, and **you, Sire, have been** selected **as an** instrument of Providence to **emancipate millions of human** beings, to foster education, **to** encourage the arts **and sciences, and to** promote free **intercourse** between man and man, by opening **the** gates **of your** Imperial Majesty's vast Empire to persons of all religious denominations.

"'Most fervently, therefore, do we invoke the Creator **of the** universe to prolong the days of your Imperial Majesty and those of your most illustrious family, so that you, Sire, may have the felicity of seeing all your wise and noble plans for the prosperity and **peace** of your Imperial Majesty's subjects realised; and likewise the gratifying opportunity of listening for a period of long duration to the hallowed hymns of gratitude **from** the millions of your faithful and loyal subjects, in which—we **venture** to hope your Imperial Majesty will graciously condescend **to accept our** assurance—none can join with more fervour than our brethren in your Imperial Majesty's Empire and the London Committee of Deputies of the British Jews.

"'Signed **on** behalf of **the Board,**

"'MOSES MONTEFIORE, *President.*'

"His **Imperial Majesty, who conversed** most fluently **in** the English **language, received me with the utmost** grace and kindness. He adverted **to the circumstance of my having had an** audience with his august father in **the year 1846, and expressed himself most** graciously **on** every subject **having reference to my Mission.** His Imperial Majesty also graciously **spoke to Dr Loewe. Nor can I here omit to** record my grateful appreciation **of His Imperial Majesty's consideration in** having come **from** the seat of **the summer manœuvres to the Winter Palace,** expressly **to** spare me fatigue **in consequence of my advanced age, and having** there received the address **of which I was the bearer. I quitted the Palace with a heart overflowing with gratitude, for indeed I am at a loss for words in which adequately to describe the gracious sentiments which his Imperial Majesty and the members of the Government evinced towards me.**"

CHAPTER XXXII.

1872.

CONTINUING his narrative, Sir Moses says:

"On my way to the hotel I was enthusiastically greeted by hundreds of our brethren who were awaiting my return from the Palace, and whose faces were radiant with joy and gladness. After a brief rest I again set out to pay my farewell visits to the British Ambassador, Lord Augustus Loftus, and his Excellency Monsieur de Westmann, left cards with those who had honoured me with visits, and then proceeded to the Synagogue, into which, however, the hour being late, I was unable to enter. Returning again to the hotel, I addressed to his Excellency Monsieur de Westmann a letter, in which I offered to his Excellency the expression of my warmest thanks for the gracious reception accorded me by His Imperial Majesty, and also for the exertions of his Excellency in aiding me to obtain the object of my Mission, requesting him at the same time, in commemoration of the happy event, to distribute a trifling sum among the necessitous inhabitants of the city.

"To this letter I received the most gratifying reply. His Excellency promised to comply with my request, and to convey to the Emperor the prayers and wishes I had expressed for the long life and enduring happiness of His Imperial Majesty.

"On Thursday morning, the 25th July, I received at the hotel many deputations and private gentlemen, who had solicited an interview; read all letters, books, and documents which had been left for my special notice, and having satisfied everyone to the best of my ability, I left St Petersburg for Königsberg, attended by the blessings and good wishes of hundreds of people, who followed us to the railway station.

"It will doubtless be a source of gratification to your Board to learn that during my short stay in St Petersburg I had the happiness of seeing a considerable number of our co-religionists in that city distinguished by decorations of different grades from the Emperor. I conversed with Jewish merchants, literary men, editors of Russian periodicals, artisans, and persons who had formerly served in the Imperial army, all of whom alluded to their present position in the most satisfactory terms. All blessed the Emperor, and words seemed wanting in which adequately to praise his benevolent character. The Jews now dress like ordinary gentlemen in England, France, or Germany. Their schools are well attended, and they are foremost in every honourable enterprise destined to promote the prosperity of their community and the country at large.

" There are three Synagogues in the city, each presided over by a Rabbi, who delivers sermons in German or Russian. The utmost decorum prevails during Divine service. In St Petersburg and throughout Russia great efforts are being made to provide education for those who require it. In order to bring it within the reach of those who are best acquainted with the Hebrew language, maps are printed with the names of the places in Hebrew letters, and educational works of all kinds are translated into Hebrew.

" Looking back to what the condition of our co-religionists in Russia was twenty-six years ago, and having regard to their present position, they have now indeed abundant reason to cherish grateful feelings towards the Emperor, to whom their prosperity is in so great a measure to be attributed ; and if there yet remain restrictions, the hope may be surely entertained that with the advance of secular education among them those disabilities will be gradually removed. And here I would place on record my earnest tribute of admiration for the marked improvements which have taken place in Russia since my visit to that country in the year 1846. I rejoiced to observe in every department of the State signs of vigour and prosperity, the happy result of the wisdom, justice, and toleration which have distinguished the Emperor's beneficent reign.

" But before resuming the narrative of my homeward journey, I would advert to the exceeding kindness evinced by Her Majesty's Ambassador at the Court of Russia, Lord Augustus Loftus, by Mr Drummond and Mr Egerton, who omitted no opportunity of facilitating the object of my Mission. I am also much indebted to Mr Mitchell, Her Majesty's Consul in St Petersburg, for his obliging attentions. I shall ever cherish towards Monsieur de Westmann and Lord Augustus Loftus sentiments of profound gratitude for their great attention and courtesy to me during my stay in the Russian capital.

" We departed from St Petersburg, travelling all night in order to reach Königsberg in good time for Sabbath. On arriving at the station at Kowno we were saluted by the Chief Rabbi, the Rev. Reuben Schnitkind, the Rev. Isaac Elkhanan Spekter, and Drs Schapiro and Klazco, who were surrounded by many hundreds of our brethren, all eager to learn the result of my Mission. I therefore requested Dr Loewe to address them in Hebrew, and they were overjoyed with the communication made to them. They referred to the address which I had presented to the Czar, and invoked the Almighty's blessing on behalf of your Board. It appeared that our route had been made known from place to place, inasmuch as we were met by large numbers of our brethren who were awaiting our arrival at each station where the train stopped. At Wilna we were greeted by the representatives of the Hebrew congregation, consisting of the Rev. Isaac Eliahu Landau, the Rev. Mordecai Straschun, and Mr Abraham Parness, son of my late friend the Rev. Chaim Nachman Parness, who were accompanied by an immense concourse of people. Here, as in Kowno, I entered into conversation with those who had come to welcome me, not only on the subject of my Mission but also upon matters relating specially to their own community, and I had the pleasure to leave them with mutual expressions of satisfaction and good-will.

" We reached Königsberg on Friday afternoon (the 26th July), and were met at the railway terminus by thousands of our brethren, who made the streets of the city ring with their shouts of joy as they accompanied me to the hotel. Mr D. H. Aschkanasi, a zealous friend of the Holy Land, presented me with a congratulatory address from the representatives of the three Russian congregations in that city, and the Rev. H. Weintraub, the well-known composer of sacred music, offered his services to invite a number of gentlemen to attend Divine service in our apartment. At the appointed hour I had the happiness of hearing the Sabbath hymn beautifully chanted by Mr

L. Löwenstein, in the presence of a full congregation, and, it is scarcely necessary to add, that after a fatiguing journey, occupying a day and night, I enjoyed to the utmost the peace and repose of the Sabbath.

" In the morning we attended Divine service, and in the course of the day the representatives of the German congregation, headed by the City Council, Dr Hirsch, Dr Samuelsohn, Mr Solomon Feinberg, and many others, called on me to offer their congratulations, apologising for the unavoidable absence of the Rev. Dr Bamberger, the spiritual head of the congregation.

"They entered into full particulars of their exertions on behalf of our brethren in Russia during the time of the great distress occasioned by the failure of the harvest, and I was much pleased with the account they gave of their praiseworthy efforts to succour their less fortunate co-religionists.

"A telegram also reached me from the Rev. Dr Rülf, and the representatives of the Hebrew congregations in Memel, expressing their appreciation of your Board's exertions in the sacred cause of religion and humanity, and tendering me their best wishes upon my safe return from Russia.

" It may not be inopportune if I refer to a pleasing incident which occurred at Königsberg, evidencing the anxiety of our co-religionists in that city to evince their approbation of the solicitude of your Board for the welfare of our brethren abroad. After dinner, on the Sabbath day, as we commenced singing the Sabbath psalm, we were most agreeably surprised by the charming voices of the first Cantor of the Synagogue and the members of his excellent choir. They had obtained permission to enter an adjoining apartment without my knowledge, and watching the moment of our commencing to intone the psalm, they took up the next verse and chanted the whole of it, in the presence of hundreds of people within the hotel and adjoining garden, all eagerly listening to the charming psalmody.

" On the following morning (July 28th) I proposed to return the visits of those gentlemen who had been kind enough to call on me ; but the number of people surrounding my carriage became so great, and the streets were so thronged, that, fearing an accident, I was reluctantly compelled to relinquish my intention, and return to the hotel.

"'The daughters in Israel,' in Königsberg, being equally desirous of evincing their appreciation of a good cause, gracefully presented me, by the hands of twelve young ladies, with a beautiful poem and a laurel wreath.

" In the afternoon we left Königsberg for Berlin, and with a view to expedite our return to England, we again travelled all night. At about four o'clock in the morning, on July 29th, whilst we halted at Küstrin, I was apprised of the presence of the Rev. Dr Hildesheimer, one of the Chief Rabbis of Berlin, who, I was informed, had purposely come there to bid me welcome in the name of his community, and to conduct me in his carriage to Berlin. This mark of attention I fully appreciated, but I could not permit the Rev. Doctor to be further disturbed. We alighted at the terminus at Berlin about six o'clock, and I entered the city in company with the Chief Rabbi and his son. The former expressed, in the name of his community, the high admiration for the active and energetic steps taken by your Board whenever the occasion for its interposition on behalf of our brethren in foreign countries existed. Early in the forenoon I called on the English and Russian Ambassadors, but unfortunately they were both absent from Berlin ; I then paid a visit to the Chief Rabbi, to express my thanks to him for his courtesy and kindness, and subsequently entered the Synagogue over which he presides. There I was told that, spacious as the edifice is, every seat was let, and that the congregation intend to build a larger one.

" Not having taken the necessary rest after an entire night's travelling, I felt somewhat indisposed from the effects of over-fatigue, but I would not delay my journey, and proceeded the next day (July 30th) to Hanover. Here

I had the opportunity of making the personal acquaintance of the Chief Rabbi, the Rev. Dr Meyer, the esteemed successor of the Rev. Dr Adler, our own highly respected Chief Rabbi. Dr Meyer had just returned from Berlin, whither he had been summoned by the Government, to assist in the deliberations of the conference held in that city, upon the subject of the improvements which it was in contemplation to introduce into the regulations and government of educational establishments. I also had the advantage of ascertaining the condition of the Hebrew institutions in Hanover. I visited the Synagogue, which is a beautiful building, and I was assured by a gentleman present that although it was at first intended to divide the Synagogue by a glass partition into a larger and smaller house of prayer, so as to enable the congregation to say prayers in the latter on week-days, yet the number of worshippers was so great that the plan was necessarily abandoned.

"On leaving Hanover we travelled *via* Cologne, Aix la Chapelle, and Ghent, to Ostend, where, on the 8th August, we embarked for Dover, and immediately on our arrival in that port I proceeded with Dr Loewe to the Synagogue, where I gave utterance to my heartfelt gratitude to our Heavenly Father for the innumerable mercies He had vouchsafed to me and my companions during our journey, and for His goodness in having permitted me once again to return to the happy shores of England, conscious of having, with His Divine aid, attained the object of my Mission.

"During my journey I had frequent opportunities of receiving from our brethren assurances of the rapid increase of their Synagogues, schools, and charitable institutions, and as indicative of the improved spiritual and social condition of our co-religionists abroad, I may notice that amongst the many thousands of Jews with whom I came into contact, I observed the most charitable and benevolent dispositions, an insatiable thirst for knowledge, a pure and religious zeal, and a high degree of prosperity."

August 10th.—Sir Moses remained at East Cliff Lodge for a few days, and then proceeded to London to attend the boards and committees of all the companies and institutions with which he was connected, the fatiguing journey to Russia not appearing to have affected his state of health at all.

September 6th.—He called on Count Brunnow to show him the report on his visit to St Petersburg before presenting it to the Board of Deputies. "The Ambassador," Sir Moses says, " having read every word of it in the most careful manner—it was more than half-an-hour before he had finished—said it was complete, but thought I should record my warmest acknowledgments to the Emperor, who, in consideration of my advanced years, to save me fatigue of going to him at the Palace, some distance in the country, came purposely to the city to receive me. I immediately made the addition his Excellency so kindly suggested."

December 21st.—Sir Moses submitted a report of the Persian Relief Fund, the total amount subscribed and collected being nearly £20,000, and he records in his Diary his great delight at the success of the appeal, and his gratitude to the Board and to all who co-operated with him and the Deputies in so good a cause.

January 1873.—The ninth anniversary of Sir Moses' visit to the Sultan of Morocco was now at hand, the day being usually distinguished by a special service and an address in Judith College, Ramsgate. This year, in consequence of the arbitrary conduct of a judge at Saffi, Sir Moses found it necessary to remind His Sheriffian Majesty of the promise he made to him on that memorable occasion. At the request of the Board of Deputies, he addressed a petition to the Sultan Mooli Abd-er-Rakhman.

The following is a translation of the principal paragraphs bearing upon the case :—

"LONDON, 10*th February* 1873 (5633 A.M.).

"May it please your Sheriffian Majesty (here follows the preamble, and a short reference to the former visit). Lately, however, rumours have reached me that one Sidi Mohammed ben Sidi Tayibbi, a judge of Saffi, unmindful of the terms of your Majesty's gracious edict, and of the duty of his high office, has ventured to oppress and ill-treat the Jews of that town, and has instigated others to injure and oppress them, whereby it has come to pass that their lives are embittered, and they have no security for their persons or their property.

"Emboldened by the gracious reception which your Majesty afforded me in the year 1280, and by the beneficent and humane terms of your Majesty's edict, I humbly entreat your Majesty to cause the conduct of the said Sidi Mohammed ben Sidi Tayibbi to be investigated, and to deal with him according to the result, so that all your governors, administrators, and judges in your Majesty's dominions may know that your benevolent designs towards my brethren remain unchanged."

The letter being written in the Moorish language, concludes, according to Eastern fashion, with a prayer for the Sultan.

May 26*th*.—A deputation from the Jews of Ispahan waited on Sir Moses to present letters from the elders of their community, giving him long and interesting descriptions of the state of their country. Sir Moses received them with great kindness, presenting them with souvenirs of their visit to him, and assured them of the great exertions made by their brethren in England, and in other parts of the world, to ameliorate the condition of the Jews in Persia.

June 11*th*.—He went to Manchester, by invitation of the representatives of the Spanish and Portuguese Hebrew Community there, to be present on the occasion of the laying of the foundation stone of the first Portuguese Synagogue in that city, and remained there several days.

In June the Shah of Persia came to England, and this gave Sir Moses an opportunity to request an audience of that monarch, which was readily granted.

Accompanied by a deputation from the Board of Deputies of British Jews, Sir Moses presented a memorial to the Shah at Buckingham Palace, soliciting His Majesty's protection for his Jewish subjects. The Shah assured the deputation that he wished for the happiness of all his subjects, and would give orders that no injustice should be done to the Jews. Later on he sent the following letter, through his Minister in London, to Sir Moses :—

"I am commanded by His Majesty the Shah to acknowledge the receipt of your memorial, praying that favour and protection may be generally extended to the Jews in Persia. His Majesty has always manifested solicitude for the welfare of his subjects, without distinction of class or creed ; and he will take care that no injustice or undue severity is shown to the Jewish community, whom you rightly characterise as loyal, peaceable, and industrious citizens. His Majesty thanks you for the good wishes you have expressed in regard to him.   (Signed)   MALCOLM."

Sir Moses, thinking it would be useful to make the good intentions of the Shah known to the Jews in Persia, as well as to the Persian public in general, had this letter translated into the Persian and Hebrew languages. He also addressed a letter of his own to the representatives of the Hebrew community in Persia ; and having had the English, Hebrew, Persian, and his own letter lithographed on one large scroll, forwarded copies to hundreds of Hebrew communities in Persia, with instructions to have the scroll affixed to the principal entrance of their Synagogues.

In his letter he calls the attention of the Jews to the good intentions of the Shah, and enjoins them to pray for his life and happiness, and the prosperity of the country in which they live.

Copies of all the foregoing are preserved in Lady Montefiore's College.

October 23rd.—In commemoration of the visit of Sir Albert Sassoon to one of the schools of the Spanish and Portuguese community in the month of May in this year, Sir Moses caused a special medal to be struck. Sir Moses was delighted to see the son of Mr David Sassoon, to whom the Jews are indebted for schools, colleges, and synagogues in Bagdad, Bombay, and other places, taking the same interest in education as his father had done before him, and he gave expression to his sentiments in a letter which he wrote to Sir Albert when sending him one of the medals for his acceptance.

CHAPTER XXXIII.

1873.

THE Board of Deputies of British Jews, on the occasion of the betrothal of the Duke of Edinburgh to the Grand Duchess Marie Alexandrovna of Russia, voted an address of congratulation to the Emperor of Russia. Sir Moses, as President of the Board, himself offered to take the address to St Petersburg and present it to the Emperor in person, but Count Brunnow, on becoming acquainted with Sir Moses' intention, persuaded him not to undergo the fatigue of travelling, and the journey was reluctantly abandoned. His Excellency himself forwarded the address to the Emperor.

Monsieur de Westmann, acknowledging the receipt of the address in the name of the Emperor, wrote to Count Brunnow as follows :—

"Les sentiments dont cette adresse contient l'expression, dans une circonstance si chère au cœur de Sa Majésté Impériale, L'ont profondement touchée. Elle a été particulierement sensible au désir manifesté par Sir Moses Montefiore de se rendre lui-même en Russie, pour être l'organe des felicitations de ses co-religionnaires. Sa Majesté Impériale n'a pu qu'approuver l'attention que vous avez eue d'epargner à Sir Moses Montefiore les fatigues d'un si long voyage. Elle m'a donné l'ordre exprès de lui faire parvenir ses remercîments par l'intermédiaire de Votre Excellence et de l'assurer qu'ayant conservé le meilleur souvenir du séjour de Sir Moses à St Petersbourg, Elle maintient invariablement les dispositions bien-veillantes qu'Elle lui a témoignées tant pour lui personnellement que pour ses co-religionnaires, dont il a plaidé la cause avec tant de chaleureux dévouement.

"Veuillez, Monsieur le Comte, faire part à Sir Moses Montefiore de ces sentiments de notre Auguste Maître et recevez, &c."

During the next three months the serious illness of his sister, Mrs Cohen, caused Sir Moses great anxiety. All the time he could spare from official duties he passed by her side, trying to alleviate her sufferings, and to cheer her by his conversation. But the dread decree had gone forth, and in spite of all that was done for her, she succumbed to the malady. On the 29th of October we read the following entry in Sir Moses' Diary :—

" It has pleased the God of our fathers to relieve my dearly beloved sister from all suffering. She was called to eternal glory this morning at seven o'clock, expiring without a sigh, passing from earth to Heaven most peaceably in a sound sleep. Oh, may my end be like hers! Peace be to her soul! ' The Lord gave, the Lord hath taken away. Blessed be the name of the Lord.'

" It is a sad loss to me. She was the youngest of nine children. I, the oldest, by the mercy of God, still remain, I hope for the purpose of doing some good.

" May God comfort my dear sister's children, bless and preserve them. Amen."

October 31*st.*—" My dear sister," he says, " looks calm and happy, free from all pain. God rest her soul! The coffin had a covering of a neatly-made glass." " My sister," he continues, " desired to be clothed in the gown and cap I gave her as a present on the New Year.

" *November* 4*th.*—Her mortal remains were taken to the grave this morning. There was a very numerous attendance of friends. I was too weak to follow to the grave."

During the seven days of mourning he received a great many visits of condolence. He sometimes felt poorly, had a cough, and his hand was unsteady for writing, but, " Thanks to the God of our fathers," he says, " My head is clear." " May God's blessing continue to me now and evermore. Amen."

November 27*th.*—The entry in his Diary reads as follows :—
" I feel very weak and low, but have had great pleasure to-day by the receipt of a most kind and pleasing letter from His Grace the Archbishop of Canterbury, written last evening immediately on his return from a visit with Mrs Tait and their family to my dear Judith College, where they had passed more than two hours.

" Believing the perusal of the letter would be pleasing to our esteemed Chief Rabbi, I have sent it to him."

The following is a copy of this letter :—

"STONEHOUSE, ST PETER'S, THANET,
November 26, 1873.

" MY DEAR SIR MOSES,—I have just now returned from a most interesting visit with Mrs Tait and all my family to the College near your house. I must write a few lines to thank you for your kindness in arranging for our reception. Dr Loewe was most kind in explaining to us all the various objects of interest and treasures accumulated in the College.

" I beg to thank you for the kind presents of the report on the famine in Persia, of the statutes of the College, and of a copy of the Shah's letter.

" It is a cause of much regret to us that you should have suffered the afiliction which has lately visited you, and which has prevented us from seeing you during our stay here. My son especially was most anxious to express to you personally how much he feels indebted for the letters of introduction with which you furnished him for his late visit to the East.

"Trusting that God may long preserve your life, and that He may keep you and guide you in all your ways.—I am, my dear Sir Moses, very faithfully yours,   "A. C. CANTUAR."

Whilst His Grace was proposing and drinking the health of Sir Moses in the College, and the latter at East Cliff was expressing his gratification at the visit of the Archbishop to the College, the people in Ramsgate were lamenting the supposed sudden death of Sir Moses. Indeed, *The Kent Coast Times*, Thursday, November 27, 1873, had a paragraph to that effect. Sir Moses, on being told of it, and having subsequently read that paragraph himself, said, pleasantly, " Thank God to have been able to hear of the rumour, and read an account of the same with my own eyes, without using spectacles."

April 16*th.*—The representatives of the several Hebrew congregations in Jerusalem addressed a sorrowful letter to Sir Moses respecting a famine which threatened to destroy the lives of many inhabitants in the Holy City.

" A wet and stormy season at its beginning ruined the prospects of the early crops, which should have been reaped on the plains of Sharon towards Jaffa and down the Ghor, the Jordan Valley, and around Jericho. In ordinary times ample food is obtained from these wide plains, but this year the Jordan flooded its banks, and all about Ramlah on the western side of the hills was a swamp. The consequence has been famine, actual famine, and in deep distress the Jews of Jerusalem utter a cry of anguish to their well-tried friend."

Sir Moses gave publicity to the letter he had received, and

several daily papers had leading articles on the subject. He and others did all they could to alleviate the distress, but seeing how often similar calamities befel the people in the Holy Land, he wished to ascertain from the best informed and most trustworthy persons in that country the best means of securing for them some permanent help either in the direction of agriculture or mechanical work or some suitable business. Accordingly Sir Moses addressed the Háhám Báshi and the representatives of the several Hebrew congregations in Jerusalem.

"It has ever been my earnest desire," he writes, "since I first had the opportunity of becoming acquainted with the state of great poverty and distress that prevailed among you, to ameliorate your condition and cause salvation to spring forth in the Holy Land by means of industrial pursuits, such as agriculture, mechanical work, or some suitable business, so as to enable both the man who is not qualified for study, but fully able (by his physical strength) to work as well as the student, who, prompted by a desire to maintain himself by the labour of his hands, may be willing to devote the day to the work necessary for the support of his family, and part of the night to the study of the Law of God, to find the means of an honourable living.

"Already in the years 5599 and 5626 I entreated you to assist me with your wise and judicious counsel, and begged of you to point out to me the right path. I then forwarded to you statistical and agricultural forms to enable you to record therein all the information required, and you most cheerfully complied with my request, and gave me all the particulars referring to these subjects.

"I on my part made known to all my friends and acquaintances the information I received from you ; but, unfortunately, from various causes I met with little success in asking for assistance to carry out this great work, and your condition remained the same as before.

"Having again this year noticed all the troubles and hardships you had to undergo from scarcity of bread, and from want of means to procure it, I thought I would again try to ascertain whether any of your suggestions regarding the best mode of ameliorating your condition, either by agriculture or by mechanical work, within or without the house, or some suitable business pursuits, if clearly and distinctly set forth to our brethren, might not, under present circumstances, be more favourably received, and induce them more readily to hasten with their succour to a most deserving class of people, so as to procure lasting comfort among you.

"Let me therefore entreat you to fully acquaint me with your views on this subject : point out to me what I am to do in order to hasten thereby the cause of bringing salvation into the land. Consider well which is the proper path, appearing most clearly to you, to produce the remedy you stand in need of.

"By doing so you will comply with the wishes of your brethren, who love and kiss, as it were, the dust of the Holy Land.

"Be strong and of good courage. Do not say 'Our words are of no avail,' but send speedily a reply to him who holds you in great esteem, and prays for the welfare of his people."

To this letter Sir Moses received replies from the congregations of Jerusalem, Jaffa, Safed, Tiberias, Haiffa, giving full particulars respecting the matters to which he had referred, and these letters he subsequently submitted to the Palestine Committee of the London Committee of Deputies of the British Jews. At the end of May the Board of Deputies of British Jews sent a deputation to Sir Moses to again request his acceptance of the Presidency over that body. Sir Moses was very reluctant to accept duties which the state of his health might not permit him adequately to fulfil, but the solicitations of the deputation prevailed upon him, and putting his trust in God to help him, he again accepted the honourable office.

During this year the Fishmongers' Company of London held a meeting, at which, on the motion of the Prime-Warden, Mr W. C. Venning, the freedom of the Company was unanimously voted to Sir Moses; and at the end of June a deputation from the Company, headed by the Prime-Warden, came to Ramsgate to present the document to him, enclosed in a golden casket of beautiful workmanship.

July 1st.—He had the honour of being graciously invited by Her Majesty the Queen to an evening party at Buckingham Palace, but was prevented by indisposition from availing himself of it.

July 6th.—"I should have been pleased," Sir Moses writes in his Diary, "had I been strong enough to go to London. I feel a deep interest in the question now under consideration of the London Committee of British Jews, for assisting our brethren to cultivate land in Palestine. I am confident if capital could be raised for the purpose, the people, the country, and the contributors would all be greatly benefited by the work. I should suggest that a million sterling should be obtained by 1,000,000 of £1 subscriptions, and I believe I could obtain, within one year, that sum for the purpose from the Jews in the four quarters of the globe."

July 26th.—"I feel deep anxiety on the subject of the projected scheme for agriculture in the Holy Land. I would suggest that a committee should be sent to Jerusalem, Safed, Tiberias, and Hebron to report. I should be willing to accompany the commissioners at my own expense, should it be the desire of the Board of Deputies."

August 4th.—Finding his health failing, he resolved to resign the Presidency of the Board. His nephew, Mr Joseph M. Montefiore, came down to him, and Sir Moses acquainted him with his wish. Before he left, Sir Moses read to him the letter which he afterwards posted to him as Vice-President of the Board, and of which the following is a copy :—

"EAST CLIFF LODGE, RAMSGATE,
"*August 4th,* 5634 (1874).

"MY DEAR JOSEPH MAYER MONTEFIORE,—It is with unaffected pain that I have to place in your hands my resignation of the Presidentship of the London Committee of Deputies of the British Jews.

"The considerations which have urged this step have reference to my state of health, which is, unfortunately, such as utterly to preclude that unremitting attention on my part to the duties of the office which their responsible nature demands.

"In retiring from a post which it has been my distinguished privilege to occupy during a lengthened period, I can only assure you that I do so with great regret, and with every earnest wish that, under your able direction, the Board may long continue to exercise its powerful influence for the good of the community, and that every blessing may be enjoyed by yourself and those esteemed friends who represent so worthily the congregations of this kingdom.—I have the honour to be, my dear Joseph Mayer Montefiore, yours very truly,
"MOSES MONTEFIORE."

I now quote from the Board's First Annual Report of its proceedings to its constituents, Session 5634, p. 9.

"Considering Sir Moses Montefiore's lengthened association with the Board, his exalted character, his potent influence in the councils of monarchs and of ministers, and the rare judgment and tact which he exhibited in directing the affairs of the Board, the Deputies contemplated with deep concern and regret the possibility of his retirement from their body."

Earnest efforts were again made to induce him to alter his determination, but unfortunately without avail, and, bearing in mind Sir Moses' advanced age, and that he had retired on the ground of failing health, it was felt it would not be right to persuade him further to retain an office involving at times arduous and responsible duties.

In parting with its venerated President, the Board expressed its sentiments in the following resolutions, which, being engrossed on vellum and emblazoned, were signed by every Deputy, and presented to him.

"Resolved unanimously—

"That this Board accept with profound regret the resignation by Sir Moses Montefiore, Bart., F.R.S., of the office of President, which he has held with so much honour and distinction since the year 1841.

"That during that long and eventful period this Board has had the proud satisfaction of co-operating with Sir Moses Montefiore in many of his numerous benevolent undertakings in the cause of civilization and humanity.

"That by his unremitting and successful efforts on behalf of the weak and persecuted, Sir Moses Montefiore has kindled a spirit of enlightenment and toleration in foreign countries, which has already led to a material improvement in the condition of oppressed nationalities.

"That by these means Sir Moses Montefiore has acquired for himself a glorious and imperishable renown, and the enduring gratitude of his co-religionists.

"That this Board will ever cherish the remembrance of its association with Sir Moses Montefiore, whose wise and discreet counsels have prompted the efficiency and success of its labours, and whose uniform urbanity and kindliness of manners have won for him the affectionate regard and admiration of his colleagues.

"That it is the earnest wish of every member of this Board that Sir Moses Montefiore may yet enjoy many years of happiness and repose, cheered by the consciousness of having devoted himself to the promotion of the welfare and prosperity of his fellow-creatures.

"(Signed)   [Members of the Board.]"

"It was still felt," the Board reports, "that something more was required to satisfy the feelings of affection and gratitude entertained by the Board and its constituents towards Sir Moses Montefiore.

"A Committee was therefore appointed to consider and report as to the best mode of recording his long and valuable services in a permanent and useful form. It was thought, moreover, that our co-religionists in all parts of the world would gladly seize the opportunity of acknowledging the invaluable services rendered by Sir Moses Montefiore in vindicating on so many memorable occasions the rights of our brethren, and in protecting and assisting the suffering and oppressed, without distinction of creeds or nationality."

Sir Moses was invited by the Board to indicate the nature of the memorial which would be most congenial to his own feelings, and, when a deputation from the Board awaited upon him at Park Lane, he at once recommended works for the improvement of the condition of the Jews of the Holy Land.

It had happened that during the session Colonel Gawler, F.R.G.S., had submitted to Sir Moses Montefiore a scheme for the promotion of agriculture and other industrial occupations in the Holy Land by means of colonisation. Sir Moses Montefiore had referred the scheme to the Board, who had appointed a Special Committee, by whom it was carefully considered. Acting on a report from this Committee, the Board came to the conclusion that, whilst Colonel Gawler was entitled to its warmest thanks for the benevolent zeal which he had evinced in the matter, his scheme was of too vast a character to be undertaken by the Board with any reasonable prospect of success; but the Committee suggested an undertaking for permanently improving the condition of the Jews of the Holy Land, by the promotion of industrial pursuits, the erection of improved dwellings, and the acquisition and cultivation of land on a moderate scale, strongly urging at the same time that the funds which might be raised should be entirely devoted to the assistance of those who were really desirous of helping themselves, and that no portion whatever should be applied in almsgiving.

These suggestions were carefully considered by the Board, and were adopted, and were found to be most pleasing to Sir Moses Montefiore.   The Deputies therefore formed themselves into a Committee of the whole body for the purpose of carrying the proposed objects into effect.

CHAPTER XXXIV.

1874.

NOVEMBER 14th.—Mr Weekes, the sculptor, who five months previously had submitted to Sir Moses a model of the bust of the Archbishop of Canterbury, which, with the consent of his Grace, Sir Moses had commissioned the sculptor to execute, now reported that it was ready for being unveiled at the Orphanage at St Peter's, Thanet. Sir Moses, believing that it would be a source of gratification to the Archbishop to see the bust of Mrs Tait placed in the same institution, wrote to that lady, asking her to allow him to give the sculptor an order to that effect. Mrs Tait's reply is as follows :

"STONEHOUSE, ST PETER'S,
THANET, *November* 15th, 1874.

"MY DEAR SIR MOSES,—Most deeply do we feel the kindness of your request in wishing me also to sit to Mr Weekes for a bust to be placed in St Peter's Orphan Home. I shall gladly comply, and thankfully accept your great kindness.

"We are truly grieved to hear of your being so unwell, and I shall be thankful if you find yourself well enough to join our party at luncheon on the 17th, without risk.

"Dr Loewe has promised to be with us, and will say a few words for you, should you be unable. He will also let me know if you have other friends you may wish to be present.

"The bust of the Archbishop is beautifully executed, and will, I am sure, be much admired.—Believe me to be, my dear Sir Moses, yours most sincerely, "CATHERINE TAIT."

"The Archbishop joins in very kind regards."

Sir Moses was too unwell to leave Park Lane, and great disappointment was felt by all present at the ceremony.

The Archbishop and Mrs Tait, however, were present to witness the proceedings. The Dean of Canterbury and most of the clergy resident in the neighbourhood, nearly all the clergy in the Westbere Deanery, many of the Sandwich Deanery, and a great number from other parts of the county, also attended. The company included several ladies. The bust was placed in the dining-hall, and the juvenile inmates of the institution were seated at one end of the room. A published report says:

"Dr Loewe attended as the representative of Sir Moses Montefiore, and unveiled the bust. It bore the following inscription:—

A Bust
of ARCHIBALD CAMPBELL TAIT,
Archbishop of Canterbury,
Primate of all England,
Presented to
ST PETER'S ORPHAN AND CONVALESCENT HOME
by
Sir MOSES MONTEFIORE, Bart.
1874.

"Dr Loewe began by reading the following letter from Sir Moses to Mrs Tait:—

"'I find with sincere regret that the state of my health precludes the possibility of my travelling, and will thus deprive me of the great pleasure and privilege of paying my respects to you and to the Archbishop at the Orphanage to-morrow, but allow me to assure you that, although I cannot be present, my fervent prayers will be united to those of your guests, who entreat the blessing of God on the noble institution in which they are assembled, and on its distinguished and benevolent founders.'

"Dr Loewe then said he was sure the regret expressed by Sir Moses at being prevented attending this interesting ceremony was equalled by that of the company at being deprived of the presence of the great philanthropist. Sir Moses, whose heart always glowed with love and zeal for the cause of humanity, had watched with deep interest the great exertions and sacrifices made by that excellent lady, Mrs Tait, and her highly-esteemed husband, the Archbishop, for the purpose of calling this noble institution into existence.

"Dr Loewe then unveiled the bust, and concluded by calling down the blessings of heaven upon the Archbishop of Canterbury, upon his most excellent consort, and his most amiable family. 'May he enjoy perfect health, and be in possession of every prosperity that this world can possibly give; may he live to see the time "when the earth will be full with the knowledge of the Lord, even as the waters cover the sea," when truth, peace, and light will be the guardian angels of every man's house, when all will be united in enjoying happiness, sitting, as it were, under their own vine and fig tree, with all the blessing that God might bestow upon them. I believe, ladies and gentlemen, I have conveyed the sentiments of Sir Moses Montefiore. I need only say that I myself, and, I am sure, all of you cordially endorse the words which have fallen from my lips in the name of Sir Moses.'

"The Archbishop said—

"'I beg to express my best thanks to all who are here present for their kindness in coming to this Orphanage to-day, and I would return my very best thanks to Sir Moses for his great kindness, and for the very flattering opinion he has formed of our efforts here. Dr Loewe has most kindly represented him in his absence. This is not the first instance of his kind consideration for this charitable work which we have received. On the very first day when the foundation stone of this building was laid, Sir Moses Montefiore was present, though at his advanced age he might have well stayed away on a bleak, wintry day. Five years ago he was present here. Although prevented from joining our religious services, he showed that he was desirous of co operating with us in every way in which he could do so conscientiously. In his carriage he drove close to where our Christian meeting was assembled, and joined in those Psalms of David which have been the solace of his life, and he ended that day by a large and handsome contribution to the charitable work which we were undertaking at that time. To-day he has kindly sent you this work by Mr Weekes, of which of course I can say nothing, except that I hope I may very faintly reflect the majestic appearance of that bust. (Laughter.) We have greatly to thank Mr Weekes for the pains and trouble he has taken with this work. We have greatly to thank Dr Loewe for the way in which he has performed his part as Sir Moses Montefiore's representative and friend of many years. But we have especially to thank the Great Giver of all good that He has so far prospered this work as to bring it to the degree of accomplishment it has now attained. I have said it was on a bleak, wintry day, five years ago, that the foundation stone was laid. I was not present, for it had pleased God to lay me on a bed of sickness, and I could hardly have expected I could live to be present five years after on such an occasion as this. Thank God, as I do with my household, this day for all His past mercies. Sir Moses Montefiore—and Dr Loewe, in expressing his sentiments—has been kind enough to speak of me in this matter. I am glad he has spoken of my wife, because I feel that it is to her that the whole prosperity of this institution is owing, and I will venture to say, though her husband, and in her presence, I believe there is scarcely another woman in England who, under the difficulties she has had to contend against, would have been able to bring the institution to that degree of accomplishment to which it has now attained. In England we still live under the barbarous law which makes the property of the married woman over to her husband, and therefore I cordially appropriate all that Dr Loewe has said of her virtues, and take them as if they were my own.

"'In conclusion I beg to return our best thanks to Sir Moses Montefiore for his kindness ; tell him we shall certainly offer our prayers that his long life may be blessed, that as he has advanced far beyond the age which the Psalmist regards as the age of man, he may have comforts and blessings poured upon him, and may be kept in such health as his age allows.'"

Sir Moses, to whom I made a full report of the proceedings at the Orphanage, requested me to call on the Archbishop and express his gratitude to His Grace for his great kindness towards him, upon which the Archbishop addressed Sir Moses as follows :—

"STONEHOUSE, ST PETER'S, THANET,
21st November 1874.

"MY DEAR SIR MOSES,—Dr Loewe called yesterday to deliver your most kind message. Kindly and well as Dr Loewe performed his part on Tuesday, there was, I assure you, a universal feeling of regret that you were not present.

"You have heard from the published account, and privately, how happily the day passed.

"It was bright sunshine, and all things seemed propitious. Your absence and its cause were the only drawbacks.

"How different a day it was, through God's goodness, from that day five years ago when you kindly attended at the laying of the first stone of the Orphanage !

"Trusting that your health will be restored, and that all the best blessings from above may rest on you and yours.—I am, my dear Sir Moses, yours very truly, "A. C. CANTUAR."

"Mrs Tait joins in all best wishes and in thanks."

Some clergymen of the Church of England who were present at the ceremony called on Sir Moses, and, in the course of conversation, the question of the conversion of the Jews was raised.

As a proof of how carefully Sir Moses retained in his memory what he had once read, I will give the reader an opportunity of hearing Sir Moses' opinion on the subject :—

He said to his visitors: "I have once read a book entitled 'Three Letters humbly submitted to the consideration of His Grace the Most Reverend the Lord Archbishop of Canterbury, Primate of all England and Metropolitan, on the inexpediency and futility of any attempt to convert the Jews to the Christian faith in the way and manner hitherto practised, being a general discussion on the whole Jewish question.' The Rev. John Oxlee, Rector of Molesworth, Hunts, is the author. In it he asks: How can it have happened that for seventeen hundred years and more the Gospel should have been freely announced and offered to the acceptance of the Jewish people without any corresponding effect? what rational hopes may now be entertained of their speedy conversion by the enthronement of a Protestant Jewish bishop at Jerusalem ; and what proper steps ought henceforth to be taken so as to lead to a happy consummation ?

"I ascertained," Sir Moses continued, "from the perusal of these letters that even Christians were enjoined not only to inculcate in others but to perform themselves the very smallest of the Mosaic precepts (p. 26).

"'The Scribes and Pharisees,' the author, quoting from the New Testament, says, 'sit in the seat of Moses; all, therefore, whatsoever they bid you observe, that observe and do.' 'Here,' he says, 'we have it explictly enjoined on the disciples not only that they should hold fast the written law of Moses, but that they should also admit the authoritative interpretations of the Mishnical doctors, so as to pay all due deference and respect to their solemn decisions.'

"With regard to the words of the Prophet Malachi, the Rector observes, 'Here in the very last of all the prophetic charges to be found in the Old Testament, the future and perpetual observance of the Mosaic Law is solemnly and emphatically enjoined on the children of Israel, as a thing never to be forgotten, together with all its special enactments whether relating to faith or discipline.

"'How then,' the Christian divine asks, 'can we conscientiously exhort the Jew (on his embracing the faith of the Gospel) to forsake and abandon the law which was not only commanded by God, and enforced by the very last of the Jewish prophets, but also strictly enjoined and practised afterwards by the founder of the Christian religion and His twelve disciples? 'Christianity,' he says, 'was never intended to supplant Judaism, nor the Christian hierarchy to interfere with the sacred functions of the Aaronic priesthood' (p. 29)."

The visitors would not argue the subject in question, but were pleased to have had an opportunity of hearing Sir Moses' views.

December 2nd.—Sir Moses suffered for six weeks from a severe and troublesome cough, requiring the frequent medical attendance of his neighbour, Dr Billing, but he was eventually sufficiently restored to health to leave Park Lane for Ramsgate.

February 8th, 1875.—The Sir Moses Montefiore Testimonial Committee, numbering 102 members, advertised their first list of 412 subscribers.

"Remitted £150 to Jerusalem to complete the Touro Houses. Blessed be the memory of Mr Touro, nevertheless his legacy has cost me £5000."—*Extract from Sir Moses' Journal bearing date 18th March* 1875.

May 11th.—He went to London to see Lord Tenterden at the Foreign Office, informed him of his intentions to go to

Jerusalem, and requested Lord Derby to give him letters of introduction to Her Majesty's Consuls.

May 25th.—Prior to his departure from England he attended the meetings of all his various companies in the city, thus, at the age of ninety, giving evidence of his intellectual powers in matters of finance. We shall now follow him on his seventh journey to the Holy Land, and find that in all matters connected with the welfare of his brethren in that country, his judgment and counsel were as clear and sound as at the time when he was in the prime of life.

On his return from his seventh pilgrimage to the Land of Promise, Sir Moses printed, but did not publish, a "Narrative of a forty days' sojourn in the Holy Land," in which he stated what his object was in undertaking so fatiguing a journey at so advanced an age, and I propose giving the reader extracts of the most important passages in Sir Moses' own words.

He says :—

"With the intention of assisting the London Committee of Deputies of the British Jews in their endeavours to improve the condition of our brethren in the Holy Land, I presented the reply which I received to my letter, addressed to the authorities in the Holy Land on the 29th July 1874, to the Palestine Committee of that Board, by whom they were subsequently published for circulation among their members.

"However satisfactory," he continues, "these letters may have been to me, and to all those who, like myself, had the opportunity of knowing the Holy Land, there were still some who expressed great doubts regarding the correctness of all the statements made therein, and being afraid lest such doubts, when spread amongst the Hebrew communities, might damp the ardour of those who appeared ready to offer a helping hand in the great object in view, I resolved, notwithstanding the entreaties and remonstrances of dear relatives and esteemed friends, to proceed at once to Jerusalem, so as to be enabled to confer personally with those who had addressed to me the letters in question, as well as with others whom I had not the opportunity of seeing during my former visits to the Holy Land."

Sir Moses continues—

"I purpose in this my narrative of a forty days' stay in the Holy Land, simply to state what I have seen and what I have heard, and to accompany all important statements by documents emanating from the several communities, or from other persons of undoubted veracity, confirming, in every respect, the highly favourable opinion I have hitherto entertained of our brethren in Palestine.

"*June 15th.*—After having offered up my prayers in the mausoleum of her who, like a guardian angel, so often sustained me on my journeys with her loving affection and judicious counsel, I left East Cliff about mid-day for Dover."

Sir Moses was accompanied on this self-imposed Mission by Ed. Aikin, Esq., M.R.C.S., Ed. Samuel, Esq., and by the writer of this.

CHAPTER XXXV

1875.

SEVENTH VOYAGE TO PALESTINE—RECEPTION AT JAFFA—
ARRIVAL IN JERUSALEM.

"IT was my intention," he says, "to lose as little time as possible, and I was fully prepared to leave Dover, *en route* for Brindisi, the next day, but a strong gale sprung up which detained us till Thursday, when, by the blessing of God, a calm sea and a blue sky made us enjoy one of the finest passages across the Channel.

"The fine weather now accompanied us all along our journey, like the pillar of cloud during the day and the pillar of fire during the night in ancient times, and with a heart full of gratitude, I may now say that during full three months, whether on land or on sea, the pleasure of the journey was enhanced by the most delightful weather.

"By the advice of my medical attendant I was only permitted to travel short stages, but I endeavoured at all places where I had to stop on the road, to confer with the Jewish communities, where such existed, and to ascertain their intentions regarding Jerusalem.

"It was in the ancient Hebrew community of Venice that a subject closely connected with the interests of the Holy Land was first broached to me. Signora F. C. S. Randegger-Friedenberg, the authoress of a work entitled 'Strenna Israelitica,' had an idea of establishing a female agricultural school in the Holy Land, at an annual outlay of thirty thousand Austrian florins, and I promised to put her in communication with those most interested in promoting industrial schemes.

"I presented my letter of introduction to the Vice-Admiral, the Hon. Sir James Drummond, who assured me of his willingness to do anything I might require for facilitating my journey, but informed me at the same time that the cholera had broken out in Damascus, and that the spread of that epidemic along the coast was greatly apprehended. This unexpected news at first somewhat startled me, for I well knew the danger to which we should be exposed in a hot climate, in the most unhealthy season, but I soon recovered my former resolution. It appeared to me that I had a certain duty to perform—a duty owing to our religion, and to our beloved brethren in the Holy Land. Nothing, therefore, I made up my mind, should prevent me proceeding on my journey. I communicated my resolution to the Vice-Admiral, who kindly expressed his hopes for my safe return.

"Returning to the hotel I heard that the sad news of the cholera being in Syria, and the necessity of remaining in quarantine on leaving that country, had also reached my *compagnons de voyage*, and they all entreated me to give up the idea of going to the Holy Land. But I would not yield, nay, with every persuasive word of theirs to make me return, my resolves to proceed became stronger.

"*Thursday evening, July 1st.*—This being the eve of the anniversary of the opening of my Synagogue in Ramsgate and the laying of the foundation stone of the College erected to the memory of my lamented wife, we proceeded to the Synagogue, where we recited the Psalms we usually read in our own Synagogue and College, at the conclusion of which Dr Loewe offered up an especial prayer for the occasion.

"I must not here omit to mention a pleasing incident which made me think of the large-hearted benevolence which our ancestors in the Bevis Marks Synagogue extended even to their brethren in remote countries. Signor Soave, the professor of a school belonging to the Spanish congregation of Venice, was engaged in searching for some ancient Hebrew, Portuguese, and Spanish documents, when he happened to find a letter addressed to the treasurer of an association known by the name 'Kuppath Pidyohn Shebuyim,' or 'Fund for the Redemption of Captives,' instituted by the Portuguese congregation of London. It is dated the 1st of Iyar 5465 (May 1705), and the treasurer therein makes a remittance of sixty ducados de Banco towards the assistance or redemption of three Hebrew slaves brought to Venice in a Maltese vessel.

"On the 2nd July we went on board the *Geelong*, and after a delightful sail of six days, touching Ancona and Brindisi, reached Alexandria on the 8th, where I experienced great kindness at the hands of Messrs Kataui Bey, Baron Menasce & Sons, Messrs Abraham Piha and Pariente.

"On the 9th of July we embarked on board the *Ettore*, an Austrian steamer. As we were steaming out of the harbour my spirits became buoyant in the extreme. God granted me His special blessing to find myself again on the road to Jerusalem. The sea was calm as a lake, not a ripple could be seen on its glowing mirror. The declining sun reminded me of the approaching Sabbath. That day has always been a particular object of delight to me. By the kindness and civility of the people on board I was never interrupted in any way in the performance of my religious duties. Every Friday as the Sabbath was about setting in, I could light my Sabbath lamp, which I always carried with me, and I often had the gratification of seeing the seven lights (emblems of the six days of creation and the seventh day of rest) burn as late as midnight, undisturbed by the motion of the vessel, even when going at the rate of eleven knots an hour.

"On the morning of July the 10th we entered the harbour of Port Said, and here I am desirous of pointing out the importance of land in the vicinity of Jaffa to the agriculturist or general trader in Palestine. The passengers from Europe to India, or from India to Europe, generally avail themselves of the opportunity to go on shore after a long and fatiguing journey, and are glad to pay a high price for a basket of strawberries, pears, or apples, or a bunch of grapes or vegetables. The stewards of any of those large steamers, I was told, pay a high price for fruit of the above description. Should it ever be in the power of the well-wishers of Zion to send a European gardener to the land they may happen to own in Jaffa, they would surely find a good market in Port Said.

"While on board the *Ettore* I had the advantage of making the acquaintance of Mr Julius Loytved, the Danish Consul at Beyrout, a gentleman who takes a great interest in the Colonies established by the Würtemberg people in Khaifa and Jaffa. He gave me a description of what they have already accomplished, the numerous houses they have built, and the land which they so successfully cultivated. He also gave particulars regarding the British Syrian schools, established at twenty-two different places in Syria, at the cost of £2372, 7s. 5d. per annum, comprising the payment of teachers, pupil teachers, Bible-women, wages, board, clothing, furniture, rent, travelling, postage, sundries, and building repairs.

"Hearing from that gentleman how liberally all the institutions for social improvement in Syria are supported by the English people, it struck me that if the well-wishers of Zion were to become acquainted with the zeal and liberality which other nations display towards the improvement of the condition of the people in Syria, they might be moved thereby, and well exclaim : 'Are we to stand in the background neglecting our Talmud-Tora schools, colleges, and benevolent institutions in the Holy Land, while the adherents of other creeds are actively bestirring themselves to make every possible sacrifice for the cause they advocate?'

" At four o'clock P.M. Her Majesty's Vice-Consul at Jaffa (Signor Amzalak), accompanied by his son, two káwásses, with their official batons and several attendants, approached our ship. It was a source of high gratification to me to see one of my brethren, a native of the Holy Land, filling so high and honourable an office. I knew his father well. He was one of the most worthy and charitable of our brethren in Jerusalem, and I was now much pleased to have the opportunity of evincing my regard for his son, whose abilities and high character had been so honourably acknowledged by the consular functions entrusted to him.

" In giving these and other particulars in connection with all my movements in the Holy Land, my object is not to satisfy any selfish feeling. I desire only to convey to the friends of Zion an idea of the kindness and attention which our brethren are ever ready to bestow on their well-wishers, and the great encouragement the Turkish Government is always prepared to offer to those who in reality seek to promote the interests of Jerusalem.

" According to our previous arrangements, we disembarked just before sunset. The boat was brought quite close to a most convenient landing, which had been expressly constructed for the Emperor of Austria when he visited the Holy Land. A detachment of soldiers, drawn up in two lines, commanded by the Kaimakam, presented arms. Deputations from the several congregations in Jerusalem, Jaffa, and Hebron bade me welcome, and tendered their congratulations on my safe arrival, and a large concourse of people almost overwhelmed me with their salutations. I entered a comfortable European carriage, which conveyed me first to the tomb of my much lamented friend, Dr Hodgkin, then to Signor Amzalak's country house, situate on the high road to Jerusalem.

" It must have been about seven o'clock in the evening when we arrived. The lady of the house, surrounded by a most amiable young family and some friends of the house, gave us a friendly welcome. A refreshing beverage, consisting of almond and rose water, was handed round, and ten minutes afterwards a dinner was served in the best European style. An almost endless variety of dishes, partly Syrian, partly French, were handed round by waiters dressed in the French style, who spoke French, Italian, Spanish, German, and Arabic. All this might have made us forget that we were in the Holy Land had we not been reminded of it every now and then, either by the overpowering heat or the bite of an intruding mosquito.

" After having procured statistical accounts from the congregation, my work at Jaffa was confined to seeing the estate known by the name of Biárá, which was bought in the year 5615 (1855) for the promotion of agriculture among our brethren.

" 13th July.—Though somewhat indisposed, I would not lose the opportunity of seeing the deputations which arrived from various parts, and gathering from them as much information as possible. With regard to the value of land, I learnt, for instance, that some land outside the walls of Jerusalem, 100 yards in length and 50 yards in breadth, sold for 25,000 piastres, equal to £207. The remainder of that property has been sold for building purposes.

" Near this property there is some land, measuring 19,000 square yards, containing seventy olive trees and five hundred vines ; also three small rooms and a cistern 10 × 16 × 12 yards ; the whole being offered at the price of £1600.

"To prevent the possibility of preparing for my reception at the Biárá, I requested Dr Loewe to go there the next day at an early hour, and report to me the state in which he found it.

"When the Biárá was bought in the year 5615 (1855), there were not less than 1407 trees, bearing oranges, sweet lemons, lemons, citrons, pomegranates, apples, peaches, almonds, dates, apricots, mulberries, pears, figs, and bananas, and I was anxious to know how many we have now in the garden.

"I also begged him to visit the Würtemberg estate, which is only a very short distance from the Biárá.

"Accordingly he started on the 14th July, at six o'clock in the morning, for the Biárá, inspected the houses, the garden, and the adjoining field, examined the well and cistern, and made a rough sketch of the estate ; went to Saroona to inspect some of the houses and fields, and returned in the afternoon with a most satisfactory report.

"From statements reported in England I expected not to find a single tree in the garden, the house in ruins, and the cistern and water-wheel destroyed, but I was now fortunately able to convince myself that such was not the case. It was arranged that I should proceed the next day to the Biárá, accompanied by the English Vice-Consul and every one of my own party, so as to be enabled to have a complete inspection of the place.

"*July 19th.*—A deputation from Khaifa came to Jaffa to present personally the statistical accounts referring to their community which I had requested them in a special letter to prepare for me. Towards the afternoon I invited the Khaifa deputation to enter my room, and I examined the valuable documents they presented to me, and there was every reason to be satisfied with the work they brought.

"Those gentlemen described the state of their congregation as being in every respect satisfactory. They have four Synagogues and several charitable institutions, maintain their poor, and do not partake of any share of the contributions from abroad. They scouted the idea that many persons came to Khaifa and Safed to escape military service in their own country, and to obtain a share of those charitable gifts which, it is said, are so abundantly offered to them by our European brethren. The Deputies felt most indignant at such a report, and on their return home the Elders addressed a letter to me, of which the following is a short extract :

"'We beg leave to inform you that we all live here, thank God, in perfect peace and unity ; all of us conjointly listen to the voice of our spiritual guides. We all consider it our utmost duty to observe the laws of God, and there is no schism whatever in our community. With regard to your inquiry respecting soldiers who, it was said, were in the habit of coming to our place to settle among us with a view of being maintained by the communal charities, allow us, sir, to assure you that there have never come such persons to our place ; any report to that effect has no foundation in truth. As for ourselves, we are all, thank God, maintaining our families by the work of our hands ; none of us partake of any charitable gift except the orphan and the widow, and even these are supported by our own charitable institutions, not by any charity coming from abroad.'

"Mesrs Jacob ibn Simool and Samkhoon called upon me for further instructions regarding the Biárá. I repeated to both the assurance of my satisfaction with their honest work, and promised to communicate with them on my return to London. Mr Jacob ibn Simool, whom I may call the father of the poor in Jaffa, called my attention to several deserving cases of distress in the community, to which I observed, 'Why do the persons in question not work?' My object in putting this question, I said, was not because I for myself ever doubted their industrial habits, but to find the opportunity of convincing others of the truth of my assertions, there being some persons who consider the Jews in the Holy Land as an idle set of people, preferring the bread of idleness to that of industry.

"On hearing this he almost burst into tears, denying the truth of such accusations. 'Well,' I remarked, 'supposing I would offer a trifle, say sixpence or a shilling, to any poor man to go out into our Biárá and there fill the large cistern, which, according to Mr Aikin's calculation, would take fifty-eight hours to fill, would any of them do it?' 'Ah!' he replied, 'there would be fifty who, without a moment's hesitation, would proceed at once to do the work.' I took him at his word, and said, 'Well, let it be done to-day.' It was about mid-day when this conversation took place. Messrs Simool and Samkhoon went to town, and I requested Dr Loewe, Mr Aikin, and every one who was with me, to proceed in the afternoon to the Biárá.

"On their arrival they found the courtyard adjoining the water-wheel almost crowded by a number of poor, not less than thirty sitting on the ground, eight of them alternately rising to turn the wheel, while the others were singing in chorus Psalm cxxviii., in which the verse, 'Thou shalt eat the labour of thine hands, and it shall be well with thee,' occurs. Presently a number of them took out of their pockets some little prayer books, and began singing Psalm cxix. ; and there prevailed as much gladness and joy among them, notwithstanding the perspiration which streamed down their faces whilst they were running round and round the wheel, as if they had been engaged in the most easy and entertaining work. As the time drew nigh the evening, Minha prayers were offered up by all present, and their melodious voices might almost have been heard by their Würtemberg neighbours in Sanoora. Subsequently they all dispersed in different corners to select a place of rest for the night, as they still had to work some time before the tank would be full of water. The next morning being fast day (17th of Tamuz), they proposed rising at a very early hour, so as to be able to do the work before the heat of the day became too overpowering. Wednesday morning the water that filled the tank was overflowing and irrigating the garden in all directions. Messrs Simool and Samkhoon were delighted to have been able to prove the correctness of their statement. As for myself, I never entertained a doubt of the persevering industry of my brethren, but my object was, as has already been stated, to convince others who were of a different opinion.

"*22nd July.*—At an early hour this morning I ascertained from my medical attendant that I might now venture, under great care, to resume my journey. Though I had but little sleep during the night, and felt very weak, I hastened, nevertheless, to give orders for our departure.

"As I took my seat in a carriage, a large concourse of people pressed around us, but the soldiers and káwásses soon cleared the way and enabled us to proceed.

"We were rather disappointed at the state of the roads, which appeared to be out of repair, and it took us three hours to reach Ramlah.

"At about four o'clock in the morning we reached Colonia, almost exhausted from fatigue, but I remained firm in my resolution, and after a stay of half-an-hour, without descending from the carriage, proceeded on my journey.

"At five o'clock in the morning we were already saluted by friends who had come forward to greet us on our approach, and half-an-hour afterwards we halted at the spot whence a full view might be had of the Holy City. There we pronounced the customary blessings, surrounded by an increasing number of people from all directions."

CHAPTER XXXVI.

1875.

WELCOME TO JERUSALEM—SATISFACTORY REPORT ON THE
CONDITION OF THE POPULATION IN THE HOLY CITY—
SIR MOSES' RECOMMENDATIONS FOR THEIR WELFARE.

"AS we now continued moving towards Jerusalem, I had continually to look
right and left to see the number of new houses, some of them very large
buildings. As we proceeded all the occupants came out of their houses, and
I had the happiness of seeing hundreds of our brethren lining the fronts of
their dwellings. Presently my attention was directed to the presence of my
highly esteemed friend, the Rev. Sam. Salant, a gentleman who had been
one of my correspondents on matters connected with the Holy Land for the
last thirty-five years. Proceeding a little further on the road, a new Synagogue was shown to me ; it was surrounded by a number of houses, occupied,
I was told, by fifty families. Again a plot of ground was pointed out to me
as belonging to a person who intended building sixty houses on it. Coming
near the Upper Gikhon pool, not far from the windmill which I had built on
the estate, ' Kérém-Moshé-ve-Yehoodit,' eighteen years ago, my attention was
directed to two other windmills recently built, which I was told gave a good
profit to the Greeks who owned them.

"Great was my delight when I considered that but a few years had passed
since the time when not one Jewish family was living outside the gate of
Jerusalem—when not a single house was to be seen ; and now I beheld almost
a new Jerusalem springing up, with buildings some of them as fine as any in
Europe.

"When my carriage reached the Jaffa gate I was obliged to alight.
Neither the streets nor the pavements in Jerusalem, the driver observed, are
as yet prepared for carriages.

"Not having given any information of the time of my intended arrival,
my friends did not order a sedan chair to be in readiness for me, so it was
a rather difficult and painful task for me to walk along the street to the house
prepared for my reception, but the káwásses soon led the way to my
apartments.

"Here the Háhám Báshi, the Rev. Meyer Auerbach, and the Rev.
Samuel Salant presented an address of welcome, and when they had concluded, I assured them of the great delight I felt in finding myself surrounded
by men of such distinction, and that I would see them as often as possible.
As soon as they left I made the necessary arrangements for the reception of
the representatives of the several communities, the wardens of the Synagogues, and the committees of all the charitable institutions, fixing the day
and hour I intended to see them.

"On leaving my apartments to inspect the adjoining rooms and tents for
the accommodation of my party, I noticed a number of porters bringing in

heavy luggage, and **speaking, or rather** shouting, as they moved along, in not less than five or six **languages—German,** Spanish, French, Arabic, Turkish, and Hebrew. I **was delighted to find that** they all belonged to the Hebrew community, because **their conduct afforded** another proof of the injustice of the accusation against our **brethren of Jerusalem that** they are unwilling to work. Looking up at the **roofs of the adjoining houses,** I observed almost as many people—men, women, and **children—as I saw in** the street below, all of them offering me their salutations. **They appeared to me** to be good-looking and neatly **dressed.** Some **of them dropped down letters** and poems, specially composed **in honour** of my arrival. **They were, however,** requested by the káwásses **to withdraw from near our** terrace, lest their presence might be considered **an intrusion.**

"Entering the large reception **room, I had a beautiful view of the east,** north, and south of Jerusalem. I **could see several** very fine buildings on the **Mount of** Olives, many new **and lofty houses all** along **the north, and some cupolas of** Synagogues. **As I looked out of the** window **I could almost see into the rooms** of **several families who lived near** the house I **occupied, and it was a source of much gratification to me** to witness **the affectionate manner in which the children were treated, and** the industrious **habits of the** inmates.

"*26th July.*—**In the course of the day I** received visits from **Mr Noel** Moore, Her Majesty's **Consul in** Jerusalem, an enlightened public servant and an accomplished **scholar, whom** I have the pleasure to number among my friends, **as well as from his** Highness Aziz Bey, the brother of his Excellency the **Governor of** Jerusalem, accompanied **by** George Balet Effendi. The former expressed regret **that no** notice had **been** given of the day I intended to enter Jerusalem, **or my friends, he said,** would have come to meet me. He brought me the cordial **welcome of the Governor,** observing, in the name of his Excellency, **that as my state of health would** not allow me to call on the Governor, the **latter would gladly come** to pay me a visit without ceremony. In reply **to this most kind offer,** I begged Aziz Bey to assure his Excellency that, however **grateful I must feel** to the Governor for his condescension, I **could not accept that honour, as I** should thereby be deprived of the opportunity to **pay that** tribute **of** respect which I **was** desirous to pay his Excellency, **as** the representative of the Turkish Government, to whom I was anxious to present the Vizierial **letter so** kindly procured for me from Constantinople.

"**Most of the gentlemen whom I** had the pleasure **of seeing were old** acquaintances, and have **been in** correspondence with me. **They gave me** pleasing accounts of their **synagogues,** colleges, and charitable **institutions, and submitted to me a number of letters** and documents **referring to com-**munal matters, which **I promised should** have my special **attention.** I was much struck with the **appearance of the** representatives **of the** Gurgistan (Georgia) **congregation.** They only settled in Jerusalem five years ago, and now number **two hundred souls, all of** whom **came to** the Holy Land by special permission **of the Russian** Government. **Some** of them wore decorations. One, **by name** Eliahu ben Israel, had **three, which** he received, **one** from the late **Emperor Nicholas** and **two from the** present Emperor Alexander. When I **enquired of** their chief how **they came by** these special marks of distinction, **he told me,** that during **the war of the** Russians with the Circassians, the **Jewish soldiers** fought most **bravely, and,** when all the people in the town **of Kutais deserted** the place, **the** Jews remained, and with their blood defended the Treasury of the Russian Government. The soldier with the three decorations, Eliahu ben Israel, said that he received, on each occasion **when** those decorations had been given to him, an embrace from **the** Emperor. It was quite **a** sight to see those handsome stalwart men, some in Caucasian and some in Circassian costume, relating the adventures of a Caucasian war.

" Considering that in the presence of these brave men in Jerusalem, certain persons should have brought forward accusations of cowardice and desertion against our brethren, it made me almost shed tears. Surely, I thought, Russia, Austria, Prussia, France, Italy, and other countries would give them quite a different character.

" I was next favoured with a visit from Dr Schwartz, Director of the Rothschild Hospital in Jerusalem, inviting me to visit all the institutions called into existence by that distinguished family, famous throughout the world for their unbounded benevolence.

" Dr Puffeles, the Director of the Hospital known by the name of ' Báté Kholim,' now entered, and in the course of conversation, gave me a pressing invitation to see the Hospital under his direction, especially as that institution had been permitted by me to take possession of the Dispensary which I had established thirty-two years ago (in 1843) in Jerusalem, and placed under the care of a medical attendant.

" Presently Astriades Effendi, the Mayor of Jerusalem, was announced. I had the pleasure of knowing that gentleman during my visit to the Holy City in the year 1866. He spoke enthusiastically of the great improvements which have taken place since that time. Under the present regulations all houses must be built, he said, according to the plan approved of by the Government, the great object being to have proper roads in all directions. It is part of his duty to see the law in question properly carried out, but he finds it difficult sometimes to convince builders of its utility and importance. Speaking of the houses which had been built by the Prussian Government for the accommodation of lepers, he observed that they were insufficient for the number now in Jerusalem.

" *July 28th.*—Preceded by soldiers and káwásses, I repaired to the Synagogue called ' Beth-Ha-Kenesset Istambooli,' presided over by the Rev. Háhám Báshi, then to the great German Synagogue, ' Beth Jaacob,' the Guedalla College, and the fine public baths.

" *July 29th.*—My medical attendant declared it impossible for me to leave my chamber, and I was most reluctantly obliged to send apologies to his Excellency the Governor, and to the English Consul, for not calling on them at the previously appointed hour. All my letters were now placed before me for my perusal, and I requested Dr Loewe to have his horse saddled, in order to go and inspect all the land outside the city which had been offered for sale. In the afternoon the Governor sent his secretary, George Balet Effendi, to express his regret at my indisposition, offering again to come to me, especially as his official duties would call him away to Gaza, where he would have to remain perhaps several days. This kind and condescending offer, however, I again begged, for the reason already stated in this narrative, with a sense of deep gratitude, to decline, as I fully hoped to be yet able to pay first my respects to him.

" Towards the evening Dr Loewe returned with full particulars regarding the land he had seen, having arranged that I should be put in possession of all the plans and exact measurements of each field, so as to enable me fully to judge of its value and usefulness for the object in view. All the various schools, institutions, foundations, trusts, soup-kitchens, and other charitable establishments were visited, and carefully inspected.

" *Friday, August 6th.*—I had occasion to see the work of eight mechanics —a watchmaker, an engraver, a lithographer, a sculptor, a goldsmith, a bookbinder, and carpenter, and all did their work most satisfactorily. The watchmaker, Joshua Fellman, into whose hands I put a valuable repeater for repairs, put it in a very short time in excellent order. The same man, in addition to his skill as watchmaker, displays also great talent as a Hebrew caligraphist. He presented me with a grain of wheat, on which he wrote nineteen lines, forming an acrostic on my name. The engraver engraved for myself and several of my party Hebrew inscriptions in the best style. The lithographer, Mr David Spitzer, a native of Hungary, lithographed a number of cards for me after a pattern I gave him of a London-made card. I could scarcely find out the difference between the one and the other. The sculptor, to whom I gave the order in the evening to prepare two stones for me, with inscriptions of the verse, ' For thy servants take pleasure in thy stones,' &c. (Ps. cii. 15), accompanied by the date of my sojourn in Jerusalem, did the work in one night. The goldsmith made a number of rings, tablets, and cases; the tinman made two large cases for my books and papers; the bookbinder bound the statistical accounts in very good style, and the carpenter gave equal satisfaction—he did his work as well as any English carpenter.

" I was again greatly disappointed when my medical attendant would not allow me to leave my apartment, and I was obliged to commission Dr Loewe and Mr Aikin to do the work I was so anxious to have done myself, to inspect the Touro almshouses, the windmill, and the whole of the estate Kérém-Moshé-ve-Yehoodit.

" On their return they told me they had been in every one of the houses, and spoken to all the inmates. They found all the apartments remarkably clean, and the occupants, with the exception of one, in the full enjoyment of health. They also entered the four new houses, for the occupation of which I have already nominated four deserving families, and assured me that they were well built, and in every respect like the old houses. They ascended to the top of the windmill, and found everything perfect, with the exception of the mill-stones, which are a little worn, but not to such an extent as to prevent grinding. The garden and the wall all round they considered to be in perfect order.

" I was particularly pleased with their account of the windmill, as I had a double object in building it—to benefit the poor and encourage industry. According to paragraphs V. and VIII. in the agreement, ' The poor shall always have their wheat ground at a reduced price ; they are to pay for each measure two paráhs less than the charge would be to any other person not classed among the poor ; and when both poor and rich come at the same time to have their corn ground, precedence should always be given to the poor.'

" I then proceeded to the Synagogue, and was there most agreeably surprised with the magnificent appearance of that noble edifice. It is a hundred feet high from the floor to the cupola ; contains a number of communal offices, a college for the study of the Holy Law, and in an adjoining building also a public bath. I was received on entering the Synagogue by the representatives of several congregations.

" I was told that the whole building had been built by the hands of Jews. Every kind of work, it was further observed—that of the carpenter, blacksmith, glazier, embroiderer, goldsmith, or engraver—all had been done by the Jews in Jerusalem. I noticed some beautiful silver ornaments for the Sepharim, especially a massive silver crown, and when I enquired where it had been made, the man who had done the work was introduced to me. The Synagogue was full in every corner, but owing to the excellent arrangements no inconvenience was felt.

" I made arrangements to start the following day for Ramlah at an early hour, but gave orders that my intentions should not be made known to any of our friends and acquaintances ; and the next day, Wednesday, 8th of August, between four and five o'clock in the morning, I was on the road to

Jaffa. My esteemed friend, the Rev. Samuel Salant, and a few more still managed to see me, so I bade him and those with him a sincere good-bye. Dr Loewe and Mr Aikin followed us on horseback.

"I found the road much better; it appeared to me as if most of the impeding stones had been cleared away. We continued our journey till mid-day, when we had a halt of two hours at Bab-el-Wad, and then proceeded to Jaffa.

"On Sabbath we again saw Port Said. On Sunday and Monday we were in the quarantine harbour at Aboukir, and the following Saturday we found ourselves in the harbour of Naples. On 13th of August we landed at Firoul; there we remained five days in quarantine. On Saturday morning, at half-past six, we entered the harbour of Marseilles, but did not land till half-past seven in the evening, when we proceeded at once to the Synagogue, and thence to the railway which took us to Paris. There again I repaired to the House of God to offer thanks for his boundless mercy to me; and on the 9th of September I had the happiness of entering my own Synagogue at Ramsgate, after an absence of three months.

"In concluding this narrative, I feel it my pleasing duty to inform all friends of Zion that I again have had every opportunity to convince myself of the correctness of those statements which had been made in the 'Replies' I received to my inquiries on the 15th October '5634.' The great regard I have always entertained towards our brethren in the Holy Land has, if possible, increased, so that if you were to ask me, 'Are they worthy and deserving of assistance?' I would reply, 'Most decidedly.' 'Are they willing and capable of work?' 'Undoubtedly.' 'Are their mental powers of a satisfactory nature?' 'Certainly.' 'Ought we, as Israelites, in particular to render them support?' 'Learn,' I would say, 'if your own Sacred Scriptures do not satisfy you, from non-Israelites what degree of support those are entitled to who consecrate their lives to the worship of God. Go and cast a glance upon the numerous munificent endowments, upon the munificent institutions, upon the annual contributions, not only in Jerusalem, but in every part of the world—not only by individuals, but by almost every mighty ruler on earth. Notice the war which has broken out within our recollection respecting the privilege of repairing a house of devotion, all for the sole object of supporting religion. And are we Israelites to stand back and say, We are all practical men; let everybody in Jerusalem go and work? We do not want a set of indolent people who, by poring over books, teaching the Word of God, think they are performing their duties in life, and wait for our support!' The Jews in Jerusalem, in every part of the Holy Land, I tell you, do work; are more industrious than many men in Europe, otherwise none of them would remain alive; but when the work does not pay sufficiently, when there is no market for the produce of the land, when famine, cholera, and other misfortunes befall the inhabitants, we Israelites, unto whom God has revealed himself on Sinai, more than any other nation, must step forward and render them help, raise them from their state of distress.

"If you put the question to me thus: 'Now we are willing to contribute towards a fund intended to render them such assistance as they require; we are ready to make even sacrifices of our own means, if necessary. What scheme do you propose as best adapted to carry out the object in view?' I would reply, 'Carry out simply what they themselves have suggested; but begin in the first instance with the building of houses in Jerusalem. Select land outside the city; raise, in the form of a large square or crescent, a number of suitable houses, with European improvements; have in the centre of the square or crescent a synagogue, a college, and a public bath. Let each house have in front a plot of ground large enough to cultivate olive trees, the vine, and necessary vegetables, so as to give the occupiers a taste for agriculture.

"The houses ought to pay a moderate rental, by the amount of which, after securing the sum required for the payment of a clerk and overseer and the repair of the houses, there should be established a loan society, on safe principles, for the benefit of the poor working-class, the trader, agriculturist, or any poor deserving man. Two per cent. should be charged on each loan, so as to cover thereby the expenses necessary for a special clerk and the rent of an appropriate house.

"If the amount of your funds be sufficient, build houses in Safed, Tiberias, and Hebron on the same plan ; establish loan societies on similar principles of security.

"And should you further prosper, and have £30,000 or £50,000 to dispose of, you will without difficulty be able to purchase as much land as you would like in the vicinity of Safed, Pekee-in, Tiberias, Hebron, Jerusalem, Jaffa, and Khaifa, and you will find in all those places a number of persons who would be most willing to follow agricultural pursuits.

"And if you now address me, saying, 'Which would be the proper time to commence work, supposing we were ready to be guided by your counsel ?' my reply would be, 'Commence at once ; begin the work this day if you can.'

"Our brethren throughout Europe, Persia, and Turkey have been roused by your promises, which have been made known to them in the most hopeful terms by Hebrew, German, French, Italian, and English periodicals. You led them to cherish the hope that you would surely make no delay in proceeding to ameliorate the condition of the Sons of Zion. They now cry out, 'Here we are, give us land, give us work, you promised to do so. We are willing for the sake of our love to Jerusalem to undertake the execution of the most laborious tasks ;' but the representatives of the community have no answer to give ; they simply, with a cast-down countenance, say, in the words of King Solomon : 'Clouds and wind without rain.'

"You are then, I repeat, in sacred duty bound not to disappoint them any longer. Begin the hallowed task at once. He who takes delight in Zion will establish the work of your hands. "MOSES MONTEFIORE."

Sir Moses now received numerous congratulations on his safe return from his seventh pilgrimage to the Holy Land, in reply to which he said, that it was a source of much happiness to him to witness the greatly improved condition of his brethren, and he would always be ready to go there again should his presence in Jerusalem be required.

CHAPTER XXXVII.

1876.

THE Executive Committee of the Sir Moses Montefiore
Testimónial, engaged since the beginning of 1876 in
promoting the object in view, held frequent meetings to consider
the best means of carrying out his wishes. They advertised in
English, German, and Hebrew papers for qualified persons to
act as their agents in the Holy Land, and succeeded in securing
the services of a qualified gentleman anxious to help the good
cause. It was decided that the fund should be devoted to the
purchase of ground in the Holy Land, to the erection of houses,
and generally to the encouragement of agriculture and of
industrial pursuits.

Those of my readers who are subscribers to the Testimonial
Fund will no doubt be glad to learn the progress which has
been made up to the present year, 1887, and I will therefore
at once give them the substance of all the information I have
received on the subject before proceeding to record any incident
of the year 1876.

A report of the said Committee, dated February 16th, 1883,
states that, " After great consideration and careful investigation
they acquired two plots of land in a very favourable situation,
outside the walls of Jerusalem, at a cost of about £1000, and
entered into contracts with two building societies for the
erection of suitable dwellings on the site.

" The members of one of their societies, the 'Mishkenoth
Israel,' belong to the German Hebrew community at Jerusalem,
and those of the other, the 'Ohel-Moshe,' to the Portuguese
Hebrew community.

" The basis of these contracts is, that as the work progresses, the Committee undertakes to make advances free of interest, in proportion to the progress, as certified by their local architect. Thus, the society, 'Mishkenoth Israel,' in consideration of sums amounting in all to £2600, to be advanced to them by the Committee, have undertaken to erect eighty single or forty double houses, as well as a synagogue, cisterns, baths, and such other buildings as may be considered necessary for the common use of the inhabitants of the houses. It has been agreed that this advance shall be repaid within fifteen years, and upon such repayment the houses are to become the absolute property of the Society, but that, on the other hand, the buildings for common use are always to remain the property of the Committee, and the name of Sir Moses Montefiore is to be inscribed on the group of buildings as a lasting tribute to his memory.

"As regards agricultural undertakings in the Holy Land, the Committee have not yet felt justified in entering upon or giving pecuniary support to enterprises of that character.

"With reference to industrial pursuits of a miscellaneous kind, the Committee, besides promoting, to some extent, wood carving and weaving at Jerusalem, have also expended various sums of money, and bestowed much attention on the manufacture of tiles and bricks in Jerusalem ; and ultimately, in December 1884, they let the machinery and plant to the authorities of the Rothschild School in the Holy City, for the purpose of aiding deserving persons desirous of being taught the art of brick or tile making. They have reason to anticipate very satisfactory results from promoting in this manner the manufacture of articles likely to come into general use in the East.

"The Committee further state the important fact that, since May 1880, no expenses whatever of management have been incurred beyond the salary of their agent at Jerusalem."

In addition to the above particulars, I am enabled to state, by the information I received on February 21st, 1887, from the present treasurer, that in round numbers the Committee have spent £6200 on 160 houses and buildings, the best of the kind in the Holy Land, and that they have now a little over £2000 left.

Since the matter has been with him (1882) not one penny has been spent in office expenses. Until last year they paid their agent in the Holy Land £200 a-year, but this has now been reduced to £100 a-year.

They are spending about £360 in erecting fences round the centre buildings, reserved as the present property of the Committee of the Testimonial Fund.

It would, undoubtedly, have been a cause of much satisfaction to Sir Moses to have seen some encouragement given to agricultural undertakings, even on a small scale, but the Committee not feeling justified in adopting this course, he expressed his appreciation of their decision with gratitude.

In a letter addressed to the Secretary of the Committee (February 28th, 1876), he says : " Conjointly with other well-wishers of Zion, I fully appreciate their labours, as well as their frequent sacrifices of valuable time and convenience to the hallowed cause of religion. May they all, I fervently pray to Heaven, reap the high reward vouchsafed unto those who seek to establish peace and happiness in the city of the Lord, and may they become living witnesses of the speedy restoration of Zion to its former effulgent glory."

However, after his return from Jerusalem, a meeting was held on the 15th of December 1875, by the Palestine Society, as a preliminary to the formation of a Palestine Colonization Fund, at which, in conformity with a resolution proposed by Mr Jacob Montefiore, it was agreed that a deputation of members of the society and friends of the cause of Palestine should wait on the Turkish Ambassador. Accordingly, on Tuesday, December 21st, by special appointment, a number of gentlemen represented to his Excellency the growing desire in this country to promote the colonisation of Syria and Palestine by persons of good character (more especially Jews), willing to devote themselves to agriculture and industry, in response to the invitation put forward a few years ago by the Turkish Government. Pointing out the great financial improvement likely to result from such utilization of waste lands, the deputation asked if the conditions originally offered to foreign settlers by the Ottoman Government, together with the various firmans published from time to time for the benefit of the subjects of His Majesty the Sultan, would now be applicable to foreign immigrants. His Excellency pointed out in reply, that foreigners were at liberty to purchase land or other property in any part of Turkey, and to remain under the protection of their own Consuls ; or they might take advantage of the offers of the Turkish Government, and receive grants of land, becoming amenable to Turkish law, and in all respects being Turkish subjects. His Excellency added that the Ottoman Government had taken great trouble to promulgate these conditions, which, he regretted to say, had not as yet been responded to. The principal points in these conditions are, that the settlers are exempt from all taxes, territorial or personal, for twelve years; they are exempt also from military service, but pay the tax in lieu thereof after twelve years. After twenty years they acquire a title to their lands, and are at liberty to dispose of them as they please. By the recent "Hát" (firman), the Ambassador said, the following privileges are secured : the power of electing judicial and administrative bodies, the power of electing the collectors of tithes, freedom to religious communities to control their own affairs, and free power of holding and bequeathing property.

The names of the members of the deputation, and of those noblemen and gentlemen who, not attending, signified their cordial sympathy and approval, revived in Sir Moses the hope that, notwithstanding the present disinclination of the Testimonial Committee to encourage agriculture, the time might yet arrive when they would gladly avail themselves of a favourable opportunity to promote his long cherished scheme.

The Diary of 1876 contains but very few entries. He complains of being weak and unwell, but his indisposition does not prevent him from seeing friends and attending to all his correspondence, which increased daily. He was occasionally present at Divine service in the Synagogue, and at the lectures delivered in the College, and often contemplated having a telephone between these two sacred buildings and his own chamber, so as to enable him to join the congregation in prayer, and listen to the lectures, when prevented by illness from leaving his couch.

He took his regular drives whenever the weather was favourable, enjoyed the fine view of the sea when in his room, telling the friends who happened to be with him of the approach of a vessel long before they were able to see it, and never failing to have at least two of the principal daily papers read to him.

June 17th.—The reader will probably remember that in the year 1874 Sir Moses requested Mrs Tait to sit for her bust, to be placed in the Orphanage of St Peter's. It was now unveiled on the occasion of the opening, by the Archbishop of Canterbury, of a new convalescent home in connection with the St Peter's Orphanage. The ceremony was performed by Dr Loewe in the name of Sir Moses Montefiore, who sent a cheque for one hundred guineas to the Archbishop for the institution.

His Grace acknowledged, on the part of Mrs Tait and the friends of the institution, in feeling language the compliment which had been paid to Mrs Tait and himself, and passed a high eulogy on the general benevolence and kind-heartedness of Sir Moses, wishing him in his old age all the blessings which God could endow him with.

Sir Moses' absence was deeply regretted by all present ; unfortunately indisposition prevented his joining the numerous assembly. I give a copy of the letter he addressed to Mrs Tait on that occasion :—

"MY DEAR AND ESTEEMED MRS TAIT,—I sincerely thank you for your and his Grace's invitation to be present at the ceremony of the 8th inst. I feel I cannot promise myself that happiness. Nothing, however, but want of health would prevent my enjoyment of that gratification.

"May you and his Grace live many years to witness the good effect of your admirable institution, which is so calculated to afford relief to the destitute and suffering. I hope you will allow me the pleasure of adding the amount of the two enclosed cheques to its funds, one in the name of my beloved wife, and one in my own.

"With my profound respects to yourself and the Archbishop, and kind regards to your amiable family.—I am, most truly yours,

"MOSES MONTEFIORE."

The Archbishop sent the following letter in reply :—

"STONEHOUSE, ST PETER'S, THANET,
June 12, 1876.

"MY DEAR SIR MOSES,—I must not delay longer to thank you very heartily for the pleasure you gave to Mrs Tait and myself and our girls and my son, not to mention all connected with St Peter's Home, by the kind present which was unveiled last Thursday.

"We regretted your own absence, but Dr Loewe kindly and efficiently represented you. Mr Weekes unfortunately was not present, but all admired the excellent way in which the bust was finished, and I hope you will assure him of our thanks.

"Your generous donation in your own name and in that of her who is so dear to you, came most opportunely to complete the payments for the new building, which, I trust, with your kind help thus given, and that of other friends, may long be a blessing to the suffering.

"I trust by God's blessing that your health continues good, and that the summer weather is favourable to your restoration.

"With kind regards from all our party here, and from my son, who is in London.—I am, my dear Sir Moses, ever yours sincerely,

"A. C. CANTUAR."

The year 1877 was charged with serious events, which fully engaged his attention.

Being informed in the month of January of the great distress then prevailing among the Turkish soldiers in consequence of the war in Bulgaria, and the great political changes following to the death of the Sultan Abdul Aziz, Sir Moses forwarded a generous donation, in aid of the sufferers, to the Ambassador of the Sublime Porte in London.

A few days later he communicated to the Board of Deputies the sad intelligence he had received, that in the villages of the district of Vaslui, Moldavia, three hundred Jewish families had been robbed of the greater portion of their effects, and driven from their homes by order of the Prefect. The Board, on having the facts verified, sought the intervention of the British Government, which was immediately accorded, the result being that the Prefect and three of his sub-prefects were superseded.

To relieve the sufferers in their distress, Sir Moses and Baron Lionel de Rothschild transmitted generous donations to the scene of trouble. The Board of Deputies also organised a fund for the relief of the sufferers, and remitted a considerable portion of the amount collected, by telegram, for distribution among the refugees.

February 1st.—He received a letter from his Excellency Musurus Pasha, conveying to him assurances of the favourable intentions of His Majesty the new Sultan, Abdul Hamid II., towards his Hebrew subjects.

" MY DEAR SIR MOSES,"—(the Ambassador writes, under the date of 17th February 1877)—" According to the intention which I expressed to you in my letter of the 4th ultimo, I communicated to the Sublime Porte a copy of the letter which you did me the honour to address me on the 1st ultimo, and I have now received the instructions of the Imperial Government to return you its thanks for your generous donation to the fund for the relief of suffering among the Turkish soldiers, and for the good feeling expressed in your letter, and to assure you, at the same time, that the solicitude of His Imperial Majesty the Sultan will be always extended to the Israelites equally with the other communities of the empire.—Believe me, dear Sir Moses, yours most sincerely,   " MUSURUS."

The Sultan has kept his word up to this day, and there is every reason to hope he will continue to do so. Some of the Jews under his rule fill high offices of State, others are employed as professors in Government schools, and all enjoy the same privileges as other subjects of his empire.

April 14th.—Sir Moses received a letter from the Secretary of the Board, in which a desire was expressed to ascertain his views as to the best mode of dealing with certain matters referred to in a letter addressed to the Board, referring to the ill-treatment of the Jews in Fez.

"I have received," he replied, "a communication from Mr A. C., of Mogador, containing complaints similar to those to which you allude, and my reply to him was that the letter which the Jewish community of Mogador had received from the Prime Minister in the name of the Sultan, appeared to me a striking proof of the Sultan's intentions to afford justice to every one of his Jewish subjects.

"In the letter Mr A. C. has addressed to me, he states that they had appealed to the Sultan, who, in reply to their petition, promised to personally investigate the nature of their complaint, and moreover added that he would in no instance suffer any injustice to be done to any of his subjects.

"I forwarded," Sir Moses writes, "to Mr C. a copy of a letter which I had addressed to all the Jewish communities in the Barbary State on my return from Morocco in the year 1864, advising them to act on all occasions in strict accordance with the suggestions therein given. If you refer to other acts of ill-treatment at the hands of the Moslems of which the Jews have to complain in Morocco, then I say, if the Board of Deputies should deem it proper to entrust me with a Mission to the Sultan, I shall regard the confidence they would thus repose in me as a high compliment, and should be ready to start at a moment's notice."

CHAPTER XXXVIII.

1877.

IN June he sent despatches to the Board which he had received,
referring to the serious persecution and cruel treatment to
which the Jews of Zargkoon, in Persia, had been subjected for
the purpose of compelling them to forsake their religion. At
the instance of Sir Moses, the Foreign Office had humanely interposed with satisfactory results, and the despatches he received
bore testimony to the satisfaction experienced by the Jewish
inhabitants of Zargkoon at the steps which had been taken to
ameliorate their condition.

In the same month, in consequence of appeals for pecuniary
assistance which had reached him from the Jewish inhabitants
of the Holy Cities of Jerusalem, Hebron, Tiberias, and Safed,
he sent £200 to be distributed among the deserving poor in
Jerusalem, and £107, 15s. for distribution among the inmates of
the Juda Touro Almshouses. To the other Holy Cities he likewise made his offerings in proportion to the number of the
inhabitants and the greatness of distress.

On July 30th Mr Weekes, the sculptor, presented him with a
bust he had made of him, and which the artist afterwards sent to
the Exhibition.

February 3rd, 1878.—He devoted some of his leisure hours
to Lady Tobin's works, and was much pleased with the varied
descriptions she gives of the land of inheritance and Bible scenes
visited by her and her husband, Sir Thomas Tobin, with the
noble object of elucidating the Sacred Scriptures.

July 16th. — Lord Beaconsfield returned from the Berlin

Congress, with the news that he had secured "Peace with Honour." Sir Moses, in common with a number of distinguished personages, met him and Lord Salisbury on their return at the railway station, and joined in the congratulations to the British Plenipotentiaries on the accomplishment of their task.

November 3rd.—The accounts of the war in Afghanistan induced him to make frequent inquiries respecting the origin of the Afghan people. He happened to know Dr Ernest Trumpp, a Würtemberg Protestant theologian and distinguished Oriental scholar, who in the year 1858 had lived for some time at St Peter's, near Ramsgate. He used frequently to visit Sir Moses' Synagogue, with the object of ascertaining the correct Portuguese pronunciation of the Hebrew language. From that gentleman, as well as from letters written by an English officer, who had been with the English army at Candahar, Sir Moses had an opportunity of learning many particulars respecting the character of the Afghans, which were not very complimentary to them. "Well," he said to his friends, "if the Afghans really are as described in this letter, they must either have forgotten the religious tenets practised by their ancestors, or have never been the descendants of that Semitic race to which it is said they belong," and he inquired no further after them, except with regard to their political position in relation to India.

Sir Moses also thanked Lord Beaconsfield for having, in the name of the English Government, caused the insertion of a clause in the Treaty of Berlin, to the effect that, on condition of Roumania conceding citizenship to the native Jews, her independence should be recognised by the Powers. Lord Beaconsfield seemed greatly pleased at seeing Sir Moses, and the meeting between them appeared most cordial.

1879.—He deplores the great loss he sustained by the death of Baron Lionel de Rothschild. "I have known him," he says, "from his earliest youth, and ever entertained the highest esteem and regard for him." He also laments the demise of their Ecclesiastical Chief, Rev. Dr Artom. It was likewise a year of great sorrow and anxiety to him, owing to a dreadful accusation brought against the Jews of Kutais, Caucasus. Letters and telegrams were sent to him from St Petersburg, Tiflis, and Kutais, stating that the trial was to take place on the 11th May. He sent a telegram to St Petersburg, to the effect that he was ready to start for the Russian capital to plead the cause of the accused before the Emperor, and also wrote to the counsel for the defence, offering to proceed to Tiflis should his presence there be desirable. Happily there was not a shadow of truth in the accusation brought against the poor Jews, and in the end they were acquitted.

He received a communication from one of the gentlemen who pleaded their cause, as follows :

"MOST ESTEEMED SIR,—Your letter, which was a pleasant surprise to me, has reached me but very recently, because being addressed to Koutais, and I being at Kiew, it has followed my steps throughout all Russia, while after leaving the Caucasus I travelled on business from town to town.

"I cannot find words to express my thankfulness for the honour and moral assistance, of which your letter has been so eloquent an expression, especially as the cause which actuated your noble heart in addressing this letter is common to us. I too am of Jewish origin, and your name was known to me from my early childhood, when I learnt to connect it with all that refers to disinterested humanity and manly championship of the cause of our oppressed brethren. How sweet to my heart to feel myself associated with the great deeds of your glorious life !

"I do not think it necessary that you should trouble yourself with so fatiguing a journey as the one to Tiflis. Our unfortunate brethren have been discharged for the present, and though the Procurator has put in his protest against the judgment, and the affair is to be tried again at the Court of Appeal early in the autumn at Tiflis, I firmly hope that it will end with a final discharge, justice working tolerably well in Caucasia. If, however, it should be otherwise, then, but not till then, we shall require your generous assistance, and beg you to come to St Petersburg. Meanwhile I will believe in the power of Truth and Reason.

"I implore you not to be disquieted, and to receive the assurance of the highest esteem and deep devotedness of yours, &c., "L. KUPERNICK."

In token of gratitude, these gentlemen sent him their photographs, which he placed in his library, the Gothic room.

Though suffering from illness, Sir Moses never relaxed his efforts on behalf of those who stood in need of his counsel and intercession, and he was constantly in correspondence with friends who were engaged in similar projects of peace and charity. Baron G. von Bleichröder of Berlin communicated to him satisfactory accounts of certain measures adopted by the Government in favour of communities in Roumania and Kutais, and Sir Moses hastened to thank him for it in a suitable letter.

April 22nd.—A telegram from Safed, Holy Land, brought the news of the great distress that now prevailed, and he at once forwarded £100 to his Excellency Musurus Pasha, with a request to send the money to the Governor of Safed as a contribution towards the relief of the distressed Moslems of that place. The following is the Ambassador's acknowledgment :

"IMPERIAL OTTOMAN EMBASSY,
LONDON, 24*th April* 1880.

" MY DEAR SIR MOSES,—I shall be very happy indeed to transmit your generous gift to his Highness Midhat Pasha, Governor-General of Syria, to whom I will send a copy of your letter, and I shall fulfil an agreeable duty in making known to the Imperial Government this fresh proof of your sympathy.

" I am truly sensible of your good wishes towards my august Master and myself personally, which are the more precious as coming from one who is known to all the world for his high character and goodness of heart, and whose philanthropy is attested by so many munificent acts.

" Our long friendship renders it unnecessary for me to dwell on the high esteem which I have for you, or to assure you of my goodwill towards the whole of the race, of whom you are such an honoured and illustrious member. —Believe me, with every good wish and the greatest respect, my dear Sir Moses, yours most sincerely and faithfully, " MUSURUS."

Subsequently he received a very kind letter from Midhat Pasha, enclosing a list of names of all the Moslem recipients of his gift, with full particulars of the mode of distribution adopted by his Highness. Midhat Pasha, Sir Moses remarked, if permitted to remain a few years in Syria, would introduce most salutary reforms in that country. But unfortunate circumstances soon called him away from Damascus, his sphere of action causing him to end his days not far from the tomb of his Prophet.

Towards the end of May Sir Moses was highly gratified by the maiden speech delivered in the House of Commons by Baron Henry de Worms. The Baron belonging, like Sir Moses, to the Conservative party, Sir Moses wrote him the following letter of congratulation :

" EAST CLIFF LODGE, *May* 25*th*, 1880.

" MY DEAR BARON HENRY DE WORMS,—I cannot refrain from expressing to you the great pleasure I derived from the speech you delivered in the House of Commons. You showed yourself as a faithful defender of the cause of religion, and I fervently invoke the blessings from Heaven upon you for having thus boldly raised the standard of Truth in the presence of the mighty of the land.

" I shall be glad to convey to you personally the sentiments of delight which fill my heart, and hope to have the opportunity of doing so by paying you a visit as soon as I am able to go to town.—With kind regards, I am, my dear Baron de Worms, yours very truly, " MOSES MONTEFIORE."

In reply to his letter, the Baron wrote :

" HOUSE OF COMMONS, 27*th May* 1880.

" DEAR SIR MOSES,—Amongst the many kind letters I have received, congratulating me on my first attempt in the House, none has so deeply touched me as yours, coming from one whose name is a household word, not only in our own community, but throughout that civilised world where true philanthropy and real religion are recognised and appreciated. Your letter has made a lasting impression on me, and in the struggles of political life, praise and encouragement are not alone the rewards of success : they are the incentives to deserve and attain it.

"As soon as you return to London, I shall do myself the pleasure of calling upon you.—I am, dear Sir Moses, very truly yours,

"H. DE WORMS."

June 13*th.*—He was informed by Baron von Bleichröder of Berlin, of the anti-Semitic movement in that city, upon which he expressed his views in the following letter, dated June 13th :

"DEAR BARON VON BLEICHRÖDER,—Your communications referring to recent Sectarian movements and Anti-Semitic Leagues in your own country and other parts of Europe present a cause of serious consideration. I entertain, however, the hope that by prudence and discretion on our part, and increased enlightenment based on principles of humanity among non-Israelites, an improvement in the condition of our brethren will ultimately be effected. In the meanwhile we must not relax our earnest activity, and, when occasion requires it, hold up high the banner of our religion, for we must always bear in mind that 'it is not by might nor by power that Israel prevails, but by the Spirit of God, the Lord of Hosts.'"

In the month of July he felt unable to address letters to his friends in his own handwriting, and on the occasion of sending the Archbishop a contribution of £100 towards the Sunday School Fund he was compelled to address His Grace through his secretary.

For the same reason he declined re-election as Vice-President of the Jews College.

"The unsatisfactory state of my health, induced by a very severe attack of bronchitis," he writes to the Secretary of the College, "precludes almost the possibility of my attending the meetings, &c.; and as I cannot do so, I consider it my duty, in the interests of the institution, to withdraw my name from the Council." He addressed a similar letter to the Secretary of the Board of the London Committee of Deputies of the British Jews, in which, for the same reasons, he resigned his honorary membership of the Board.

The Jews at Bach Kali, in the Vilayet of Van, Asia Minor, whose unfortunate position required his immediate intercession, made him, however, forget his resolution to withdraw from the sphere of communal work, and we find that in the same month he addressed Lord Tenterden on that subject in eloquent and powerful language.

His Lordship having transmitted to him a letter from the Hebrew community of that place, Sir Moses writes to Lord Tenterden : "I will not fail to give its contents my earliest and best consideration. I have a vivid and grateful recollection of your Lordship's kindness to me when I had occasion some years ago to seek the powerful aid of the Foreign Office in behalf of my suffering co-religionists in Persia."

In the month of October he was deeply grieved by the sudden death, whilst almost in the prime of life, of his nephew, Mr Joseph Meyer Montefiore, who had succeeded him as President of the Board of Deputies.

On March 15th, 1881, the news of the terrible death of Alexander II., Emperor of Russia, gave a great shock to Sir Moses, and he hastened to express deep sympathy with the Russian Ambassador in London and his friends in St Petersburg, recalling the gracious reception given to him by his late Imperial Majesty when in the Russian Metropolis, and deploring the awful calamity.

April 10*th.*—The dreadful earthquakes in the Island of Chios pressed with peculiar severity upon the poor, and Sir Moses immediately sent £300 to his Excellency Musurus Pasha, with the request to transmit the sum to the Governor of the Island for the relief of the distressed, irrespective of race or creed. Sir Moses availed himself of this opportunity to convey to the Ambassador his sentiments of deep gratitude towards the Government of His Imperial Majesty the Sultan for the protection which the inmates of the Juda Touro Almhouses and the lessee of the windmill had enjoyed. "From the time," he says, "when I laid the foundation stone of those buildings up to the present day there has not been a single complaint made by them, as far as I know, of any unjust act, and I feel the greatest pleasure in congratulating your Excellency on the very satisfactory state of the administration of justice in the Holy Land.

"It is more than twenty years," he continues, "since those almhouses and the windmill were built, and it was said at that time that there could be no security for people living outside the walls of the Holy City, but I always relied on the justice and protection which the Turkish Government so often manifested, and it has now been proved that I was right."

Musurus Pasha in reply says :

"MY DEAR SIR MOSES,—Manifold feelings of pleasure were evoked within me by the perusal of your kind letter of yesterday, enclosing a cheque for £300 towards the relief of the sufferers by the earthquake in the Island of Chios, irrespective of race or creed ; pleasure at knowing that the noble heart of a friend for whom I have ever felt the highest esteem still responds to the call of suffering humanity ; that his spirit of justice still impels him to bear testimony to the tolerance and impartiality shown to his race by my Government and country; that his good wishes are again offered for the welfare of my Sovereign and myself ; in a word, that time has not dimmed the feelings or judgment of one whose virtues are known to all.

"I have already sent the cheque to be exchanged for a draft on Constantinople, and, by to-morrow's post, it will be my grateful duty to forward the latter to my Government, with a copy of the letter by which your munificent donation was accompanied.

"I shall also not fail to bring to the knowledge of His Imperial Majesty the Sultan, personally, the feelings which you have expressed towards his person and throne.

"Meanwhile, with best wishes and the highest consideration and respect, I have the honour to be, my dear Sir Moses, yours very sincerely,

(Signed)   "MUSURUS."

April 11*th.*—He received a letter from the Jews of Safed, Holy Land, enclosing an address to Her Majesty, in which they humbly expressed their gratitude for the protection granted to them by the English Government. On the same day he complied with their wishes, writing to Earl Granville, as follows :—

"MY LORD,—I beg leave to hand your Lordship the accompanying letter addressed to Her Majesty, which has been forwarded to me by the representatives of the Jewish community at Safed, Holy Land, with the request to have the same transmitted to your Lordship for Her Majesty's gracious reception.

"The letter expresses their sincere gratitude for the renewal of protection which has recently been granted to them by Her Majesty's Government.

"I still remember with heartfelt thanks the kind sentiments your Lordship was pleased to evince towards me on the occasion of my intended journey to Persia, and hope your Excellency will extend that kindness to me for the sake of my brethren in Safed, by causing their letter to be placed before Her Majesty, for whose long and glorious life they fervently offer up their prayers to Heaven, in which I most sincerely join.—I have the honour to remain, my Lord, your Lordship's most obedient and humble servant,

"MOSES MONTEFIORE."

CHAPTER XXXIX.

1881.

NUMEROUS letters now arrived from all parts of the
Continent describing the Anti-Semitic movement in
Germany ; hundreds of communications reached him also from
Russia, describing in heartrending language the attacks made
upon the Jews during the riots in various towns and villages.
Some of his Russian correspondents attributed them to the Anti-
Semites in Germany. These people, they said, had entered
into a league with similarly prejudiced persons in Russia, who,
discontented with the results of their own business transactions,
or of their professions, gave vent to their disappointment by
attacking the Jews who peacefully followed their own pursuits.
Others of Sir Moses' correspondents traced these disasters to
the neglect of local governors and other officials to afford protection to those who stood most in need of it. There can be no
doubt that the Anti-Semitic movement in Germany very greatly
assisted those engaged in sowing the seeds of hatred, and in promoting ill-feeling against the Jews in Russia. Towards the end
of April the Jews were openly attacked by the populace at
Argenau, in Prussia, their intention having been publicly advertised before-hand, and the instigators of the riots having signed
their names to the placards. It appears that this was the signal
for the members of their league in Russia to begin the attack,
for, on the same day, four hundred Jews were plundered at
Elizabethgrad, many of them ill-treated and some killed, the
riots continuing in various towns and villages. According to
a tabulated statement, giving full particulars of the persecutions,
the number of places where the Jews had to suffer in Russia
amounted to 167.

A writer in the *Times* says : " Ever since the German Anti-Semites raised an outcry against their Jewish fellow-citizens, it had been feared that the movement would spread to Russia, and there take a form more adapted to the less civilised state of the country when, before the assassination of the Czar on March the 3rd had roused all Russia to the highest pitch of excitement, it was confidently predicted that the approaching Easter would see an outbreak against the Jews.   It was said afterwards, that the prediction was aided in its fulfilment by Panslavist emissaries from Moscow, who planned all the subsequent troubles.

"It is at least certain that rumours of a rising had reached Elizabethgrad, and caused the heads of the Jewish community, who form a third of its thirty thousand inhabitants, to apply for special protection from the Governor.   No notice was taken of the appeal, and on Wednesday, April 27th, the dreaded outbreak took place."

Numerous meetings were held in London, Manchester, Liverpool, Birmingham, and other important towns in England, on the continent of Europe, and in the principal cities of America, to consider the position of the Russian Jews, with special reference to the necessity of sending delegations of their respective committees to Russia.   Some thought emigration from Russia would be the best means of helping the sufferers.   A million sterling, they said, could easily be collected from the Jews of the whole world, which would go far towards meeting the expenses of emigration; and many of the emigrants would be able to furnish a portion of the necessary funds themselves ; but the question rose : " Will the Government permit the emigration of so many subjects ? "   Then it was asked : " Where are our brethren to be sent to ? "   Some suggested Bosnia, some America, others the Holy Land.   There was a great difference of opinion among the members of the various committees, as to what should be done in the present terrible crisis.

May 23rd.—A numerously attended deputation of the Representatives of the Board of Deputies, conjointly with those of the Anglo-Jewish Association, waited on Lord Granville at the Foreign Office, for the purpose of invoking the good offices of the British Government to stop the outrages on their co-religionists in the Russian Empire.

His Lordship, referring to certain questions which had been raised by the deputation, said :

"It appears to me that the questions which have been raised are three. It is quite clear, as stated, that they are more or less connected one with the other. The first is the general question of the laws imposing great disabilities upon the Jews in Russia. Now it is clear that, however intolerant, however unjust, however impolitic such laws are, yet it is competent for any independent state to maintain those laws, if it seems fit to them. I maintain with regard to myself, that one of the strongest political convictions I have ever had in a public life, now extending to a good many years, was that in favour of the great measure of the emancipation of the Jews—(cheers)—and all I need say of that is, that it has been a source of great satisfaction to me to see the enormous change which has taken place since that was effected. Why, I have seen melt away like snow all those prejudices, not only political but social, which certainly, when I first came into public life, were extreme. I am glad to find that the members of this deputation have followed the example of their predecessors ; and I think I can say for myself, that I am not aware of not having taken advantage of any opportunity in my power of doing what I thought judicious for the improvement of the position of the Jews, in countries where they are less favoured than in our own. At the same time it must be remembered that all nations are jealous of interference with their internal concerns, and this is especially so with regard to the great Powers of Europe. I had only last week to make a speech connected with Russia, with regard to our refusal to join in a conference on another subject, and I then pointed out how exceedingly sensitive we are in this country in anything which appears like compulsion from foreign countries, with regard to our internal legislation. I even quoted an instance where a popular Minister was turned out of office for proposing that which every one agreed was quite right, merely from the idea that he had been instigated to the task by a foreign power. While remembering this, we may consider what is the best to be done. Now I am myself perfectly convinced that it would not be judicious to make official representations on this subject to the Russian Government. I agree with the speaker who said that the prejudices are greatest amongst the mass of the people ; but I do not agree with those who have said that a strong representation from a foreign Government would strengthen the hands of the Russian Government. I think that in many instances it might weaken the hands of the Government, who, I believe, are infinitely more enlightened than the mass of the people on the subject. I feel very strongly that if any representations are made, they should not be official representations, and moreover, that they should not be public. With regard to the second question of the fearful riots, and the destruction of the property of the Jews, I can only say I believe the statements that have been made, and that I share the feeling of sorrow that must be common to all that have read them, and I cannot help believing that that is the feeling of the Russian Government, and of the higher classes of that country." The noble earl then read a short extract from the information received from Mr Wyndham and our Consul at Odessa in regard to these riots, which were believed to be instigated by the Nihilists, and which had led to great destruction of property and some loss of life. "It is announced that the riots have been suppressed, and that no less than 1000 persons had been arrested on account of them. After that I do not think you can be of opinion that the Russian Government has any complicity with these outrages. No better proof can be afforded of the good feeling of the Russian Government than the cordial reception lately given by the Emperor to a deputation of Jews. Such a thing as that would have been absolutely impossible in the reign of the Emperor Nicholas, and I think you may take it that the Emperor is horrified at these proceedings, and is desirous of putting them down."

Mr Arthur Cohen, Q.C., M.P., who had now become President of the Board of Deputies, gave Sir Moses a full account of all that had passed at the interview with his Lordship, and subsequently at the meeting of the Board. Sir Moses wrote to him under date of 24th May, as follows:

"MY DEAR ARTHUR,—It was most kind of you to devote so much of your valuable time to furnishing me with particulars on a subject which has occupied my mind for many years.

"When I had the honour of an audience with the Emperor Nicholas in the year 1846, His Majesty observed the laws of Russia did not permit Jews to sleep in St Petersburg. I said, 'I trust your Majesty will see fit to alter them,' and the reply was, 'I hope so.' Twenty-six years later, on my again visiting St Petersburg to seek an audience of the late Emperor Alexander, I found 12,000 of my co-religionists settled there; many of them had decorations, and a goodly number filled high offices in the University and public libraries; some were bankers, others merchants. On my arrival there, I was asked by a person of high authority what my object was in seeking an audience of the Emperor. I replied that it was to convey my gratitude to His Majesty for having realised the hope expressed to me by his father. The Prime Minister then assured me, in the presence of three or four Ministers of State, that the Russian Jews, if qualified by their abilities and moral character, could attain any high position in the Empire.

"I am fully convinced that it is only by mild and judicious representation —relying in advance, as it were, on their kindness and humanity—that you have a chance of your application reaching the throne of the Emperor.

"You have, I conceive, acted most wisely in all you have done with reference to the movement, and I perfectly agree with the opinion entertained by Lord Granville on the subject.

"If it be thought advisable, I am quite ready to go again to St Petersburg. I should, in the first place, ascertain whether my visit would be agreeable or not to the Emperor and his Government; and, in the next place, I should apply to the British Government for letters of recommendation to the British Minister, and thus equipped I should have every hope of smoothing the unfortunate position in which our brethren are placed in that country."

Here we have a man, nearly ninety-eight years old, speaking seriously of setting out again on a Mission to St Petersburg. When his friends said to him, " How can you think of proceeding to Russia at your advanced age, and in your present weak state of health?" he replied, "If necessary, I will be carried there. Take me in my carriage to the train, put me on board ship, then again in the train, and when in St Petersburg I will be carried into the presence of the Emperor. Nothing," he added, " shall prevent me from serving my unfortunate brethren if I can be of use to them."

Although deeply grieved by the sad events to which so much

public attention was being directed, Sir Moses did not withdraw his attention entirely from other matters, and was much pleased to read in the *Times* of the success of Mr A. F. Saunders, who had just gained the prize medal for Hebrew, which Sir Moses had founded years before at the Merchant Taylors' School. Many of the students who had gained this medal used, while pursuing their studies at the universities, to address Hebrew letters to Sir Moses, to show him the progress they were making in the sacred language, and he never failed to encourage them further in their studies.

The death of Dean Stanley was another shock to Sir Moses, whose relations with the Dean were of the most cordial character. He would frequently have read to him the reply of the Dean to Canon Jenkins, who proposed the establishment of an " Appellate Tribunal, to which the question of the treatment of the Jews should be referred."

The Dean regarded the scheme as impracticable, but expressed his abhorrence of the cruel persecutions, and his conviction that they were impossible in a country like ours.

"We stand much in need of such advocates for right and justice," Sir Moses remarks, " and the loss we have sustained by his death is great."

The news of the attempt on the life of General Garfield, the President of the United States, caused him also much sorrow. He always entertained a high regard for the Americans, and admired their numerous noble institutions. " How many millions of our fellow-beings," he used to say, " found a happy home there when all hope for an honourable maintenance in their own country had to be given up, because the land which gave them birth ceased to give them shelter and protection ? "

September 19th.—On hearing that the life of the President was in danger, he immediately sent a telegram to the Spiritual Heads of the Spanish and German Hebrew Congregations of Jerusalem.

" Let prayers be offered up," he telegraphed, " in all Synagogues for President Garfield's speedy recovery."

Mrs Garfield, to whom Sir Moses subsequently addressed a letter of sympathy, several Senators, and many prominent American citizens, acknowledged this mark of attention most gratefully, and expressed their high appreciation of it.

When the President died Sir Moses sent £100 to Mr Marcus of Boston for distribution among the most deserving charitable institutions of that city, without distinction of race or creed, in memory of the esteemed and lamented President.

September 28th.—The following telegram appeared in one of the papers, under the heading " Anti-Semitic Agitation," dated Vienna, Tuesday night :

" According to a Russian paper, Sir Moses Montefiore has forwarded an address to the Jews in South Russia, informing them of the measures provided for their emigration to the United States, and stating that no obstacle will be raised by the Government to their leaving the country."

This report having no foundation in truth, Sir Moses immediately addressed the editor on the subject, who in return published a correction the next day. As a matter of fact, Sir Moses never expressed an opinion on the matter, sent no address to the Jews of South Russia, and did not even reply to letters written to him on the question of emigration.

On the 8th day of Heshvan Sir Moses celebrated his ninety-seventh birthday.

A few days afterwards there is an entry in his Diary, in which he says : " I have been very unwell for several days, and this day unable to take a drive in my carriage. Blessed be God for His manifold gifts, and, I hope, renewed strength."

December 30th.—Letters reached him from America referring to a meeting of the citizens of Harrisburg, Catahouli, and Louisiana, reporting that resolutions had been passed cordially inviting the Russian emigrants to settle in the district, and promising every assistance. Three representatives of the emigrants made an inspection of the land offered to them, and gave a very favourable account of it. At New Orleans every assistance was given to the emigrants, numbering about a hundred, and the President of the West End Railway placed a special train at their disposal.

The Local Committee leased the Continental Hotel, capable of lodging over five hundred persons, and placed it under the Ladies' Hebrew Sewing Society.

" I wish," Sir Moses said, " facilities like those offered by the Committee at New Orleans could be secured for emigrants who select the Holy Land for colonisation."

CHAPTER XL.

1882.

THE REIGN OF TERROR IN RUSSIA—INDIGNATION MEETING IN LONDON—THE LORD MAYOR'S FUND—THE TISZA-ESZLAR TRIAL — ANTI - JEWISH CONGRESS AT DRESDEN—A PRE-TENDED SPEECH OF SIR MOSES—DEATH OF ARCHBISHOP TAIT.

THE Anti-Jewish Riots in Russia continued to excite the greatest indignation. All the daily papers had leading articles on the subject. Relief committees were formed in the principal towns and cities of Europe. The Governor-General, A. von Drentlen, sent Sir Moses full accounts of the work done by the Committee under him, reporting that contributions from all sources had amounted to 218,482 roubles, and that upwards of five thousand sufferers had already been relieved. By January 20th, Messrs Louis Cohen & Sons had collected £16,658, and on the following day the subjoined requisition was made to the Lord Mayor, Sir J. Whittaker Ellis, to call a public meeting at the Mansion House.

Requisition.

"January 21st, 1882.

" To the Right Hon. the LORD MAYOR OF THE CITY OF LONDON.

" MY LORD,—We, the undersigned, consider that there should be a public expression of opinion respecting the persecution which the Jews of Russia have recently and for some time past suffered. We therefore ask your Lordship to be so good as to call, at your earliest possible convenience, a public meeting for that purpose at the Mansion House, and that you will be good enough to take the chair on that occasion.—We are, your Lordship's faithful servants,

"A. C. CANTUAR.	ARTHUR OTWAY.
SHAFTESBURY.	JAMES MARTINEAU.
J., LONDON.	SAMUEL MORLEY.
C. J., GLOUCESTER AND	M. BIDDULPH.
BRISTOL.	B. JOWETT.
J., MANCHESTER.	H. D. M. SPENCE.
F. LEVESON-GOWER.	

<table>
<tr><td>" CHARLES MAGNIAC.</td><td>DONALD CURRIE.</td></tr>
<tr><td>W. J. COTTON.</td><td>HENRY RICHARD.</td></tr>
<tr><td>JAMES CLARKE LAWRENCE.</td><td>W. ST JOHN BRODRICK.</td></tr>
<tr><td>JOHN TYNDALL.</td><td>H. R. HAWEIS.</td></tr>
<tr><td>MATHEW ARNOLD.</td><td>J. J. STEWART PEROWNE.</td></tr>
<tr><td>F. A. INDERWICK.</td><td>F. W. FARRAR.</td></tr>
<tr><td>JOHN LUBBOCK.</td><td>W. PAGE ROBERTS.</td></tr>
<tr><td>HENRY EDWARD, CARDINAL MANNING.</td><td>J. G. HUBBARD.</td></tr>
<tr><td>SCARSDALE.</td><td>W. LAWRENCE.</td></tr>
<tr><td></td><td>ERASMUS WILSON.</td></tr>
<tr><td>MOUNT-TEMPLE.</td><td>CHARLES DARWIN.</td></tr>
<tr><td>J. F., OXON.</td><td>A. M'ARTHUR.</td></tr>
<tr><td>EDMUND FITZMAURICE.</td><td>C. M'LAREN."</td></tr>
<tr><td>ELCHO.</td><td></td></tr>
</table>

The Lord Mayor complied with the requisition, and on Wednesday, February the 1st, at three o'clock, his Lordship presided over a large and most enthusiastic meeting. The Egyptian Hall was crowded in every available part, and the reserved seats on the platform were altogether inadequate to accommodate those who were invited to take part in the proceedings.

The representatives of the churches of England and Rome, together with Dissenters and Unitarians, leaders of thought in science and philosophy, representatives of the aristocracy and finance, trade and commerce, all, with equal eagerness, stood up for the cause of the suffering Jews.

It was resolved, "that a fund be raised at the Mansion House for the purpose of contributing to the relief of the distress among the Jewish population of Russia, and among the refugees therefrom, which distress has been caused by the recent outrages of which they have been the victims, and also for the purpose of effecting some permanent amelioration in their condition, in such manner as the committee may deem expedient, whether by emigration or otherwise;" and, "that the Right Hon. the Lord Mayor be requested to receive contributions on behalf of such fund."

The total amount collected through this fund was £108,759. On the day following, Sir Moses, in token of deep gratitude to the citizens of London for the sympathy they had manifested with his unfortunate brethren, addressed the Lord Mayor, sending £500 as a contribution towards the building fund of the City of London College.

His Lordship, much pleased with Sir Moses' attention, replied to his letter in the following terms :

"THE MANSION HOUSE, LONDON.
"*February 8th*, 1882.

"MY DEAR SIR MOSES MONTEFIORE,—It is with a sense of great satisfaction that I received your considerate letter and generous contribution to the building fund of the City of London College, and I feel assured that the whole of the citizens of London will appreciate the nobility of sentiment which has dictated this liberal gift.

"It will be a source of great pleasure to me to be enabled to report to the Committee to-morrow, that the fund raised here under their auspices for your suffering co-religionists in Russia amounts to nearly £40,000.—Assuring you of my sincere esteem and respect, believe me, my dear Sir Moses Montefiore, yours very truly,   "J. WHITTAKER ELLIS, Lord Mayor."

The late much-lamented Lionel Louis Cohen wrote to Sir Moses as follows:

"I know you are so deeply interested in the results of the great demonstration of last Wednesday, that I think a few lines may be agreeable to you, as to how it is judged by the world at large.

"It was undoubtedly the most imposing meeting which in modern times has been held at the Mansion House. Its moral effect will be very great; not only in Russia but in Germany, and even in France it is already evident that it has thrown back for a time the rising tide of prejudice against the Jews.

"I had the honour, on Wednesday evening, of being invited to the Goldsmiths' Company, and met at dinner men of all parties, who concurred in thinking the moral effect of the demonstration as considerable.

"Probably ten thousand persons will speedily by its means (the Mansion House Fund) be removed from Russia to American and British possessions; they will be the advance guard of a host; and thus the Almighty may turn what to us seems a calamity into an engine of civilization and prosperity.

"Your name was received with enthusiasm at the Mansion House, none the less genuine because, as became him in that place, the Lord Mayor coupled it with your long connection with civic work, and especially with the Merchant Taylors, of which, he said, you were the oldest living member.

"I hope you continue in good health and spirits, and do not worry yourself at your enforced seclusion at home. We all know how active your sympathies are, and how imperfectly we can follow the excellent example you set, but it is well to see a generation, even younger than my own, striving, however inadequately, to do their little best for their poor brethren."

The Archbishop of Canterbury wrote as follows:—

"ADDINGTON PARK, CROYDON,
"1882.

"MY DEAR SIR MOSES,—I cannot refrain from writing to you, knowing how your heart must be torn by the distressing news from Russia. It is as if the enemy of mankind was let loose to destroy the souls of so many Christians, and the bodies of so many of your people.

"I cannot but hope that a united cry of indignation from England will, by God's blessing, stop this mad wickedness.

"With my daughter's kindest regards and my own.—Ever yours,
(Signed)   "A. C. CANTUAR."

His Grace expressed himself on that subject in a similar

spirit in his letter to the Lord Mayor, which his Lordship read to the meeting. It ran as follows :

"MY DEAR LORD,—It is a distress to me that I am forbidden by my medical attendant to take part in the meeting your Lordship has undertaken to call together to enter an emphatic protest against the recent outrages to which the Jewish people had been exposed. Unable to attend myself, I have asked Canon Farrar to be present and express the horror with which I contemplate the disgrace brought on the Christian name by these shameful persecutions.—Yours sincerely,   "A. C. CANTUAR."

The number of emigrants exceeded all expectation, and the committees had to contend with the greatest difficulties in order to meet the requirements of the various cases. Heavy contingents came from all parts of Europe to London *en route* for America, but soon the order came from the United States only to forward working men and mechanics. Others were dispatched to the Holy Land, and on May 4th, 1882, Sir Moses received letters reporting the foundation of the first Colony, "Rishon Lezion" ("The Pioneers of Zion"), 3550 doolams of land having been purchased for the purpose near Jaffa for the sum of 42,900 francs.

In the course of time the London Committee was able to cope with the distress by means of its admirable arrangements, and by a wise distribution of the emigrants in different directions, with a view to stemming the current, which at first threatened to resist the efforts of the band of philanthropists who worked night and day to help their unfortunate brethren.

The attention of the reader is now again directed to the records of Sir Moses' Diary. Under date of March 2nd he expresses his sorrow at an attempt on the life of Her Majesty the Queen, and on hearing that she was mercifully spared, he immediately sent a telegram to Jerusalem, requesting the Spiritual Heads of the several congregations in the four Holy Cities— Jerusalem, Hebron, Tiberias, and Safed—to have special services held in their Synagogues for the purpose of offering their deep gratitude to heaven for the preservation of Her Majesty's life. A few days later a reply reached him from Jerusalem, in which he was informed that all congregations had cheerfully joined in their attendance in the house of prayer, and that they were preparing special letters of congratulation, which they asked Sir Moses to present to Her Majesty.

Knowing the great interest the Archbishop of Canterbury took in the Holy Land, he informed his Grace of the result of his recent communication with Jerusalem, and the Archbishop, in reply, promised to report the circumstance to Her Majesty.

On the 1st of April an event took place at Tisza-Eszlar, in Hungary, which gave rise to one of these most extraordinary trials ever recorded in the annals of modern administration of justice. " A series of sensational incidents," says A. Hartleben in his " Chronik der Zeit," "forcibly brought together in order to lend to the proceedings the imprint of something unusual, an apparently inextricable coil of intrigues and machinations awaiting a strong hand ready to loosen it. Personal malice, religious hatred, national prejudice, ignorant superstition—these, and many other circumstances, unite to make the whole of the trial a most extraordinary one.

" We are not exaggerating," he continues, "in saying that for years no trial has kept the whole of the civilised world in such breathless suspense as that of Nyiregyhaza."

The press of all nations followed the proceedings of the court with the utmost attention, and even before sentence was given, the *Journal des Debats* considered it necessary to protest against the proceedings of the court, describing them as a horrible result of the then prevailing Anti-Semitic agitation in Germany—a raging fire devouring thousands of innocent lives, which even a number of intelligent and enlightened men in that country did not hesitate to stir up and fan.

I am alluding to the Tisza-Eszlar trial, instituted to discover and punish the murderer of a girl, fourteen years old, named Esther Solymossi. She was a native of Tisza-Eszlar, in service with one of her relatives, the wife of Audreas Hury, who was living at Nyiregyhaza. This girl was sent by her mistress to make some purchases from a shopkeeper in Ofalu, the old part of the town. She was seen at his house in the middle of the day, and made her purchases there, but never returned to her mistress, although later her own sister, who was in service in the neighbourhood, and other people saw her running fast, as if returning in great haste. The Jews were subsequently accused of having killed the girl, in order to make use of her blood for the approaching feast of the Passover. Sir Moses naturally took a deep interest in this trial, and the revival of the old familiar blood accusation.   The trial was not instituted until the following year, but soon after the disappearance of the girl a fearful agitation arose against the Jews.   A large number of them, said to be implicated in the murder, were put into prison, and the outcry against them generally was so great that Christian girls serving in Jewish families left their situations, and could not be persuaded to remain, although previously they were perfectly happy and contented.

In many parts of the country violent disturbances took place. Jewish houses were plundered, and the Jews themselves illtreated.   These occurrences were the cause of stormy debates in the Hungarian Parliament, where some of the Anti-Semitic Deputies tried to fix the guilt of the murder upon the Jews, and by way of confirmation again brought forward the exploded story about the Jews of Damascus having, in 1840, murdered a priest to use his blood for Passover.   When Sir Moses received a report of these debates, he immediately addressed the following letter to the Minister President:—

" EAST CLIFF LODGE,
" RAMSGATE, 9*th June* 1882.

" To His Excellency COUNT TISZA, Minister President of the Imperial and Royal House of Representatives in Buda-Pesth.

" May it please your Excellency,—My attention having been drawn by the perusal of a paper, entitled *Neues Pester Journal*, to a debate held on the 25th of May, in the Imperial Royal House of Representatives in your city, referring to an interpellation made by one of the honourable deputies, in which that gentleman introduces the subject of an accusation brought against the Jews of Damascus in the year 1840, to the effect that the Jews of Europe on that occasion had offered large sums of money to the members of the Austrian and French Consulates in Damascus to gain their favourable services ; that the accused had been subsequently liberated by an act of grace from Mohhamed Ali, and that notwithstanding his firman all the people in the East were convinced of the truth of the accusation.   I deem it my sacred duty to entreat your Excellency's permission for bringing the following statement to your knowledge, trusting that, for the sake of truth, justice, and humanity, which so pre-eminently distinguish your noble career, you will forgive the intrusion.

" It was in the year 1840 that I had the honour of being entrusted by my brethren in the British Empire with a Mission to Damascus, when I pleaded the cause of the accused first before His Highness Mohhamed Ali in Alexandria, and afterwards in Constantinople before His Imperial Majesty the Sultan Abdel Mejid, from whom I obtained Khát Shérif, in which the Sultan not only declared the innocence of the accused, and that all charges made against them and their religion were nothing but pure calumnies, but His Majesty, in conformity with the Hatti Sherif which had been proclaimed on a former occasion at Gulhane, repeated that the Jewish nation should possess the same advantages, and enjoy the same privileges, as are granted to the numerous other nations who submit to his authority. I am for this reason in a position to assure your Excellency that no other means were used to obtain the liberation of the Jews in Damascus than those of justice and truth.

"Mohhamed Ali granted them freedom and rest (*Itlâk î tarwich*). These are the words used by him in his firman : 'Every one shall follow his former pursuits and enjoy the utmost protection.' This was no act of grace but of justice, and it is with the feeling of the greatest indignation that I reject the accusation brought by the author of that interpellation against the Jews of Europe.

"I request the favour of your Excellency's kind acceptance and perusal of the accompanying copy of the Sultan's Khát Shérif, also of a book treating on the subject of the accusations, and beg to subscribe myself with profound respect, your Excellency's most humble and obedient servant,

(Signed)   "MOSES MONTEFIORE."

Almost immediately on the receipt of the letter, the Prime Minister Tisza issued a circular to the local authorities all over the country, couched in the strongest possible language, appealing to the patriotism, love of peace, and impartiality of the Hungarians, impressing upon them the untruth of the accusation and the impossibility of such proceedings, and calling upon the guardians of the public peace to prevent the publication of such absurd superstitions, and to forbid meetings being convened by the instigators.

The Anti-Semites, however, had set their mark upon Sir Moses; three months later they introduced his name in one of their reports, in such a manner that had the allegations been true it would have formed a convenient weapon of attack on the Jews by their enemies in general.

On the 11th and 12th of September 1882, the first International Anti-Jewish Congress met at Dresden, and by virtue of a resolution published a manifesto, addressed to the "Governments and peoples of Christian States endangered by Judaism" (subsequently printed at Chemitz, Saxony, by Ernst Schmeitzner).

Therein we read on p. 15:—"The Congress finally appointed a Committee, whose next task will be to procure pecuniary assistance for the establishment of an Anti-Semitic press. For bearing in mind the words of the Jew 'Montefiore,' uttered by him in a Rabbinical Assembly at Krakau in the year 1840, the Committee have come to the conclusion that as long as the Christian Aryan natives do not reconquer the press in order to enlighten the people and show them the true state of affairs, they will not be able to effect any good."

Now, as I happen to have been with Sir Moses from the beginning of the year 1840 to the end, I can positively declare that Sir Moses never was at Krakau, never attended a Rabbinical Assembly in that city, nor in any other part of the world, and never spoke the words attributed to him.

As a matter of course, Anti-Semitic journals speedily copied the statement made in the manifesto, but when a copy was sent to me by a gentleman at Elberfeld, I immediately, with the sanction of Sir Moses, contradicted the statement, and, to the credit of the editor of the Elberfeld journal, on receiving our letter he published a paragraph in his paper, to the effect that he had been mis-informed regarding the presence of Sir Moses at Krakau, and the words said to have been spoken by him.

At this time of public trouble, Sir Moses was also much pained to hear that the health of the Archbishop of Canterbury had become such as to give great anxiety to his friends. Sir Moses sent telegrams or letters of inquiry almost daily. For many weeks the illustrious patient bore his sufferings with the pious resignation which he had shown under previous exceptionally severe trials, his even temper and amiable disposition never forsaking him, until it pleased the Almighty to release him from all earthly trouble. Sir Moses felt the loss most acutely, and wrote a most touching letter to the family. He sent a wreath to be placed on the Archbishop's coffin. Miss Tait, one of the Archbishop's daughters, acknowledged its receipt in terms of gratitude.

CHAPTER XLI.

1883.

THE coronation of the Czar Alexander III., at Moscow, afforded to Sir Moses an opportunity of writing a letter of congratulation on behalf of himself and his co-religionists, to one who was the son and grandson of two monarchs who had nobly responded to his appeals in days gone by, on behalf of the Jews in their vast Empire. The following is Sir Moses' letter :

"To His Imperial Majesty ALEXANDER THE THIRD, Emperor of all the Russias.

"May it please your Imperial Majesty,—Among the many millions of your Imperial Majesty's faithful subjects,—numerous representatives of States and Kingdoms of the world,—and a multitude of admirers of your Imperial Majesty's rule of justice, blended with mercy and benevolence, who this day, the great and glorious day of all the Russias, offer their congratulations to you, Sire, on the most auspicious event of your Imperial Majesty's coronation, your most humble servant, prompted by an ardent desire to join that host of well-wishers, very respectfully approaches your Imperial Majesty, to lay at the foot of your Imperial Majesty's throne his most sincere and heartfelt felicitations.

" Having had the distinguished honour of hearing, in the year 1846, from the lips of his late Imperial Majesty, the Emperor Nicholas, and subsequently in the year 1872, from his late Imperial Majesty, the Emperor Alexander the Second, your Imperial Majesty's august father, the noble sentiments of their paternal love towards all true and loyal subjects, irrespective of creed and nationality, it is an especial cause of great felicity to me to have been permitted, by the mercy of God, to attain the advanced age of nearly one hundred years, to hear of the exalted and ever memorable event of your Imperial Majesty's coronation, and to read with my own eyes the glorious manifesto, in which you, Sire, bend your merciful glances upon all your subjects, and, in accordance with the inmost dictates of your Imperial heart, turn towards all who are specially in want or oppressed : preserving the rights and privileges of all men, and shedding the radiant light of your Imperial Majesty's great wisdom, justice, and humanity over myriads of people under your Imperial Majesty's sway.

"Conjointly with the latter, including **several millions of my brethren,** your Imperial Majesty's Hebrew subjects, I invoke **Him, who is the Eternal Ruler** of the Universe, the King of Kings, **to cause His most choice blessings to** alight on the crowned head of your Imperial **Majesty, likewise on the crowned** head of Her Imperial Majesty the Empress, **and on your Imperial Majesty's** most illustrious family.

"May your days, Sire, be prolonged ; May **you rule for** many **years** in refulgent glory **over** your vast Empire ; May **you, Sire,** have the happiness **of** seeing all your fervent wishes for peace **and lasting** tranquillity among the nations realized, **so that your** Imperial name may for ever be indelibly inscribed on the tablets of the **heart** of your Imperial Majesty's faithful subjects, and on those of every friend of justice and humanity.

"Deign, Oh Sire ! graciously to receive the fervent and most sincere felicitations expressed by your Imperial Majesty's most humble and obedient servant, "MOSES MONTEFIORE."

"EAST CLIFF LODGE, RAMSGATE,
28*th May* 1883."

In reply to the above letter, His Excellency, Monsieur de Giers, Minister of Foreign Affairs, by order of the Emperor, addressed Sir Moses as follows :—

"ST PETERSBOURG, *le* 2 *Juin*, 1883.

"MONSIEUR,—J'ai placé sous les yeux de mon **Auguste Maître la lettre** destinée à Sa Majesté que **vous** m'avez transmise.

"**Sa** Majesté me charge de vous **assurer** qu' Elle **apprécie** les sentiments que vous temoignez à la mémoire de **Son** Auguste Père et **de** Son Grand-Père, ainsi que les voeux de felicitations **que** vous Lui addressez à l'occasion de Son couronnement.

"J'ai l'ordre de vous **en remercier en Son Nom, et en** m'acquittant de cette volonté Suprême, je vous prie, **Monsieur de recevoir** en même temps l'assurance de ma consideration la plus distinguée. "GIERS."

Translation.

"ST PETERSBURG, 2*nd June* 1883.

"SIR,—I have **placed** before my august master the letter which **you** have transmitted to **me for** His Majesty.

"His Majesty charges me to assure you that he appreciates the sentiments **which** you entertain **for** the memory of his august father and grandfather, likewise **the** felicitations **which you offer** him on the occasion of his **coronation.**

"I am commanded to thank you for the same in his name, and **in acquitting** myself of this supreme will, I have the honour to remain, &c., &c.

"GIERS."

Sir Moses was much **pleased with the** gracious reply given to his letter, and **expressed** the **hope that** the condition of his brethren under His Majesty's sway **might** soon improve.

June 19*th.*—The Tisza-Eszlar trial **having** commenced at Nyiregyhaza, Sir Moses deemed it his duty to send to each member **of** the Hungarian House of Representatives a copy of the Damascus paper translated into the Hungarian language, accompanied by a copy of the following letter :

"EAST CLIFF LODGE, RAMSGATE, 21*st June* 1883.

"SIR,—Prompted by an ardent desire to serve the cause of justice and humanity, I beg to transmit to you, for your perusal, a copy of the Firman Khát - Shereef, issued by His late Imperial Majesty the Sultan Abd-ool-Medjid to the Chief Judge at Constantinople in the year 1840, and the address which I delivered to His Majesty on that occasion at the Palace of Beshik-Tash.

"With fervent prayers to our Heavenly Father that the light of truth may ever illumine our paths, and speedily dispel the dark clouds of calumny and fanaticism, I have the honour to be, sir, with great respect, your very obedient servant, (Signed) "MOSES MONTEFIORE."

This letter brought him warm acknowledgments from many members for having enlightened them, as they said, on subjects which hitherto had not been quite clear to them.

The Anti-Semites, however, would not rest, and one of their leaders, Professor Rohling of the University of Prague, accused Sir Moses of having had a book printed under his auspices, referring to the charge of ritual murder among the Jews as being true.

The reader may well imagine the indignation of Sir Moses on hearing so false a charge, and I did not lose a moment in addressing the following letter to the Editor of the *Daily Telegraph*, in which it appeared on Thursday, July 12th, 1883, under the heading of "The Tisza-Eszlar Mystery."

"SIR,—I have been requested by many readers of your journal to lift, if possible, the veil of an apparent mystery in a letter written by Dr Rohling, Professor of Theology in the University of Prague, on the 19th ult., and addressed to Herr Géza von Onody, Deputy of the Hungarian Diet. It is published in the *Westungarischer Grenzbote*, Presburg, of the 24th ult., and in other papers in Hungary and Germany. For the sake of the vindication of truth, I beg you will kindly give publicity to the following statement. Dr Rohling writes :

"'Having said in my "Antwort an die Rabbiner" (Reply to the Rabbins) that I did not find in the Talmud, as far as we know it by printed copies, any proof of ritual murder among the Jews, the Rabbins maintained that such proofs are generally not to be found in their literature. But, as there is now such a case before the Court, I deem it my duty to give you to understand that, after having written the above "Reply," I came into possession of a Hebrew work, which has been printed under the auspices of Sir Moses Montefiore so late as 1868, in which it is written (page 156a) "that the shedding of the blood of non-Jewish maidens is considered among the Jews a very sacred act ; the shedding of such blood is most agreeable to Heaven, and obtains mercy for them." This is but a short extract of the passage, which I shall shortly give to the public in its entirety. The truth of what I have said I am, in case of need, ready to confirm by oath before the court.'

"This is signed by Dr Rohling as Professor in the Imperial and Royal University of Prague.

"It makes my heart shudder, and will, I have no doubt, outrage many who read the above letter, that the character of the man whose name, whether mentioned in the house of Jew, Christian, or Moslem, is always received with the deepest respect and veneration, should be defiled by the foul breath of so terrible a slander at the very moment when it is a question of life or death.

"With an evil ingenuity the professor gives the page but not the name of the book, to puzzle the mind of the reader, depending for his success more upon the ignorant people of Nyiregyhaza, before whom the Deputy will most probably read his letter, than upon the judgment of those who are far away from that place.

"Now, all the Jews in the world, including even those who became apostates from their religion, as well as the high dignitaries of the Church, nay, bishops and professors of theology, have declared, and will again solemnly declare, if necessary, that there is no such statement, there can be no such statement, in existence. Neither in the Bible nor in the Talmud, nor in any book treating of the Kabbala, could be seen even the shadow of the tracing of such a rite to which the Professor alludes ; but his great object is, as he gives it to be understood in his letter, to guide the Court in their judgment.

"To clear up the mystery in question I will simply give the words of Dr Franz Delitzsch, Professor of Theology in the University of Leipzig, published in the *Pester Lloyd*, March 16, which, as the reader will see, have reference to the very book of which Professor Rohling, in his letter, concealed the title :—

"'The 'Paderborner Judenspiegel" (second edition, 1883), forming a part of the "Bonifazius-Broschüren" [of which Dr Rohling, in his "Reply to the Rabbins," page 52, says : "the texts which Dr Justus"—this is the name by which the masked author goes—"offers are taken directly from original sources "] concludes with three quotations from cabalistic works, on which he bases the blood accusations. One of these works appeared, as stated before, in Jerusalem, the other in Bagdad. Professor Rohling had undoubtedly these books in his mind when he said, p. 53: "If the high authorities were to make it possible for me to spend several years in the East, I think I could also find texts of the same kind." The passage of the Jerusalem book which bears the title of "Halikutim," by Chajim ben Joseph Vital of Calabria,* refers to an observation made therein on verses 18 and 19 of chapter xxx. in the Book of Proverbs : "There be three things which are too wonderful for me, yea, four which I know not : The way of an eagle in the air ; the way of a serpent upon a rock ; the way of a ship in the midst of the sea, and the way of a man with a maid." By this he seeks to establish the right of accusing the Jews of ritual murder ; that the shedding of the blood of a non-Israelite maid is deemed by the Jews a sacrifice agreeable to the Deity. If an observation from which such inferences could be drawn were really to exist, it would certainly prove an awful prejudice against the Jews at the Tisza-Eszlar trial. It might be said, "Why should such a passage not exist in that book?" Does not Dr Justus give the name, page, and place of printing? Thousands of people will believe him—because who can easily procure a book printed in Jerusalem? And, if they do procure it, how very few would be able to read it, or be sure to have a correct translation of it. But because I am one of those few who have that book, and, as a Christian, consider, in the words of my Lord (St Matthew xv. 10), as false witness all that which defiles man before God, the holy and true one, I herewith

---

* Born 1543, died 1620. He resided at Safed, Palestine, and was a disciple of Isaac Luria. The book in question, which forms part of the book Etz Chajim, was printed in Zolkiew, Wilna, and Jerusalem.

declare before all the world that the rendering of the passage in question which Dr Justus gives is not a translation, but a bungling work of infernal falsehood. Into the sacred text of Deuteronomy, chapter xxii., v. 17, which treats on a subject of chastity and purity, the falsifier, in the spirit of the before-mentioned incendiary paper, " Paderborner Judenspiegel," introduces his own idea—the invention that the words in question were meant to recommend the murder of a maid for ritual purposes. Who is that Dr Justus by whom the "Bonifazius Verein" allowed itself to be made a dupe? Does it behove a Christian association to cast the dragon-seed of such falsehood into the heart of a Christian people? The "Judenspiegel" concludes with the wish that God may open the heart of the Jews to the truth of Christianity. This is also my wish; but, for the same reason, I abhor a controversy which, blinded by the hatred of races, unites itself with ignorance and malice, and does the work of hawking about false witness as a matter of business. Philologists professing the Catholic religion, such as Professor Birkoll of Innsbruck, Professor Scholz of Wurzburg, the Priest Knabenbauer, and others of my colleagues, will confirm what I say regarding the disgraceful falsification made by Dr Justus.'

"So far the words of a Christian scholar of great eminence, Dr Delitzsch.

"With regard to the statement of Dr Rohling that the mysterious book had been printed under the auspices of Sir Moses, I have to explain that, nearly forty years ago, with a view of encouraging industry in the Holy Land, he presented a person of the name of Israel Back with an English printing press, and the recipient in token of deep gratitude to the donor named it ' Mássát Moshe Ve Yehoodit '— a present from ' Moses and Judith ;' since that time all the books printed by the use of that press bear that name on the title-page. Sir Moses himself has not the remotest idea of the printing of that book, nor has he ever heard of the existence of it, but it pleased Dr Rohling, and he thought it would answer his purpose exceedingly well, to interpret these words by ' Under the auspices of Sir Moses Montefiore.'

"The name of Sir Moses sheds too bright a lustre over all his acts to require any further explanation on my part; but my object in writing this letter is to rouse the indignation of all friends of truth and justice, and point out to them the cruel means of slander which are used to influence this trial. Sir Moses has sent a letter to every one of the deputies of the Imperial and Royal Hungarian Diet, enclosing for their immediate perusal a copy of the Firman Khat Shereef issued by his late Imperial Majesty the Sultan Abd-ool-Medjid to the Chief Judge at Constantinople in the year 1840, and the address which he delivered to his Majesty on that occasion at the Palace of Beshik-Tash, translated into the Hungarian language, at the conclusion of which he uttered a fervent prayer 'that the light of truth may ever illumine our paths, and speedily dispel the dark clouds of calumny and fanaticism.' In this prayer you, Sir, every Englishman, every friend of humanity all over the world, will most assuredly cordially join him.—I have the honour to be, Sir, your obedient servant,

"L. LOEWE,

"One of the members of the Mission to Damascus and Constantinople, under Sir Moses Montefiore, Bart., in the year 1840.

" 1 OSCAR VILLAS, BROADSTAIRS, KENT, *July* 10."

August 3rd.— The Tisza-Eszlar trial, after thirty-two days pleading in open court, terminated this day, "all the accused being declared innocent of the accusation brought against them." The accusation of murder the court declared to be entirely without foundation; "as for ritual murder in general," it declared, "such does not exist."

"The trial terminated," the *Chronik der Zeit* says, "as we expected. We strongly relied upon the idea that there were still true judges in Hungary; judges whose calling it is to uphold the law, who in spite of agitation, creed, hatred, and prejudice, would not at the decisive moment allow themselves to be blinded to the truth."

Sir Moses, a few hours after the decision of the court had been given, received a telegram informing him of the result of the trial. He was greatly rejoiced, and immediately addressed letters of congratulation to all the liberated prisoners, enclosing to each of them a handsome present, on account of the sufferings they had undergone. A few days later he had the satisfaction of receiving their acknowledgments, couched in terms of deep gratitude, for the sympathy he had evinced towards them, from the beginning to the end of the sorrowful days during which the trial lasted.

Although nearly three months had still to elapse before the dawn of the day on which he was to celebrate the ninety-ninth anniversary of his birthday, poems, books, works of art, and numerous letters from distant parts of the world had already reached London; the authors and donors requesting their friends to present the gifts to Sir Moses when the day should arrive. The state of Sir Moses' health varied. It depended to some extent upon the weather, but there was seldom a case of serious illness. He complained of weakness, but was still able to go out for a drive now and then, and was cheerful in conversation with his friends and general visitors. He had all his letters read to him, and signed as many replies as were required. He himself wrote the principal part of the cheques he drew on his bankers, and signed them in his usual style.

The weeks and days were now counted impatiently by his friends for the advent of his ninety-ninth birthday, which was to be publicly celebrated on the 8th November (8th Heshvan, Hebrew date), but the celebration already began on the 24th October, the last day of the Jewish Feast of Tabernacles. For upwards of fifty years Sir Moses had every year on this festival held the

office of Hattan Thora (Bridegroom of the Law) in his own
Synagogue, and in honour of the occasion received a large number of friends and relatives to luncheon at East Cliff, after the
morning service in the Synagogue.   On this particular day the
company was more numerous than ever, many having come
from London to congratulate Sir Moses.   After the luncheon
most of the visitors were admitted, a few at a time, to Sir Moses'
room, to offer him their good wishes, and were delighted to find
him so cheerful, happy, and grateful to Heaven for the mercy
bestowed upon him.   In the London Synagogues the preachers
from the pulpit spoke of the auspicious event, holding out the
high aim of Sir Moses' life as a noble example of virtue.   Immense numbers of telegrams began to arrive from all parts of
the world, in many different languages, some of them containing hundreds of words.   The post-office officials had a
heavy task in transmitting them.   Large packages containing
choice flowers and costly fruit were continually being sent by
friends and admirers far and near, some even from perfect
strangers.   Visitors also began to call day after day, and,
although numerous, formed, with the apparently endless arrival
of letters, telegrams, and bouquets, only the vanguard of what
was intended for the 8th of November.   Early in the morning
Sir Moses was serenaded by a party of sixty ladies and gentlemen stationed on the lawn, under his bedroom window, who
sang hymns and songs composed in honour of the day.   Sir
Moses was greatly pleased by this attention, and had his window
thrown open in order to hear the singing better.   While sitting
there listening, he had the honour of receiving a special telegram
from Her Majesty the Queen, which was couched in the most
gracious terms, congratulating him on the happy day, while
complimenting him on his noble and useful career.   As soon as
Sir Moses had read it, he requested the ladies and gentlemen
to sing " God save the Queen," which they did, following it up
by hearty cheers for Her Majesty.   Soon afterwards equally
kind telegrams arrived from their Royal Highnesses the Prince
of Wales and the Duke of Edinburgh.   So many deputations
from various towns, corporate bodies, and religious, charitable,
scientific, and mercantile institutions were waiting to present
addresses to Sir Moses, that it was quite impossible for him to
see them all, although all were hospitably entertained at his

house, and received every attention from Mr Sebag and Mr Guedalla, the relatives of Sir Moses, who, together with their wives, assisted him to receive the numerous visitors during the day. Whole vans full of boxes were brought to the house from the railway, containing works of art, choice flowers, costly fruit, and other presents. The telegrams arrived by hundreds, so that they could not even be opened, much less read, on that day. The post-office and railway companies had to engage a large number of extra officials to cope with the work. There were extra trains run, not only from towns in Kent, but even from London, to bring down the crowds anxious to witness the proceedings, or to take part in them. Ramsgate and all the neigbouring towns made the day a general holiday. All the shops and schools were closed; the streets were tastefully decorated with flags and garlands; handsome triumphal arches had been erected, with inscriptions containing good wishes for Sir Moses, and fervent blessings for all the good he had done in his long and noble life; the ships in the harbour were dressed with flags, and salutes were fired. Even the street lamps had been ornamented with the initials of Sir Moses' name in English and Hebrew letters of gold. Many thousands of visitors had arrived by train, and the authorities of the town had requisitioned one hundred extra constables to keep order in the crush that was expected. The streets of Ramsgate were filled with people, and the immense fields between the house of Sir Moses and the Synagogue soon became so crowded that when the hour came for the special service in the Synagogue, which was to be attended by the friends of Sir Moses and the heads of the deputations, it seemed impossible for them to get through the crowd. By the help of mounted constables a way was cleared, and the building was soon filled to its utmost capacity. Handsomely printed copies of the order of service were handed to the visitors. After the usual afternoon service, the Rev. Dr. Herman Adler, the Delegate Chief Rabbi, opened the ark, and offered up a fervent prayer composed by him for the occasion. As soon as the service was concluded the visitors had to hurry back to East Cliff Lodge to witness a grand procession, which was one of the principal features of the day, and which had been arranged most successfully by Messrs Ben Twyman, of Ramsgate, and Mr Hodgman, the Chief of the Post-Office of the town. The procession was two miles in length, and took nearly an hour in passing through the grounds of Sir Moses' estate. It was composed of military bands, detachments of firemen and police, mayors and members of town councils, lifeboat men, Foresters, Oddfellows, Druids, allegorical groups, and members of deputations from Jewish communities in different parts of England and the Continent. The rear of the procession was brought up by several thousand school children from nearly all the schools in the neighbourhood. Sir Moses stood on the balcony of his drawing-room, overlooking the garden, to witness the procession. It was a touching sight to see each separate part of the procession, as they came to the balcony, make a halt, lower their flags before the venerable hero of the day, and send up ringing cheers for him. Sir Moses lifted his cap and waved his hand in response. He several times attempted to address a few words to them, but was too deeply moved to give them utterance. The scene made an indelible impression on the heart and mind of the writer of this memoir, and few of the many hundreds of friends who surrounded Sir Moses on that day are ever likely to forget it. After the procession more deputations were received by Sir Moses, and in the evening a lecture was delivered at the Montefiore College by the Principal on the words of the Psalms, " With long life will I satisfy him, and show him my salvation," and of the prophet Isaiah, " He gives power to the faint, and to them that have no might He increaseth strength. Even the youths shall faint and be weary, but they that wait upon the Eternal shall renew their strength ; they shall mount up as with the wings of eagles, they shall run and not be weary, they shall walk and not be faint." The Hall was brilliantly illuminated, and filled to its utmost extent, many being unable to find room. A grand banquet was given in honour of the day at the Granville Hotel by Mr Vale, the Chairman of the Ramsgate Improvement Committee. The poor also had their share in the festivities. The proprietor of the Granville Hall gave a dinner to 300 sick and poor people, and the Rev. J. C. Collins entertained a like number of poor children at tea. The Commemoration Committee also gave a large number of dinners to the poor ; at Grave's Hotel nearly 400 were entertained, besides 150 at Christ Church Parish Hall. St Luke's Parish gave a dinner to 120, and a still larger number sat down at St Lawrence. The Congregationalists, the Baptists, the Wesleyans, and the Primitive Methodists all did honour to Sir Moses in this way, knowing that it was the way he would most approve. Naturally, the Jewish poor were not forgotten on this occasion. In the evening the whole town of Ramsgate and the harbour were splendidly illuminated, and large bonfires were lighted. The rejoicings were brought to a close with a grand display of fireworks in the vicinity of Sir Moses' residence.

Anything so grand had never before been witnessed in Ramsgate, and it was unanimously conceded that the inhabitants of the Isle of Thanet had done honour to themselves by sparing neither trouble nor expense in showing honour to him who for upwards of half a century had been one of their most respected fellow-citizens, and during all this time had never allowed an opportunity to pass without giving substantial proofs of his goodwill, wherever required, without distinction of creed or nationality.

It was a source of great thankfulness to all the friends of Sir Moses that he bore the extraordinary excitement and fatigue of this ever memorable but trying day so well. He received one deputation after another until midday, saying something pleasant to each, and thanking them all most heartily. From two o'clock until three he stood on the balcony to view the procession, and after it had passed, continued receiving deputations until five o'clock. So many visitors were anxious to shake hands with him that all the rooms of his house, with the stairs and passages, did not suffice to contain them; many had to remain in the garden for hours until there was room for them upstairs. No one seemed to mind waiting. The costly and beautiful presents were spread out in every room; the lovely flowers and choice fruit turned the house into a veritable paradise, although only those could be displayed which had arrived before the day, upwards of a hundred boxes not having been opened for want of time. The addresses from all parts of the world are too numerous to be named singly. Many of them were splendidly mounted. One was from America, an album of immense size, mounted in velvet, with silver ornaments; another, from Warsaw, in ivory, most artistically carved. Several contained lovely pictures by noted artists; others in exquisite needlework covers. They are all kept in large glass cases at Judith College, and are the admiration of all who see them. In every synagogue throughout the world special services were held in honour of Sir Moses, and large benevolent institutions were founded in his memory on the Continent, in America, and in Australia. It was universally acknowledged that before this time no such honour had been shown to any private individual, but that Sir Moses had received no more than his just reward.

CHAPTER XLII.

1883.

*T*HURSDAY, *November 22nd.*—The City of London presented an address to Sir Moses. This was unanimously voted by the Court of Common Council, on the motion of Mr Loveridge, seconded by Mr Alderman Isaacs, and a beautiful specimen of modern illumination on vellum was accordingly prepared. The words of the resolution, skilfully engrossed, made mention of the fact that Sir Moses Montefiore was Sheriff forty-six years ago, and the writing was enclosed in a handsome and elaborate border.

This richly ornamented address was conveyed from London by a deputation of the Common Council, composed of Mr Loveridge, the mover of the resolution, Mr Alderman Nottage, and twelve or fourteen deputies. Mr Alderman Isaacs, the seconder of the resolution, was unfortunately prevented by illness from accompanying the party.

* The vivacity, the heartiness, the wit, the cheerful readiness of repartee with which Sir Moses Montefiore welcomed his visitors defy all description. Vital force and high animal spirits seemed heightened rather than diminished in this truly marvellous centenarian. He was begged again and again to sit down, but said, " When all my guests are seated I will be seated also." Thereupon the greater number sat down, and Sir Moses took his seat on a couch beside Mr Alderman Nottage, but this was only for a minute or two. Seeing that a few yet stood, he was on his feet again in a moment, protesting his ability and his desire to stand also. Mr Sebag introduced the deputation, and Sir Moses could hardly wait for any formalities, so impatient

---

* Description of presentation taken partly from *Daily Telegraph.*

was he to pour forth his gratitude and goodwill in simple, earnest, and impulsive words. That he was greatly moved may be supposed by all who know his sympathetic nature. The address was read by Mr Loveridge, who added some appropriate words, and presented a magnificent bouquet, with the inscription, "Jerusalem," in golden characters across it, this appropriate gift being due to the thoughtfulness of Mr Courtney.

Then Sir Moses, with great feeling, uttered his evidently heartfelt thanks. He spoke of the dear old city with which he had been connected long ago; said it gladdened him to see the blue gowns of the Common Council; that there never was a city more loyal to that Sovereign whose portrait hung before them, and whom he prayed God in Heaven long to protect. He said that he truly wanted words to express all he felt. He could assure the deputation, one and all, that from his heart he thanked them. As a matter of fact, no such assurance was needed, for the voice in which it was expressed swelled with emotion, and the hearers also were visibly affected. The pride with which Sir Moses Montefiore showed his treasured chain of office, the gold casket containing the freedom of the Fishmongers' Company, and other civic souvenirs, was delightful to witness. All present passed before the aged baronet and shook hands with him, and to each who addressed him in turn, he replied with some apt and gracefully turned sentence, which showed a freshness of heart and clearness of brain not frequently found among men of any age. One member of the Common Council said he was eighty. "Is that all?" exclaimed Sir Moses, and then he gravely added, "You have much work before you, sir." The deputation of Common Council was followed by one from the Merchant Taylors' Company, with which Sir Moses was long connected. Subsequently all the guests were entertained at luncheon, Mr Joseph Sebag presiding in place of Sir Moses, who deputed him to say how cordially he felt the pleasure they had conferred on him. Mr Loveridge, Mr Sebag, Mr Arthur Cohen, Q.C., M.P., and Mr Alderman Nottage, spoke after the repast, and whether the immediate subject was their host or the City of London, the former was remembered by name in every sentence, the last speaker quoting language originally uttered in praise of Milton, to the effect that "if he were sent to another planet from our globe he would be regarded as the representative of a race who were the favourites and heirs of Heaven."

The writer having been requested to say grace after the repast, made use of the ancient and venerable Hebrew language, the same being well understood by most of the guests present.

Before leaving, the civic party, at the earnest entreaty of Sir Moses, returned to his room to shake hands once more, and bid him adieu.

Sir Moses, being desirous of expressing his gratitude to those who honoured him with their congratulations, addressed a letter to the editors of the principal journals in the following terms:—

"SIR,—May I ask the privilege of expressing through your paper my heartfelt thanks towards the very large number of friends and public bodies who have so considerately offered me their esteemed congratulations on the occasion of my entering this day into my hundredth year?

"Grateful to Providence for the merciful protection vouchsafed to me during my long life, I rejoice in the reflection that any feeble efforts I may have made to advance the happiness and welfare of my fellow-creatures have been so kindly judged.

"With a fervent prayer for the health and long life of our gracious Queen, whose beneficent sway over this great and free country has caused so much happiness to all classes of her subjects, reiterating my thanks to my numerous friends, and acknowledging your courteous and flattering remarks, I have the honour to remain, yours faithfully,   (Signed) "MOSES MONTEFIORE."

Subsequently he addressed letters of thanks to all who favoured him with their congratulations, at the same time enclosing cheques in many cases for charitable institutions. The following is a copy of his reply, which was in most instances translated into the language of his correspondent:—

"Your most esteemed letter, conveying to me your felicitations on the occasion of my entering, by the blessing of God, upon my hundredth year of life, has reached me on the eighth of Heshvan, and I feel great pleasure in expressing to you my warmest acknowledgments for the kind sentiments you were pleased to evince therein towards me.

"In appreciation of the honour you conferred on me by your communication, I have placed the same among the important documents I keep in Judith, Lady Montefiore's Theological College, with a view of making known to those who attend there for the study of our Holy Law and the Hebrew literature, the kindness which prompted you to address me on the auspicious event.

"Most fervently do I pray to Him, who has ever been, and ever will be, the Guardian of Israel, to cause His choice blessing to alight upon yourself and your respected family, so that you may be permitted to continue in your praiseworthy work of benevolence for many years to come in full enjoyment of every happiness.—With reiterated thanks, I am, &c."

Up to the last day of December, letters, books, poems, and costly presents continued to arrive. In Austria, Galicia, Roumania, Russia, Russian Poland, Italy, and many towns in America and Australia, charitable institutions were established bearing his name, and reports of the same, accompanied by photographs of the buildings and of the principal officers, were sent to him.

Even in 1884, when he had attained his hundredth year, Sir Moses would not give himself the rest he deserved. He continued to take the liveliest interest in charitable and educational institutions, and even signed documents sent to him by his favourite companies—the Alliance, and the Imperial Continental Gas Association.

Sometimes in the course of conversation with his friends he would say, " Can I believe that I am a hundred years old ? "

What interested him most this year was the movement at Warsaw by the promoters of agriculture in the Holy Land. They formed themselves into a society, adopting the name of " Chovavey Zion " (the friends or lovers of Zion), and had an excellent likeness made of him by a distinguished artist, which they sold in Russia, Holland, and Germany, the amount realised being intended for the benefit of Jewish colonists in the Holy Land. Many thousands of copies were sold, and the names of the purchasers and the amounts received were published in the Hebrew and German papers. Most of the purchasers gave considerably more than the stipulated price, in order to manifest their high appreciation of Sir Moses' character, and of the object the society had in view. It was a source of very great happiness to him to hear of the progress made by the Jewish agriculturists in the Land of Promise, where there were now seven colonies.

That for which he had been longing full sixty years of his life he now saw being realised by the strenuous efforts of the society " Chovavey Zion," by the agricultural Hebrew associations in Roumania and elsewhere, and by private gentlemen, who individually exerted themselves for the good and great cause. Foremost among them stands the great friend of colonisation, Baron Edmond de Rothschild in Paris.

Sir Moses had the satisfaction of being enabled to send his contributions on his ninety-ninth birthday to six colonies, viz. :—

Ge-oni, near Safed ; Rishon le-Zion, two and a half hours from Jaffa ; Beney Bilu ; Sámárin, near Haifa ; Yahood, two and a half hours from Jaffa ; Pe-kee-in, near Safed, the Bokea.

He also had the satisfaction of receiving Mr David Gordon, a delegate from twenty-three congregations in Russia, who presented him with an album, containing fervent wishes and prayers for the prolongation of his life, with the signatures of 1562 representatives of fifty societies bearing the name of " The Friends of Zion," all branches of the above-named society at Warsaw.

They celebrated his centenary by holding a general meeting of the members in the town of Kattowitz, in Upper Silesia, a place chosen by them on account of its vicinity to the frontiers of Russia, Austria, and Prussia, for the purpose of arranging all the particulars referring to a " Sir Moses Montefiore Institution," having for its object the cultivation of land in Palestine.

In America, in Pratt Country, Kansas, a colony bearing the name " Montefiore," and consisting of refugees from countries in which the blessings of liberty have not yet been allotted to their brethren, sent him an address in pure Biblical Hebrew, conveying the expression of their gratitude for his exertions to ameliorate their condition, and forwarded for his acceptance specimens of the produce of their colony.

His regular medical attendant and others paid him frequent visits, but he seldom left his room. Sometimes great anxiety was felt by those round him when attacks of bronchitis or a severe cough disturbed his nights, but he would rally again, so strong was his constitution. Sir William Jenner once came down. Sir Moses was not informed he had been sent for, or he would not have consented. The eminent physician, after a careful examination, made the satisfactory statement that his pulse was wonderfully well for a man of his age, but, of course, he observed, his life was, as it were, hanging on a thread. However, by great care and unceasing attention, he might yet, comparatively speaking, continue to enjoy health and good spirits.

Very frequently, as I walked from Broadstairs to East Cliff Lodge, I was stopped on the road by rich and poor, eagerly inquiring, " How is Sir Moses ? " and whenever he took a carriage drive, which was now but very seldom, many groups of people might be seen awaiting him on the roads through which he would have to pass, so as to catch a glance of him.

His Synagogue and College continued to engage his mind. To visitors, who purposely came from London or elsewhere to Ramsgate to see him, he would say, " Have you been to see the Synagogue ? Have you seen the College ? " Not being able to attend the College himself, he had copies made of the lectures, and on a Friday night or Sabbath morning he would invite the lecturer for the day to come and read the same to him.

The order for writing a scroll of the Pentateuch was again sent to Wilna, in accordance with his custom ever since his first visit to that place in the year 1846, and he awaited its arrival with impatience. He often expressed the wish that he might soon have the happiness of again writing the last verse in the sacred manuscript.

He used to join his friends at the dinner table, although, for the last two years, he could no longer partake of the same food as was prepared for them, but he would remain on the sofa and join them in drinking the healths of some of those present.

He still enjoyed the Friday evenings (the commencement of the Sabbath) to a high degree. When his Sabbath lamp illumined his chamber, and prayers were being recited, he would join in singing the hymns and psalms ; afterwards he would drink the wine out of the Sabbath cup, over which the benediction of the hallowed day of rest had been pronounced, and partake of the Sabbath bread. He would then be in the best of humours, and would delight every one with his conversation.

Thus the weeks and months glided away on the path of time, and the hundredth anniversary of his birthday drew near.

CHAPTER XLIII.

1884.

ALREADY in the beginning of the year, "Sir Moses Montefiore Memorial Committees" had been formed in many parts of the world, also in London. By the kind permission of the Right Hon. the Lord Mayor, a public meeting was held in the Egyptian Hall, at the Mansion House, in January, for the purpose of considering the best means of celebrating the approaching centenary. The Ramsgate Memorial Committee sent a special deputation to attend the meeting, but at the request of Sir Moses, it was indefinitely postponed.

Sir Nathaniel M. (now Lord) Rothschild, Chairman of the Montefiore Memorial Committee, issued the following circular countermanding the meeting :—

"NEW COURT, *21st January* 1884.

"DEAR SIR,—The newspapers will have announced to you this morning that the public meeting convened for to-morrow, at the Mansion House, under the presidency of the Lord Mayor, will not be held.

"It had reached me that Sir Moses Montefiore had manifested to those around him, considerable disquietude as to the proposed movement by which his friends had intended permanently to commemorate his great services, and that while deeply appreciating the kindness of his friends, and touched by the feelings of regard, he was very unwilling, even tacitly, to sanction the collection proposed to be made. Under these circumstances, two members of the Executive Committee, Mr Joseph Sebag and Mr Lionel L. Cohen, went to Ramsgate, to ascertain Sir Moses' exact wishes on the subject.

These were expressed in terms so distinct and so decisively adverse to the contemplated movement, that, as previously arranged with me, they put themselves in immediate communication with the Lord Mayor, who, acquiescing in the desire to conform to Sir Moses' wishes, decided to countermand the meeting.

"It only remains for me, therefore, to thank you for your intended co-operation.—I am dear Sir, yours faithfully,

"N. M. DE ROTHSCHILD, Chairman."

Meanwhile, biographical notices were published in English

and foreign papers, and preparations on a grand scale were made to celebrate the centenary, especially in Synagogues, schools, colleges, and charitable institutions. Dinners, teas, treats of every description were to be given to the aged, the poor, and the school children of various communities. Charitable institutions were raised in most parts on the Continent, bearing the name of Sir Moses Montefiore. The tide of offerings once more flowed in upon Sir Moses.

The Freemasons all over the world sent their fraternal salutations. Some of these are on scrolls, with handles to them in the form of Hebrew Pentateuch scrolls for Synagogue purposes.

The number of addresses delivered at East Cliff Lodge was very great, and to sort and arrange them generally, as well as according to the various languages in which they were written, occupied the time of a diligent worker for several months.

On Monday, 27th October 1884, according to the Hebrew date, 8 Heshvan, 5645 A.M., Sir Moses completed the hundredth year of his life.

Religious services were held in all the Synagogues of the United Kingdom. In London the principal service was at the Synagogue of the Spanish and Portuguese congregation in Bevis Marks, which was decorated with flowers and brilliantly lighted. The Delegate Chief Rabbi delivered a sermon, and the principal reader offered up a special Hebrew prayer composed by the Chief Rabbi.

Mr Joseph Sebag (now Mr Sebag-Montefiore) entertained a large party at dinner; the Jewish Working Men's Club gave a grand entertainment; six hundred poor were invited to a dinner at the expense of the Bevis Marks Congregation, and treats were given to the pupils of nearly all the Jewish schools in London.

Sir Moses forwarded a sum of £100, corresponding to the number of years in his life, to the late Mr Lionel L. Cohen, M.P., President of the Board of Guardians of the German Congregation, and a similar sum to the Board of Guardians of the Spanish and Portuguese community, to the Mansion House Poor Box, to each of the four Holy Cities in Palestine, and to various Continental congregations.

The proceedings at Hereson, Ramsgate, began with the ordinary service in his Synagogue at 8 o'clock A.M. and at 1.30 P.M. there was a special service at which the Delegate

Chief Rabbi recited the prayer composed by his father, the Rev. Dr N. M. Adler.

Most of those who were present then proceeded to East Cliff Lodge. One of the local papers which I copy says:

"The festivities of the day commenced with the delivery of coals to the houses of poor people, and this was followed a couple of hours later by the distribution of a hundred pairs of blankets by the new Mayor, Mr Kennett, at the Town Hall, to as many necessitous individuals. All the blankets bore the motto of the day, "Think and thank," upon them.

"During the night workmen had been busy, and by the early morning the newly incorporated town had undergone a complete transformation. Almost every street was a mass of colour. Flags of every nationality hung across the streets and draped the houses, interspersed with appropriate mottoes. Red and gold were the prevailing colours, and the motto of the house of Montefiore, 'Think and thank,' was frequently repeated. In the harbour all the ships, including the Trinity yacht *Galatea*, were dressed in honour of the event. Even the stolid boatmen were obliged to give way at last, and joined the festive throng, admiring the profusion of flags and banners, and the complimentary inscriptions upon arches of evergreens, castellated trophies, and shop facias. The houses round about were gay with bunting, kept in constant motion by the wind. Harbour Street, High Street, King Street, and Queen Street were alive with the colours of all nations, paramount among them the Union Jack. The crowds of excursionists from the neighbouring towns and villages strolled along singly and in groups, stopping ever and anon to recite from the suspended banners such legends as, 'The man whom the people delight to honour,' and 'Europe claims his birth, all nations own his worth.' Two triumphal arches had been erected. That in High Street was most solid in appearance, being built to imitate a tower and a battlement, which were tastefully adorned with evergreens, while the one in King Street was entirely floral, and was decorated with flags. The Town Hall was prettily hung with banners across the front. Then came the procession, which marched with bands and banners from one end of the town to the other. The newly presented mace was carried at the head of the procession, and was greeted with loud cheers.

After the mayors and officials of the neighbouring towns of Margate, Deal, Sandwich, and Broadstairs had driven past, came the Mayor of Ramsgate, the Deputy-Mayor, the Aldermen and the Councillors of the town. Then came what were called ' Illustrations of trades.'

"One of the most interesting features in the procession was the travelling carriage in which Sir Moses rode when on his philanthropic missions in Russia and Poland, France and Italy, in the old stage-coach days. It was drawn by six horses. The route was crowded with sight-seers."

I now take the reader to join the party, who on leaving the special service in the Synagogue, proceeded to East Cliff.

On being introduced into the presence of Sir Moses they found him surrounded by his nearest relatives and friends, with whom he conversed in high spirits. His voice was clear, his memory perfect.

It is a strange and fascinating picture! There, in the right-hand corner of a large high-backed, old-fashioned chintz sofa sits a patriarchal figure supported by pillows. This impressive picture of age, tended by love and respect, is lighted from the right by a stream of sunshine, which pours through the upper panes of a large angular bay window, and rests gently upon a grand head, full of character, fringed with a short, closely cut, snow-white beard. One hand of Sir Moses is thrown negligently across a tall arm of the sofa, the other rests upon the ample skirts of a purple silk dressing gown. Close to the head of the sofa stands a table covered with baskets and great bouquets of flowers. Around on the walls are pictures of the Queen and the Royal family, and of scenes in the Holy Land, and a beautifully carved tablet with the inscription of the Decalogue over a standing desk, for the use of the reader when reciting the daily prayers; also a palm branch and a citron, over which he pronounced the blessings at the Feast of Tabernacles.

The Delegate Chief Rabbi now recited the prayer which he had previously offered in the Synagogue. Sir Moses insisted on standing during the greater part of it. He was much affected by several passages alluding to Lady Montefiore, and joined fervently in the prayer for the Queen.

At the conclusion of the prayer he expressed his thanks to

the Delegate Chief Rabbi, and spoke highly of his father, the Chief Rabbi.

The representatives of the Anglo-Jewish community were next introduced to him, and he expressed his thanks to them in touching language.

I then introduced the scribe of Wilna, who had brought with him the Pentateuch scroll. Sir Moses kissed the scroll, almost overpowered with happiness. On opening it, the well-known blessing pronounced by the priest happened to be written in the column before him. He read it aloud, and expressed gratitude to Heaven for having permitted him to see it on this his day of joy.

It was now nearly two o'clock, and the procession from the Town Hall drew near East Cliff. A deputation from the town visited the Lodge, in order that Sir Moses might invest the new Mayor with his present of a new gold chain of office for the service of the newly-made corporation in perpetuity. The members of the Commemoration Committee soon followed. They all, together with a number of ladies and gentlemen, after having partaken of Sir Moses' hospitality, proceeded to his room. There the Vicar of Ramsgate read an address to him. Sir Moses was much affected by it, and expressed his thanks to the Vicar with great warmth, speaking kindly of the Ramsgate inhabitants.

The new Mayor then stepped forward, and Sir Moses placed over his head a magnificent gold chain of office, bearing prominently on a shield the Hebrew letter " Mim " (corresponding to the English letter M, the initial of the name of the donor), saying, " May Almighty God give you and your children and children's children happiness. You are the first Mayor in Ramsgate. May God in His mercy protect you! I am sure He will!"

The Mayor replied, " I do not know what to say, Sir Moses, to thank you for all your kindness." " Do not thank me," Sir Moses rejoined. " What I have done gives me sincere pleasure. As to the praise which has been more than lavished upon me, I take it as a compliment to my co-religionists." The Mayoress then presented him with a bouquet, and Sir Moses received the congratulations of a considerable number of friends. He spoke to most of them, and continued in excellent spirits ; but he felt weak, and his medical attendant advising that the room should be cleared, all present withdrew.

It being now near the time when the evening prayers are offered in the Synagogue, the visitors repaired there, and met a large congregation.

Subsequently they proceeded to Judith, Lady Montefiore's Theological College, where the lecture hall was brilliantly illuminated. A profusion of choice flowers, tastefully arranged between numerous lights on steps in the bay window, gave it a charming appearance.

The Principal of the College held a special service, and addressed the assembly on the events of the day, concluding with a heartfelt prayer for the life of Sir Moses, in which all fervently joined.

With this service the religious celebrations of the day terminated.

The residents in the town and neighbourhood, the relatives and friends of Sir Moses, now assembled at a public banquet given in St George's Hall, under the presidency of the Mayor. During dinner the latter received a message, which he read to his guests. "Sir Moses wishes to send a message of friendly greeting to the Mayor of Ramsgate, and to his guests assembled this evening. He desires to drink a glass of wine with them, and wishes good health and prosperity to them and to the town. He regrets much that be is unable to be present with them to-night." The message was received with hearty cheers, and the Mayor proposed the toast of the evening, which was received with much enthusiasm, and acknowledged by Mr Joseph Sebag.

In the course of the evening a torch-light procession was formed at the Town Hall, and marched up to East Cliff, where a grand display of fireworks took place, the spot specially selected for it being not far from the bay window of Sir Moses' bedroom, to enable him to see it from his chair. The whole town was illuminated.

Thus the day passed in perfect happiness for Sir Moses and those who had taken part in the festivities. For the latter the sight of this grand old centenarian, who had won so much honour, esteem, and friendship, will never be effaced from their memory.

Great and numerous, however, as were all these manifestations of veneration and affection for Sir Moses in England and other parts of the world, the feeling must surely have arisen in the minds of many that the lights which illuminated the streets would soon be extinguished, the voices of the brilliant orators again be silent, the flowers which had this day decorated many a Synagogue become faded, and the words of the preachers forgotten; while the numerous charitable and educational institutions, which the recipient of so much homage had called into existence all over the world, will remain, and, while benefiting mankind in a high degree, will serve to keep alive the memory of his unselfish devotion.

The following morning he was better than could reasonably be expected after such an exciting event, but he was anxious to convey his sense of gratitude to the thousands who had honoured him with their congratulations, and at once gave orders for the purpose. His medical attendant, however, strongly advised him to refrain from too much exertion, and he wisely consented to remain quiet for some time.

Relatives and friends suggested that measures should be adopted by which he should be relieved of the necessity of answering his many correspondents. When weak and ailing he agreed to what they proposed, but the moment he felt a little stronger he invariably insisted on continuing his good work.

CHAPTER XLIV.

1885.

JANUARY 29th.—The Board of the London Committee of Deputies of the British Jews having been among the first in England to convey to him its congratulations, signed by the Honorary Officers, he this day addressed the following letter to them :

"EAST CLIFF LODGE, RAMSGATE,
"29th January 5645 (1885).

"To Arthur Cohen, Esq., Q.C., M.P., President ; Joseph Sebag, Esq., Vice-President ; Henry Harris, Esq., Treasurer ; and the Members of the London Committee of Deputies of the British Jews.

"DEAR AND ESTEEMED FRIENDS,—I have the honour to acknowledge the receipt of a copy of the resolutions unanimously passed at a special meeting, held on the 14th October 1884, in which you were pleased to express your kind sentiments and sincere felicitations on the occasion of the centennial anniversary of my natal day.

"My heart is overflowing with thankfulness to the Most High for having tended me all my life unto this day, and there will for ever remain enshrined within my memory the grateful sense I entertain for the manifestations of kindness which I was permitted to receive on my entering, as well as on my completing, the hundredth year of my existence, from many valued friends. To none of them, however, will my gratitude be more intense than to the distinguished members of your Board, with whom it has been my privilege to be associated in their unceasing endeavours to promote the interests of the communities at home and abroad for so long a period.

"I appreciate highly the renewed assurance of friendship by which you have greatly honoured me, and earnestly pray that the Most Supreme may shield and protect you and your families, so as to enable you to continue your noble exertions in the cause of our holy religion, in the cause of suffering humanity, and in the vindication of truth and justice. I invoke Him who is the Eternal Disposer of events to inspire you with holy zeal, that you may not rest until all the innocent sufferers from oppression shall be relieved.—I am, yours faithfully, "MOSES MONTEFIORE."

He next addressed the Anglo-Jewish Association, the Wardens of the Synagogues, Schools, and Colleges, and numerous public companies ; but at times he was compelled by weakness to desist, and could only resume his work after a lapse of three or four days.

It was always a pleasure to him to hear of matrimonial engagements, and he never failed to send costly wedding presents to all who invited him to be present at the solemnisation of the marriage, or to the customary breakfast afterwards. He often received letters from young persons signing themselves " Moses Montefiore," who had been so named by their parents as a mark of respect to Sir Moses.

Like most persons of affluence, he often received letters from strangers in various parts of the world who claimed relationship with him, and were not satisfied with a simple assurance on his part that there was no foundation whatever for such a claim. He frequently had to write strong letters to them before he could succeed in convincing them of their error.

Many persons in this country and abroad appeared to forget that they now addressed a centenarian, and used to write to him on various subjects, asking his advice on communal or other important matters, just as, with greater propriety, they had done twenty years before. Sir Moses, on giving his orders that a reply should be sent to them, expressed the strongest desire to avoid as much as possible any phraseology that might be interpreted as a disinclination to remain in peaceful relation with his correspondents, even when he had to disapprove of the measures proposed by them.

He found especial pleasure in persuading friends and acquaintances to take a trip on the Continent for a change of air and scene, and often presented them with as large a sum even as £100 to enable them to do so. Even persons who could hardly have expected such a favour were sometimes indebted to him in this way.

To those whom he entrusted with the carrying out of his orders, he would say, " I wish to continue doing just as I have always done with regard to benevolent institutions and individuals."

His weakness, however, often manifested itself to a degree which caused considerable uneasiness to his relatives and friends, and, by the advice of his medical attendant, additional nurses were engaged, so that he might be attended by them day and night, and never left alone for a moment.

He now gave special orders "never to allow any of his letters to leave the house before an exact copy had been made of them, however insignificant they might have been."

He still signed all his cheques, and added his usual motto, "Think and thank," on the face of them. He took special care never to express his immediate agreement with any suggestion made to him, and would say, "I will consider it," or, "I will do it to-morrow;" but it often happened that the person counting on this promise was disappointed, as Sir Moses frequently altered his mind upon consideration.

Speaking sometimes to me on his own advanced age, he would say, "I have endeavoured to do the best I could; no doubt I have often failed, but I rely on God's goodness; He forgives those who approach Him with a contrite heart." "Death," he would say, "is like going to sleep for a while, to awake again spiritually invigorated. When I pass the mausoleum of Judith I always read the Hebrew inscription above the entrance—

> 'Into His hands my Spirit I consign,
> Whilst wrapt in sleep that I again awake,
> And with my spirit, my body I resign;
> The Lord with me, no fears my soul can shake.'

" Let my mortal remains be taken through the grounds to my last resting-place quietly by the way I always used to go to my Synagogue with my dear wife."

After a long pause he would talk of more cheerful subjects. "Do you remember," he said, "when we crossed the Dwina near Riga, and the ice broke under our feet? We had many a narrow escape on our missions; praised be God for His numerous mercies."

He would then begin to recite a psalm, the Song of Moses, or a favourite hymn of his, commencing with the Hebrew words, "El Norá 'Aleelah," generally sung in the Spanish and Portuguese Synagogue on the day of atonement, before the conclusion service.

Often, when in conversation with me during the evenings, at a time when he was comfortably resting in bed, he would review the numerous pleasing incidents which happened on his Missions, in the company of Lady Montefiore, during the last fifty years of his life. His observations induced me to remind him of a number of occurrences which just at the moment appeared to have been forgotten by him, and he was delighted in recalling them again to his memory.

In reflecting upon the actual state of the Holy Land, the great changes which had taken place there since his first visit to Jerusalem, and its favourable prospects in the future, his countenance would become illumined with satisfaction.

Fifty years ago, very few persons in England and France manifested any particular interest in the Land of Promise —there were persons in both countries who laughed at the idea of even mentioning that country. "Now," he said, "some of them are numbered amongst the great benefactors of its inhabitants."

"Look," he would continue, "at the great improvements which have been made in Jerusalem, and, after all, fifty years is but a short time, if we consider the number of years it takes even in Europe to improve the condition of different classes of people."

Suddenly he would turn his head, and put his finger on the stone from Jerusalem which he had under his pillow, bearing the inscription, "For thy servants take pleasure in her stones, and favour the dust thereof" (Ps. cii. 17). "This," he said, "you will put under my head when I am placed in my last resting-place. Now go into the Gothic Library, take a good supper, and we shall have a glass of wine together in pleasing remembrance of what we have seen and endeavoured to do for our brethren."

On the 24th April the first bulletin appeared in the newspapers regarding his health. It was issued by his medical attendant, and was to the following effect :—" For several days in the early part of the week Sir Moses Montefiore suffered much from weakness." He recovered his strength a little, but not sufficiently to enable him to remain unaffected by the weather, which had become a little colder, although the month of June had now arrived.

Meanwhile he continued to take a deep interest in current events. In honour of the Queen's Birthday he gave orders to provide a dinner for the poor in the Union at Ramsgate, and tea and refreshments for the pupils and teachers of the Jews' Infant School in London. At dinner he took up his glass, and requested his friends to join him in drinking to the health of our good Queen. "God bless her," he said, "and all the Royal Family."

June 19th.—The bulletin stated that the condition of Sir Moses caused some anxiety, but happily, on Saturday morning, his medical attendant was able to report that the alarming symptoms had passed away.

June 26th.—No more weekly bulletins were issued. Sir Moses is fairly well. He signed cheques, but for large amounts; for small payments, bank notes and gold were procured from the bank. Before singing his name, he generally tried the strength of his hand on a sheet of paper. Sometimes the writing was remarkably good; but his eyesight was failing him, and he would request some one to put the pen which he held in his hand on the spot where his signature was required, and he was then able to sign his name.

July 10th.—Although already in such a weak state of bodily health, the mind and heart of Sir Moses were still animated by their old impulses, and he showed the deepest interest in whatever concerned his friends or the progress of humanity. He was delighted to hear that Lord Rothschild had taken his seat in the House of Lords. It will be readily understood that he insisted in having every word of the account of the proceedings read to him.

Sir Moses, with feelings of fervid loyalty to our Queen, and deep devotion to the members of the Royal House, highly appreciated the honour which Her Majesty had done to the Jewish community through Lord Rothschild.

July 17th.—Sir Moses felt rather better; he was delighted to have another opportunity of evincing his loyalty at this time to Her Majesty, by sending a wedding present to the Princess Beatrice. It consisted of a massive silver tea and coffee service with tray, the monogram, "H. B.," being beautifully engraved on each article, and the tray having an inscription in Hebrew, of which the following is a translation :—

"'Many daughters have acted virtuously, but thou excellest them all.' May He who dwelleth on high cause His light radiantly to shine on thy head. May joy and gladness meet thee; the voice of the bridegroom and the voice of the bride. May there be peace within thy walls, and tranquillity within thy palace, for now and for evermore, is the fervent prayer of him who reverentially subscribes himself,

"MOSES MONTEFIORE, 5645 A.M."

The affixing of his name to the above inscription was one of his latest acts, and may be regarded as the closing deed of his active life.

Her Royal Highness acknowledges the receipt of the same in the following most gracious terms :—

"*July 21st*, 1885.

"Princess Beatrice has just received the magnificent present Sir Moses Montefiore has so kindly sent her, accompanied by his good wishes, and she is anxious to express at once her heartfelt thanks for the valuable pieces of plate she greatly admires. The Princess is much touched by his kind attention on the occasion of her marriage, and will ever remember it gratefully."

Sir Moses, on hearing the above lines read to him, felt greatly pleased.

Day after day, whenever I saw him he would say, "Have I anything more to do? if so, let me do it. If there is any cheque to be written for charitable purposes, tell me, and I will sign it the moment I am able." On being assured that I would not hesitate to remind him, but that up to the present he had discharged all his self-imposed obligations in connection with benevolent institutions, he would raise his hands, saying, "Thank God for having been enabled to do so."

He felt extremely weak, and sometimes he was unable to hold a pen in his hand for several days. His medical attendant frequently slept in the house, or called two or three times in a day, and great uneasiness was felt by all round him.

July 24th.—An alarming bulletin was issued : "The condition of Sir Moses during the past week has caused serious anxiety. On Friday last there was extreme prostration, and the rallying power during the three following days was sensibly diminished."

July 25th.—Congestion of the lungs set in, but the day following he felt somewhat better, and the symptoms were less grave.

July 27th.—This being one of the days when I generally reported to him on subjects relating to his foreign correspondence, I entered his room, and coming near his bedside, he took my hand, saying, "My dear, dear Dr Loewe, do not leave me ; you must not leave me." I replied that if such was his wish I would certainly comply with it, and he rejoined : "I tell you, do not leave me ; sleep here."

I accordingly remained with him, but at eleven o'clock his medical attendant came for the purpose of sleeping in the house.

Under the impression that Sir Moses might pass a good night, those of his relatives round his bedside wished me to retire, Dr Woodman promising to call me if necessary, and I did so.

At two o'clock in the morning Dr Woodman knocked at my door, saying that Sir Moses had taken a change for the worse ; it was doubtful whether he would live till the morning.

I immediately entered his room, finding him surrounded by his near relatives and faithful attendants. He appeared to be asleep. He breathed heavily, and every now and then opened his eyes, looking steadily at those near him. He kept his right hand continually on the right side of his chest, as if he felt some pain there.

Telegrams and messages were sent to relatives and friends, to the gentlemen of Judith College, and to the ministers of the Synagogues, requesting their immediate attendance.

In the course of the morning he was asked now and then to take a glass of wine or some beef tea. He would then say "wait," while he endeavoured to hold the glass till his breath would allow him to drink. Then feeling apparently a little refreshed, he would say, "God bless you, God bless you." A little while later he would turn to me, asking if he had still anything to do, and moving his hand, as if he wanted to sign more cheques for benevolent purposes.

As he held his hands up, I thought he wished to pray, and commenced reciting prayers out of the very book which he had put aside to be used in the last moments of his life on earth.

He followed every word I said, and frequently joined in the principal sentences. I then remained silent for a time, when I noticed again his raising his hands in prayer, or invoking the name of God ; and I again recited prayers, in which he joined by moving of his lips or raising of his hand.

His medical attendant came in and spoke to him, and he appeared still conscious of all around him. The doctor again tried to make him take some wine, but he could only take very little. His hands now became very cold, and he would not allow them to be covered ; he remained almost in a sitting posture, supported by cushions.

Relatives and friends now arrived. The gentlemen of the College, the ministers of the Synagogues, and several members, of the congregation were in the room. All his faithful attendants entered to take leave of their good master.

Mr Joseph Sebag Montefiore, Mrs Guedalla, Mr Guedalla, and the writer were also at his bedside.

We recited part of the daily Morning Service : " My God ! the soul which Thou hast given unto me is pure. Thou hast created, formed, and breathed it into me. Thou dost also carefully preserve it within me, and Thou wilt hereafter take it from me to restore it unto me in futurity.

" During the time that my soul continues within me will I be making acknowledgments to Thee, O Lord, my God ! and God of my forefathers, Sovereign of all Creation, Lord of all Souls. Hear, O Israel, the Eternal is our God, the Eternal is One ! "

With the last word his soul took flight to heaven. The heart which beat so warmly for all that is good and noble had stopped for ever.

Serene calmness, peace—heavenly peace — lay upon his countenance, lit up by the glorious sunset of a life illumined by the love of God.

" The Lord has given, and the Lord has taken away. Praised be the name of the Eternal now and evermore." According to ancient custom, all present rent a portion of their attire, saying, " Praised be the name of Him who is a righteous Judge."

The sad intelligence immediately spread through the town. The Mayor of Ramsgate, who was presiding at a meeting of the Town Council, at once communicated it to his colleagues, and it was forthwith resolved that the town should be draped in black, and the meeting broke up.

As soon as the news became known, the customary signs of mourning appeared on all sides, and a wish was generally expressed that the funeral should be made as public as possible, in order that the townspeople might have an opportunity of showing their regard to one who, though truly a citizen of the world, yet took a deep interest in their town.

In the city of London, at a meeting of the Common Council, held the day after his death, the Lord Mayor said that, since last they met, one of the most distinguished—he thought he should be justified in saying "the most distinguished citizen of London" had been called away. He referred to the late Sir Moses Montefiore, whose life the Almighty had mercifully spared so long. The extreme old age to which the honourable Baronet had lived must soften, in a great degree, the feelings of regret which all present entertained at the loss; but, at the same, they must feel the highest pride in being able to say that Sir Moses, during his long and honourable life, always took the deepest interest in the affairs of the citizens and their ancient Corporation. In works of charity and philanthropy no man stood higher; he was not only the dearest friend, but the firm supporter of every good cause connected with that community—that venerable race—to which he belonged, and setting aside creed or race, he sympathised, it might be said, in a most practical manner with every popular movement throughout the world. No doubt it would be agreeable to the Court to have placed on record their sense of the great loss which not only the city and the metropolis, but the world at large, had sustained in the death of that eminent man, and he should ask the Chief Commissioner to move in the matter.

Mr Dresser Rogers accordingly proposed, " That this Court sincerely joins in the national sympathy evoked by the decease of their distinguished fellow-citizen, Sir Moses Montefiore, Bart., ex-Sheriff, who, after an exceptionally long and useful life, had passed peacefully to his rest, full of days and of honour, and leaving behind him a memory which will be long cherished in many lands." Mr Rogers, as one of the deputation who had the privilege to visit Sir Moses last year for the purpose of congratulating him on his one hundredth birthday, spoke of the kindly and courteous manner in which they were received by the honourable Baronet on that occasion, and of the great pleasure which their presence evidently afforded him.

Mr Alderman Lawrence, M.P., seconding the motion, also alluded to the eminent services which Sir Moses rendered to the city, and the many philanthropic acts which he performed during his long and honourable career. The epoch in which the deceased Baronet lived was distinguished for its improvements and inventions, for its progress in every way, and for the comfort and welfare of the great masses of the people at large.

The motion was adopted unanimously.

Mr H. L. Phillips proposed that a small deputation of the Council should be appointed to attend the funeral of Sir Moses this afternoon, for he was sure that all wished to honour the memory of the good man who was now deceased.

Mr M'Geagh seconded the motion, and it was decided that Mr Alderman Cowan and the mover and seconder be the deputation accordingly.

The Council also agreed, as a graceful act, to invite Mr George Faudel Phillips, the junior Sheriff, to accompany the deputation to Ramsgate this morning.

A few hours after the death of Sir Moses, telegrams were despatched all over the world, announcing that the great philanthropist had breathed his last.

Innumerable messages of condolence reached the family. Deputations arrived in London to attend the funeral, which was fixed for Friday, July 31st, at two o'clock P.M.

Memorial services were held in synagogues and churches. Ministers from the pulpit addressed their congregations in all parts of the world, every one claiming him to be a member of his own congregation, for " the principles," they said, which he advanced and practised are those which we teach, and which every human being ought to adopt, to secure peace and happiness—that which is good for himself and good for his fellow-beings.

CHAPTER XLV.

1885.

FROM the moment of his death to the hour fixed for the
funeral, the members of the College, conjointly with some
friends, remained with the body, reciting prayers and certain
psalms, which he so often liked to hear chanted in his Synagogue.

On Wednesday evening his body was taken from his room
and placed in one of the libraries below stairs, where, when
Lady Montefiore was still alive, he used to enjoy his frugal
repasts in the company of friends.

Here, in my presence, the ministers of the Spanish and
Portuguese congregations, and the members of the Hebrew
Association known by the name of "Lavadores," reverently
prepared the body for its last resting-place, and whilst thus
engaged, one of the gentlemen present recited appropriate
passages from the sacred text bearing on the subject.

Prompted by the great love he ever felt for Jerusalem, he
had desired to have his head covered with a cap which had
been specially worked for him in the Holy City; he also wished,
in commemoration of his happy union with Lady Montefiore,
to have the prayer-shawl which he used during the solemnisation of their marriage in the Synagogue, placed on his shoulders,
in addition to the customary plain linen attire used in the case
of all the dead, poor and rich alike.

Mementoes from the Holy City, papers referring to certain
recipients of his benevolence, which he did not wish to destroy,
but only to hide from the sight of the world, were also in compliance with his request, placed with him. He had likewise

expressed a desire that the dust from the Holy Land, which he himself had brought with him from the Valley of Jehoshaphat, should be placed in his coffin, and that some of this should be sprinkled on his face in token of his deep veneration for the Land of Promise.

I need not say that all his wishes were scrupulously fulfilled.

When the solemn proceedings of the Lavadores were concluded, his near relatives entered the room to take leave of their beloved kinsman. Little change had taken place in his countenance, his benign features leaving a lasting impression on the mind of all present.

The body was now placed in a coffin made of plain deal boards, and covered with black cloth, on the lid of which two lighted wax candles were placed, light being emblematic of the soul of man (Prov. xx. 27).

After the intelligence of Sir Moses' death reached London, great numbers of people arrived in Ramsgate, most of them walking round East Cliff Lodge, or up and down outside the gates. Then with the morning trains of Friday (July 31st) all the Representatives of the Spanish and Portuguese Jews' Synagogue, to which Sir Moses belonged; their elders, wardens, ministers, and most of the members of their congregations; special deputations from most of the charitable and educational institutions in London; clergymen belonging to various Christian churches, and others, all came to pay the last token of respect.

It was the desire of Sir Moses that his funeral should be plain and private, and that no carriages should follow, yet the line of roadway from East Cliff Lodge to the College was crowded with people, among whom were thousands who sincerely mourned for the departed.

Precisely at two o'clock the coffin was placed on a bier, and borne out of the house by ten of the Lavadores and friends. The senior minister of the Portuguese Synagogue in London, accompanied by his colleagues and the ministers of the Ramsgate Synagogue, preceded the bier, chanting in mournful tones appropriate verses from the Sacred Text.

The chief mourners were Mr Joseph Sebag Montefiore, Mr Arthur Cohen, Q.C., M.P., Lord Rothschild, Mr H. Guedalla, Mr A. Sebag Montefiore, Lord Rosebery, Mr S. Montagu,

M.P.; Mr Lionel L. Cohen, M.P.; Mr Henry L. Cohen, Mr Jacob Montefiore and his son, Mr L. I. Montefiore, Mr H. Montefiore, Mr C. Montefiore, Sir Julian Goldsmid, M.P.; Sir Albert Sassoon, K.C.S.I.; Baron H. de Worms, Dr Woodman, Mr William Johnson, the Rev. Dr H. Adler, Delegate Chief Rabbi; the ministers and representatives of all the London Synagogues, and the ministers and wardens of the congregations of Edinburgh, Dublin, Manchester, Liverpool, Brighton, Bradford, Newcastle, and other provincial Hebrew communities from all parts of the United Kingdom, as well as the Rev. A. Vivanti, representing the Hebrew community of Ancona, and gentlemen from Brussels and Jerusalem. Following them were the representatives of the city of London in their official robes, the Mayor of Ramsgate, wearing the chain presented to him by Sir Moses, accompanied by his two chaplains, the Vicar of Ramsgate, and the Vicar of St Laurence. After them came the representatives of the Town Council, the Mayors of Margate, Sandwich, and Deal, and the Broadstairs Local Board. These were followed by the Magistrates, the clergy, and hundreds of gentlemen who came in their private capacity.

As the mournful procession entered the outer field it was met by a guard of honour, composed of persons representing several local institutions, and deputations from religious and other bodies.

The cortege passed through the grounds, and proceeded to the front of Judith, Lady Montefiore's Theological College, where a halt was made. The doors of the institution having been thrown open, the writer for the moment left his place at the side of the bier, and placing himself in his capacity of Principal and Director of the College in the doorway, offered up a prayer, referring to the service the deceased had rendered in the promotion of the study of sacred literature, and beseeching Him who is the God of spirits of all flesh, that peace, justice, and righteousness, which the departed so fervently fostered during his life, might now, even as guardian angels, walk before him, pleading in his favour before the Throne of Mercy.

The body was then taken to the Synagogue, and placed in front of the Ark; Psalm xvi. was intoned by the chief minister, and the congregation joined in it verse by verse. At the conclusion the bier was taken out and borne along a path, lined right and left with masses of choice wreaths, and numerous floral tributes from friends, to the entrance of the mausoleum.

There the air was perfumed by the fragrance of tuberoses, gardenias, and azaleas, in addition to the scent wafted thither from wreaths of coloured lilies suspended from the railings and gates without. The walls were decked with tablets bearing Hebrew and English prayers and psalms ; a lamp was suspended from the cupola above, with a Hebrew inscription, " The soul of man is the light of God." At the sight of the open grave, with the Jerusalem stone therein ready to give rest to the mortal remains of him who had worked all his life for the good of others, the eyes of the bystanders were dimmed with tears.

It was with considerable difficulty that the coffin could be removed from the bier and carried into the mausoleum, hundreds of persons being anxious to be present at the interment, whilst there was scarcely room in the mausoleum for twenty persons. Ultimately the multitude yielded to the entreaties of friends, and the coffin, having been brought near the grave, was placed in straps for the purpose of being lowered, but owing to some misunderstanding of the instructions respecting the excavations on the part of the sexton, it met with obstacles in its descent. For a moment it seemed as if even the grave were unwilling to sever the last link which bound the departed to the world of the living, and it was not until the grave had been considerably enlarged that the coffin reached its last resting place. The officiating minister thereupon pronounced a last farewell, " He enters his place in peace," a sentiment which was feelingly repeated by all the bystanders.

The orphans from the Spanish and Portuguese Hebrew schools in London, headed by one of the ministers of the Synagogue, now intoned one of the psalms, the nearest mourners, emblematically teaching the living the lesson, " Dust thou art, and unto dust thou shalt return," sprinkled " Terra Santa " on his coffin, and friends and strangers followed their example. Presently nearly all left the mausoleum. I myself, however, could not help thinking of the last wish of my revered friend, " Pray do not leave me," and I remained near his grave till it was completely filled up and a slab had been placed over it. I then lighted two candles and placed them at the head of the grave. It was the eve of Sabbath, and for many years he and his wife had been in the habit of lighting candles on the Sabbath eve while on earth, even while travelling on their philanthropic missions in distant climes.

During the first seven days after his death prayers were offered up at East Cliff Lodge every evening in the room in which he died, and in the Synagogue, Divine service was held every morning, with the addition of a prayer for the repose of the soul of the departed head of the community. On the expiration of the thirty days of mourning, I considered it a solemn duty to hold a special service, and to deliver an address in Judith, Lady Montefiore's Theological College. There was a numerous congregation.

Abstracts of his will were published in the daily papers, some of which gave a complete copy of the whole document. It will only be necessary here to give the introductory portion, which is a reflex of the sentiments he entertained throughout his life, and the paragraph referring to the appointment of the executors of the will, and the institutions which the testator so richly endowed.

"This is the last will of me, Sir Moses Montefiore, of Grosvenor Gate, Park Lane, in the county of Middlesex, and of East Cliff Lodge, Ramsgate, in the Isle of Thanet, in the county of Kent, Baronet, F.R.S., son of Joseph and Rachel Montefiore, of happy memory, and for more than fifty years the happy husband of my deeply lamented Judith, daughter of the revered Levy Barent Cohen and Lydia, his wife, deceased. I desire, in the first place, gratefully to acknowledge the goodness of Almighty God, the Lord of all beings, for the abundance with which he has blessed me, and for having allowed me the enjoyment of it for so many years. When it may please Him to call me away from this world to eternal life, may our Heavenly Father pardon all my sins, and have mercy on my soul, and may those persons whom I may in any way have offended forgive me. I desire that my remains may rest by the side of those of my beloved wife in the mausoleum near our Synagogue at Hereson, and that my funeral may be as private as may be, and without carriages to follow.

"I appoint my esteemed friend Sir Nathaniel Mayer de Rothschild, Baronet, M.P., and my nephews, Arthur Benjamin Cohen, of the Inner Temple, Esquire, Queen's Counsel, M.P., and Joseph Sebag, of Westbourne Terrace, in the county of Middlesex, Esquire, and my friend Dr Louis Loewe, of Oscar Villas, Broadstairs, Executors and Trustees of this my will, and I give to each of them the sum of £1000 free of legacy duty.

"The testator bequeaths £3000 Bank stock, 300 Alliance Assurance shares, £10,000 Imperial Continental Gas Company stock, to the Trustees of the Synagogue and College at Ramsgate, founded by him in memory of his late wife, Judith, Lady Montefiore ; he also bequeaths to the said Synagogue and College four pictures from his house in Park Lane, all his Hebrew books and MSS., a piece of plate presented to him by the late Viceroy of Egypt, and all his English, French, and German testimonials ; £1000 Bank stock,

550 Alliance Assurance shares, and £5000 Imperial Continental Gas Company stock, to the Trustees of the Spanish and Portuguese Synagogue, Bevis Marks, upon trust, to apply two-fifths of the income to or for the benefit of learned and necessitous Jews of every congregation residing in the Holy City of Jerusalem, and one-fifth of the income to or for the benefit of learned and necessitous Jews of every congregation in each of the Cities of Safed, Hebron, and Tiberias. He also bequeaths £100 to be distributed within three months of his decease among the learned and necessitous of each of the said four cities; £1000 Bank stock and £5000 of the said Gas Company's stock to the Trustees of the Spanish and Portuguese Synagogue in Bevis Marks, upon trust, to apply the income in the purchase of blankets and coals to be distributed annually among the deserving poor of the Spanish, Portuguese, and German communities; £1000 to the Trustees of the United Synagogue for the poor; £500 each to the Synagogue in Bevis Marks and the Synagogue at Leghorn, in augmentation of their respective repairing funds; £500 each to the Jewish Convalescent Home and the Beth Holim Hospital; £300 to the Jews Hospital at Norwood; £250 each to the Ladies' Lying-in Charity for the relief of Jewish women, the Bread, Meat, and Coal Charity, of which his father-in-law was one of the founders, and the Jews College; £200 each to the Samaritan Fund of St Bartholomew's Hospital, the London Hospital, and Mrs Palmer's Cancer Hospital; £100 each to Mrs Tait's Orphanage, St Peter's, Thanet, the Royal Sea Bathing Infirmary, Margate, the Seaman's Hospital, Ramsgate, the Fishing Boys' Home, Ramsgate, the Sailors' Home, Ramsgate, and the Ramsgate and St Lawrence Dispensary; and £100 each to the principal officiating Ministers of the Parishes of St Lawrence and St Peter, in the Isle of Thanet, of St Luke, St George, the Vale Church, the Roman Catholic Church of St Augustine, and the Parish Church of Broadstairs, to be applied for the benefit of the poor of their respective parishes and congregations."

The dividend on Sir Moses' legacy sent this year (the second after his death) to the learned and necessitous Jews in the Holy Land, amounted to £1251, 2s. 5d., which, in compliance with his instructions, was divided as follows:—

$$
\begin{array}{llll}
£500 & 8 & 11 & \text{to Jerusalem.} \\
250 & 4 & 6 & \text{to Hebron.} \\
250 & 4 & 6 & \text{to Tiberias.} \\
250 & 4 & 6 & \text{to Safed.}
\end{array}
$$

On Sunday, March 14=Adár 7, the 3158th anniversary of the death of Moses, the son of Amrám, the ceremony of setting the tombstone took place in the presence of Mr Joseph Sebag Montefiore, Mr Háim Guedalla, and other relatives, the Wardens of the Spanish and Portuguese Synagogue in London, many members of the community, and a large assembly of strangers.

At the conclusion of the ceremony at the mausoleum, the company proceeded to the Lecture Hall of the College, where I held a special service and delivered an address.

The tombstone of Aberdeen marble is similar to that of Lady Montefiore, and bears the following inscription :—

In memory of
Sir MOSES MONTEFIORE, Bart., F.R.S.,
of East Cliff Lodge, Ramsgate,
Born the 8th Heshván 5545 A.M.,
Died the 16th of Menákhem Ab. 5645 = 28th July 1885,
In the hundred and first year of his age.
" I have set the Lord always before me."

(This verse, which is the first part of verse 8, in Psalm xvi., is in Hebrew.)

This inscription was composed by Mr Joseph Sebag Montefiore. It is in all respects very appropriate, as in every occurrence of his life Sir Moses set the " Lord before Him," and recognised the direct hand of Providence.

The year of mourning rapidly passed, and the anniversary of his death was solemnly observed in his own Synagogue, and in those of Hebrew communities all over the world. In many churches and chapels likewise his name was reverentially remembered by his friends and admirers.

Thus was Sir Moses Montefiore honoured in death as he had been in life.

The impartial reader of these Memoirs, in closing the book, and recalling to his mind the varied scenes portraying the life and work of Sir Moses and Lady Montefiore, and the moral to be derived therefrom, will acknowledge that the practice of justice, truth, and virtue towards his fellow-beings, and staunch loyalty to the Sovereign, will ensure an ample reward. At the same time, he cannot fail to contemplate with intense admiration the life's work of the hero of a hundred years, who fought so sturdily in youth the battle of life, and who afterwards devoted himself with such unwearying ardour to the task of combating hatred, persecution, and fanaticism, of severing the bonds of physical and moral slavery, and of aiding in the establishment of religious toleration all over the world. His unparalleled devotion to the sacred cause of humanity in general, and the unclouded halo of a spotless integrity which encircles his name, will ever afford a splendid example for emulation no less than the dauntless courage with which he set to work for the rescue of the suffering and the oppressed, whilst the bright guiding stars which lighted all his actions were the fear of God on high, and deeds of charity and loving kindness on earth.

The retrospect of the lives of Sir Moses and his honoured spouse brings joy and gladness to the minds of all who care for the welfare of the human race. It is calculated to inspire increased hopes for the future, to implant and confirm in us the love of heaven, and to cause us to rejoice in the victory of truth and justice over falsehood, and to make us devoutly thankful for all the blessings vouchsafed to us by Providence.

May we ever bear in mind that the life-work of Sir Moses and Lady Montefiore was based upon the lesson taught by the Wise King—"Fear God and keep His commandments, for this is the duty of all mankind" (Eccles. xii. 13).

אֶת־הָאֱלֹהִים יְרָא וְאֶת־מִצְוֹתָיו שְׁמוֹר כִּי־זֶה כָּל־הָאָדָם

The power adequately to fulfil this behest is in itself a noble reward, and constitutes the happiness of every human being created in the image of God.

APPENDIX.

Genealogy of the Farkhi Family, translated from the Arabic.

RAPHAEL and Mordecai Farkhi being among those accused of the murders of Padre Tomaso and his servant at Damascus in 1840, I here give the genealogy of their family, which will show the great esteem in which they had been held for generations, and the high Government offices with which many members of the family had been entrusted.

In the year 5491 A.M. (1731 of the Christian era) the ancestors of the Farkhis came originally from Tyria, in Asia Minor. About 120 years ago Haim Farkhi (grandfather of the late Haim Farkhi) came to Damascus, together with his brother Joseph. Both were then employed as bankers (sariffs) by the Governor of Damascus. They were likewise entrusted with the offices of keeping the accounts of the Government revenues, and of those connected with the pilgrimage to Mecca and its expenses, also the expenditure required for keeping the army. The revenues derived from farms and villages were also entrusted to them.

When the Governor of Damascus was called away from there to go to another place, his successor, seeing that the management of the brothers Farkhi had given general satisfaction, confirmed them in their office, as did every succeeding governor coming to Damascus during their lifetime.

Haim had two sons, Solomon and Nathan. The latter being the more clever of the two, succeeded his father in the several offices he had held, and surpassed him in importance by the influence which he had with the Governor and in good reputation among the people. Nathan had five sons, Haim, Menahem, Joseph, Raphael, and Moses, and one daughter, Reina. Solomon had two sons, Jacob and Meir, of whom the first only held public appointments. Nathan, being once requested by the Governor of Haina to send him a person of talent, in whom he could place entire confidence, and whom he could employ as banker, sent his eldest son Haim. The latter was at that time very young, but gifted with such extraordinary capacity that, after a few years, he was recalled from Haina to Damascus to superintend all the members of his family in their different public offices. When Haim was twenty years old he was sent to Constantinople to supervise the accounts with the Ministry of Finance. The ability shown by Haim on this occasion roused the jealousy and hatred of some very influential and fanatical persons in Constantinople, who caused him to be thrown into a dungeon, where he remained for many years, without even having been examined; and he was subjected to the most cruel tortures, without being allowed the opportunity of answering the charges brought against him. His sister Reina, though at that time only fourteen years of age, undertook to go to Constantinople, with the intention of procuring justice for her brother.

When there, she awaited the Sultan in a street through which he was about to pass. On his arrival she approached, took hold of the horse's bridle, and presented her petition, in which she related how unjustly her brother had been treated. The Sultan investigated the matter, and, becoming convinced of Haim's innocence, ordered him to be liberated, and reinstated in all his former offices.

Haim now returned to Damascus, sent for his brothers, and employed them again in the functions of his public calling. Some time after his return Ahmed Pasha Djezar was made Governor of Damascus. He was known for his cruelty and the merciless manner in which he compelled his subjects to provide whatever money he chose to demand from them. Haim Farkhi tried to intercede on behalf of some of the unfortunate sufferers, and remonstrated with the Governor for his merciless proceedings. By so doing he offended Ahmed Pasha to such a degree that the latter commenced to harbour in his heart the desire to kill Haim ; but, finding that he could not do without him, he was obliged to leave him in his various offices, and he took his revenge by persecuting Haim's brothers to such an extent that they were compelled to leave Damascus and go to Aleppo and Bagdad. Ahmed Pasha was subsequently also made Governor of Sidon. He took Haim Farkhi with him, the latter leaving some of his relatives in his place at Damascus, so that both provinces were under Haim's control and direction. Ahmed Pasha, fearing the punishment of the Porte for his cruel treatment of those under his jurisdiction, fortified Acre, and made it his residence. Thinking himself now secure, he gave way still more to his barbarous instincts, and contrived fresh tortures, killing women, and hanging them by their breasts, throwing children into the wells, putting out persons' eyes, cutting off their ears and noses, putting hot irons into their flesh, and crushing their foreheads with small bones. All this he did to induce his unhappy victims to give up their property to him !

The officers of the Pasha seeing, that all the public offices were in the hands of the Farkhis, and that Haim Farkhi did his best to alleviate the sufferings caused by the inhuman treatment of the Pasha, became very jealous of his good name, and tried to incite the Pasha to have him killed ; but the latter, well knowing how indispensable Farkhi was to him, told his officers he could not kill him until they had procured another man of equal capacity to fill his place. They thereupon brought to the Pasha a man from Haina, to whom were entrusted all the offices held till then by Farkhi, who was then put in prison. This new man, however, proved so incapable for his responsible office, that he had to be forthwith discharged. Those who had recommended him to the Pasha were disgraced, while Haim was liberated from prison, and once more reinstated in all his former offices and honours. This roused the jealousy of his enemies still more ; they continued to persecute him, and to urge Ahmed to kill him, until the Pasha became afraid that Farkhi would take flight. To prevent this he had him closely guarded in his house every night, and brought to his office in the day time under an escort ; he also ordered one of his eyes to be put out, and part of his nose and ears to be cut off. In a short time the Pasha repented of this order, and sent in haste to countermand it ; but Farkhi's enemies had had everything prepared beforehand, and the cruel order was so quickly carried out, that the counter order came too late.

The Pasha then called on Farkhi, and tried to comfort him by good words, saying that what had happened was the work of evil-disposed persons, and giving him new robes of honour. Poor Farkhi had to submit, and to promise that he would serve the Pasha faithfully again. Haim continued in the Pasha's service till the latter died.

Ahmed Pasha Djezar's death caused general joy throughout the country, and the people praised the Almighty for having delivered them from such a tyrannical ruler.

Ismael Pasha, one of his slaves, and the organiser of the brutalities of his predecessor, then took the reins of government, and Farkhi was compelled to remain in his service. A few months later, however, the Sublime Porte appointed Suleiman Pasha as Governor of Acre and Zidon. He informed Farkhi of his appointment, and the latter gave notice of this to the officers, who immediately delivered the town over to the new Governor, and he afterwards also took possession of Zidon.

Suleiman, who loved justice, entrusted Farkhi with all that concerned the administration of the place, directing him to arrange all the matters according to his ability.

Farkhi then, under the auspices of the Pasha, took the direction of affairs, introducing everywhere principles of justice and equity, showing honour and respect to every individual according to his deserts. By his conduct he attracted the attention of the Sublime Porte, and was also much esteemed by Mohhammad Ali Pasha in Egypt. The secret correspondence between the Sublime Porte and Suleiman Pasha was conducted by Farkhi, he being well versed in the Turkish language.

It had been the custom formerly, that the chiefs of the districts were allowed (if they thought fit to do so) to practise extortion and order capital punishment at their own discretion, but now that Farkhi was at the head of the administration, he caused such authority to be withdrawn from them. Any officer who had allowed himself to take any money in the way of extortion, was made to undergo due punishment for the offence, and no one could be put to death unless the crime of which he had been accused had been brought to the knowledge of a Court of Justice, and there condemned by the Law. Every fine, payable in money by the transgressor, was to be distributed amongst the poor of the country, by order of the judge.

Farkhi was also charged to maintain the security of the high roads, and in his time both women and children could travel without incurring any danger.

He always kept the accounts of his administration in the hands of his Christian employés, in order to make it evident to every native or stranger in the country that there was nothing in all his acts requiring concealment from the eye of the public.

Haim Farkhi's good name and strict integrity caused the inhabitants of Palestine to appoint him as treasurer of all contributions sent to them from abroad for the support of the poor and the learned students in the Holy Land. He attended to this office most zealously, and often himself advanced large sums, without interest, when the donations did not arrive in time. His benevolence was known far and near, and applications for assistance came to him, not only from the inhabitants of Turkey, but also from his co-religionists in Russia and Austria. He founded, at his own expense, institutions for the support and maintenance of learned teachers and pupils in schools; also imported large numbers of Hebrew books for distribution among poor Jewish children, and purchased every year quantities of new clothing, which he divided among the poor of all denominations. He was extremely well educated, and in addition to his knowledge on various secular subjects, he was also learned in theology, astronomy, and the Mohammedan laws. He was perfect in the Turkish and Arabic languages, wrote Hebrew well, and also possessed some knowledge of Persian. His courteous manner, his benevolence and learning, commanded general admiration. People of all denominations blessed his name. His brothers imitated his good example, and were also greatly respected.

Haim Farkhi, as well as his brothers, showed the utmost hospitality in their houses at Damascus to all strangers, and were always ready to give them every assistance in the settlement of their affairs.

Suleiman Pasha, the Governor, had appointed Ali Pasha, one of the

Djezars of the Mamelukes, as his Lieutenant. This man was taken ill, and on his deathbed sent for Haim, requesting him to act as guardian to his son Abdallah, and recommending the young man to his particular care and favour. Haim promised to do his best, and after Ali's death, introduced the son to Suleiman Pasha, and obtained for him the appointment to succeed his father. Haim remained for nineteen years in Suleiman Pasha's service without incurring any blame, and gave the utmost satisfaction by his management of State affairs.

After Suleiman's death Abdallah's mother came to Haim and entreated him to grant his protection to her son, that he might be appointed Governor of Acre. Abdallah was at that time very young, but Haim, thinking that as he had brought him up and tried to instil into his mind the principles of virtue, he would be able to lead him in the right path, and also being mindful of his promise to the dying father, recommended Abdallah to the Sultan, and procured him the Governorship.

After Abdallah's promotion the Turkish Government required him, as was the custom, to give up the property of his predecessor, Suleiman having left no son. Haim again interceded for him, so that he was only required to give up a portion of the property, being permitted to keep the remainder for himself. During the time in which Haim had directed the affairs of State, there had been no necessity for maintaining a large army; all was conducted so fairly that the people were perfectly satisfied, and called him Haim Pasha !

But Abdallah had surrounded himself by young and profligate companions, who soon caused him to forget the teachings of Haim, as well as to be jealous of his influence over the people. If Haim ventured to remonstrate with Abdallah for leaving the paths of virtue, that only succeeded in rousing the latter's wrath.

Haim soon found that all his influence over his pupil had vanished, while Abdallah's low companions became paramount. He repented, but too late, of having raised Abdallah to power. Abdallah's companions told him that as long as Haim lived he (Abdallah) was not safe, as Haim was likely to report his doings to the Sultan. Haim, they said, ought therefore to be put out of the way. They brought false reports to Abdallah about Haim, which enraged him to such an extent that he would no more listen to anything Haim said.

Abdallah's mother tried to reason with him, and reproved him for his ingratitude towards Haim, to whom he owed position, fortune, and everything in life, but all in vain. Several persons told Haim that the Pasha meant to kill him, but he would not believe that one to whom he had been more than a father could act so basely. At last his enemies triumphed, and procured from the Pasha the order for Haim's execution. Before giving the order the Pasha had sent for the Mufti, and tried to get from him a Fetwa against Haim, saying that this Jew had succeeded by illegitimate means in obtaining great influence over the Mussulmans, which is against the Laws of the Koran, and punishable by death ; but the Mufti refused to give a Fetwa, and on the contrary praised Haim, saying he was a most useful servant of the State, upright in all his dealings, and that to kill him would be not only an injustice but a great injury to the State. Abdallah was greatly incensed by this refusal, but decided in spite of it to have Haim executed.

He sent to call him suddenly in the middle of the night. Haim arose to obey the summons of the Pasha, and when he came to the door of his house he was met by the Pasha's lieutenant and five hundred armed men. The barbarous decree of the Pasha was shown to Haim, who, having read it, said with sublime resignation, " Let the will of the Almighty and the order of the

Pasha be fulfilled, but I entreat you to allow me time to say my prayers first." They granted his request, and as soon as he had finished his prayers he was strangled at the door of his own house, and his lifeless body was brought to the Pasha.

When this shocking event became known in the town it caused general mourning and lamentation among all the inhabitants, Jews, Christians, and Mohammedans, but his inveterate enemies were not yet satisfied. They said to the Pasha, "Let Haim's body be thrown into the sea, otherwise the people will make his tomb a place of veneration and pilgrimage." Abdallah thought this very probable, and therefore permitted the body of his benefactor to be thrown into the sea, at the same time giving strict orders that the whole proceedings should be concealed from his mother, who, he knew, would be outraged at his depravity. Haim's house was shut up and his property confiscated by the Pasha.

After Haim's corpse had been thrown into the sea it was seen swimming on the surface, and Abdallah then ordered it to be thrown in again with heavy weights attached, so that he might not be troubled again by its reappearance. The next day, greatly repenting of what he had done, he offered a large reward for the recovery of the body in order to have it decently buried, but it could not be found.

When the Viceroy of Egypt, Mohhammad Ali Pasha, heard of the murder he was very indignant. "What a madman," he exclaimed, "must Abdallah be to deprive himself of such an assistant, a man endowed with such qualities ! Had he resigned him to me, I would gladly have given him many thousand purses in return." Abdallah afterwards felt great sorrow for his crime, and the remainder of his life was embittered by undying remorse. He gave up to Haim's family the greater part of the property which he had confiscated, and also permitted the widow and brothers to leave Acre for ever. They went to Damascus, but the widow, overcome by grief and sorrow, succumbed on the journey.

The brother Moses obtained employment with his cousin Solomon, and his brother Raphael at the Treasury office in Damascus. Abdallah then sent a confidential messenger to Constantinople to report his own version of Haim's death to the Sultan, to whom he also sent many valuable presents, but the Sultan indignantly rejected the presents and the report, and threatened the Pasha with his vengeance. Upon this Abdallah suspected Haim's brothers of having sent a true report of his death to the Sultan, and greatly regretted having allowed them to go to Damascus. To avenge himself, however, he sent decrees to all his officers, telling them to hunt down the Jews in all their districts. He himself set the example by inflicting horrible tortures upon the Jews of Acre, sending many of them to hard labour, condemning others to death, and confiscating the fortunes of all on whom he could lay hands. The Jews in Palestine had likewise to suffer from his tyranny. His misconduct was so unbearable that in 1825 Dervish Pasha, the Governor of Damascus, was sent with three other Pashas and 40,000 soldiers to decapitate him. Dervish Pasha took his Saraf, Solomon Farkhi, a relative of Haim, with him. When Abdallah heard this he sent secret emissaries to poison Solomon, saying that Solomon prevented any reconciliation. So Solomon was poisoned, and his brother Raphael had to take his place. When Abdallah's mother found that no benefit resulted to her son from Solomon's death, she went to Mohhammad Ali, Viceroy of Egypt, and entreated him to intercede at Constantinople for her son, who promised in future to rule with justice. In this she was successful, the troops were withdrawn from Acre, and Dervish Pasha returned to Damascus, taking with him Raphael Farkhi.

Abdallah no sooner felt himself free, than he sent his own troops to

Damascus to attack the Governor, in revenge for his having carried out the Sultan's order, and behaved again so shamefully with the people under his jurisdiction that he received the name of " Mad Abdallah."

After Solomon Farkhi's death, Abdallah spread the report in Constantinople that the family of the Farkhis was still very opulent, and their riches were not honestly earned. In spite of all that was known to the contrary, some officers of the Porte could not withstand this bait, and Saleh Pasha was sent to confiscate all the property. Raphael was put in prison and utterly ruined ; Saleh Pasha likewise ordered the imprisonment of all the Jewish notables in Damascus. They were not liberated until very heavy ransoms had been paid for them. Raphael then went to Bagdad with the intention of remaining there, but after some time Saleh Pasha sent for him to return, as he had been reinstated in his offices of trust and honour.

Raphael held this appointment for many years until the Egyptian invasion. In 1833 the great contest took place between Abdallah and Mohhammad Ali, Viceroy of Egypt, in which Ibrahim Pasha defeated Abdallah, and took possession of the whole of Syria. Ibrahim confirmed Raphael in his office, giving him many distinctions and proofs of confidence ; but after many years evil-disposed persons, jealous of Raphael's influence, intrigued against him, and obliged the Pasha to give the office to another, but as a proof that Raphael had not lost his personal regard, he made him a member of the municipal council of Damascus.

As soon as the Egyptian Government was expelled from Syria through the intervention of the English, Raphael was restored to his place. After his death the office was given to a Christian, but the whole responsibility was placed under the direction of the Defterdar Effendi, who is always sent direct from Constantinople, thus depriving the office of its dignity and trust. Since that time no member of the Farkhi family could get employment from the Government, although they were all honourable and many capable men among them, the services of their ancestors being entirely disregarded.

Names of the surviving members of the Farkhi family :—

Meir Farkhi, at present member of the Municipal Council (not paid).

Solomon, Moses, Jacob, sons of Meir Farkhi.

Joseph and Nissim, sons of Menahem Farkhi, and Solomon, son of this Joseph.

Ezekiel and Nathaniel, sons of Joseph Farkhi.

Aaron Farkhi, their nephew.

Mordecai and Menahem, sons of Moses Farkhi.

Judah, Meir, David, sons of Raphael Farkhi.

Israel H. Farkhi, son of Solomon, who was poisoned at Acre.

Of these sixteen persons, only seven are tolerably well off, the others can with difficulty earn a scanty living.

EXTRACT FROM THE LETTER OF THE REV. C. A. SCHLIENTZ.

On the 11th August 1840 Mrs Schlientz and I had the pleasure of dining together with the Rev. Mr Marshall and Lieut. Shadwell of H.M.S. *Castor* (who had been our fellow travellers from the mountains of Lebanon to Damascus) at the English Consul-General, Mr Werry's, whom we requested to ask the Governor for permission that we might visit the Jews imprisoned on the charge of having murdered Padre Tomaso and his servant. Our request was granted, and our whole party went the following day to see the persecuted sufferers. Their prison was amidst the barracks of the soldiers, and had just been made a little more tolerable than it was before. They showed as the marks of their stripes and tortures, and told us with much emotion that their fearful sufferings were made more cruel for them by having been deprived during the whole time of their confinement of the comfort of seeing any of their relatives. The last of the prisoners we saw was a venerable Rabbi, who, as one means of torture, had not been allowed any sleep nearly the whole time. Amongst the prisoners was a young man, who, unable to endure the tortures, had turned Mohammedan, and upon the strength of whose testimony the others were prosecuted and judged. It is indeed surprising that the Government, knowing this fact, could act upon the declaration of such a man! After leaving the prisoners we were conducted to their houses, which were of elegant construction, and showed that the prisoners were very wealthy persons. The poor females appeared to be in great distress. In these dwellings we were shown the place to which the Magicians had been brought, to find out by astrological calculations the persons guilty of that supposed murder. We saw, too, the place where the Padre was said to have been cut to pieces, and where there is a mark of something on the wall, which, judging from the colour, may be anything but blood. We also saw a young girl of remarkable beauty, whom one of the French officials had succeeded in wresting from her mother by the promise that he would interest himself in the deliverance of her father. The poor mother related to us with deep emotion the great grief of her heart in this affair. What a pattern of Christian justice must this appear to others!

We saw the spot where the bones of the Padre were said to have been found, as well as the place where they are said to have been deposited in the chapel of a convent. Upon this they have put the inscription : " The bones of Padre Tomaso, murdered by the Jews !" They did this without any satisfactory inquiry whether the Padre had indeed been killed ; and if so, by whom? whether these were really his bones? &c. As long as no legal investigation by competent judges has taken place, I will never take these for the bones of Padre Tomaso, and I trust that the inscription on that tombstone will be altered, and deprived of an assertion which has never been proved in any satisfactory way. I visited some of the convents at Damascus, and at one of them I had a long interview on this subject with the Superior. He was a Frenchman, and the light-minded and frivolous way in which he spoke of this serious subject, affecting, as it does, not only many individuals, but a whole nation, and the principles of its religion, showed me that he could not be trusted in that matter. To him it did not admit of the slightest doubt, even without evidence, that the Jews must have been the perpetrators of this crime ; no one but they in their wickedness was capable of such a deed. I do not know in what relation these missionaries stood to the accused Jews, but I perceived distinctly that they laboured under very unhappy prejudices, and that their assertion would bring no conviction to my mind. The proofs of wealth which we saw in the dwellings of the persecuted sufferers rather suggest that motives of envy and hatred have given rise to a story which almost exceeds that of John Calas of Toulouse, during the last century, or the accusations brought against the Christians in the first centuries of their ecclesiastical history, and against the Jews in after times, all of which were proved to be diabolical calumnies. I have not entered into the question whether the Jews sacrifice Christians in order to obtain their blood, as this has been answered satisfactorily already by Jewish and Christian writers, especially so during this year, on account of the Damascus affair. Even if such a horrid custom had existed, I deem it most unlikely that persons of wealth and liberal sentiments, such as these Jews of Damascus are, would lend themselves to the perpetration of such a deed.—With my heartfelt desire for the real welfare of Israel, I remain, dear sir, yours most truly, C. A. SCHLIENTZ.

August 6th, 1847.

To Mons. VATTIER BOURVILLE,
    Consul at Damascus.

SIR,—Sir Moses Montefiore has forwarded to me some documents, from which I learn that in the month of April last a Christian child having disappeared in one of the quarters of Damascus, a rumour arose that it had been stolen and put to death by the Jews in order to obtain its blood for their religious ceremonies. This, in the eyes of prejudiced and credulous people, formed a pendant, due to Hebrew fanaticism, to the sad history of Father Thomas.

From the same documents I find that upon this idle rumour alone, and without any reliable information whatever, the agent of the French Consulate, Mr Baudin, hastened to accuse the Jews formally before the Pasha of having caused the disappearance of the child. In his letter to this high functionary of the Porte, Mons. Baudin writes something to this effect :

"We ask your highness to institute an inquiry regarding this strange affair ; to order the sheiks of the different quarters to search for the lost child, and to remind them particularly that, according to a tradition worthy of belief, the wicked Jews are in the habit of killing children who are in their power during the time of their religious solemnities, for which reason the master of the child who has disappeared strongly suspects that it is in the Jewish quarter."

The child has been found, and its reappearance seems to have put an end to the disturbance, and also to the conjectures of which it was the object.

Monsieur Baudin not having written to me on this subject, I beg you, sir, to forward me most explicit details, in order that I may be able to ascertain the true facts of the case. If his conduct and language have been such as they have been represented, they cannot be sufficiently condemned, and you should express to him my strongest disapprobation.

The Government of the king has constantly refused to give credence to the atrocities imputed to the Jews, and could not blindly accept accusations against them which in the East are but too well explained by the hatred and rivalry of religion.

Without wishing absolutely to impose its own views on its agents, it is at least entitled to demand that they should abstain from manifesting openly inimical sentiments, and above all should not deliver up for persecution to the Moslem authorities a whole population and a whole people on nothing more than vague suspicions without any substantial evidence. It is a duty, a principle of equity, and a natural reserve to which I should much regret to learn Mr Baudin had not strictly conformed.

PARIS, *Le* 23 *Aôut* 1847.

MONSIEUR,—Le Roi M'á reuvoyé une lettre que vous lui avez adressée le 9 de ce mois au sujet du préjugé malheureusement répandu en Orient contre les Israëlites et qui les accuse de verser le sang humain dans leur sacrifices. Vous exprimez le désir qu'il soit prescrit aux agents de sa Majesté dans le Levant non seulement de s'abstenir de tout ce qui pourrait contribuer à accréditer un tel préjujé, mais encore d'employer tous leur soins à le combattre et a le détruire.

Le Gouvernement du Roi regarde l'imputation dont il s'agit comme fausse et calomnieuse, et ses agents en général sont trop éclairés pour songer à s'en faire les organes. Il le regretterait vivement et n'hésiterait pas à les en blâmer de la manière la plus expresse. C'est ce qu'il s'est empressé de faire relativement au cas particulier que vous m'avez signalé touchant un enfant chrétien de Damas qui avait disparu dans le courant d'avril dernier, et à l'accusation que le gérant du consulat de France n'aurait pas craint de porter à ce sujet auprès du Pacha, contre les Juifs. Aucun avis ne m'étant parvenu directement à cet égard, j'ai demandé des éclaircissements au consul du Roi à Damas, eu lui ordonnant, si le fait qui vous a été rapporté était exact, d'exprimer de ma part le blâme le plus sévère, à l'agent qui sur un simple bruit, aurait hazardé une pareille imputation contre tout un people.

Recevez, Monsieur, l'assurance de ma consideration trés distinguée,

GUIZOT.

Sir MOSES MONTEFIORE.

LONDON COMMITTEE OF DEPUTIES OF THE BRITISH JEWS.

Copy of Letter addressed by Sir MOSES MONTEFIORE, Bart., to J. M. MONTEFIORE, Esq., President *pro tem.* of this Board.

GROSVENOR GATE,
PARK LANE, 30*th June* 5627 (1867).

MY DEAR SIR,—It is with deep regret that I have to place in your hands further despatches received from Jassy, from which it would appear that the position of our unfortunate co-religionists in Moldavia still continues most distressing. You will be pleased to submit these communications to the Board of Deputies without delay.

The several memorials which I have received from Moldavia, solicit so frequently and so urgently my personal presence there, that if, in the opinion of your Board and that of our Community, it should be considered that my presence in Moldavia might prove of utility to those who in their misery apply to us for sympathy and aid, I should feel it an imperative duty, at whatever personal risk and sacrifice, to respond to the appeal thus piteously made.

There can be no doubt that, as the delegate of our community, any representations that I might be intrusted to make as its organ would acquire great force and significance, while I should be encouraged by the consciousness that I should be acting, not only in accordance with my own sense of duty, but also as the exponent of the earnest wishes of your Board and of the Jews at large, that so unhappy a state of things as is now existing in Moldavia, as affecting the Jews of that Principality, may, under the blessing of the Almighty, speedily cease.—I have the honour to be, my dear Sir, yours faithfully,   (Signed)   MOSES MONTEFIORE.

Copy translation of the despatches above referred to.

JASSEY, 6*th June* 5627 (1867).

*To the Defender and Champion of Israel, who is zealous
in their cause, the Crown of Israel!*

Sir MOSES MONTEFIORE, Bart.,
&c., &c., &c.

GREETING,—At these tidings your ears must tingle, the hair of your head stand on end, and your heart melt with anguish.

Within the last few days, the head of the enemies of Israel has prevailed. The object is to drive the Jews out of the provinces of Moldavia and Wallachia,—to take for spoil all their wealth and possessions without let or hindrance. We get no protection from the Minister ; on the contrary, he aids our enemies against us by all manner of evil decrees, and imposes upon us all kinds of oppressions without measure.

On the 4th May last, a decree was issued by the Minister Bratiano to expel all the Jews from the villages of Moldavia as coming under the category of vagabonds. Scarcely was the edict made known when the Minister arrived here ; in another moment the enemies of Israel filled the streets and public places, seized every man of Israel without distinction that came in their way, crying out, "He is a vagabond ;" bound him hand and foot with chains, beat him unmercifully, drove out alike old and young, chased them out of the city, and delivered them over to the mercy of the soldiery, to drive them to the boundaries of the land.

A cry of anguish from the women, and like lamentations from the men, went up to heaven. Old men and children, women with suckling ones cry aloud, but there are none to pity, none to look with compassion. They have been driven from all the villages, made to leave their possessions, their goods and chattels, in the hands of their enemies, and have escaped only with their lives.

The heads of the congregation here have entreated the Minister to withdraw the decree, but in vain have they supplicated. Non-Israelites have also sought justice for the Jews, but they have pleaded to a deaf ear. He seeks only their expulsion.

In three days the prisons were overcrowded with our brethren ; the persecutions for awhile abated, still we were in fear and trembling, lest every moment they should be renewed with fresh rigour, for the decree has not yet been recalled.

A great evil threatens us, the hatred increases every day and every hour, —there is none to stay the hand. I therefore make known to you, these our troubles and distresses, beseeching you with scalding tears to aid us all in your power, and to defend the cause of oppressed Israel, who are driven from the land of Moldavia.

May the Creator of heaven and earth, the God of Israel help us !

Trouble upon trouble ! During the last three days soldiers have been going about the streets molesting the Jews, and with their swords they injured a woman with child. Her cries brought persons to her rescue, and those who endeavoured to take the weapons from the soldiers were seized, thrown into prison and charged with attempting to murder the military authorities. We have no one to look to for help except our Father in Heaven and His servant Moses. The chief matters we dare not venture to write, out of dread and apprehension, for we are as sheep in the hands of the slaughterer.

May the Holy One have you in his keeping, bestow upon you strength, energy, and will to save the residue of His flock, and reward you a thousand fold, the prayer of your servants, &c., &c., &c.

By the help of God.

JASSY, *Monday, 15th Sivan,* 5627.

To the benevolent of heart, the desire of the eye of Jacob,
Head of the children of Israel, Prince of our brethren,

Sir MOSES MONTEFIORE, Bart.,

&c., &c., &c.

The eyes of all Israel in the province of Moldavia are directed to you for salvation and consolation, to deliver them out of the power of their enemies, for no violence is to be found in their hands.

Surely the man Moses will rouse himself as a lion for the rescue of his people, as he has done in days of old, and in former years, to deliver his brethren, the house of Israel, from their sorrow and distress.

May Heaven's blessing rest on his head, inspire his heart, and prosper all the works of his hands.

(Signed)   JESIAS BHOR,
Chief Rabbi of Jassy,
On behalf of the whole congregation.

END OF VOL. II.

TURNBULL AND SPEARS, PRINTERS, EDINBURGH.

½ M.—S.—12/89.